Bad & Bossy

A Secret Baby Enemies to Lovers Romance

Boulder Billionaires

Mia Mara

Copyright © 2024 by Mia Mara
All rights reserved.
No part of this book may be reproduced in any form or by any electronic or
mechanical means, including information storage and retrieval systems,
without written permission from the author, except for the use of brief
quotations in a book review.

It was a *bad* idea from the start.
A wild night with a bad boy in a suit.
And now a bun in the oven to prove it.

Six months later, I'm a struggling single mom with new curves and a new job.
I never thought I'd see him again.

Until today...

I'm at work and the mysterious owner shows up after a lengthy absence.
A shocking realization hits me:
I've been working at his company all along.

I frantically try to stay out of sight.
But I can't avoid my new boss forever.

"Mr. Pearson wants to see you in his office now."

Every nerve in my body is on edge as I stand before him. And then he brings his face inches from mine. **"I won't let you out of my sight, Dana."**

Sparks fly between us and he asks me to stay late.

But one thundering question haunts me:

How do I tell him I have to get home - *to his baby boy?*

Chapter 1

Cole

Returning to Boulder so soon was a *bad* idea.

Seeing it from above the breaking clouds had never before caused so much anxiety. The fields my friends and I used to explore, the restaurants I used to frequent, the cars, the people, they all looked like ants from the jet's window. I wondered how much of a difference my disappearance would cause, how many people I'd inevitably hurt.

White fluff shielded my view as the plane split a cloud in two. We had reached our main altitude and I sat back in my seat, looking away from the window, staring instead at the rattling cup of water on the table in front of me. Turbulence never bothered me before, but this time it was making my nerves fray.

The movie that had been playing on the widescreen television ended and another had started, one I didn't recognize. I stared at the screen as a distraction, hoping the unfamiliar faces would be enough to keep my mind off of the upcoming rocky descent.

Mia Mara

———

"Ah, man, you look so good."

Grayson's hand clapped hard against my shoulder as he pulled me in for a hug on the tarmac. Six months was long enough for me to almost forget the way his voice sounded—deep and gruff ever since it dropped when we were about fifteen. "I do?" I chuckled, surprised. A few hours on a plane usually only made me look worse.

How bad did I look when I'd left, then?

"Yeah, Cole. You look... healthier."

I watched the back of Grayson's black mop of hair as he led me toward the car. He'd upgraded since I last saw him; the entirety of the hood of his new Porsche was covered in a black buffalo outlined in gold, the letters CU overlapped in the center. I guess he was taking his mentorship of Boulder's football team at the University of Colorado more seriously now.

"Dinner?" Gray asked as I slid into the passenger seat beside him, the sun hanging low just above the peaks that skirted the edge of Boulder. I'd missed sunsets like that. "A great new grill just opened up. We could get some ribs, watch the football—"

The car roared to life. "I'd rather head to the brewery, if that's okay," I politely cut him off.

Cole turned to me as he shifted into drive, his foot on the brake. "You want to go to the brewery?" he asked, speaking each word with a heavy pause.

"I can't avoid it forever, Gray."

"You just got back. Surely throwing yourself into that environment isn't—"

"It's my business. I need to see how it's doing." I sighed, and slowly, gently, he let off the brake. "I haven't heard a single thing about it since I left. I need to make sure the place is still standing and hasn't burned down in my absence."

He watched me for a few seconds more before the car slowly started to drift forward, a heavy silence falling between us. I knew he was worried about me—knew he had been for a while—but I couldn't avoid my business any longer. I already had for six months. The time I'd been gone only caused the worry to grow that much more with every second I wasn't there.

"You've missed a lot while you were gone," he said, his voice low. If he thought I wouldn't catch the subliminal meaning behind those words, he was wrong.

"With you or with everything?"

Grayson chuckled. We turned onto Valmont Road, leaving the municipal airport behind us. "Both. But mostly me."

Either the newly-opened grill he spoke about was in the same direction as my brewery or he was giving me what I wanted. He's always been a better friend than me.

"I ditched Amy about a week after you left," he said, the engine revving with power as his speed picked up. "Weird girl but damn do I miss fucking her sometimes."

I snorted. "She seemed nice, though."

"She kept insisting I help her meet famous people at the matches, as if I would do that for her even if I could," Gray laughed. "But at least Penny's happy about it. She hated Amy."

Penelope, his daughter, was almost nine and somewhat able to understand her father's actions. I wasn't surprised she was becoming vocal about the women he brought around. "You're lucky Halsey hasn't chewed you out for having your flings around her."

Grayson shrugged. "Halsey's going through her own quarter-life crisis or whatever you want to call it."

"Don't think you can call it a quarter-life crisis when she's the same age as us."

"Yeah, well, thirty-four isn't exactly in mid-life-crisis territory." Every turn Gray took drove us closer and closer to the brewery. The tips of my fingers began to buzz, anxiety creeping its way through my bones. "If my ex-wife has an opinion about who I date, she can keep it to herself."

I wasn't going to tell my best friend how to parent his child, even if it didn't sit completely right with me that he was bringing his flings around her. I would keep my mouth shut for now. Hell, I'd been keeping it shut for the last six months.

The two-story, red brick building came into view as the car slowed. He parallel-parked in the spot meant for me, letting out a long slow breath as he turned off the engine. "Are you sure you want to do this, man? You literally just got home."

"I'll be fine."

"You're supposed to be taking it easy for a few days," he sighed. "They emailed me a pamphlet and—"

"Look, man, I... I know. But I also know what's best for myself and being alone in my house for a few days is only going to drive me insane. It's better for me to keep busy, to show my face around the brewery and squash any rumors that might have popped up about why I was gone."

"Are they really rumors if they're true?"

I shot Grayson a glare sharp enough to cut bone.

The smell of boiling wort hit me the moment I opened my door. Releasing a chocolate-like aroma, it poured out of the metal vents on the side of the massive complex. Soon the hops would go in, and it would transform into something different, something deeper. The scent of it all was what had drawn me to brewing in the first place.

Grayson followed me inside in silence, his hands fisted in the pockets of his hoodie. For a Thursday night, the on-site bar was packed, music pumping from the speakers, a college basketball game playing on the wall-mounted TVs throughout the space. The scent of spilled beer almost masked the boiling wort and made my spine stiffen.

"Mr. Pearson?"

Wide eyes met mine as I turned my head toward the waitress carrying a tray of our signature pale ale. Long blonde hair flowed over her right shoulder, frighteningly close to the tops of the glasses. Apparently no one had been enforcing the rule that servers with long hair needed to wear it up.

"Hey, Candace," I said, forcing a small smile.

She blinked at me a few times before plastering her signature customer service smile back on her face and passing out the beers on her tray to a rowdy group. She hurried back over to me the second she'd finished, her smile faltering. "Are you... are you back? Or just stopping in?"

"Both," I grinned. "Is Ben here?"

"Uh, yeah, yeah he is." Her eyes darted to the bar where a couple of men leaned over the counter, clearly waiting for service. "I'll grab him."

She disappeared before I could direct her toward the bar instead, her blonde waves bouncing behind her back as she slinked through the swinging black door.

"She seems surprised to see you," Gray said, his eyes wandering about the bar.

"Well, I did disappear without saying a word to anyone but Benjamin, the guy I left in charge." I sighed.

My gaze caught on the stacked barrels along the far right wall. Definitely a new addition to the bar portion of our campus, and as I stepped closer, I couldn't help but notice the faintest sheen of dust covering them. Pressing my finger against the wood, I dragged it down, watching the barely-there line form in its wake.

When was the last time the staff cleaned?

I made a mental note to bring down the hammer on cleanliness tomorrow morning. My inner perfectionist wouldn't be able to handle these imperfections for very long.

The more I looked around, the worse it got. Stray bottle caps on the floor behind the bar and under tables, a handful of tears in the leather-bound seats, a small crust forming under the beer taps. All of these things meant little on their own but together, downgraded the entire establishment. If they weren't addressed, small problems would build into big problems.

My feet itched to walk the length of the campus to the restaurant on the other side and inspect that as well. Doing so would allow me the chance to check out the brewery and ensure all of it was up to code. Despite my six-month absence, my focus would be entirely on this come tomorrow. I only hoped my concerns would dwindle and not grow as I continued on my walk-through.

"Cole!"

The black door swung both ways as Ben burst through it, walking toward me, his best black button-up tucked into his trousers. His long, wiry brown hair was tied back in a ponytail, and as Candace stepped back through the door, I noticed she'd tied hers up as well.

Convenient.

"Hey, man," I grinned, holding out my hand in offer toward Ben. Gray looked on from the sidelines, his gaze bouncing between us and the bar. I wondered if he was fighting the urge to grab a drink.

"Good to see you." Ben grabbed my hand and gave it a firm shake, a bit stiff in the wrist. "I was wondering when you'd be back."

"Now," I chuckled. "Flight landed about thirty minutes ago."

Ben's mouth tightened briefly before a smile returned to his lips. He was technically my acting CEO while I was away, and although I didn't intend to rip that title away from him entirely, he'd be losing control of the business with my return. I knew he wouldn't be happy about that, but it was unavoidable. Besides, he knew he was only filling in and that his role as CEO was temporary.

"I appreciate you looking after the business while I was gone," I continued. "But I'll be taking over from here."

Benjamin cleared his throat. "Of course," he said.

"Could you get the team together in the back? Whoever is here. I'd like to speak to them."

"Cole," Gray hissed. "We were just supposed to pop in."

I shrugged. "I've changed my mind."

"This isn't good for you—"

I shot him a glare sharp enough to cut steel. I didn't need any more fuel igniting the fire of rumors.

"Fine. Whatever."

Ben glanced between us, his brows raising slightly. "Yeah. I can do that."

"Great," I grinned. I watched as he turned, his fingers

forming into a fist as he headed back toward the swinging door.

———

Thirty minutes later, I stood with my arms crossed in front of a group of about fifty people, the scent of boiling wort long gone, the smell of hops surrounding us. I could see the evidence of stains on the floor from spilled beer and yeast, could smell a tang in the air from uncleaned metal. My jaw stiffened.

Whispers made the already noisy room come to life in the most uncomfortable way. I knew exactly what they were talking about. I fumbled with the medallion in my pocket to keep my mind calm.

"Thank you all for coming down on such short notice or staying past your shift," I said. I scanned the crowd, taking in familiar faces as well as new ones. "I appreciate you all for stepping up while I was away. I know it's not easy when management makes a sudden shift."

In all honesty, I felt nervous speaking to them. Having a group of people standing in front of you, several of whom likely knew exactly why you were gone, was nerve-wracking to say the least, especially when you were out of practice of being in charge. But I did everything in my power to not convey that nervousness. I wasn't even sure if this was a good idea, but the more I spoke, the calmer I felt. I was home. Things could go back to normal, for the most part.

I was the boss. The brewery belonged to me. I had started the company and was single handedly responsible for making it the best brewery and most loved beer in the state. I was Cole Pearson of CP Beers and this was my rightful place.

"Benjamin has done an incredible job leading you all for the last six months. But I intend to fully return to my position tomorrow morning," I continued, my voice strong. "I ensure we'll make this as smooth of a transition as we can. Smoother than when I left—"

A flash of familiar brown wavy locks ensnared my vision.

My head whipped to the side and I watched as the woman silently pushed her way through the crowd, her face hidden, her body language stiff.

Every ounce of confidence I'd built came to a screeching halt.

She glanced in my direction.

Those bright hazel eyes locked on mine.

Dana.

What the fuck was she doing here? Last I'd heard, she was working for Lottie and Hunter Harris on their horse ranch. When the hell did she make the jump into brewing?

The uniform that clung to her form told me she'd been hired on as a tour guide. It must have been while I was gone; I would have noticed her file on my desk, would've ensured that I was the one to conduct her interview. But I didn't get the chance to do that, and here she stood, her face paling the longer she looked at me.

She was just as shocked to see me as I was to see her.

The collar of her shirt rested against her neck, the fabric hugging her breasts, her nipples just barely poking through making them that much more appealing. Her high-waisted slacks cinched in her waist, and I could just barely make out the outline of her hips. She was curvier than I remember but that made her all the more attractive.

I already knew what she looked like underneath her clothes.

I knew how she felt.

How warm she was.

How good she tasted.

I needed to stop myself. I couldn't go down that road, couldn't keep looking at her, drinking her in. If I did, everything I'd worked so hard on would start to unravel.

Everything about her was intoxicating, and the more I fingered the medallion, the more I worried she was as bad for me as what it symbolized.

Her breath caught as I turned away from her, addressing the group once again. I tried not to let her presence get to me, tried to pelt out my voice as I had before I had seen her.

Today I had returned to Boulder, to restart my life, finding strength in the support of my best friend, in the company of my employees, within the walls of this building that signified my triumphs and my successes.

But now, my fragile confidence was turning to shit.

Because that woman symbolized everything that I had destroyed in my life, my weaknesses and my failures.

And now I was face to face with the mammoth endeavor of making things right.

Even if she didn't want anything to do with me, I still had to find the strength to try.

Chapter 2

Dana

My heart started pounding. I put my hands in my pockets so no one would notice how they were shaking. *Why is he here?*

The crowd slowly dissipated, splitting into two recognizable groups—one that clearly knew Cole, and one that had likely been hired on without meeting him. How I'd gone five months without knowing he was in charge was beyond me.

I watched as people milled about. Those who knew him slipped away from the room soundlessly while others stayed behind to introduce themselves and speak to him, shake his hand, meet the man who apparently was in charge of us all.

I'd heard whispers about the supposed runaway owner. Everything from an unplanned extended vacation right down to an alien abduction had floated around the office. I'd paid no mind to it under the assumption that he was never coming back.

Maybe I should have.

My feet didn't follow my brain's commands to move. Partly because the floor was so sticky and moving my shoes would take effort, but mostly because I just didn't have the willpower. I wanted to go with the rest of them, pretend like maybe he hadn't clocked me despite our stupidly prolonged eye contact.

Benjamin stepped up next to me, nearly making me jump as I ripped my gaze from Cole. "Come on, I'll introduce you," he said, one arm extended toward the line that was forming to fucking shake Cole's hand.

"I-I'm fine," I said, forcing a smile, my eyes looking towards the door. "I don't need to meet him."

"He's insisted," Ben replied. His voice had dropped, an air of irritation dripping in his tone. "Just get it over with so we can all finish up and go home."

It wasn't that he didn't have a point. I was taken away halfway through a guided tour to listen to this bullshit. I had to leave my group in the restaurant with a stack of free meal vouchers as an apology, and it was already pushing against my time to clock out.

"Fine," I grumbled, finally peeling my boots from the floor and stepping into the line.

I discovered I was sorely mistaken with my hopes that he hadn't noticed me. He glanced at me between each person, each time lingering for half a second too long.

It only made my heart pound stronger.

And make me want to escape.

I just wanted to get home to my son. My shift was already too long for my liking, and the nanny wasn't exactly thrilled whenever I was late picking up Drew. At this rate, he'd be asleep by the time I got there, and I didn't even want to consider how easy he could go from peacefully sleeping at the nanny's house to a screeching baby in the backseat. But the pay here was insane, more than what Lottie could give me.

I should've known there was a catch.

I wouldn't have taken it, no matter the pay, if I knew Cole ran the fucking company.

The line was moving too quickly for my liking. I was caught between wanting to go home and wanting to stay at the back of the line to avoid having to shake his hand and speak to him.

Mistakes had been made.

We'd parted ways.

And now he was my boss.

What the fuck?

I quelled the shaking in my hands as I got closer by picturing Drew sleeping soundly in the backseat. If I thought about calm and peace then I could get through this. I could shake his hand, rush back to my group, finish the last twenty minutes of their tour, and head home. Surely it would be fine.

The woman ahead of me, someone I didn't recognize but wore the uniform of the bar staff, stepped out of the way and, suddenly, I was face-to-face with him.

Cole fucking Pearson.

The Pearson of Pearson Beers. How did I not put two and two together? God I was an idiot.

He loomed over me, his dark blonde hair looking far too perfect for having supposedly just gotten off a plane. The suit he wore clung to his arms, not a wrinkle in sight. His eyes—those stupid, goddamn perfect, green-as-grass eyes that drew me to him in the first place—seemed to be looking straight into my soul. He was far more attractive than any man I'd managed to grab in my twenty-eight years on this earth.

He was going to be the fucking death of me.

I hoped he could see every ounce of discomfort I was

feeling, that my awkward stance and forced smile would clue him in. I hoped he could replay that horrible scene when we had last seen each other, echoing in his head like a bad pop song on repeat. Maybe it haunted him as much as it did me.

Cole dared to smile, that same infuriating, charming smile that had once made me melt. But I had already made up my mind. I would never forgive him for the bullshit that had happened the morning after that hot night.

The man behind Cole, one I'd seen around the brewery a handful of times but knew definitely didn't work here, looked like he'd rather be anywhere else. I could relate.

But nothing could change what was happening. I was here, standing before the man who had hugely impacted my life beyond just a one-night stand.

I had imagined this moment hundreds of times in hundreds of different scenarios. Running into him at a restaurant on Pearl Street. Seeing him at a party at Lottie and Hunter's. Even bumping into him in the mountains. What they all had in common was that my son, Drew, was never present and I counted my lucky stars he wasn't here now either.

Without me even offering my hand, Cole grabbed it in his.

His touch was warm and firm, a stark contrast to my own hand, which instantly turned into a floppy fish.

A shiver ran up my spine as his fingers wrapped around mine, his grip both familiar and unsettling. "Nice to see you," he said, his eyes drilling into mine with an intensity that made my heart do somersaults. His hand felt strong and reassuring, yet it ignited a flutter of nerves that I couldn't quite control, making me painfully aware of the goddamn chemistry sparking between us.

"Mmm-hmm." I faked a smile so wide it probably came off as psychotic as I pulled my hand away.

Cole's expression wavered, a mix of nervous excitement and uncertainty crossing his face as he realized I wasn't falling at his feet.

But there was something else lurking behind Cole's stare — something that made my pulse quicken. An unmistakable familiarity, a reluctance to pretend he hadn't seen me naked, and worst of all: a desire to actually talk to me.

His mouth opened as if to say more, but I turned away from him as quickly as I could without raising any red flags to the rest of the staff and scurried toward the back of the brewhouse. There were at least four people behind me still in line, not a single chance of him getting through them all before I was gone.

Or so I thought.

Footsteps echoed behind me, clacking against the sticky floor. I glanced over my shoulder as I grabbed the door handle, those wild green eyes meeting mine once again. He stopped in his tracks the moment I got through the door.

About half of my tour group had gone home instead of waiting around. I couldn't blame them. I did, however, hate the idea that those people might leave me a bad review and Cole would be the one dealing with it.

The campus was massive. It stretched an entire block of downtown Boulder, with a bar at one end and a restaurant at the other. In between was the brewhouse, with its high ceilings taking up two floors of the center of the building. The second and third floors consisted of mostly offices and storage for the bar and restaurant.

From the top level of the brewhouse on the overhead walkway, I could see Cole and the man that had been standing behind him during the meet and greet on the lower level. Cole's hands were flying as he spoke, but with the sounds of the machinery, I couldn't hear what was being said.

"Is the brickwork original?"

"Huh?" I turned, my hand gripped on the metal railing. One of the men at the front of the group, an older guy who smelled horribly of cigarettes, held his hand up to claim the question. "Oh. Right. Yes, it is. The building was built back in the early 1900s. It was meant to be a brewery back then, too, but prohibition hit in 1916 and it was forced to close."

"What's this?"

A woman who was absolutely old enough to know better reached far over the railing, her hand wrapped around a pipe I knew next to nothing about — and I did not want to be the reason the entire brewhouse came to a screeching halt.

"Stop, stop!" I pushed through the people between us, forcing them up against the railing. The woman recoiled, her eyes going wide, and slowly but surely she brought her entire body back to the catwalk.

The fact that this was the third time this month that this same thing had occurred made literally zero difference. I didn't know how to handle it the first time, and I still didn't know how to handle it now.

"Please don't... touch anything," I said, loud enough for the people in the back to hear. "Everything in here is important. There's a reason we're not down on the ground."

Bad & Bossy

"Right. Sorry," the woman mumbled.

I glanced down toward Cole, hoping to God he hadn't seen that, but of course, he was staring directly up at me.

Twenty minutes. I'd only run over by twenty minutes. I could still make it to the nanny's before Drew fell asleep.

I pulled on my leather jacket from my old riding days and zipped it up. My purse was somewhere in the sea of hanging bags, and as I searched through them, the door opened behind me. Immediately, my spine stiffened.

"Dana? Can you hang back a minute?"

Not Cole. Breathing a sigh of relief, I unhooked my purse and turned. "I really need to get going."

Allison, my manager, shifted on her feet uncomfortably, her eyes darting back out into the hallway. "I know. I'm sorry. But the owner wants to meet with you."

For fucks sake.

"Me?" I scoffed, trying to play it off as if it wasn't a big deal, as if the thought of being alone in a room with Cole didn't make my stomach sink. There was a questioning glint in her eyes, though. "Why?"

"He saw your employee of the month photo—"

"Seriously? Goddammit. Why do we even have those?" I groaned, throwing my head back in frustration as I stepped through the door. "Drew's not gonna sleep tonight if I leave much later."

"I know, I'm sorry," Allison sighed. "I tried explaining that your shift had already run over but he's very... well, no nonsense. You haven't worked under him yet, Dana. He's more of a hard ass than Ben."

Somehow that didn't surprise me in the slightest.

She walked with me in silence to the elevator, briefly giving me directions to Cole's office as the doors closed and separated us. As the elevator lifted me higher, it felt like my freedom was slipping away.

How fucking convenient that the moment I found a job that paid well, and one I actually enjoyed when tourists weren't actively trying to destroy machinery, that this had to be the outcome. I'd finally been able to stand on my own two feet competently and my brief fling, my one-night stand that ended in disaster, turns out to be the boss. If there was a god, he certainly had it out for me.

Those eyes found me the moment I stepped out of the elevator.

"You actually came."

I didn't do Cole the decency of meeting his gaze as I stepped around his hulking frame. "Not like I had much of a choice," I mumbled.

Whatever conversation he wanted to have absolutely wasn't going to be done where someone could stumble upon us, and I was going to make damn sure of that. I followed Allison's directions to his office and let him trail silently behind me. The floor was clean and shiny; not a chance that a single spec of stickiness would be clinging to my shoes. The only sound was our heavy footfalls and the swing of his office door as we entered it.

I wondered where the other guy had gone, if he'd sent him home or if he was waiting around downstairs.

The door clicked shut behind me. "Been a while. Don't you think?" he asked, his deep voice trailing around me as he weaved his way to his dusty desk and office chair. As he sat, a cloud of it puffed up, dancing in the low light around us. Had the sun been out, the view from his office would've been incredible—all mountains and trees with only a trace of the street below. But all that filtered through now was a lonesome streetlamp, reflected headlights, and a hint of the stars above.

"Can we please not do this?" I asked, not caring how badly it came across. I didn't want to be in here and it wasn't like he couldn't tell already. I didn't even bother sitting, didn't care to bring home any dust or make him believe I was staying long.

His lips curled into a thin, harsh line. "When did you start working here, Dana?" he asked, avoiding my question as if it were the plague. And as much as I didn't want to play into his interrogation game, I knew him well enough to know it was the quickest way out of this situation.

"About five months ago," I said, crossing my arms over my chest. "You didn't need to bring me up here for that. Surely you could just check my file."

Avoiding the heaviness of his gaze, I gave myself a moment to take in the expanse of his office. Exposed brick, just like Allison's office and like every other wall in the building. The only difference was the sheer size and the ornate furniture that littered it. A solid, perfectly carved wooden desk, a chair that likely cost more than a year's worth of my rent, lamps that looked like the original fixtures in the bar.

Even in the poor lighting and the far too wide silence, it still screamed wealth.

"You didn't tell me," he said, breaking the quiet he'd created. But his voice wasn't quite as booming, wasn't quite as demanding as it had been before.

I forced myself to look at him, to take him in for a

moment. The line between his knitted brows was juxtaposed by the softness of his eyes, and in his expression I saw who he was before that night we'd shared that had changed everything. It hit me more than I thought it would. In my wildest dreams, when I considered the possibility of running into him out in public, I always imagined he'd be the way he'd been that night — not the way he'd been before. Maybe that was my mistake. "Why would I, Cole?" I sighed. "I had no idea this was your business."

"You never noticed my pictures on the wall in the restaurant?" he smirked, leaning forward into the pile of dust on his desk. Little particles clung to the sleeves of his suit jacket. "You didn't notice my face three photos down from yours where you've been hung as employee of the month?"

A memory flashed in my mind from the stupid hanging ceremony they'd had for me, and sure enough, nope — I couldn't remember even looking at the other photos on the wall. I'd avoided looking at them ever since it'd be hung my second month here because I hated that picture of me, taken just a few months after my son was born.

How had I missed this?

"Do you think I look for you everywhere I go?" I crossed my arms, trying to mask the tremor in my voice.

He snorted. "I don't know, Dana. But if you think it wasn't obvious that you knew who I was the moment you locked eyes with me downstairs, then you're dead wrong. I saw your face go as pale as a goddamn ghost. You haven't forgotten my face just as much as I haven't forgotten yours."

Warmth spread across my cheeks, betraying me as I tore my gaze from his. My mind was a whirlwind of emotions, the memory of our one night together clashing with the urgent need to keep a wall between us.

"I'd even hazard a guess that it excites you just as much as it used to."

"Don't—" I cut myself off and searched for the words I wanted to say, but everything fell flat. I stared at the brickwork to the left of him, counted the odd ones that looked like more recent replacements, focused in on them to give myself a moment to breathe and find myself. "Please. I actually like working here, and I really, *really* don't want you to sully that."

"How would I?" he asked, and I could *hear* the grin in his voice. "If anything, I'd bet that my presence would only magnify that."

"Don't be an ass," I snapped, pulling myself back to his piercing green stare and the little lines beside his eyes brought on by his shit-eating smirk.

"I only mean because you have an *in* with the boss."

"If I wanted an *in* with the boss, I would have stayed working for Lottie." As much as I loved the independence that came from working a job where I didn't get pity-paid, I *did* miss seeing my close friend as often as I used to when I worked on the ranch. And if Cole made my life hell here... "I'm sure she'd be plenty happy to have me back, though."

I didn't expect him to move the way he did.

He pushed up from his desk, sending dust flying into the air in the low lamp light. Three steps and his height was already rounding it, moving far quicker than I was capable of as I took a step back toward the door.

His presence enveloped me, stealing the air and leaving it dry, demanding that I try to reclaim it. At one point in time, that had been enticing to me — the back and forth between us, the fight for who was really in command. Even now, a part of me still responded to it, still clung to it, and as he brought himself inches from my face, his light cologne filling my nostrils.

"You don't want that," he said, that thickness back in his voice. I could feel the depth of it in my chest and in my stomach, but somehow, I doubted it was loud enough to even make it through the door. "You've made that irrevocably clear."

I swallowed. He wasn't wrong, and I almost wished I hadn't said how much I enjoyed it here. It gave him power over me — gave him the power to hold my employment above me and dangle it like a cat toy, too tempting to ignore but with the possibility of it disappearing the moment he decided my presence wasn't worth the effort.

I didn't know what to do. Didn't know how to handle him like I used to, and in my flailing, I found my tried and true get-out.

"I need to go home," I said, the warble in my voice only slightly noticeable. The moment after I started my sentence, I realized that I couldn't finish it — I couldn't use that excuse, no matter how true it was. I couldn't tell him why I had to go home or who was waiting for me there. *Shit.* "It's late." *Please let that be enough.*

His eyes flicked between mine, studying me, watching every minute movement I made. "Fine," he smirked. "But know this... " He moved his face an inch away from mine. "I don't intend on letting you out of my sight, Dana."

Chapter 3

Cole

Being at home alone was certainly my first hurdle to get over.

It was nearly one in the morning, and I hadn't felt an ounce of exhaustion sweep over me yet. Instead, I found myself in the kitchen like I used to most nights whenever I was here. The space was too large for just me, and despite the temptation itching at my bones, I decided to make it even larger.

Grabbing a far too expensive bottle of wine from the top shelf felt like a solid place to start.

I plucked the cork out with my bare fingers, my nails catching in it and stinging as I pulled. I didn't give a shit if it broke, couldn't care less if little bits of cork swam in the wine like marshmallows in a cup of cocoa. I pulled and pulled until it gave way with a pop.

The scent of it alone was staggering. Perfectly fermented, crisp, apple-like and tangy. I almost lifted it straight to my lips.

Almost.

Instead, I poured it directly into the drain of my sink.

Over and over again, I emptied bottle after bottle. Thousands of dollars entering the sewage system felt like a goddamn waste. I could've given it away, offered it to employees or friends and family, but I needed it gone. I wanted to drink it. I wanted to forget the day and pretend like seeing her hadn't thrown me for a loop.

But it had thrown me for a loop. I hadn't expected to see her again anytime soon, and certainly not the day I came back to Boulder. She was unlike anyone I'd ever been with, even if it had only been one date and one extra night together. I'd thought about her often, thought about what had happened between us.

It played again in my head as the bottles broke in my glass pulverizer.

"Lottie's going to kill me," Dana had said. That part I remembered clear as day. The way she laid back on my queen-sized bed in my barely furnished apartment downtown, her wavy brown hair framing her face, nothing but her bra and underwear covering her body. Her knees were up, swaying back and forth, and I was so transfixed on them I could barely breathe. They'd kept my gaze from her lips—the ones I'd devoured in the elevator on the way up.

She'd always been so fucking beautiful.

The ache in my cock begged me to drive my zipper down and climb on top of her. I'd worked on my shirt instead, though, taking my time despite the buzzing in my head.

"Why?" I'd asked. "Who you sleep with shouldn't affect her."

"You were her dad's client, Cole. Do you honestly think that won't bother her? I mean, yeah, Brody's gone now, but she heard enough from him about your... *type*. Enough to tell me about it." Her lower lip had folded in beneath her upper teeth, her eyes tracking every movement of my hands. "She'll think I've gone insane."

"So's her husband but she still married Hunter, didn't she?"

"Are you proposing to me on our second date?" she'd laughed.

The sides of my shirt had slid down my shoulders then onto the floor. "Don't get cocky," I'd warned, a faint smile forming on my lips. "I'm just saying that it's perfectly natural for wedding guests to, well, do *this*."

I'd climbed onto the bed, her knees falling apart so easily, welcoming me, almost beckoning me.

"If Lottie has an issue with it then she can bitch about it to her horses," I'd mumbled.

I could still hear her giggle before the sound of her breath catching as I pressed my lips against her jaw, just beneath the little beauty mark between her lips and chin. She'd smelled of salt spray and coconuts, like a piña colada on the beach at sunset. I'd wanted nothing more than to drink her in entirely.

Her chin tipped down, catching my lips on hers. I'd kissed her for the second time, tasted the leftover hints of wine and mixed drinks on her tongue, and savored every second. We hadn't been roaringly drunk, at least, not anymore by that point. But there was still a lack of inhibitions, a buzz that had settled at the base of my skull and told me it was time for more.

She would be my *more* that night.

I hadn't been invited to Lottie and Hunter's first wedding. According to Dana, it was a quick, private event solely for the benefit of Lottie's father before he passed. But when they'd decided to have another—one that I would be in attendance for—Dana had reached out to me a few months after our first hangout to ask me to go with her.

And thank fuck she had. She wouldn't have been in my bed if she hadn't.

I'd been thinking about her since the moment we'd met at Lottie's house. I'd barely been able to take my eyes off of her then. Her tanned skin, those far too bright hazel eyes, the way the sun glinted off her flushed cheeks. But there, in my bedroom, she was almost otherworldly.

Her freckles peeked through her minimal makeup. The low light of the lamp on my bedside table coated her in a different kind of warmth, one that made her eyelids heavy and my cock ache. The soft glow of the streetlights outside the window of my apartment filled the room with light blue and yellow. I was grateful I'd sobered up enough by then to remember it, and enough to ensure my driver brought us there instead of to my house in the mountains, too far away. And I couldn't wait that long.

"Cole," she'd breathed, her chest rising and falling against my chin.

"Hmm?"

"Are you going to... you know?" She'd giggled as her cheeks turned red. "You're not doing anything."

Oh. Shit, she was right. I'd gotten lost in my own head.

"I'm just taking you in." I could still feel the way my lips had twitched up into a smirk. "And imagining all the ways I'm going to make you scream."

Her flush had deepened as her hips lifted just an inch, a silent request for something, anything.

The memory halted, and by the time it picked back up, her bra and underwear had been discarded somewhere on the floor, my slacks hung off one foot, and my cock was rubbing against her entrance.

I'd lost the time. I'd hesitated as the realization of that settled in and stared down at every inch of her.

Holy fuck. Even remembering it now, I knew then that her breasts would be the death of me.

Wrapping my fingers around the little pockets of skin at her hips, I'd used them like handles to hold her steady as I slowly, achingly, sunk myself inside of her.

Warmth invaded my senses like wildfire. Her body had swallowed me whole, her little grunts and mewls only making me harder. She'd stretched for me perfectly, so slick, so desperate. "Oh, fuck," I'd groaned, bottoming out inside of her as I brought my body over hers again. "You're going to kill me, Dana."

Her little giggle had made her insides shake. "Why?"

"Because I've never felt something so good in my goddamn life."

I didn't know why, didn't know what had come over me, but the words I'd spoken were true. I'd searched for the same thing in countless women after her, searched for someone that fit to my body like a glove, in the exact way that she had, but none had come close.

She'd ruined me.

I'd lost count of how many times I spilled myself inside of her, on her, in her vicinity. I'd lost count of how many times she shrieked her release, her hands fisted in the pillows or her lips around my length. We'd fucked like animals, insatiable and constant, writhing and needy, far too late into the morning.

And I stored every fucking second that I could in my memory. I didn't want another blip like I'd had at the start, no, I wanted to remember her in every position, in every vixen-like gasp and cry.

It was easily one of the best nights of my life.

But when I woke that morning with her lightly snoring frame wrapped in my arms, my head pounded. It *screamed*. I couldn't count the number of times I'd been hungover in my life, but this one had been one of the worst. I hadn't drank enough water throughout the night.

I'd slid my arm from under her and slinked out of the bed, careful not to wake her, then stumbled my way down the hall toward the kitchen as I clutched my head. The world had felt shaky, hazy, like I was stuck between reality and dreams. Everything seemed so far away, so without consequence.

I could have taken a Tylenol. I could have drank a glass of water, eaten something greasy, prayed to whatever god would listen to kill the hangover before it could get worse.

But I had taken the easy route.

Shaking fingers had wrapped themselves around a glass and a bottle as if they had a mind of their own. I'd watched from somewhere far back in my mind, barely understanding what I was doing but knowing it wasn't abnormal for me. *Couldn't be hungover if you're drunk.* I guess that could have been my motto.

For what had felt like the first time in my life but was probably somewhere closer to the two-hundredth, I had slung back a glass of whiskey in one gulp, starting the morning routine.

The burn of it had eased the throbbing in my brain. I

remembered looking out the window and noticing how the sun was just starting to crest over the mountains, its rays cutting through the sky like the way the throbbing headache had shot pain streaking across my head. It had to have been somewhere around seven in the morning.

One glass was enough. It should have been enough.

But then it was two.

Then three.

And by the third, I didn't even hear Dana approaching. The room seemed to sway slightly, but in a pleasantly energized way, not the overwhelming dizziness of being too drunk, and I felt a warmth spreading through me. My hands were steady now, and I was definitely feeling the buzz.

How much had I poured into my glass? I remembered the whiskey almost reaching the rim, a sign of my growing enthusiasm.

"Cole?"

I swear, her voice had echoed. It was beautiful, like a song, and as I'd torn my gaze from my too-full glass and looked at her, she came into focus.

Shit. Even through the buzz, I could tell that she had clocked it, could tell that she saw and internalized the drink in my hand.

"Are you... still drinking?" she'd asked, her brows knitting as she studied me. "Did you not go to bed?"

I'd approached her, doing a little dance. "No. Went to sleep with you. It's fine."

"It's not fine." Her face had contorted, her body retreating. "It's like, eight in the morning, Cole. Why the fuck are you drinking?"

I'd plastered a smile on my face, mustering up the lie. "It's just one."

"You don't sound like you've only had one," she'd said, her fingers twitching where they clung to the hem of my button-up shirt that she'd put on. It was so large on her — the image of her like that was burned into my mind.

"Shh, don't worry about it," I'd grinned. I'd reached out for her, her body within grasping distance, and pulled her toward me. She'd stared at me, concern and irritation coating her features, and god, I wished I'd picked up on it then. I wished I hadn't taken the gentleness she regarded me with as she placed her hand on my cheek as something it wasn't. "Fuck, you look so good in my shirt."

The look of abject disapproval on her face was something that had burned itself into my mind. Even through the buzz of the alcohol, that was what stuck with me the most, what flashed in my mind too many times a day. Of course I couldn't forget her face. I feared I never would.

"You could have made yourself a coffee, you know?" she finally said.

I knew I had royally fucked up but I tried to keep the mood light-hearted. "It's never too early to pick up where we left off last night. Come on, join me. Hair of the dog, they say." I grinned, hoping she'd see the humor in my suggestion.

Dana raised an eyebrow, clearly not convinced. "I think we've had enough 'dog' for a while, don't you?"

To that I didn't have an answer. All I could do was watch her as she left the kitchen and hurried into the bedroom and, from what I could hear, she was frantically getting dressed and collecting her things. I sat down and rolled the full glass in my hand, staring deeply into the sea of amber.

"I need to go," she'd breathed when she came back, her eyes wandering to keep herself from looking at me. "I have to get out of here."

"Why?"

"Don't. Just don't, Cole."

"Then I'll continue the party without you."

In two seconds, she was down the hall and at the front door. "Don't even think about calling me," she yelled out to me, her voice echoing through the apartment.

And the door slammed shut.

The silence that followed was all consuming, enveloping me in a blanket of loneliness.

What happened after that was something I'd gone over multiple times, something that haunted me in the early hours of the morning when I couldn't fall asleep, something I'd spoken about multiple times just to try to get over it.

I'd downed the nearly full glass, searing my insides with every gulp. I remembered, clear as day, setting it down on the table and placing my open palm over the entirety of the thin rim of it. I used it as leverage to steady my unbalanced frame as I pushed myself up out of the chair.

I remembered it shattering under the weight I placed on it.

What I didn't remember in the slightest was the pain of the glass slicing into my palm, but the little drops of blood that fell onto the table beneath were clear as day.

I stared down at the last empty bottle from my cupboard. I'd ruined so many things that morning, probably said things to her I couldn't even remember. I'd searched for that feeling I had with her at the bottom of every bottle, in the arms of women I couldn't even remember the names of, in the sickness in my gut that flared with every drink I had.

It had only gotten worse after that.

Seeing her again had only made the need to make amends with her stronger. From the way she'd looked at me, I knew there wasn't a single inkling of forgiveness in her bones, but I'd apologize to her somehow. Even if it physically pained me to do it. But would she even accept it? We'd both ghosted each other after that night. I'd been far too ashamed to reach out, and assumedly, she hadn't wanted to contact me again. I didn't judge her for it in the slightest. But the idea of apologizing for things that had happened after, the things that had gotten lost in the heavy fog of the drink, felt almost worthless when I didn't even know what I'd said. All I had left was the *feeling* of it, the venom in words that would forever evade me.

God, I hated apologies.

A text from Lottie lit up my phone on the counter. I shoved the last bottle into the glass crusher.

You still up? Brody won't let me sleep.

I swiped down on her name and hit the call button.

The sound of wailing met me before her voice did. "Sorry! Sorry," she sighed, the wail cutting off with a little coo. "He's been so goddamn hungry lately I can barely keep up."

Damn it felt so good to hear her voice. I'd meant to call her earlier—she knew I was coming home—but it had slipped my mind in the transition from plane to work to home to throwing away bottles of ridiculously expensive alcohol. We'd texted frequently while I was away, and even though she was Dana's friend first and foremost, she was impartial when it came to me. She knew me through her father, Brody, whom she'd named her son after. I think in some way it provided her a last little connection to him.

She also was one of two people who knew where I'd been for the last six months.

"It's okay." I couldn't hide the smile from my voice. The freedom of being able to use my phone however I wanted was hitting me like a fucking freight train. "I don't mind. Honestly."

"How have you been?"

"Me? What about you?" I chuckled. "I still haven't met Brody. He's, what, seven months? How's Hunter? The ranch? The company?"

"Whoa, whoa, whoa," she laughed. "Brody is almost exactly seven months. Two more days until he hits that milestone."

"And Hunter?"

"He's good. Exhausted. He's been an absolute dream with Brody, letting me have the last week off of nighttime duties so I'm trying to return the favor," she sighed. "We've both been wildly busy with work but honestly, I'm... I'm really happy."

"That's good, Lots."

"And you?"

"I... yeah. You know your friend is working for me?"

The end of the line went silent except for a quiet little coo. "Shit. She does. I didn't even think about that."

"That was a fun discovery," I snorted. Pulling a shitty ready meal out of the freezer, I chucked it into the microwave. "She's not happy about it."

"I imagine not." Lottie huffed as Brody's little coos

started to turn more into cries again. "For fuck's sake. I'm sorry, I've got to go. I don't know how long he'll be like this."

"That's alright."

"You should come out to the ranch sometime. Meet Brody. Horses can be very therapeutic, you know." The wails grew louder, angrier.

"I will."

"Bye, Cole."

"Bye."

———

A microwave meal on the balcony of my expansive home at two in the morning was certainly a new form of rock bottom.

At least I wasn't drunk.

The wind whistled through the trees as the stars hung brilliantly above, blocked out only by the outlines of the mountains. I lifted spoonful after spoonful of macaroni and cheese and overcooked chicken with gravy into my mouth, wishing more than anything it was the lip of a bottle instead.

The house was far too large and I was far too small. I hadn't even begun to crack into the stashes of bottles throughout the property. I'd still be finding them for months, and I knew damn well that every single one would be a test.

I felt the imprint of my medallion and let out a sigh.

There had been so many times over the years that I wished I could turn back the clock and stop time before any of it started or changed my behavior, but now more than ever, it loomed over me like a giant raincloud. I wished I could take it all back. Every person I'd hurt, every event I'd ruined, the damage I'd done to myself and others...

I glanced down at my right palm, zoning in on the little scar from the shards of glass that morning with Dana. I wished I could take that back, too.

Is there a world where we could have worked?

The more I stared at it, the more it morphed into the split-open skin and blood.

Would she give me a second chance?

Surely not.

An alert from my doorbell camera buzzed on my phone, someone had triggered it. For a short, split second, I wondered if it could be her. If she'd heard where I'd been and wanted to talk. But the face on the live video feed was someone else entirely, someone I knew far too well.

"What are you doing here?" I laughed down the phone, pushing my way into the house and through the maze of corridors toward the front door. Shoulder-length black hair, a stout frame, a shorter stature than me. My sober companion, my friend from the last six months. A chaotic man with a chip on his sleeve. A brightness in a sea of clouds. Somehow, he was exactly the person I needed.

Bobby grinned at the camera. "Came to the rescue, didn't I?"

Chapter 4
Dana

My tendons felt like they were on fire. Every step, every slam of my feet onto the cement felt like I was going to snap like a twig.

Drew's little whimpers in his stroller told me I was coming up on time to call the run, but I didn't feel like I was ready. I still hadn't run away the incessant thoughts about Cole. I hadn't dispersed the memories, and it almost felt like to stop would be to let it all flood back in.

I wanted to quit my job. The temptation was nagging at me, scratching at the back of my mind like an incessant cat. Run away and avoid him for as long as I could. But the money was too good, and as much as I loved Lottie and knew I could ask her for anything, I didn't want to have to. Crawling back to her and asking for a pay raise felt like forfeiting the life I was trying to build for me and my son.

But Cole.

Fucking Cole.

I couldn't stop the onslaught of the memories from that night.

The weight of him on top of me had felt like a warmth I didn't know I needed. His nose pressed against my neck, his lips flush with my skin. I wasn't sure where he'd gone—if he was lost in his thoughts, if he was just content, or if he had fallen asleep on me. Whatever it was, it didn't bother me.

I'd dragged my nails across his bare back, over the ripples of muscle and bone, up to the base of his neck. Something about it felt so easy, so natural, in a way I hadn't exactly experienced before.

We hadn't seen each other in months. That first date had gone amazingly, but we were both busy, and I had a million things to help Lottie with after her father passed and a thousand things to do in my own life before I could genuinely think about a relationship. But when Lottie told me she'd invited him to the wedding... well, I didn't stand a chance. *Might as well embrace it,* I'd told myself.

The inevitability of Lottie's irritation with me for seeing him was a contributing factor in my hesitation, as well. We'd grown so close while we were in Hawaii. I'd been there on a work deal, learning the ropes with the lead stable hand, and she'd come in a month after me. We'd clicked instantly, even to the point of her insisting on hiring me when she landed the job managing the breeding side of her future husband's business. But Cole was her late father's client, and after the chaos they'd gone through with losing him, and the whispers of infidelity and womanizing tendencies being passed down to her from her dad, I knew she'd be mad at me. But

Cole had been right—ultimately, she'd ended up with the same sort of person.

"Cole," I'd said softly, my impatience for more getting the better of me.

"Hmm?"

"Are you going to... you know," I'd laughed. I looked up at him, my eyes meeting the swirling seas of his. "You're not doing anything."

"I'm just taking you in," he'd said, a little smirk spreading across his lips. "And imagining all the ways I'm going to make you scream."

I'd felt my cheeks flush as I lifted my hips just a little. Anything for friction, anything for attention in the place I needed it most. I already knew he could deliver; he'd worked his magic with his hands on the first date.

A shift had happened in him then. His lips met mine again, igniting a fire in my gut that traveled south and pooled into my panties. The way his hands moved was almost carnal as he quickly and deftly unlatched my bra, pulling it off my chest in one quick motion and leaving me bare. The cool air only briefly kissed against my skin before his chest was pressed to mine, the small tuft of hair rubbing against my nipples. I'd moaned into his mouth.

His hands wandered lower at the same time as mine. I found his belt as he found the band of my underwear, his fingers teasing the hemline and threatening to pull them down. I wanted him to. God, I fucking wanted him.

I'd lifted my hips, giving him clearance to tug them over my ass, and soon those were gone too. The pads of his fingers had slid between my parted thighs, coating themselves in what he'd ignited, and before I could even think straight they were inside of me.

"Oh my god," I'd gulped, barely able to form a coherent

thought as he moved inside of me so perfectly. He curled his fingers, flexed them, fucked me with them as his thumb thrummed precisely against my clit. I'd lost track of my hands—shit, what were they doing?—and instead, found them covering my mouth, my eyes, pulling at my hair. He'd had his fingers in me no more than a minute before I felt my need for release building.

"So fucking eager for me," he'd muttered, his free hand tugging at his belt and slinging it off. "And so goddamn pretty when you get so flustered. Tell me, Dana, does this feel good? Is this what you wanted?"

"Fuck, yes," I'd cried. My back began to arch, my hands fisting into the sheets. Why was this so easy? Why was I so comfortable? Nine times out of ten, I was lucky if I came once with a man, but that, that time with him was so different...

My release had ripped through me, nearly splitting me in half as I shook and clenched onto his hand. He'd dragged me through it, forcing me through every ripple of excruciating pleasure as if it fueled him, and by the time I'd come back down from whatever plane of existence I'd ascended to, his slacks were out of sight and all that stood between us was an inch of air.

I could still feel the gulp I'd made.

He was big. Bigger than any man I'd ever been with before. It was almost comical how well-endowed he was in comparison to the other men I'd been with. I wondered if he tanned naked, it was warm in color like the rest of his skin, but deeper at the tip with a hint of reds and purples as it dripped precum. Little veins crept up the edges, the base neatly trimmed and groomed, but that fucking girth...

"Like what you see?" He'd laughed, his irises blowing so wide I could barely see the ring of green around them. I'd nodded. "I'm going to fucking ruin you, baby."

His head had pressed up against my entrance, steady yet a little demanding. He'd blinked, his vision lost for a moment, roaming across my bare body beneath him. But then his hands had wrapped around my hips and pulled me onto him, sinking into me far too easily for his size, splitting me in two.

I swear I saw goddamn stars that night.

He'd stayed true to his words. He did ruin me, in too many ways to count. I've never been fucked like that since, never experienced the hours of desperation and gluttony we shared. I drank him in as if I was dying of thirst, savoring every fucking second of it. Release after release, too many to count. Soon after, my head was swimming with more than just the lingering effects of alcohol, something stronger, something different between us. It was as if neither of us wanted it to end.

I'd had plenty of one-night stands in my day. But none of them, absolutely none, had come anywhere close to that night with him.

But when I woke that morning in cold sheets and a quiet room, everything came slamming down at once. I wish I'd known then that when he promised to ruin me, it hadn't ended with just the sex. I had been sore everywhere, especially between my legs, in that way that only felt satisfying the next day. But I was alone. And that wasn't so satisfying.

I'd told myself he was just making breakfast, or coffee, or doing his morning routine, whatever that entailed. But each passing second had felt more and more worrying. I didn't know if he was even still in the apartment. He could have slipped out in the night, perhaps not feeling a single thing I did during it all.

I'd checked my phone. Twenty percent battery. Eight in

the morning.

I'd slipped from the sheets, shrugged on his button-up from the night before, and stepped out of the dull, lifeless bedroom. At night, illuminated by the glow of the streetlights, it hadn't seemed so empty. But in the daylight I noticed there was nothing on the walls, barely any furniture, and not a single touch of it looking like it was lived in properly.

The hallway was much the same. Wooden floors gave way to new but stained carpet. Cole was wealthy—I knew that much—so I couldn't help but wonder why he'd live in a place like that.

I'd stepped through the opening at the end of the hall into a kitchen I hadn't seen until then. He sat at the table, naked, save for a pair of boxers, a glass in his fist and a bottle of whiskey I didn't recognize. Behind him, littered across the countertops, were old liquor bottles and varying cans of beer.

What... the... fuck.

"Cole?"

I'd tried to make sense of what I saw. Maybe, just maybe, he hadn't gone to sleep last night — maybe what we'd done had kept him up, and he'd kept his own little party going into the early hours, losing track of time. I didn't like the way it sat in my gut regardless— I knew the road this led down. Knew it far too well, grew up surrounded by it, and then, when I'd finally thought I could give myself time and get to know someone, someone I felt like I had a deeper connection with than I originally intended...

"Are you... still drinking? Did you not go to bed?" I'd asked, taking a step toward him hesitantly.

He abruptly stood up and moved towards me as if he were dancing, probably trying to hide his shakiness on his feet. "No, I went to sleep with you. It's fine."

I couldn't stop myself from retreating, from taking a step back from what was unfolding in front of me. He'd laughed. I was not amused. "It's eight in the morning, Cole. Why the fuck are you drinking?"

He waved a solitary finger in front of my face. "It's just one."

"You don't sound like you've only had one," I breathed. I clutched the bottom of the button-up nervously. I hadn't imagined that the way I'd felt hours before would become Pompeii so quickly, but there I was.

He'd shrugged, and it only made me angrier. His face had crumpled in on itself for a split second before he'd looked back up at me.

"How many glasses, Cole?" I'd asked, desperately trying to sound calm as I reached for the bottle and took it in my hand. Some kind of silvery material made a raised emblem of an antlered deer across the front of it, and the label read *The Dalmore, 2007 Vintage Highland Single Malt Scotch Whiskey, 46%*. It was strong, and it looked fucking expensive.

Cole's hand grasped my shirt and pulled me toward him. "Shh, don't worry about it," he'd grinned. He stared at me almost longingly, and if it wasn't for what was playing out, that look would have done things to me that I wouldn't be proud of.

I'd placed my hand on his cheek, pushed the short strands of dark blonde hair out of his face. But god, the knot in my stomach telling me to run, to disappear before he could become another presence in my life that only disappointed me, was strong.

"Fuck, you look so good in my shirt," he'd rasped, his eyes raking over my frame the way they had last night. But it didn't feel the same, didn't feel like two people meshing together too well — this was not the Cole from last night.

"You could have made yourself a coffee, you know?" I didn't know what else to say.

He curled his hand around the back of my neck in a way that would have made me fall fucking lifeless in his arms the night before. "It's never too early to pick up where we left off last night. Come on, join me. Hair of the dog, they say."

He was grinning and it was kind of cute.

But the sirens in my head made me freeze. "I think we've had enough 'dog' for a while, don't you?" I'd pulled away from him and he shrugged and glanced over at the bottle on the kitchen table.

I turned from him and headed toward the bedroom, my feet going from sticky linoleum back to carpet. Strewn all around the room on the floor were my dress, my shoes, my underwear, along with my handbag, proof that the previous night hadn't been my imagination. I frantically got dressed and went back to the kitchen.

"I have to go," I'd breathed, lifting my hands in surrender as I stepped back. "I have to get out of here."

"Why?" Cole had asked, his brows coming together as he watched me stand there, disappointed and far more confused than he was. He'd taken the bottle from the table as he took a step toward me, and I moved two steps back.

"Don't," I'd said. "Just don't, Cole."

"Do you hate me?" he'd asked.

"This is bad, Cole. Really bad. I need you to understand that," I'd said, my hand sweeping beneath my hair to free it from my dress.

"Not into bad boys?" he'd asked, snorting at his own joke.

"This isn't *bad boy* behavior."

His eyes had turned hard as I slid my heels on, the rejection switching right on. "Fine. Then this fling is over and I'll continue the party without you."

I'd stiffened my jaw and pushed past him, the backs of my eyes burning. It hadn't felt like a fling, like a one or two night stand like he was implying, but if that's what he wanted to pretend that it was, then fine. "I'm going home," I'd said, but the words had come out croaky through the knot in my throat.

I'd held back the tears as I blindly found the exit of his apartment with no help from him, shouting out to him to not bother calling me. I'd held them back as I descended the stairs and called for a taxi. I'd held them back the entire ride home, looking a mess and doing the walk of goddamn shame.

But in the safety of my house with no one else around to see me, I'd let myself feel everything.

―――

My knees gave out from under me. I gripped the stroller's handle as my right shin and kneecap hit the cement, a bright bloom of acidic pain lancing out from under my leggings. Drew's seat tipped back—he didn't weigh nearly enough to counteract my stumble—and as he started to kick and cry from the sudden shift in his world, the pain dissipated. He could cry for me.

I picked myself up from the ground and clocked a bench about ten feet ahead. Pushing Drew and limping my way to it, I collapsed onto the cold decrepit wood and caught my breath.

Drew's little whimpers and cries had a pull on me that I had never thought possible. Every time he cried, a pit formed in my stomach, an ache to soothe and calm him at all costs. I wasn't sure what I thought motherhood would be like, but there were parts of it that surprised me nearly every day.

I scooped him from his stroller, passing a quick glance at my knee as I bent over. My leggings had torn, the skin beneath raw and bleeding, but I would deal with that later. Instead, I leaned back with his little body in my arms, rocking him gently enough so that he calmed and my body didn't protest too hard.

It was strange looking down at him and seeing his plump little face, the tiny bit of blonde hair that ghosted his head, the little specks of blues, greens, and browns in his eyes. He'd changed so much in the three months since he'd been born. No longer was he this intensely fragile, wrinkly little infant. Now he was an intensely fragile chubby baby.

And god dammit, I loved him.

The more I watched him settle in my arms, the more it cemented in my mind that I couldn't quit my job. It worked too well for both of us when Cole wasn't interrupting my shift schedule by making a surprise appearance. As much as I loved my job at the Harris Ranch, this one paid so well and was understanding when it came to childcare duties.

I knew Lottie would have gone above and beyond to make the ranch worth it as well. But I couldn't lean on her generosity. There was only so much she could do anyway. Being with the horses meant being there at the crack of dawn and doing that with a baby on my hip seemed almost impossible. I could have been moved to admin, but again, I needed to figure out my own path and my own way instead of relying on Lottie's help to make things work.

Plus, I'd barely given the brewery a chance. I'd only been there a couple of months before my water broke mid-tour, and after my almost two-month long maternity break, I'd come back before I was needed to make ends meet. I couldn't just abandon it after only working there for about three months total.

I had to make it work. I had to do this myself—for Drew, for both of us. No matter what.

———

A familiar head of wavy deep brown hair was looking in my front window as I jogged up to the house, my right knee screaming at me.

With her hands cupped around her eyes and her face pressed against the glass, I couldn't help but chuckle under my breath. If she'd just called me instead of appearing out of the blue I would've just told her I was out, maybe then I wouldn't have arrived home to find a "peeping Veronica" at my windows.

As silently as I could, I pushed Drew's stroller with his sleeping body up the little hill of my driveway. "It's a bit creepy to be looking in someone's windows, Vee."

She jumped, her tanned, freckled face meeting mine with a hint of blush on her cheeks. "I thought you were dead!"

My sister could be dramatic, to say the least. Always expecting the worst-case scenario. I was shocked she hadn't overturned all of the rocks in front of my porch searching for a hidden key.

It was in the little wooden mallard, she would've never found it anyway.

"And you didn't think to call first?" I snorted. I picked up the little mallard and flipped it over, plucking the key out of its belly and giving her a wink. I hated taking my keys with me on runs. "I'm sure if I was dead, you would've heard Drew screaming his little head off."

"Or giggling up a storm," Veronica countered, side-eyeing my child as if he were the spawn of the devil.

I shoved the key in the lock and opened up the door before replacing the spare in its ducky home. "For the last time, Vee, he's not the anti-Christ."

She followed me inside, the screen door slamming behind her and nearly falling off its hinges. For a rental, it wasn't the worst place imaginable, but it wasn't exactly very well-looked after by previous tenants. Or me. I had bigger things to worry about.

"Sorry it's a mess," I sighed. She hadn't visited me in about two months. The last time she swung by was when she was visiting our parents, and thankfully, she hadn't ended up at my house. We'd met up at the park instead and then she was off again. She lived out in Miami the majority of the time, but she was always bouncing from place to place. I hoped she wouldn't judge my home and had spent time in worse. "It's a bit hard to keep on top of everything while taking care of Drew."

"Hmm. I'll have to work on that," she mumbled, collapsing onto the sofa in a heap. "What happened to your leg?"

I glanced down at the open wound poking out of my leggings. *Shit, it's swelling.* "Tripped on my jog. Just need to wash it out."

"Looks nasty."

"Thanks," I deadpanned. I glanced down at Drew as he drooled over his little white shirt, his eyes practically glued shut. I knew I needed to move him to the bassinet, but god, I didn't want him to wake up and kick off. "Are you visiting Mom and Dad?"

She blinked up at me. The dull, ugly brown of my sofa almost made her seem less lifelike than she normally did. "No. I came to help."

"What?"

"You said you were struggling to juggle work and Drew and that the nanny wasn't always available. I came to help you out."

Did I tell her that?

"Maybe he'll be less, uh, evil when he's not on Face-Time," she said, glancing at him warily.

"He's asleep, Vee. He's not going to start babbling demon summons."

My sister didn't know the first thing about looking after children. She had none of her own and often avoided them as much as she could, though, to be fair, I was the same way before I found out I was pregnant. Maybe it wouldn't be so awful if she double-teamed it with the nanny the first few times.

Though I did have a worrying suspicion she'd try to have him exorcized behind my back.

"So where am I staying?"

I snapped my gaze to her quickly. "What?"

"Mom and Dad said I couldn't stay with them."

"Jesus," I sighed, pinching the bridge of my nose between my eyes. Her need to insert herself without asking permission beforehand was something she'd carried with her since adolescence. The number of times she'd weaseled herself into my sleepovers and parties sat heavily on my mind. "Well, I've got a spare room but I don't have a bed—"

"That's fine. I'll buy a bed," she grinned as she cut me off. "I can sleep with you tonight and then tomorrow morning I'll have one delivered. Problem solved."

Problem solved. More like a problem created.

The stinging in my knee throbbed. "Fine. Whatever."

Chapter 5
Cole

I'd made a horrible mistake with my decision to go back to work so quickly. Waking up at six-thirty in the morning was never easy, even when I could drink the exhaustion away. But after months of waking up when my body said it was time, not the alarm, was even harder.

Day one had been agonizing. Day two had been painful. Day three, today, was only slightly better but still had a nagging sting to it.

"What's on the docket for you today?" I asked, glancing across the center console of my dark green Rolls Royce.

Bobby shrugged. "Figured I'd check out what Boulder has to offer. Your house gets a bit lonely."

I knew that feeling far too well.

The reds of the cobblestone streets reflected the morning light back up toward the sky, the college students shielding their eyes from the harshness of Boulder in the early fall. The clubs and restaurants had long closed down from the night before, but there was a tickling in my spine that wanted me to pull up to one of them, bang on the door, and force my way in.

But I wasn't going to do that.

I pulled to a stop at a red light, my car idling quietly, and tried to focus anywhere but the bar I used to frequent located on my left. Bobby hit my leg gently, and I glanced at his hand, following his pointed finger beyond the hood of the car to a group of young, college-aged women crossing the road in front of us. They stared at the car, their mouths agape and grinning. One of them waved and another shouted something I couldn't hear.

"Looks like they're interested," Bobby chuckled.

Six months ago, I might have shut off my car and gotten out in the middle of the intersection to try to convince one of them to get in and go anywhere with me. But not today. Not anymore. The thought that I used to be that way made my stomach churn.

"They've got fucking backpacks, Bobby."

"Yeah, but they're clearly students here."

"Too young. Too naive."

The girls passed and the light turned green. I couldn't hit the gas fast enough for my liking.

A few minutes down the road I pulled into the parking lot of the cafe I used to frequent before I left. I hadn't yet built up the nerve to stop in over the last couple of days, and with Bobby by my side this time, it felt much more doable.

The door chimed as we walked in. There were a handful of people waiting around for their coffee while others sat with their laptops open, ready to spend the day immersed in their work from the comfort of the cafe. I wished I could do that instead of going into the office.

"Cole!"

The owner, Eric, stood behind the counter. His graying hair and wide-eyed smile were always so welcoming, but after six months of being gone, it felt almost like an uncertain homecoming. "Hey, Eric."

"Long black with an extra shot?"

I don't know why I was surprised that he still remembered, I'd done my fair share of working behind the counter. I knew regular orders. But six months was a long time to remember. "Yeah," I grinned.

"Can you tack a latte onto that?" Bobby asked.

"Sure can." Eric got to making the drinks quickly, knocking out the old coffee puck into the trash and starting the process over again. "Where've you been? Missed your face."

"Uh—"

"Working on himself," Bobby grinned. "Me too. That's where we met, actually. This great place out in Cali—"

"He doesn't need to know the details," I snapped, the uncomfortableness of it creeping up the back of my skull. I didn't want that following me around, and Bobby's big fucking mouth was only going to make it worse.

Eric looked between Bobby and me, his brows knitted. He must've known, though. I couldn't count how many times I'd walked in here still drunk from the night before.

"What?" Bobby whispered.

"I don't want to tell everyone, okay? It just feels weird."

"All right," he sighed, eyeing me warily as if I was crazy. "My driver is about a minute away anyway."

"Driver?"

"Yeah, I'm going to head out to the golf club just outside of town. One of my friends sent in a recommendation for me, and they're going to let me in." He shrugged, taking the latte from Eric with a half-hearted thanks. "Maybe I'll check out what else Boulder has to offer to guys like us."

Guys like us. I knew he didn't mean drunks; Bobby was

the kind of person who truly enjoyed having money to an annoying degree.

The door chimed as I paid for our coffees. We turned to leave but within a split second I wished I could just fucking teleport instead of having to step toward the door.

"No shit." Adam, a tall, dark-haired, wiry man I used to drink with at the bar down the road grinned at me, the yellowing of his teeth and eyes making my stomach turn. "Where the hell have you been?"

I had two options: I could push him away and tell him the truth, or I could pretend like nothing had happened and get out of there faster.

I chose option two.

"Out of state for work," I lied, painting the fakest smile across my cheeks. "Good to see you."

"You too, man." Adam's hand clapped against my shoulder, shaking me just a little too hard, a little too rough. "You should've called. We can make plans to meet, catch up."

My throat tightened as I looked at Bobby. He seemed none the wiser, his nose buried in the top of his takeout cup instead of having to smell the strong scent of booze emanating from Adam. "Yeah, sorry. I'll call you."

Adam studied me. I knew I didn't look like I used to. I was more put together now, less sloppy, less of a mess. "You on the straight and narrow now too?" he asked, his brows knitting as he gave me a whiff.

I swallowed. "I—"

Adam snorted, his hand abandoning my shoulder. "Whatever, man. Good luck to you. It never lasts."

Before I could say a word he stepped around me and up to the counter, spouting his order to Eric the way I used to when I didn't give a shit. I booked it before he could ask me anything else.

Bobby followed behind me, waving absentmindedly at the black Porsche that pulled up alongside my car. "Don't worry about him," Bobby said, his gaze caught somewhere far off in the distance. "He's a shit. We'll get through this together."

I kind of wanted to get through it alone.

Bobby nodded at me as he stepped off toward the car he'd hired. I didn't know how I'd managed to get myself into this situation—my old friends looking down at me, my new friend someone I barely knew but seemed to be on this journey with me regardless. I didn't know how I even considered Adam a friend. It's not like we did things together outside of drinking, and I was fairly sure he and his group only liked me for my house, but still it stung, nonetheless.

Work helped to keep my mind sharp and to keep me distracted from giving in to the things I wanted, all right there in front of me. However, here, I could stare at the alcohol and not see it as a temptation, instead seeing it as nothing more than chemicals in the different stages of creation.

My start to the day still sat heavy in my mind, and as I made my way out of the main chamber of the brewery and toward the elevator back to my office, all I could think about was how much it made me sick to see Adam still drunk when I wasn't. He was definitely easier to be around when I was also inebriated.

The stack of papers in my hand did absolutely nothing to distract me from my thoughts. As I continued to think about Adam and my previous situation, something warm collided with me, nearly knocking me off my step. I wrapped my arm around it to keep my balance.

"Shit, sorry," a small voice mumbled.

I looked down, moving the papers out of my line of sight.

Shit, indeed.

Long brown hair, a tour guide uniform, freckles, and hazel eyes. That little beauty mark between her lower lip and her chin.

Dana.

My body froze. My hand around her waist, warm and soft against my skin, felt like an electric current. She looked as mortified as I felt, and as the seconds ticked by and things became even more awkward, I didn't know what to do or say. But something about holding her, the way her body curved against mine...

"Cole," she hissed.

My heart leaped in my chest as I released her without another word, snapping back to reality. She hurried off behind me but my legs were frozen in place, and it wasn't purely from the sticky floor that still hadn't been taken care of.

No, it was the little ache in my heart, the one that I'd felt when I'd sobered up after that horrible morning between us. The one I'd pushed down with drink after drink.

Fuck.

Chapter 6

Dana

I stood outside Cole's office with a clipboard, paper and a pen in my hand, bouncing from foot to foot. All I had to do was knock. That was it. I just needed to get inside, ask my questions, and go.

The amount of incessant inquiries I was getting with every tour about Cole's background was becoming tedious. I didn't know the answers outside of the standard ones I'd been told to give when I first got the job—he had a passion for beer. I laughed thinking about it now. Passion was one way to describe it.

I wished they'd told me who I was talking about before finding out the hard way.

But by going straight to the source, I could answer the questions the visitors presented with confidence. I hated having to avoid queries and conversations because I didn't know the proper thing to say, so my manager, Allison, had suggested having a conversation with him. If only she knew how fucking difficult that would be for me.

Taking a deep breath to steady myself, I knocked three

times on his opaque glass door, almost hoping he wasn't in there.

"Come in."

Godammit.

I pushed the door open, trying to breathe through the warmth that filled my face. "Do you have, like, ten minutes?"

His green eyes went wide as he shut his laptop. "Yeah. I do."

I wanted to go inside. Truly. But my feet betrayed me and stayed where they'd grown into the ground.

"Do you want me to follow you somewhere?"

"No, I... I'm coming in."

"Okay."

He blinked at me. I still didn't move.

"Dana—"

Finally, my body responded and I made the move into his office, softly shutting the door behind me with a click. What a great way to kick this off.

Silence hung in the air between us, awkward and heavy, and all I could do was fucking stare. As if I hadn't taken him in enough when he'd shown up unannounced the other night.

A sleek, shaven, chiseled jawline and a muscular neck were always my downfall, but with him, it was almost otherworldly. Maybe it was because I knew how well he knew how to handle a woman in the bedroom, or maybe it was just how attractive he was overall. His button-up clung to his chest, tight against the ripples of his pecs, his biceps, and his forearms. He wasn't quite as bulky as he'd been last year, but it was still enough to make my knees weak. His dark blonde hair, pushed back and to the side, was neatly groomed in a way I hadn't noticed last time. All that was missing was that little dimple that punctuated his cheek whenever he grinned too wide.

I shouldn't have felt the roar of butterflies in my stomach or the sinking heat between my thighs caused by the fleeting memories of his words to me as he caged me in on his bed, his cock ready, his eyes wild. *I'm going to fucking ruin you, baby.*

Truth is, he would have ruined me regardless, even if things hadn't ended the way they did.

"Can I ask what this is about?" he looked directly at me, his chin resting on his upturned hand as he leaned forward onto his desk.

I cleared my throat, hoping the heat in my cheeks wasn't nearly as noticeable as it felt, and sat down in one of the plush leather chairs directly opposite his workspace. The cleaning crew had done a great job—not a speck of dust anywhere. The mountain view outside the window behind him almost snagged away my attention but I forced myself to be present.

"Well, uh, I was wondering if it was okay for me to ask you a handful of questions about... you. I keep getting asked a bunch of shit on the tours and I don't have anything to tell them other than you have a passion for craft beer and the process of making it perfect."

A ripple of something that looked like shame crossed his eyes before he spoke. "Oh. Sure, I guess. Though I don't want you to tell them every detail of my life."

My throat closed a little. "I won't, I don't. Don't worry about that."

His mouth turned into a straight line as he nodded once. "Thank you."

I glanced down at my list of questions. I wished I'd

included a few extra ones such as: *What happened after that morning? Do you still drink like that? Can't you just fucking apologize?* Now wasn't the time, or the place, so instead, I started with the first one I'd written down.

"Why craft beer?"

He snorted out a laugh and leaned back in his chair, his body visually relaxing just a bit. "Because I'd done some home brewing and found it fun." His eyes lingered on me, flicking back and forth between the clipboard and my mouth. *Oh, my god.*

"Okay." *You're good. Calm down. Stop, for fucks sake, stop getting turned on.* I could work with that answer and capitalize on it. I jotted it down on my paper.

"Why Boulder? Did you grow up here?"

He shook his head. "No. I grew up in Austin."

"Texas?"

He nodded. "Yeah. I moved to Boulder as a teenager and my aunt took me in. Then I met Brody Harris and he agreed to mentor me on business after I graduated, I wanted to stay close to my new home," he explained. The way he looked at me was piercing, almost as if he was tearing me apart or fucking undressing me with just his eyes. It was hard to hold eye contact; it felt like a predator staring at his prey.

I swallowed and jotted down his answer as quickly as I could. I threw out an additional question, one that popped into my head. "Did you have an accent?"

"Everyone has an accent, Dana," he purred, his lip twitching up and flickering the hint of his dimple. "If you're asking if I sounded more southern than I do now, yes."

God, why did it sound so good when he said my name? "What happened to it?"

"Faded. As most things do."

He ensnared me again, catching my gaze and holding it for far longer than I should have allowed. It was foolish of me to even try to pretend that I didn't find him attractive. There was a reason I'd fallen in with him so quickly before, but I needed to keep myself at bay here. He'd fucked me over once, and he was more than capable of doing it again.

No way was I going to let that happen.

"Are you going to write that one down?"

I narrowed my eyes at him. "No," I said, my mouth feeling like it was full of sand. "I was just curious."

He chuckled darkly as he shifted in his seat. "Do I get to ask you questions just because I'm curious?"

"Absolutely not," I deadpanned. "Why this building?"

"At the time, I liked that it had originated as a brewery right before prohibition. Did you know they continued brewing in secret here during most of that period? They moved everything to the basement," he explained. "It wasn't on the blueprints. It still isn't. The only reason we know is because of the abandoned machinery down there. I thought it was really brave of them and I wanted to continue the legacy."

I took a deep breath. "And do you still feel that way?"

His gaze lingered a second too long once again before he turned from me. "Next question."

A chill went down my spine. I wasn't expecting that. "Okay. How did you fund the business?"

"Trust fund and an investment from my aunt," he replied. The words were quick, snappy, inattentive. I wondered if the previous question had gotten under his skin.

"Do you have any plans for expansion?"

"No."

"Is your aunt involved in the business?"

He winced. "No."

Was it just the questions I was asking that made his answers become so short or had I done something to ruin it? I couldn't tell. I wanted to know more, wanted to ask more questions that weren't on my list. "What's your family like?"

Again, that piercing glare met mine. "Next question, Dana."

"What do your parents think of the business?"

Silence fell over us in a quick, startling wave. I could hear the footsteps passing in the hallway, the sound of my breathing, the honking of horns three floors below on the street.

A storm brewed behind his eyes, menacing and angry, and I knew then that I'd royally fucked up. My heart pounded in my chest, aching and expanding, and my grip on the pen grew loose enough for it to fall from my hand and clatter against the hardwood floor.

"That's enough for now," he said, his voice like gravel as he broke his gaze and flipped open his laptop again. "If I were you, I'd leave before you regret coming in here more than you already do."

What the fuck did that mean? "Okay," I breathed. But I didn't move from the chair, couldn't find the will. I hated that this happened with him, this freezing up, this immobility that felt like a fucking trap. I wanted to stay. I wanted to know the answers to the questions he'd avoided. But more than anything else, I wanted to ask for an apology. I also wanted to give him one.

"I'll go," was what came out instead.

Finally willing myself to stand, I turned to the door, feeling his gaze like an iron barb in my back as I turned the handle.

"Dana," he said.

I halted, glancing over my shoulder. His mouth, perfectly symmetrical and far too inviting, opened and closed a handful of times before he spoke as if the words he wanted to say got stuck behind his teeth. I'd take anything— the smallest mention of what we'd shared, a brief apology, an acknowledgment of *something*. But he couldn't seem to find it in him.

"Close the door on your way out, please."

———

I sat down in my chair, the cramped space of my office almost suffocating. That had been far more intense than I'd imagined it in my head, even when one of those scenarios I'd come up with had ended with him fucking me over his desk. I shook the thought away.

My attraction to him was still strong, maybe even stronger. That was a problem in and of itself, because my god, I could not handle him. The moods, the hot and cold, those were quite the put off. Though I could understand the topic of family being triggering for him, I probably would have responded much the same to the question had someone asked me that.

Halfway through typing out a summary of the answers to send to my manager, my phone rang. For the smallest of seconds, I wondered if it was him. An apology, maybe. A text. Anything. But instead, Lottie's name flashed on my screen, and I answered it as I sent off the email to Allison.

"Hey," I said, a smile spreading across my cheeks. We hadn't spoken in almost two weeks, and with Drew and work and everything else piling on top of me, time had gotten away.

"Oh my god, I've missed you," Lottie gushed down the phone. "How are you? How's Drew?"

"I'm okay. Drew's good. I've missed you more."

"I swear, we need to get Brody and Drew together for a playdate soon. I need Dana time so badly," she chuckled. "I'm sorry I haven't called."

"It's okay, no worries." I leaned back in my chair, my eyes turning to the mop slouched against the wall on the other side of the tiny office. I had a sneaking suspicion I shared a space with the custodian. "We definitely need to get together. I miss the horses."

"Maybe sometime this weekend? If you're available, I mean. I know your shifts can be a bit weird. Oh! How's work? I heard he-who-must-not-be-named is back."

My blood ran cold. "You knew he ran the business?"

"Uh..."

"*Lottie.*"

"Look, I," she sighed. I could hear Brody's giggles in the background. "Please don't be mad."

"Seriously?"

"I didn't know how long he'd be gone. And I thought maybe, when he came back, you guys could, like, talk. Or make up. Or make out. I don't know."

"Jesus—"

"I know, I know, it was childish. But I just thought with everything that maybe it was worth it. I didn't want to meddle and stop you from leaving Harris Ranch just because he owned Pearson Beers. You wanted out and it was a good offer." The way she rambled made my head spin. "But I'll hire you back if you want to leave. I don't want you to feel trapped."

I sighed and kicked the base of the wall with my boot. I could tell her I was pissed, I could shout at her, but I just didn't have the energy. But it still hurt a little that she knew what had happened between us and hadn't said anything to me when I started working here. "It's okay. I'm not mad. Just a little taken back."

An incoming email from Allison made me pause.

Meet me in my office in five.

"I've got to go," I said. "And not because I'm annoyed—which I am, a little—but I have to meet with my manager."

"Promise?"

"Promise. I'll see you soon."

The short walk to Allison's office gave me time to think far too hard about the situation with Cole. The more present he was around here would inevitably cause complications. He seemed more in control, much more confident in a way he hadn't been before. He was always a light in the dark somehow, but now, he was shining even brighter.

I wondered what caused the change, wondered where he'd been.

A buzz in my pocket had me checking my phone with hope again, but this time, it was a text from Vee. A photo of her and Drew in the park, his giggling face lighting up my world for just a moment. The nanny stood behind them, her eyes off in the distance, almost as if she were standing guard. It was nice to see Vee getting along with Drew. Maybe she didn't think he was the anti-Christ after all.

A thought hit me like a sinking stone as I slowed to a stop outside Allison's door. If Cole was going to be around more often, he'd find out fairly quickly I had a son. I didn't exactly keep it a secret—it was plastered all over my time-off requests, my schedule, and my emails.

How the fuck was I supposed to tell him Drew was his?

Chapter 7
Cole

Six months was long enough for the plans I'd enacted before my departure to reach fruition.

Rows and rows of prototypes lined the table in front of me. Sours, pale ales, and IPAs infused with different tropical fruits. A new expansion on our already significant product lineup.

And I couldn't even taste it.

Lines of small cups sat in front of the new beers, each filled about halfway with testers. The tour guides, bar staff, and wait staff stood before me, shuffling awkwardly on their feet. Toward the back on the righthand side, Dana looked anywhere but directly at me.

"Anyone that would like to try the new lineup can come up and grab one," I said, lifting my chin just a hair to keep the air of being in control. "Please only take one of each. Don't need anyone getting drunk at work."

Whispers flitted around the room as the majority of them formed a line behind the table, including Dana. I couldn't blame them for the gossip, plenty of them were aware of my old habit of drinking at work. It was hard to miss.

The goal now was to create enough buzz that the products would fly off the shelves and taps. The tour guides would focus on the brewing aspect of it, which we'd already gone over, and the bar and wait staff would push it to newcomers and regulars alike. I watched each one take their cups and drink, my mouth salivating at the idea of finally getting to try what I'd wanted to make for years. I felt like a fucking sham.

Dana met my eyes briefly as she sipped at each one, tossing away a mostly full cup after each sip.

As the group filtered back into their positions, questions began flying at me left and right. *How long is each one brewed for? Is the fruit fermented separately? Will there be testers for those on the tour?* I handled each with as much care as I could before rapid firing into the next.

But it was seeing Dana's hand raised that stopped me in my tracks and made me pause.

"What do you think of them?" she asked, her voice booming over the others in the room. Everyone went dead silent.

It wasn't a bad question despite the intent behind it. A quotable endorsement from myself would benefit all of them. I just didn't have an answer. And from the look on her face, her honey-hazel eyes wide and her mouth parted just enough to entice me, she knew damn well she'd stumped me.

And she liked it.

"I think it's exactly what I've been dying to make for years," I said, each word carefully chosen.

"What's the percentage?" Dana asked, using the quiet to her advantage.

"Seven."

She nodded, her hair bouncing forward then falling back. She didn't break eye contact once, holding my gaze in the same way I'd done the day before with her. There was a heaviness, a staggering weight between us that made me hungry for her.

My cock twitched.

Fuck.

I was thankful the table was high enough to cover my lower half as hazy memories from that night flitted across my mind. Her, naked, full of my cum, and begging for more. Her mouth, that same one that asked me angering and perfect questions, split open wide and waiting on her knees. The way she'd tasted as I'd devoured her pussy over and over, like fucking honey, like overripe strawberries—

Stop, for fucks sake.

I took a seat and let them mingle amongst each other, trying more of the beers. The sample stock wouldn't be sold, and I was happy for them to take as much home as they wished. The alternative was taking it home with me, and that simply wasn't an option, no matter how much I wanted it.

How fucking ironic that I owned a brewery and couldn't taste what we made.

A handful of people came up to ask me personal questions and I let them, hoping for the blood in my cock to dissipate enough that it wasn't noticeable. But just when I'd figured I was calm enough to make my rounds, Dana's face shined through the crowd as she approached, her hands clasped together in front of her. I wondered if she even realized her arms were pressing her breasts together, creating a luscious cleavage.

"Hey," she said, a tight-lipped smile flashing across her

face. "I'm sorry about the question. That was kind of rude of me. Especially in front of everyone."

I shook my hand and waved it off, standing from my seat. "Don't worry about it. It was a good one, and in fairness, I think I gave a pretty quotable answer."

A little chuckle seeped past her lips. "Yeah, I can definitely use it to my advantage. 'What does Mr. Pearson think of his latest lineup?'" Her voice deepened as she pretended to be a questioning guest, that silly, goofy attitude making its first appearance in months. "Well, sir, he thinks it's exactly what he's been dying to make for years!"

I laughed at her impression of me, less because it was funny and more because it was the first genuinely pleasant interaction I'd had with her since I'd returned. Maybe the first pleasant interaction with anyone. "I don't sound like that," I chuckled.

"Oh, you totally do. If only I could grow, like, nine inches taller, then I could look down my chin at them and puff out my chest—"

"God, I'm not that bad."

Her giggles were infectious. The version of herself that she'd been hiding under a mask was slowly coming out, and fuck, I loved it. "You so are. Do you ever look back on interactions and think, *hmm, maybe I shouldn't have been that big of an asshole?*"

Her words came crashing down for both of us at the same moment. The life drained from her, the light in her eyes dulling. Her smile faded. And I could feel each of those things happening to me too. *Yes,* I wanted to say. *Every fucking day I think I shouldn't have treated you that way.*

On the nights when I felt the worst about it, I took comfort in pushing away the memories of what happened after the smashing of the glass. But I also knew that was probably a privilege only I possessed.

She glanced down at her watch as she noticed a handful of people leaving the room. I could tell she wanted to follow them by the way her eyes lingered, but before she could make a run for it, I grabbed her attention. "Can I take you out?"

Wide, angry eyes snapped to mine. There she was again, the angry girl that had become her new normal.

"Not like that. Not a date. I'll draw that line now," I clarified.

"Then what is it?" she asked, a breath of hesitation to her tone.

"We can have dinner. Hash things out. Clear the air," I suggested, taking a small step toward her, careful not to scare her off with my proximity. "If you're going to be working for me, the least I can do is make things more comfortable for you."

She glanced at her watch again and back to the doors before finally looking up at me. "I don't know, Cole. That sounds like a recipe for disaster."

"Or it could make your life easier."

She scoffed. "My life isn't easy to begin with. I don't expect it to become any easier just because you take me on a date."

"Not a date," I corrected. "Just a casual chat and some food."

"In public?"

I knew what she meant by that. There was an air of safety with being in public—I couldn't get too drunk and I couldn't verbally attack her, at least not without repercussions. "In public. Yes."

Her lower lip slipped between her teeth. I couldn't help

but think of other things I'd like to see between her teeth instead.

I took another step toward her, crowding her just a little. "Do me this favor, Dana, and I'll make as many things easier for you as I possibly can."

Her lashes fluttered absentmindedly as she looked me up and down. "Fine. Text me where and I'll meet you at seven. I've got things I need to sort out at home first."

I sat in my desk chair, my knee bouncing nonstop and driving me insane, but I couldn't stop. I felt like a teenager who'd just asked a girl he'd been crushing on to go on a date, even though that wasn't what this was.

Not a date.

Two more hours. I could wait that long. But damn it felt like forever.

Four thirty-minute segments.
Six twenty-minute segments.
Eight fifteen-minute segments.
Twelve ten-minute segments.
Twenty-four five-minute segments.

Somehow, looking at it that way, didn't make it seem any quicker.

I couldn't focus on work, so that was out of the question. I could go home, but I'd only have about ten minutes before I'd have to head back into town. I could go to my apartment, but the thought of stepping in there after six months of emptiness and the countless bottles that waited felt more like hell than watching paint dry.

Instead, I sent Bobby a text.

Won't be home until late.

Immediately, he responded.

Hot date?

I chuckled.

Something like that. I'll fill you in later.

―――

Fifteen minutes before Dana was meant to arrive, I found myself stepping foot into a restaurant I was far too intimately familiar with.

The hostess was the same woman I assumed it would be. She was always friendly with me, always professional, and of course, she remembered me.

"Mr. Pearson! So lovely to see you," she grinned. "I was beginning to think you'd moved away."

I smiled, shoving my hands in my pockets. "No, just busy."

"Your table is available. I'll move your reservation," she said, giving me a sly little wink as she jotted something down.

I followed her to a table in the back, one I always requested. I'd wanted to be as far from the front windows as possible in case I got a little too drunk, a little too rowdy. I didn't need it for those reasons anymore, but either way, I was flattered.

"Whiskey sour to start?" she asked as I slid into the chair.

I almost said yes. Almost. "Actually, can I get a glass of water?"

"As well as the whiskey sour?"

"Instead of it."

She blinked, and for a moment, I think she was genuinely concerned she remembered the wrong person. "Of course. I'll get a pitcher for the table."

Before she could return, the door opened and a breeze blew in, taking my breath at the same moment she did.

With her hair swept up into a neat updo and a silky, strappy black dress covering her from the tips of her breasts to a couple of inches below her ass, I knew I was absolutely ruined for the evening. I held no ground as hazel eyes met mine across the room and her upper chest and cheeks darkened into a shade of pink. I had half a mind to run to her; I couldn't wait for her to get closer.

My gaze never left her as she slowly walked toward our table. Every inch of her was explosively intoxicating. I didn't notice the hostess dropping off the pitcher of water, the glasses, or the menus. The other people in the room faded into the background, becoming a simple, meaningless blur that I couldn't give less of a shit about.

As she sat down in the seat next to me, her scent surrounding me in a fog of honeysuckle, I wondered if I could get drunk off of her alone.

"Hi," she said, one brow raising. She looked me up and down, waiting for a reply, and the realization that I hadn't spoken a single word to her yet hit me.

I cleared my throat. "Hey."

"Stop staring at me like that," she hissed, reaching

forward over the table and picking up the pitcher. "I'm not a piece of meat."

"I'm not staring," I lied. I could feel the corner of my lip twitching, a smile begging to sprout. "Am I not allowed to appreciate how nice you look?"

"No, because it's not a date."

"I knew I shouldn't have said that when I asked you," I chuckled. I lifted the pitcher from her hands and poured us each a glass of water. "Fatal mistake on my part."

"I wouldn't have come if you didn't say it," she retorted.

I couldn't help but watch her as she flipped open the menu, her delicate little fingers wrapping themselves around it gently. Seeing those same fingers brought back too many images, nails painted a slightly different shade of red, wrapped around the shaft of my cock instead.

I knew she was mad. I knew that in the pit of my stomach and in the way she glared at me from the corner of her eye. That moment of joking earlier was a blip. I'd royally fucked up with her, worse than I had with any woman in my life, and although I knew I'd said some awful things to her after the glass shattered that fucking awful morning, they had vanished for me the moment they left my lips. I couldn't even apologize for them, not without context, not without knowing how deeply I'd cut her.

And something told me she wouldn't dare consider anything more with me until I apologized.

Everything I ordered, sans the water instead of the whiskey sour, was what I always requested when I came here. A house salad, bread to share, a filet mignon cooked medium rare, dauphinoise potatoes, and asparagus. Dana had taken longer than I expected to choose something, and when she'd asked what I recommended, I couldn't give her a genuine answer. The truth was I had no idea what to recommend—I was too much a creature of habit to be able to suggest anything else.

In the end, she ordered the blackened tilapia with lime and coriander rice, a side of Mediterranean mixed vegetables. She shot me another scowl as she handed the menu over to the waitress. "You're paying," she said. It wasn't a question.

"Did you think for a second I'd ask you to cover your half?" I scoffed. "You're my employee. This is... loosely considered work. I wouldn't have let you pay if you tried."

Her gaze lingered on my lips for half a second too long to be natural. "Thanks, then."

Thanks. My throat closed in and I tried to contain my shock. I couldn't imagine a world in which she said that to me outside of the bedroom, but here we were. Having a conversation with her in a restaurant was awkward, to say the least.

"You didn't have to do this, you know. I could have handled being around you without the awkwardness of dinner," she said, a sneaky little smile crossing her lips. "I'd say I've done a fairly good job of avoiding you when I need to."

I tilted my head side to side, weighing up her words. "True. But then you wouldn't have had this spectacular not-a-date with me."

She snorted, her hand instinctively covering her mouth and nose. "Spectacular is certainly one way to put it."

"Well, you know, had you actually dressed up instead of wearing pajamas maybe it could have been truly spectacular," I laughed, my eyes dragging over her far too beautiful frame and the gorgeous dress that covered it. Teasing had always come easy with her.

Her mouth popped open in faux disgust. "Well if *you*

hadn't shown up in just your boxers, maybe I'd have dressed for the occasion," she giggled, the tips of her fingers grazing the edge of my suit jacket's sleeve. Her lips curled into a positively shining grin, little specs of shimmer catching the light from her deep red gloss.

God dammit, I wanted to kiss her.

Our food arrived a moment later. We spoke idly as we ate, mostly about work and the people who had been hired on in my absence. She filled me in on the drama between tour guides, how one of the newbies was more intense than the rest, and insisted on taking as many people as he could in one group. She told me about how a woman had leaned so far over the railing on the overhead walkway of the brewhouse, about how panicked she was knowing I was twenty feet below. I hadn't been aware of what was happening though I do remember looking up at her from the floor, watching her anxious face as she stared back at me. I hadn't even realized.

Despite the elephant in the room, I was genuinely surprised at how easy it was to speak to her. We'd always gotten along well since that first time I'd met her in Lottie's backyard, but we didn't have weights on our shoulders then. As simply two people who had just met, we meshed almost too well.

The more she offered me stolen glances and gentle, barely there smiles, the more I lost my hold on myself. I touched her, my fingers just barely grazing her knuckles, and she hadn't recoiled. I wondered if she was fighting demons over what was happening, but if she was, they mustn't have been too hard to overcome—she touched me back just as eagerly. A knee and a forearm against mine as she laughed while she told me something her manager had said to her days before. I hadn't even caught what it was. I was too transfixed in how agonizingly beautiful she looked as she tipped her head back in a fit of giggles, her shoulder bumping against mine, her grin unmistakably genuine.

God, I'd fucked up with her.

I was moving before I even realized it. In the same way I used to end up with a drink in my hand without remembering pouring it, I was crowding her, my hand around the back of her neck, my lips against hers. I didn't remember the journey but I didn't regret it, either. Not when the stiffness in her body softened, not when she melted against me far too eagerly. Her lips tasted of blackened seasoning and strawberries, an odd combination from her dinner and her lip gloss, but I didn't mind.

The sound of a plate being set down on the table in front of us didn't faze me as I pressed my tongue between her lips, parting them. She didn't protest, instead welcoming me like a long-lost friend, a haven in a storm, a glass of whiskey to my aching chest.

This wasn't good for us. I knew that. Not when we had history between us.

She pulled back, just enough that her lips parted from mine but our breaths still mixed. Almost reluctantly, her eyes fluttered up to mine, a look of resignation hanging over her. "My sister's staying with me," she breathed.

I studied her eyes. *What the fuck does that mean?*

"Can we go to your place instead?"

Chapter 8

Dana

I knew I was making one of the worst decisions of my life. I knew it the moment he'd kissed me and I didn't push him away, knew it in the forty-minute car ride out to god-knows-where, knew it as I stepped onto the gravel driveway and looked up at the monstrosity of the home before me. It was like something out of Beverly Hills or Malibu, tucked into the corners of the mountains. A massive estate with floor-to-ceiling windows, large, ornate pillars, expertly maintained shrubbery, and a goddamn infinity pool.

I knew it when he'd taken me inside and the double staircase took up half of the foyer. I knew it when he'd lead me up the stairs and through the winding halls, when the double doors to his massive bedroom opened up, when my dress hit the floor.

He kissed me hungrily, his hands grasping at my waist and jaw as if he were afraid I'd run. I wondered why he hadn't brought me here a year ago, wondered if he even owned this then, but in fairness we were so desperate at the time that it probably wouldn't have even fazed me. Now, though, as the doubts and worries sunk into the pit of my stomach, I couldn't help but notice how different this house was.

This place, this home, didn't smell of booze. *He* didn't smell of booze. He hadn't had a single drink the entirety of dinner, and I couldn't help but wonder if he was planning on drinking like last time after I'd fallen asleep.

My decision to go home with him may not have been the best one but I was lonely. I was a single mom, constantly on the go, too busy for men and their bad habits to consider taking time for myself. But I wanted, *needed*, to feel desired. I hadn't slept with anyone since Cole, and with memories from the last time he'd fucked me still fresh on my mind, I knew he'd do a damn good job of making me feel like I was more than just a one-night stand. Even though that's what this was.

His mouth left mine to explore my neck, his heavy breaths warming my skin. My fingers traced the lapels of his suit coat and latched on, pushing it back and over his shoulders. It fell to the ground in a heap beside my dress.

"This is a bad idea," I gulped, but I didn't let it stop me. I pulled on his tie, freeing it, and dropped it. I plucked open his buttons, my knuckles grazing the warm, hard skin beneath.

"Tell me to stop then," he rasped, his teeth sinking into my skin with a nip of pain before he soothed the ache with his tongue. "I'll drive you back. Just say the word."

"I don't want you to stop."

"Good, because I don't want to," he replied. One hand gripped the side of his shirt and pulled, popping and freeing the remaining buttons. They littered the floor as he pushed the fabric from his chest.

Fuck, he still looked amazing.

His muscles had shrunk since the last time I'd seen him, but they were still there, hard as stone and rippling out from under his skin. I dragged my fingers along them, resisting the urge to kiss, lick, and bite the way he loved to do to me.

He sprang into action the moment I took his belt in my hand.

"Don't even fucking think about it," he snarled, his arm cupping me beneath the shelf of my ass, lifting me up. Before I could get too comfortable, I was falling, landing firmly on my back in a heap of plush sheets. His hands pushed me down when I tried to sit up, then they were moving around my chest to free the clasps of my black strapless bra. He tossed it somewhere behind him then focused on my black lacy panties, pulling without an inkling of warning, and discarding them just as quickly. "I need to taste you."

His hands wrapped around the backs of my thighs and pushed them upward at the same moment he fell to his knees.

A wave of self-consciousness hit me. In my year of celibacy, I'd grown an entire baby and pushed him out of me. I'd spent some time looking in the mirror and noticed that the color around that area had changed a bit. I also knew from personal time with myself that I didn't get wet as easily as I used to.

If he noticed any of it, though, he didn't let on.

His mouth closed in on me, licking and nibbling at the inside of my thighs. I wanted this. God, I wanted this. I didn't care if I regretted it tomorrow morning or immediately after. The words he'd said to me a year ago didn't fucking matter.

Just when I thought I couldn't take anymore, he finally found his way to my aching clit, sucking it into his mouth.

The movements from his lips and tongue, the nibbling on my thighs, had caused me to grow wet and his saliva seeping into my folds added delicious extra lubrication.

I breathed out a moan as his fingers slid inside of me. I'd been too nervous after childbirth to put anything up there, not even a tampon, and the one time I'd done it had resulted in a bit of bleeding. The feeling of it was almost otherworldly from how long it had been.

"You moan so pretty for me," he mumbled, his words muffled from how full of me his mouth was. His fingers curled up, pressing on that godsend of a spot inside of me, drawing sounds I hadn't made in over a year.

My hand knotted in his hair, pulling at the strands, needing something steady to hold on to. Over and over, his tongue dragged over my clit, nipping and sucking at the little bundle of nerves, and far too quickly I was falling over the hurdle of my first release. My thighs closed in on his head as my body spasmed, my breathing stagnant, and good *god* he kept going, pulling me through every wave and drowning me in it.

He only stopped when my legs fell away from him.

"I need to be inside you," he rasped, his eyes wild, his pupils dilated so far I could barely see the hint of green. Without saying another word he stood, stepped around the side of the bed, and opened his dresser, fumbling for something I couldn't quite see.

"Cole," I breathed. My voice was weak and broken, my vision hazy. I wanted more and fuck, what was taking him so long?

He turned and shut the drawer, something I couldn't quite make out in the low light in his palm. I blinked through the fog of my orgasm and watched as he dropped it on the bed next to me.

A bottle of lube.

My chest tightened. He'd noticed. But he didn't seem to have a problem with it.

He took his trousers off, his tight, black boxers hugging that magnificent bulge of his. Just above the hemline, two lines were carved down his lower stomach, forming a deep V that pointed exactly where I was desperate to see and feel.

He pushed me back further onto the bed and came over me, freeing himself from the fabric and kicking it off. His cock sprang to life against my pubic mound. Long, girthy, veiny, with a hint of reds and purples at the glistening, dripping tip.

My mouth watered.

"I haven't been able to stop imagining this," he rasped. He plucked the bottle of lube from beside me and popped the top, pumping a glob onto the top of his shaft and another just below my clit. It was freezing, but his hands warmed it quickly, rubbing it around the entrance and pushing it inside as his other hand spread it over himself. "Remembering what you sound like. How much you'd been aching for me."

I gulped as his tip pressed against my opening. "Is it what you hoped for?"

"It's fucking better." Hands pressed my legs back, positioning me perfectly, just like he had that first night. "It's so much fucking better."

Slowly, gentler than he was before, he eased himself inside of me. The sting of the stretch hit me immediately, and as I sucked in air through my teeth, he paused, leaning down to kiss me as his knuckles rubbed against my clit. "Sorry," I mumbled against his lips. "It's been a while. I'm a little, uh, out of practice."

He sank to his full length, burying himself so deeply that I couldn't imagine a world where I wasn't full of him. "I've got you, baby."

He made me feel like I was melting.

Once I'd finally stretched enough to accommodate him easily, he finally began to move. Blinding pleasure bloomed in my veins, and *oh my god*, I missed this. I missed this so goddamn much. All of him, the way he touched me, the way he moved inside of me.

He kissed and fucked me voraciously. It was as if something snapped inside of us, something that made us want—no, need—more. His thrusts were devastating, the perfect angle and pace, and with every shift of my hips it felt like we were building something more than just a release inside of each other. His mouth assaulted my own, his tongue exploring every inch of me, and the moment his fingers returned to my clit I knew I was fucking done for.

"Fuck, Cole," I moaned, my back arching and forcing my lips to part from his. He dropped his head lower, kissing and nipping at the skin of my breasts. *Shit, shit, shit, please don't go for my nipples. Please.* I didn't want to think about the possibility of leaking onto his tongue. It was a miracle they hadn't fired up when he was kissing me; thankfully I had pumped before dinner.

His lips closed in over the peak, and I panicked.

My hand flew to his throat, forcing his head up. I pulled him back up to my face, absentmindedly wiping away any potential residue on my hand and trying to disguise it as self-pleasuring. "They're sore," I lied, my cheeks heating astronomically.

He nodded, lost in his own need, and I thanked my lucky stars that he didn't push any further. Instead, he kissed me, burying himself in me over and over, and within seconds, I was rapid-firing closer and closer to another orgasm.

"I'm close," I whimpered, my nails digging into the skin on the back of his neck.

Everything about him became sharper. His thrusts, the kneading of his fingers, the way he kissed me. It was as if he hyper-focused on what he was doing, ensuring every bit of it stayed the same, keeping his pace and touches exactly how I needed them. "Come for me then, baby," he whispered, his grunts growing. I could feel him twitching inside of me, hardening further to a degree I didn't think possible. "I want to hear you scream."

I tipped over the edge, sounds ripping from my throat, leaving it raw and aching. He took complete control, holding my hips steady, plowing into me as if his life depended on it as he threw himself over the cliff at the same time, panting and grunting his desperation against my lips. All it did was light that fire again for me.

We stilled our breaths, our bodies finally coming down from the heavens, a sheen of sweat coating our skin.

How did I already want more?

The ache in my breasts forced my eyes to open.

The room was pitch black, the only sound that of Cole's deep breathing as he clung to me, his chest pressed against my back, his arms encasing me. I grabbed for my phone to check the time and was not surprised at all to find it was two in the morning. I swear, my body's internal clock was shockingly accurate.

The realization hit me all at once. I'd left my pump in my car which was still parked in the restaurant parking lot. *Fucking idiot.* I shined my screen's light on the sheets beneath me. A little wet puddle was forming.

I needed to go.

As silently and gently as I could, I slipped from Cole's hold, squirming my way off the bed. I pressed down on my breast, hoping for just a little relief, and felt the slow trickle run down the curved flesh and over my stomach. I needed to get Drew on formula if this was going to be a recurring theme.

Turning my phone's brightness down, I requested an Uber and began the hunt for my clothes. One by one I managed to find them, and as I slipped my dress over my head, I noticed the leakage was already seeping out of my bra. *Shit.*

Scrambling for something to cover myself with, I pulled open one of Cole's drawers and found something soft and warm with graphic letters written across the front. I could only hope it was a hoodie. I couldn't tell what it said in the darkness but it didn't matter, it would do the trick.

Clutching my heels in my hand and slipping out of the bedroom, I got my first real look at the house without being overwhelmed and distracted by how much I wanted him. It was beautiful—unique and ornate, as if an architect from the 1920s had designed it. Massive windows framed most of the rooms, with exposed wood beams jutting through the ceiling or running along the corners. Reddish-brown hardwood floors ran the expanse of the hallways, and as I took a turn that I thought might be familiar, the floor turned to smooth, cool stone on my bare feet as I stepped into the kitchen.

"For fucks sake, Christian! You're supposed to be the goddamn medic!"

I jumped at the unexpected noise in the darkness. It didn't sound like it was coming from upstairs where I'd left Cole. No, this was further down a hallway, maybe a floor below in the basement. I set my shoes and my phone down on the massive kitchen island and took a step toward the noise, worry creeping up my spine.

"Then take a fucking MP potion, you moron! Don't let us suffer because you're shit at the game!"

I stopped. Okay, less worrisome if it's a game.

But who the fuck is that?

I didn't think it was in Cole's character to have a roommate. Though I guess in a house this large, you could easily have one and pretend you didn't. But there was no mention of him on the drive over, no heads up, and if this was said possible roommates' normal state—shouting about a video game in the middle of the night—surely a heads up would have been nice.

But what exactly was I expecting of Cole? It wasn't really my place to ask questions about his roommate if indeed he had one, was it?

I pulled the hoodie over my head and glanced down at it in the low light. A logo bearing the Kansas City Chiefs emblem decorated the front of it, and although it looked ridiculous over my dress, it wasn't stained to shit from my breast milk. It would do.

My phone dinged on the countertop. The Uber had arrived.

I just needed to find the exit.

Waking up at seven in the morning after not falling asleep until nearly one, waking up at two, making my way home by three, pumping, crawling into bed, and passing out would have meant I couldn't function had it happened a year ago. But I'd grown used to surviving on barely any sleep after Drew was born. It wasn't easy by any means, and if last night was anything to go off of, I was absolutely going insane.

But as I looked at myself in the mirror, taking in every little bruise and bite mark, soreness blooming between my thighs, I couldn't help but not care. If anything, I was happy about it. Sex with Cole had been the best sex of my life the first time it happened and was only more so now. Maybe I could have my cake and eat it, too.

Pulling my satin robe tighter around my body, I turned the handle on the shower and it roared to life.

"Where were you last night?"

I glanced behind me as I stuck my hand into the stream of water, waiting for it to warm up. Veronica stood in the doorway, a giggling Drew on her hip, her hair wild and pajamas crooked. My lips tugged upward seeing Drew so happy in her arms. I stepped toward her and placed a little kiss on the top of his head as I did my daily smell check. *Still smells like heaven.*

"Dana."

"I went out with some friends," I lied, grinning as Drew's little hand wrapped itself around my finger.

"Friends?" Vee asked, one brow raising. "Is it normal for your friends to give you hickeys?"

"What, yours don't?"

Her glare pierced through me, her face stoic and dull. I wondered if Drew had kept her up late.

"Thank you for watching him," I sighed, relinquishing my cheery mood. I could feel it slipping from my grasp the moment she appeared, dragging me back down to reality.

Sliding my hands under Drew's arms, I hoisted him out of Vee's grasp and into my own. He cooed happily, still a little sleepy. "You're going to shower with him?" Vee asked.

I nodded. "Yeah, I've got a little tub thing for him. He loves it."

She eyed me warily and slowly backed out of the bathroom, mumbling something about Drew being the spawn of Satan. If only she knew the half of it.

Veronica hadn't shut up since I'd walked out of the bathroom with a naked baby and my hair up in a twisted towel. Apparently, she'd met up with some friends she'd made online over the weekend and there was drama, but if I had to sit through another second of hearing what Kyle had said to Natalie and how crazy it had been, I might have kicked off worse than Drew does when he's tired.

"You know, Mom thinks they need to just suck it up and get married," she continued. That word, that single word, brought my entire body to a fucking halt.

Drew's mouth searched for the bottle as it slipped from his lips. He glanced back and forth around his bouncer. My knife froze against the bagel, cream cheese half smeared, my mug of coffee burning the skin of my other hand. "You've been talking to Mom?" I breathed, slowly turning my gaze to her.

"Of course I've been talking to Mom," Vee said, her brows knitting together. "She's not happy you haven't brought Drew around to see them."

As carefully as I could manage, I set the mug and knife down before I broke something. Thought after thought raced through my mind, blurring into incoherent sentences, and all I could muster was a quiet, "You told them about Drew?"

"What? No. He's all over your Instagram, they figured it out."

"My page is private," I snapped. I'd made sure it was seven million times before I posted a photo of Drew. I didn't need my parents snooping, and even more than that, I didn't need Cole snooping.

Vee shrugged. "I don't know what to tell you. Maybe you accepted Mom by mistake. Either way, they have a right to meet their grandson—"

"Fuck no, Mom does not have any rights."

Drew's babbles went quiet as he watched the two of us. I thanked my lucky stars that he had no idea what we were saying.

"I don't want them around him. Or me, for that matter."

"Dana. Come on. You can't still be mad at them—"

"I am!" I snapped, my hands seizing into fists as I tried to contain the irritation boiling inside of me. "You think just because Mom is blood she deserves to meet him? After everything we went through together as kids, do you honestly think I would feel comfortable with him around her?"

"Calm down. She's not as bad as you remember," Vee pushed.

Not as bad as I remember. "You must have wiped your fucking memory then!"

A choked little sob pierced through the air and within a second, my coffee and bagel were no longer important. I went to Drew before I'd even realized I was moving, scooped him up out of his bouncer, and tucked him against my chest as he started to cry.

"You'll have to forgive her one day," Vee grumbled, sipping at her tea as if nothing at all had just happened. I wanted to tell her to go to hell. Wanted to tell her to grab our mother and drag her down with her on her way.

But more than that, I wanted Drew to calm down.

Chapter 9

Cole

I couldn't stop thinking about how cold the bed had been when I woke up yesterday morning. Despite the screaming crowd around me and the shouts from the cheerleaders down below, it was barely enough to hold my attention. Instead my mind crept toward the memories of Dana—how soft she felt beneath my fingertips, how warm and fucking heavenly her pussy felt, how easily I'd slept with the heat of her pressed against me.

Until last night, I hadn't had a good night's sleep in almost six months. And even so I still barely slept at all. But the little I did sleep was restful, with her body next to mine.

Grayson had convinced me that a day out watching the Colorado Buffaloes play their second home game of the early season would help me feel more alive and less like a shell of myself. I'd done everything in my power to conceal that feeling, so his ability to pick up on it had shaken me more than I expected it to.

He didn't really give me the chance to say no.

And although it certainly gave me a much noisier environment to stew in my thoughts, it didn't quiet them. *Why did she leave? Why not wake me? No note? No text? Nothing.*

"You've got to stop this, man," Bobby grunted, one hand on my shoulder and one clutching a hotdog as he came around the side of me. The amount of ketchup on it made my stomach churn. "I can see it in your eyes. It's the same look you got during group sessions."

I raised an eyebrow at him. His long black hair swayed in its ponytail as he cast his gaze at me, shaking his head.

"Overthinking. Retreating."

"Ah," I sighed, resisting the urge to roll my eyes as a glob of ketchup fell onto his jersey. He didn't even notice. "I'm fine. Don't worry about me."

"Look, it's like Angie would say every time as we packed up after counseling. One step at a time."

Buzz words. That's what they were. Thrown around, pounded into us day after day. "Angie was a nightmare," I deadpanned.

With a mouth full of hotdog, he laughed, spewing bits of the red condiment against the glass of the private viewing box. "Yeah, I fucking hated her. But some of the stuff she said was true."

"She always gave me shit for coming in late even though she knew I had therapy just before her session," I said, leaning back in the far too rigid seat for how much the private box cost. I should have brought cushions. "I swear, she hated us."

"Sometimes I think she would have rather us relapse than be there in her group therapy," Bobby chuckled.

The crowd erupted into cheers, and as I turned my attention back to the game, I noticed someone had scored. From the look of the jersey, I assumed it was the Buffaloes, but I wasn't really a football guy. I could have sworn our goal post was on the other end.

The band played some kind of rallying song as the color guard spun their batons and flags. The cheer team shook their pom-poms and moved into formation. "What's happening?" I asked.

"UC won."

I turned in my chair toward the sound of the unknown voice. For a moment, the smallest of split seconds, my brain convinced me it was her. But the blonde hair and the toddler at her feet were anything but Dana.

Gray's ex-wife, Halsey, stood with their three-year-old, Penelope, at the back of the box. I hadn't even heard them come in.

"Say hi, Penny," she said, patting the little girl on the back as she clung to her stuffed rabbit. She was wearing an oversized Buffaloes jersey and she looked just like her mother, more so than the last time I'd seen her.

"Hi," I offered. Giving her the friendliest smile I could muster, I did a little wave. She only tucked herself in closer to her mother. "It's nice to see you, Hals. Sorry I didn't realize you were here sooner, I would have said hello."

Halsey rolled her eyes as she leaned back against the wall. "It's fine. I didn't expect anything from you."

The door cracked open and in walked Grayson, the volume of the cheers louder from the lack of a sound barrier. Penny's hands covered her ears instinctively, her little stuffed rabbit falling to the floor, and Halsey took advantage of the moment to take a stab at Grayson without her hearing. "Surprised you're not on your way to fuck a cheerleader after that win."

Grayson shut the door behind him, ignoring her completely.

"Daddy!" Penny grinned, her rabbit long forgotten as Gray scooped her up in his arms. "You won!"

Gray laughed, his smile unparalleled. "My team won. Not me, sweetheart." He glanced at Halsey, his face falling for the briefest moment. "Thank you for bringing her."

"To be honest, I wouldn't have if I knew he'd be here," Halsey said, her chin jutting out in my direction.

My mouth popped open but words failed me, the shock of it hit me like a brick. She said it as if I were the plague, as if I were the spawn of the Grim Reaper himself and was here to influence her daughter into becoming the next Hitler.

"Don't look so surprised," Halsey deadpanned. "I heard you were off galivanting all over Vegas the last six months. Who knows what you picked up there."

Bobby snorted as he shoved the last of the hotdog into his mouth. On the one hand, I was grateful for Grayson covering for me and keeping my whereabouts a secret but come on—Vegas?

"So what if I was?" I joked. "Don't want my wicked ways to rub off on your ex?"

Her glare could have cut right through me. "Keep an eye on him," she grumbled to Grayson, leaning forward to plant a kiss on her daughter's cheek. "Love you, sweetheart. I'll see you later."

"Love you too," Bobby grinned.

I swear, she nearly gagged.

―――

The cheers and cries of the fans in the stadium had been left behind and exchanged for ones from children and adults alike, all clinging to the handrails of rides like their lives depended on it. As I walked through the gates of the state fair, the scent of cotton candy and fried dough filled the air, the sounds of victory bells and plastic guns firing overwhelmed my hearing, and the lights and crowds triggered a flood of memories that I had fought hard to leave behind.

It had been two years since I'd been to the annual local fair. It was a shock to me, Gray, and Bobby that they'd even let me in—the last time I was here I'd left in handcuffs, coated in my own vomit after having fallen face first in the dirt. I was charged with drunk and disorderly conduct. Thankfully, I was able to wipe it from my record, but the memories were still there.

Bobby and Grayson talked idly as Penelope dragged us around, her infectious laughter the only thing keeping me grounded. The two of them seemed to be getting along fairly well, and although Grayson had his worries about me living with another alcoholic, I couldn't help but feel like it was the right thing to do. We could hold each other accountable without judgment. We knew what the other was going through. Hell, I'd spent the last six months living with him. It only made sense.

It didn't make it easier being at the fair, though. Temptation was at every corner. Nearly every adult carried a plastic cup of beer, and somehow that sounded miles more refreshing than the contents of my bottle of water. Stand after stand was packed with Pearson Beers. I'd kill to taste it again. But having Bobby, Grayson, and Penelope by my side reminded me of the purpose behind my recovery. I wanted to be present for moments like this, to experience the joy and wonder of life without the haze of alcohol turning me into someone I didn't recognize.

My thoughts drifted to Dana, and part of me wished she was here, too.

A handful of rides and a giant wad of cotton candy later, we sat at a picnic table with Penny happily picking at her sugar-coated funnel cake.

"Your ex is a looker," Bobby snickered at Gray. He dipped a tortilla chip into a massive vat of liquid cheese and passed it to me. "Sour attitude, though."

Gray gave him the side-eye before double-checking that Penny hadn't picked up on what was said. "She's just protective of our daughter."

"Yeah, but she's rude about it," Bobby continued. "Like, what was that comment about you fucking a cheerleader?"

Penny's little giggle told me she'd picked up on his swearing. "Don't curse in front of Pen," I said, before Gray even had the chance.

Gray sighed, his eyes meeting mine quickly, conveying way too much information. I knew he wasn't overly fond of Bobby, but it didn't seem too bad between them until that moment. "I get around. That's all she meant. It's not a big deal."

"Seems like she's got a stick up her ass," Bobby grumbled, and thankfully, Penny didn't snicker that time.

"How's things with Dana?" Gray asked, taking his chance to change the conversation. If only he knew how intense things were at the moment.

I sighed. "I don't know. She fu—freaking left in the middle of the night," I explained, sneaking a hand across the table toward Penny's funnel cake and stealing an edge that her grubby, three-year-old hands hadn't yet touched. "Normally, that wouldn't bother me, but it does. And there's a part of me that already wants more with her, and that's confusing in itself, considering what happened."

"Of course it would bother you. There's history there," Gray offered, his voice dropping and filling with sincerity. "You really liked her when you first started seeing her."

"Yeah, but I fucked that up," I snapped, quickly covering my mouth the second I realized I'd cursed. "Sorry, Pen. Don't repeat that."

"Mommy cusses all the time," Pen giggled.

"Oh, great," Gray mumbled, ruffling the top of her hair and dragging a laugh out of her. "Look, man, you just need to apologize and start fresh. She's probably just as confused as you are."

"How am I supposed to apologize when I don't even remember what I did?"

"Just show her how you've changed. Show her that's not you anymore."

"That's what I said," Bobby interjected, nodding along.

The rest of the day passed in a haze. A haze that, for once, wasn't brought on by alcohol but instead by mixed feelings and confusion. When I'd left six and a half months ago, Pen had been smaller, and I'd only seen her in passing a handful of times during the time leading up to rehab. But she was bigger now, smarter, and was becoming her own little person as she clung to her father. Their relationship was something I'd not witnessed properly until now, and seeing Gray fully in dad mode was certainly something that I hadn't quite gotten used to.

But they shared a bond. More than my parents and I ever did. Watching them tugged at my heartstrings—the way she screamed with excitement as we all got onto the Ferris wheel and she wrapped her arms around his neck, the way her face lit up with joy when he'd won her the biggest prize at the ring toss. It was something I'd never been sure I could ever have, certainly not with my issues.

But I was clean now.

Maybe, just maybe, it was something I could have someday.

I could make up for the way I'd been treated in my youth. I could be the parent I'd always needed but never had. Gray was already showing me how, my parents had never taken me to the fair. I'd grown up being sent off alone with a driver or going out with my friends, sneaking in bottles of alcohol I'd stolen from my parent's expansive liquor cabinet.

They could never be too bothered with raising me. Couldn't even be bothered to spend any amount of time with me, if they had any say in it. I couldn't remember a single childhood family vacation but god, could I remember them taking plenty and leaving me behind.

I needed to keep my mind off things like that. I was ten times better worrying about why Dana had abandoned me in the middle of the night than worrying about why my parents had done such a shitty job. It was my biggest trigger.

If by some miracle I was going to get a second chance with Dana, if I even deserved that, I needed to get my act together. I needed to hold onto my sobriety and keep myself sane. She didn't need me at my worst, I'd already done enough damage there. I'd need to be stable, strong, and focused if I stood any fucking chance of winning her over.

But a part of me still wondered if I could make it last, if I could make it the rest of my life without falling victim to my vices.

Chapter 10

Dana

The waiting room of Drew's pediatrician was a nightmare. Sneezing, snotty, screaming kids surrounded us on all sides. Somehow, despite the noise, Drew napped quietly in his carrier on the chair next to me.

Vee had told me she was happy to take him instead, but everything she did lately had been getting on my nerves to the point of me not even considering it. It was his four-month checkup. Besides, I should be the one to take him, the one to be there. But mostly, I wanted to take him out of spite for my sister.

She hadn't shut up about how I should let my parents meet him, how I should forgive them, give Mom the chance to show me that she had changed. It was incessant, and with every passing hour, I was starting to regret letting her stay with me, even if it was helpful to have another set of hands with Drew. I didn't think there was a single bone in my body capable of forgiving Mom, or Dad, by extension.

Had she forgotten everything we'd gone through? Had

she dismissed our entire childhood, looking at it through rose-colored glasses?

Looking down at Drew and focusing on him helped to drown out the cries and shouts of the other kids in the waiting room. He was so peaceful, so calm, his little nose just barely beginning to leak. His lips and eyebrows twitched as he slept. My everything, all bundled in one tiny package.

How was anyone capable of not caring about something so perfect?

The biting cold was nothing against my warm cheeks, overly puffy jacket, and determination.

I'd wanted Mom to come with me. Stranger danger, and all that. But Jenny only lived a few houses down, Mom had said, and I'd be fine. She'd done that weird thing again where her words had all slid together into one string of consciousness, but I was getting better at deciphering it when it happened.

Making a mental note to ask about it during the health portion of class, I jumped from the bottom step of our front porch into the winter wonderland before me, making an indent into the snow that nearly reached my shins. Dad hadn't shoveled our walkway, he said we didn't need to seeing as we walked over it every day. But the snow had picked up since Dad and Vee had gone to the mall, their tracks barely visible in the uneven slush beneath my feet.

To Jenny's and back. Ten minutes. I'd be fine.

She was in the grade above me and had offered to let me borrow one of the books she had to read when she was in my class last year. Mrs. Stein had assigned us the project on Friday, and with Monday quickly approaching, I needed that book.

I tried to treat the walk like an adventure. Each little snowflake was a wonder, no matter how small. The Christmas lights our neighbors had decorated their houses with weren't on yet, and I found myself wishing they were so I'd have something other than a wall of white to look at as I trudged along, the wind howling and stinging my cheeks. If my parents had the time or energy to hang Christmas lights, I'd definitely make sure they were on all the time.

I counted the houses as I walked. One, with a deflated Santa Claus blow-up decoration lying limply on the lawn. Two, with hanging icicle lights and plastic reindeer in the front yard. Three, with a trash can sitting on the edge of the road filled with half-used wrapping paper. I stopped for a moment, considering plucking out one of the plastic tubes so I could wrap up Vee's gift in something other than printer paper. The longer I looked, the more the patterns on them stuck out to me.

Huh. One of them was the same pattern I'd seen on Santa's gifts to me last Christmas.

Weird.

Four, with nothing but a wooden sign out front that read, "Santa, stop here!"

And five, Jenny's house, with intricately placed Christmas lights along every edge of the house and wrapped around the dying bushes and trees. Blow-up decorations littered the lawn, a waving Santa and a swaying Rudolph in the heavy wind.

I sprinted up the front steps and knocked on the door.

Jenny's mom, Ms. Alice, opened the door with Jenny's book in hand.

"Hi, Dana," Ms. Alice cooed, a smile spreading across her cheeks before falling abruptly. "You're all alone?"

I nodded. "Yes, ma'am. Mom said I was big enough to go on my own," I grinned, putting my hands on my hips like a superhero. "She's napping."

"Oh. Okay," Ms. Alice said, her brows scrunching together and creating lines on her skin just like my parents. "Do you want to come in? I was just about to make hot chocolate for Jenny."

"Oh, no thanks, Ms. Alice. I've got to get home and start reading." The idea of a hot chocolate and Jenny's clean house was tempting, but I didn't want to worry Mom by being gone longer than she'd said it would take. So instead, I gratefully took the book from Ms. Alice's hand and waved her goodbye with my mitten-covered fingers as I skipped off her snow-shoveled walk.

The cold had started to settle into my jacket as I began the short walk home. I didn't bother to count the houses this time since I knew the front of ours like the back of my hand, even covered in heavy snow. Maybe if I was lucky I'd be able to convince Mom to get up and make me a hot chocolate like Ms. Alice.

Wiping the snot from my nose, I followed my own footsteps through the front yard and up to the door, trying to line them up perfectly backward so my boots wouldn't be covered in snow. I pulled open the noisy screen door and turned the handle, but it didn't give way.

Confused, I tried again.

And again.

"Mom?" I called, shoving my shoulder against the door

before trying the bell. She must have turned the lock while I was gone, but she knew I'd be back...

"Mom!" I tried again. I knocked, rang the bell, and shoved my face against the window trying to look in before my breath fogged it up. But there was no movement inside.

I bounced from toe to toe, trying to warm up a little. Why wasn't she answering? Something had to be wrong.

I banged on the door again, harder this time. It hurt the side of my palm. "Mom!" I shouted. "Mom, let me in! It's cold!"

I don't know how long I stood between the screen and the front door, pounding on it and shouting. But by the time Dad's car pulled into the driveway with Vee in the front seat, my fingers and toes had gone numb and my body had started to ache. I was shivering, my face burning from the lack of shelter or warmth, and I almost envied the redness on Dad's face when he stepped out of the car and slammed the door. At least his was from heated anger, not from the biting cold.

"Why are you outside?"

I gestured weakly to my pocket where I'd shoved the book once my hands had started to hurt from holding it. "I had to get a book for school from Jenny's house. Mom's not—"

"So you just left?"

"No, I asked Mom to come with me and she told me I was big enough to go alone that she was tired," I explained, my words sounding a little funny from my chattering teeth. "But then she locked me out."

"For fucks sake, Dana," Dad grumbled. "How long have you been out here?"

I shrugged. I didn't know, time was still confusing for me and it had felt like an eternity. "I left at two," I said.

"You've been out here nearly an hour?" Dad fumed, his

nostrils flaring as he fished his keys from his pocket. "Why didn't you go to a neighbor's house? Or back to Jenny's?"

I watched as he shoved the key in the lock and twisted the door open. Quiet music filtered through the open door along with the sound of the television and that sickly scent I'd been smelling a lot lately when Mom was acting weird. "I..."

Vee looked at me in bewilderment as she stepped into the house.

"I just wanted Mom," I breathed.

The memory stung as I watched Drew begin to squirm in his carrier. I didn't know until later what had happened that day. Mom had been drinking, and after I'd left she'd entirely forgotten I had stayed home with her instead of going with Dad and Vee to the mall. So when she'd noticed the unlocked door, she locked it, drank herself stupid, and passed out on the bed. She'd been dead to the world until Dad woke her up.

I didn't want Drew to have to grow up experiencing things like that. He'd never have to question whether I loved him, whether I cared. And he didn't need her or anyone like her in his life.

"Andrew and Dana Beechings?"

Shit. I'd almost forgotten where we were.

I gently picked up Drew's carrier and followed the nurse back to our allocated room. The doctor, clad in his white jacket and greying hair, beamed at us with a customer-service smile as we walked in.

The doctor weighed him, examined him, checked the little red spot beneath his left ear that I'd noticed the night before, and gave him the all-clear. Apparently, babies can get pimples. All in all, it was an uneventful checkup, and although I was glad that he was in a good percentile, I couldn't shake the irritation from Vee and the memory off.

"Before you go," Dr. Sinclair said, catching me off guard as I packed up the diaper bag, "I wanted to check if you'd been able to get any more medical information from Drew's paternal side. We still need to update that portion of his record."

"I haven't had the chance to speak to his father yet." *Lie.* "I doubt there's anything significant."

"If Andrew's dad is in network, we could obtain his medical history fairly easily—"

"I'll figure it out," I snapped, the words coming out harsher than I intended.

Dr. Sinclair's brows rose as he jotted something down. "If you don't want to, that's fine. It would just be useful to know if there's anything on Dad's side that we should be looking out for."

I huffed a sigh and lifted Drew in his carrier. "I'll figure it out," I repeated, hoping that maybe that time, he'd heard me.

———

The brewery loomed over me like a sleep-paralysis demon, inescapable and unmoving. This would be my first shift back after my recent night with Cole. I wasn't looking forward to the inevitable awkwardness or the potential conversation—I just wanted to keep to myself and get back home to my son.

Vee had apparently canceled the nanny's shift for the evening to take Drew on her own. I'd chewed her out for it when we'd gotten home from the pediatrician, telling her that she couldn't just take a shift away at the last minute, that it could unexpectedly impact the nanny's income. In truth, I was more concerned about leaving her alone with him after all the talk about our parents. In the back of my mind, I worried that she might try to take him to meet them without my knowledge.

By that point I didn't have much of a choice, though.

Pushing my way through the doors, I walked over to the tour guide closet, hung my purse, and slid on my vest with Pearson Beers printed across the chest and back. I tried not to appear annoyed as I clocked in, giving a courteous nod to my manager, Allison, and the handful of waitresses showing up at the same time as me. I didn't want to bring my frustration with Vee to work.

As I slipped out and through the hall, down past the elevator and through the doors into the main brewery space, I caught a glimpse of dusty blonde hair and a neatly pressed black suit.

I froze, half-hidden by one of the massive metal tanks, and watched as Cole spoke casually to a man I didn't recognize. He grinned eagerly, almost as eager as he looked before his mouth devoured every sensitive inch of my skin, and out popped a single dimple on his left side.

God dammit.

Okay, so it wasn't a one-time thing. It's okay. It never was. We knew this, I tried to tell myself. But god, why did he have to be within reaching distance nowadays? I'd already proven to both of us how easily I folded when it came to him. I didn't need it going any further, didn't need that temptation and the potential for another drunken blowup.

His eyes locked with mine.

As I watched his lids drop and his smile turn into a smirk, I knew I'd been caught. I sprinted across the brewery, hightailing it to the other side where the break room was. I still had five minutes until my next tour was scheduled to start and I'd rather spend it in there than being preyed upon by the one person I didn't have the guts to speak to right now.

A handful of waitresses and a fellow tour guide stood in the corner, cups of water in hand, giggling amongst themselves. I collapsed into one of the chairs and stared at the door, hoping he wouldn't follow me in.

"There's no way he was in rehab," one of the girls snickered, lifting her cup of water to her lips. "I bet he just learned to hide it better."

Rehab.

"No, I'm positive," another said. "I heard him mentioning it to his friend the other day. He was talking about things he'd learned while he was gone, and the guy asked if those were things they taught in rehab. Cole nodded yes."

Cole. I turned my attention to them, fully listening, no longer caring about who walked in the door.

"He was probably joking, Sarah."

She shook her head. "No, he was definitely serious. I'm positive he was in rehab."

"For drinking?" I blurted. The girls turned to me, quizzical looks on their faces as if I should already know the answer.

"Oh shit, that's right, you didn't see him before he left," Sarah said, her mouth popping open as if the cogs were turning in her head. "He used to drink here all the time. It got out of control—a lot—but most of the time he was barely functioning. Like he was constantly on autopilot. Definitely an alcoholic."

And just like that, everything clicked.

The bottles strewn across his counter a year ago. The drinking first thing in the morning. The anger. The way he always smelled faintly of booze when I met up with him despite not appearing drunk. I don't know how I'd never put two-and-two together considering my experience with it, but realization sank like a stone in my gut.

Cole was an alcoholic, just like my mother.

Chapter 11
Cole

"I was young when I started drinking," I spoke carefully, monitoring the faces of those in the circle around me for any sign of recognition. I'd worn a surgical mask under the guise of worry about illnesses, but in honesty, it was more in the hope that no one would recognize me.

It was my first AA meeting since getting back, and although I had Bobby beside me, it was more intimidating than the circular meetings we had back in rehab. I knew everyone in those, had heard their stories countless times and they'd heard mine. Here, I was starting from scratch.

"Probably fourteen, maybe fifteen," I continued. I took a deep breath, trying to steady my trembling hands. "My parents never noticed any of their liquor missing from the cabinet and probably wouldn't have cared if they did. I was an afterthought for them, really. An inconvenience at best."

"Is that what drove you to the bottle?" Emily, the leader of the group, asked gently.

I shook my head. "Maybe eventually. But it was my friends' influence, at first. I realized how much I liked how it made me feel, how easily I was able to forget about everything else, and so when things started to get really bad at home, it was the first thing I turned to."

"Your parents never realized you were drunk?" Emily asked.

"No. They barely paid any attention, and by the time it started to become a real problem for me, they dropped me off at my aunt's with a single suitcase and a bank account. They told me I was old enough to leave them alone." I shoved my hands under my thighs, needing to calm them. Bobby scrolled through social media beside me.

"How old were you, Cole?"

"Sixteen," I said simply, watching as the most minuscule flicker of surprise rippled across her aging features. "My family is my biggest trigger."

Bobby didn't share his story. I didn't mind—we all take things as slowly or quickly as we need to—and Bobby being himself with a new group wasn't completely within the norm for him anyway. He chatted idly about some game he'd been playing lately as he sipped at his mug of coffee in the back of the meeting room.

I stood by him instead of mingling and getting to know the others. Although I'd grown comfortable enough to remove the mask, I wanted to stick by Bobby. I didn't want to veer him off course by ostracizing him.

"Cole?"

Emily stood behind me, clipboard in hand, a soft smile

on her face. Her gray hair flowed around her features in ringlets, bouncing as her head tilted to one side at Bobby, probably curious about his lack of participation.

"I'm really glad you guys came today. It's always nice to have new faces around here," she said, offering out a hand. "How long have you been sober now? I missed that part."

"Seven months yesterday for both of us," I said, shaking her hand. I pulled my coin out of my pocket and held it up. "Still carry my six-month chip, though."

"Ah!" She reached into her purse, fumbling around for something before pulling out fresh coins with red paint on them. "Lucky for you, I've got a couple of seven-month ones you can have."

She grinned as she held them out to me. I took them hesitantly and passed one to Bobby. "Thank you."

"Look, I know this is a little forward," she said carefully, "but I know you said your original sponsor is out in California. If you're looking for a local one, I'm happy to sponsor you. I've been at this for over ten years now, and I sponsor some of the others, as well."

Sponsor. My sponsor from rehab had been assigned to me. To have someone offering it with such ease seemed almost foreign. "Really?" I asked, glancing at Bobby who was far too distracted with his phone and his cup of coffee. "I'd love that."

"Of course. The first year is the hardest, you know. You need someone reliable that you can meet on a whim if needed," she explained. "Doing this kind of thing is honestly what keeps me away from the bottle the best."

I huffed a chuckle and turned the seven-month coin in my hand. "Thank you. That's... that's exactly what I need. My life is really hectic at the moment and having someone I can see in person when things go south would really help."

"Why's it so hectic?" she asked, her head tilting again and sending her curls bouncing. "If you don't mind me asking."

I shook my head. "It's fine." I stuffed the coin in my pocket and picked up my cup of coffee out of instinct. "I've just gotten into a romantic situation, I guess you could say. It's a bit confusing."

"A new relationship?"

"Not exactly," I laughed. "But I guess something along those lines. It's... complicated."

Her lips pursed into a thin line. "Be careful with that," she said, her voice dropping in volume. "Experiencing the highs of a new relationship—or whatever it is—when you're new to sobriety is generally not ideal. It's exciting, of course, to want to pursue something with your newfound freedom and outlook on life, but it can keep you searching for the next good high, if you know what I mean. The honeymoon period can only keep you distracted from temptation for so long."

"Don't worry about that, miss," Bobby piped up, his eyes still zoomed in on his phone. "I'm keeping him on the straight and narrow."

Emily gave me a sympathetic smile as she reached for my arm, pulling me off to the side far enough so that she could speak without Bobby hearing. "How did you two meet? At the facility?"

I nodded. "We came in at the same time. He's kept me in check and I've done the same for him," I explained, glancing at him briefly. "He's a bit of a character, I know. But he's a good guy. Kept me sane while I was in there and we have a lot of similarities in our stories, but that's not for me to share."

She nodded, her gaze continuing to snag on him. "Just...

keep yourself in check. And keep an eye on him. I know it's his first meeting here, too, but he seems a little less focused on staying sober than you do. I don't want to seem pessimistic, but if you're serious, you need to watch your temptations."

Towel drying my hair as I stepped down the stairs, the music playing from the kitchen was a song I'd never heard before. It was pop, a female singer, and for once it didn't bother me. I was feeling on top of the fucking world after the AA meeting; it had been far too long since I'd had a group setting like that. I was used to having two a week back in rehab, so going a month without felt like a missing limb.

"I think I burned the eggs," Bobby grunted as I came around the corner. Smoke and the scent of charcoal filled the massive space.

"You think?" I coughed. I whipped the towel around, actively trying to keep the smoke away from the alarm. The pan on the stove was practically black. If there were ever eggs in it to begin with, it was impossible to tell. Instead it looked like he'd tried to cook some kind of sticky, black goop. The plastic spatula was stuck to the center of the pan, half melted.

"I don't get how that happened," he said, his gaze cemented to the black goop. He wrapped his fingers around the handle of the pan and lifted it, the flame underneath at the highest level, and turned it upside down. Nothing moved, not even the spatula. "Shit."

I turned the knob of the stove off to extinguish the flame and took the cooking utensils from him, throwing them directly into the sink and turning on the cold water to cool them down. I had every intention of tossing them into the trash once they were cool enough. "Did no one ever teach you how to cook?"

Bobby's head shook, his shoulder-length hair flying. "Nah. Never needed to. Angie did all the cooking." Angie. He'd mentioned her before. If I remember correctly, she was one of his family's maids.

"I'm shocked you managed to get the flame going," I said, giving him a side-eye as I pulled a fresh pan from the cabinet.

"I googled it."

"Ah." Fetching the box of eggs and a container of sausages from the fridge, I got started on breakfast for us both. His copious amounts of ready-made meals in the fridge made a lot more sense now, and although I wasn't a cook by any means, I could handle the basics. My aunt had always said I made a mean spaghetti. "For future reference, you don't need the flame all the way up to cook eggs. And you definitely don't leave them unattended once they start cooking."

Bobby grunted some kind of thanks before hopping up onto the counter beside me. "We should just hire someone to do this shit. At least they cooked for us back in rehab."

I shrugged. "You can if you want, but honestly, I feel like it's part of the recovery. Taking the time to learn things you wouldn't have before because you were too drunk to handle it or your family never taught you." I caught the little wince he made as I mentioned family. "Sorry."

"It's fine."

Bobby's triggers were shockingly similar to mine, and

our stories aligned so closely that it was like looking in a mirror. Except he'd never had an aunt he was shipped off to that actually seemed to give a shit. He just had an absent family altogether who simply ensured he was fed, dressed, and taught right from wrong. Outside of his teachers, all he had was Angie.

He was a trust fund baby with excessively rich parents who were never around. At eighteen, they loaded up a bank account and sent him out into the world. Three years later, they died in a plane crash over the Himalayas, and Bobby inherited every cent they ever made. I was almost positive he had more money than me and considering my own trust fund and the wild success of Pearson Beers, that was really saying something.

My phone dinged on the counter behind me and I grabbed for it, hoping it was Dana, but was met instead with something almost as good. A text from Lottie.

Lunch at the ranch this weekend?

"Dana?" Bobby questioned, one brow shooting up as he kicked toward me playfully.

"No," I chuckled. I shot a message back to her.

Sounds like a plan.

Shareholder meetings, as important as they were, made me want to bash my head into a wall every time they were held. Usually, I'd sip at a coffee during them and spike it while no one was looking. But I couldn't do that this time. I just had to sit and suffer while drinking boring, non-alcoholic coffee.

The temptation was there. The wall behind the projector was lined with bookshelves filled with old, sealed prototypes, bottles of liquor, and our current range of offerings. It would be so easy to just take one.

My fingers twitched.

I shoved them into my pocket, wrapping them around the new, shiny, seven-month-coin. I could make it through the boredom of the meeting; I should care about the content anyway. Apparently, a new law was coming into effect in Colorado. One that would mean we'd need to change the recipe on our new, unreleased lineup of infused beers.

The amount of waste that would cause made my stomach sink to think about. We'd already made almost an entire batch for production, and now it would need to be disposed of or given out for free to the staff.

Seven months ago, I would have taken all of it.

I hadn't spoken to Dana since the night she left and hadn't seen her since the other day at the brewery. I found myself lost in thoughts of her to distract myself from the meeting, and the more I imagined her on her back, on her front, on her knees, the less the boredom seemed to take hold and the less the cravings hit me. A part of me knew I should speak to her, but the other part of me, the part that wanted her as the distraction, told me I didn't need to.

I could just take her.

The moment the meeting ended I found myself slipping from the room and checking the timetable for employees on my phone. She should be here—she was scheduled three to ten in the evening.

As luck would have it, she didn't have a tour right now.

My mind fogged with the idea of her. I paced down the hall to the elevator and rode it down. If I didn't see her, fine.

I could play it off like I was checking on things in the brewery. But if I did...

Ding. The doors parted and within a second my eyes zeroed in.

There, at the end of the hallway with her back to me and her hair up in a ponytail, was the woman I couldn't get out of my head.

I beelined for her, sidestepping Ben and Allison and anyone else who tried to get my attention. She didn't even notice me coming. She was so wrapped up in whatever conversation she was having with the girl in front of her that she barely even noticed my hand wrapping around her wrist.

One swift tug was all it took before her protests began.

"What the fu—?"

"I need to speak to you," I said. I didn't have half of mind where I was taking her. I just let my gut lead the way.

"Cole," she hissed, pulling at her wrist but following me anyway. I glanced behind me, aiming to make sure that no one else was watching but instead becoming far too transfixed in how her brows nearly touched with how irritated she was, with how her lips parted to release an angry huff.

God she looked sexy when she was pissed.

I opened the nearest door and pulled us both in, shutting it behind me.

Fucking janitor's closet.

"I was only five minutes late—"

"Shut up," I grumbled, and before I could think it through, my mouth was on hers.

Her hands pushed against my chest but her body relaxed into me, a war within herself that I could physically feel. Her lips tasted of strawberries and were slick with ChapStick, and I devoured them, tasted them, sucked at them. Maybe Emily was right—maybe this was a high I was chasing in the same way I used to chase the haze of alcohol, but *fuck*, I didn't care. She was too perfect, too right for me in too many ways that made no sense. If she was a drug, she'd had me hooked from the first time I saw her.

In the darkness of the closet, I felt her hands slip between the strands of my hair. I shifted myself, kissing her jaw, nipping at the skin of her throat. She smelled so fucking good, sweet, like pancakes with maple syrup. Blood rushed from my head and down between my hips, my cock already beginning to strain at the front of my suit trousers.

"Cole," she squeaked.

"Hmm?" My fingers teased at the waistband of her jeans, desperate to slip beneath and feel what I was doing to her. I knew damn well that she could feel my cock against her side, it was only fair I got to feel her wet pussy.

Slick dampness coated my digits as I eased them beneath her underwear and between her lips. "Fuck," she hissed, her grip on my hair pulling taut. "This isn't appropriate."

"Have I ever been appropriate with you?" I chuckled. Sliding my fingers across her clit, pulling a little 'yelp' from her, only made my cock harder.

Her hips pressed forward into me, forcing my fingers just a little further back to her entrance. Two easily sunk inside of her, and her answering moan nearly turned me feral. *Control yourself.*

She writhed against me with every motion of my hand. Two inside, my thumb on her clit, and my lips just beneath her ear. "Keep quiet, baby," I rasped. I knew how fucking loud she could be when she came, and god dammit, we didn't need someone thinking I was murdering her in here.

She bit down on her lip and rode against my hand, her

nails digging into the skin of my scalp. Every plunge, every stroke had her clenching around me, her breaths coming short and quick or not at all. All I wanted was to sink myself into her, wrap my throbbing cock in her damp heat. But I'd give her this and save myself for later.

"I-I can't, I—"

Too loud. I covered her mouth with my free hand and brought my nose against hers, breathing with her. Her walls closed in, her hips moving frantically, and I could tell just how close she was. "Come for me," I ordered, dropping my forehead and resting it against hers. "And try not to scream."

A muffled shriek ripped from her at the same moment her knees gave way, and I took the brunt of her weight with my knee and the hand she rode. Frantic little breaths came from her nose, and only when I was completely convinced she wouldn't alert everyone to exactly what was happening, I removed my hand from her mouth.

"Good girl," I cooed, pressing my lips to hers to absorb any other little sounds. Her body shook, little aftershocks sending spasms through her as I finally stilled my fingers.

Chapter 12
Dana

My body was on fucking fire.

Cole's hand slid from between my thighs and out of my jeans. In the low light of the janitor's closet, I watched as he sucked his two middle fingers into his mouth, licking every little drop of me off of them. My cheeks heated.

This wasn't a good idea and I fucking knew that, but he was too good at dragging me down with him.

"Cole," I breathed, my legs shaky and my mind fully in a haze. *Think straight. Come on.*

"You have no fucking idea how good you taste," he grunted. He wiped his saliva-covered hand on the inside of his suit jacket.

"Cole, stop," I said, my voice far weaker than I intended. His body went rigid for a split second before he took a step back, releasing me entirely, and I took that moment to catch my breath and try to organize my thoughts.

I was in dangerous territory. The need for him was growing stronger, and even though I'd tried to keep my distance, it wasn't going away. A part of me was terrified of this becoming a regular thing—if the rumor of him being in rehab was true, I knew the likelihood of relapse. I knew every part of this journey from the ten or so times my Mom had tried to conquer it and failed.

And I didn't want Drew anywhere around it.

But another part of me was desperate for a proper connection with the father of my child. And a deeper, guiltier part of me was screaming to tell him that Drew was his son so that he could have a father figure.

"Was that...?"

I shook my head. "It's fine. I would have fought you if I didn't want it," I rasped, pushing the little stray hairs that had fallen from my ponytail out of my face. "I just.... This shouldn't happen here."

Cole's eyes went wide for a second as he watched me fumble for my phone in the darkness. I checked the time, I still had ten minutes before my tour. "What do you mean?"

"I mean, that was really fucking obvious," I said. "If *this* is going to happen here, we need to be discreet. I don't want to get shit from my coworkers."

"If they give you shit, I'll talk to them—"

"No. *No.* I don't want them to give me shit in the first place. I don't want them to know. You talking to them will only make things worse."

"Right. Fine." His expression turned sour as he reached for the door handle, but then he paused. "Why did you leave?"

I blinked at him. Well, I guess we were having that conversation here in the janitor's closet. I could only avoid it for so long. "I wasn't feeling well," I lied.

His brows knitted together as he flicked on the light. His cheeks were tinted pink, his lips swollen from kissing me. "Why didn't you just wake me up?"

"I didn't want to bother you with it."

"You couldn't have just texted me to let me know? I mean, you've been dodging me at every opportunity—"

"I didn't think it was that big of a deal," I pressed. "We're not really a thing, so I felt weird about it. I figured we'd just go back to being awkward again and figure it out from there." It wasn't entirely a lie, even though I did want more. But there was only so much more I could handle while keeping things from him. "Unless you want it to be a thing?"

"Is it bad if I want to see you more often?" he asked, the corner of his lip twitching up into a smirk. "I mean, I don't want to just fuck you and abandon you."

"What does that even mean, though?" I crossed my arms over my chest, suddenly feeling far too vulnerable. "I have things I have to consider here, Cole. Future plans and people in my life. I have responsibilities. I can't just fuck you whenever you want it then go about my day-to-day life, especially when what happened between us still hangs over my head every time I see you."

Everything about him softened at my words. "I'm sorry about that," he sighed. "Genuinely. I was at a fucking low point in my life and I burned a lot of bridges because of it. I'm working on myself and I'm doing a lot better, but I never wanted you to get hurt."

I eyed him warily. *Working on myself.* He seemed sincere, but they were quick, easy words. Words that didn't erase what he'd said before. I needed time to think over his apology before actually accepting it. "Look, I have a tour in a few minutes and I need to get out there. But maybe we can talk about it later, okay?"

He watched me for a moment before letting out a breath and opening the door, gesturing to it. "Alright."

I'd spent nearly every second of the three consecutive tours far too deep inside my head. Every thought was either a replay of how he touched me or a panic about how I was going to make this work, if I even wanted to make it work. I could only hide Drew for so long, and soon enough, Cole would find out and do the math. Every fucking day, he was starting to look more and more like his father.

The easiest solution was to just tell him. I knew that, knew it would solve the majority of my problems, even if it created new ones. *What if he wants to be actively involved? What if the rumors are true? Do I want Drew to have a father who's an alcoholic?*

And if he didn't want to be involved, what then? Continue working for him indefinitely while raising his son, occasionally sleeping with him, and pretending that Drew didn't exist for his sake? No fucking way. I couldn't do that.

I leaned against his office door, resting my head on it. I had no idea what to fucking do.

"Busy," a voice called from the other side of the wood.

I stood up straight. I didn't realize he'd hear that. "It's me."

"Then come in."

I turned the knob and slid through the narrow opening I gave myself, shutting it quickly behind me. Cole stood facing away from me, his black suit so neatly pressed it was infuriating. He gazed out the window that faced the start of the Rocky Mountains, a cup of black coffee in his hand, his body motionless as the sun slipped beneath the top of the slopes.

"Hey." I hesitated before moving toward him, just a step.

"You done for the day?" he asked, turning his head slightly, just enough to look at me over his shoulder.

"No, but I've got about an hour before the next tour. I figured we could talk properly, not in a closet."

He turned to me fully, gesturing to the plush chair I'd sat in before in front of his desk.

"Do we have to do it over your desk?" I asked. The double meaning hit me and my cheeks flushed. "I'd much rather this be informal."

A hint of a smile cracked through his demeanor, and he set his coffee down before stepping around the massive piece of oak to my side. He leaned back on it, resting his rear against the edge. "Whatever you want."

I crossed my arms over my chest, my vest tugging at the back and reminding me just where I stood when it came to him. "It's going to take me some time to forgive you," I said, the words feeling like ash on my tongue. "And I'm not getting into a full-blown relationship with you. Not after that."

He took a deep breath and watched me, giving me a little nod. "That's fair. And to be clear, I wasn't asking for a full-blown relationship, Dana."

"I know. But I have to think about what could happen down the line, and that's not something I'm comfortable with," I explained, the rawness of it feeling way too personal to say out loud. "But I also don't want to avoid you or to avoid... this."

"I'm not sure I'm following."

"Can we just start over?" I asked. I rubbed the top of my

left arm, squeezing it just a little to calm me down. "Forget what happened a year ago and be cordial."

Something shifted in his eyes, but I couldn't quite tell what it was. "Can you do that?"

"I can try," I offered. "We can just be normal. I won't avoid you. And then, whatever happens, happens. I'm not going to pretend like I'm not attracted to you or that I don't want to be around you because we both know that's a lie, and you can do the same. But let's not put any expectations on it. That way, we don't end up in a relationship."

He huffed out a chuckle, his fingers trailing the rim of his mug. "That seems like a lot of steps just to let me touch you, Dana."

"Are you okay with it or not?" I deadpanned.

He nodded. "Yeah. I'm okay with that."

"Great." I shifted to my feet, unsure of where to go from there. I hadn't thought that far ahead.

"What are you doing this weekend?"

My gaze snapped right back to those annoyingly piercing green eyes. "I was planning on going out to Lottie's, maybe go riding. I haven't really had the time lately with the whole new job thing." *And the four-month-old baby.* "Why?"

He eyed me carefully before shifting onto his feet and taking a step toward me. "I'll come with," he said. "I've been meaning to see Lottie anyway."

"Are you inviting yourself?"

He grinned as he took another step, getting uncomfortably close. "Is that a problem?"

Is it? I thought for a moment. It wasn't necessarily bad, but it meant I couldn't bring Drew for a playdate. But I could use a day out and about without him, and I knew Vee would happily watch him. "No, it's not."

He leaned in closer, his face just an inch from mine, and my heart leaped in my chest. He'd been this close earlier, it shouldn't affect me. But it did. "This will be good," he breathed, his lips pressing lightly against my cheek and lingering a second too long. "A fresh start."

I could only hope that I could keep Drew a secret for a little while longer.

Chapter 13

Cole

Horse riding was not my strongest ability.

I clung to the horn of the saddle with a death grip, the reins in my free hand, doing my best to remember the leg motions for controlling the supposedly loving horse beneath me, Darcy. He didn't seem to like me very much.

Dana, Lottie, and her husband, Hunter, all seemed to ride as if they'd come out of the womb on the back of a foal. I'd told Lottie at least ten times that I'd rather stay on my own two feet, but apparently, I would be ruining the fun if I did that.

Dana shot past me at lightning speed, the widest smile across her lips as her long hair flowed in the breeze. It startled Darcy enough to whinny and raise his hooves. I held on for dear life, throwing myself forward and wrapping an arm around his neck, shooting a death glare at Dana as she laughed ahead of me.

"Struggling a bit?" she called back to me, as Darcy finally began to calm down. "You scared him!" I shouted back. The reins shifted as the horse shook his head in frustration at my attempt to squeeze my thighs.

Lottie and Hunter raced past Dana, shouting profanities at each other as they tried to gain the upper hand, and Dana chuckled at them. I wished I were more practiced at riding so I could join in the childish behavior with the rest of them, but no matter how many lessons I took, I'd never quite gotten the hang of it.

Dana looked far too confident as she sat up straight and directed her horse toward me, approaching slowly enough so Darcy didn't get spooked again. Her smile morphed into something a little more sinister. "Feeling left out, pretty boy?"

A chuckle bubbled up my throat. "Surprisingly, no, not too much," I admitted. Darcy shifted forward and turned, saddling up next to Dana's horse. Our knees brushed against each other. "It's nice seeing Lottie and Hunter this happy after everything they went through. I don't mind your smugness, either."

Something akin to surprise flashed briefly in her eyes before her little smirk returned. "Good. Don't want you to be pouting the whole way back to the stable."

Before I could blink, she'd taken off ahead of me, heading back toward the barn outside of Lottie's late father's house, leaving me and Darcy to figure it out on our own.

The moment my feet hit the ground, Lottie was shoving a brush into my chest. "You're not putting him away dirty," she said, her shit-eating grin far too wide for comfort.

Dana grumbled in the stall to my left, her horse already cleared of gear but her brush half tangled in the knots.

"Don't tell me you've lost your touch already," Lottie joked.

"You need new brushes," Dana said, her boot colliding with the bucket at her feet as she kicked it beneath her horse's head. He happily drank from it. "This one's old as shit."

"Can you two try not to bicker?" Hunter grunted, his hands wrapped tight around the plastic handles of the hay bale he carried. He'd buzzed his hair since I last saw him, and every time he turned the corner, I'd had to do a double take. We'd met a handful of times before he and Lottie got together at various events hosted by her father, who had been a business mentor to both of us.

"When's your mom dropping off Brody?" Lottie asked, avoiding his comment entirely.

He dropped the hay bale at her feet and sliced the plastic straps with a box cutter. He checked his watch, squinting through the dripping sweat. "About thirty minutes or so."

The time passed fairly quickly with all of us focused on our assigned tasks. I brushed down Darcy with a little help from Dana, and with every soothing stroke, he seemed to grow a little more fond of me. I almost wished we'd started with this; maybe it would have given me a moment to actually bond with the massive horse before me.

I actually felt like this had been good for me.

We made our way into the house together, Dana walking beside me as Lottie walked backward next to

Hunter, rambling on about all the improvements they'd made to the house since I'd last been here. It was apparent as soon as we stepped through the sliding glass door—all-new hardwood flooring, a remodeled kitchen that combined modern with homey, brand new carpets spread throughout the living room and entry area. The walls had been repainted a dusky green, and altogether it formed a cohesive, farm-style house that looked like it had been plucked from a magazine. Brody's old recliner still sat in the living room, standing out like a sore thumb, and I assumed she didn't want to get rid of her dad's favorite spot.

Hunter started prepping lunch as Lottie, Dana, and I sat around the kitchen island. I always looked forward to Hunter's cooking—he was definitely meant to be a chef in another life.

"How's the brewery?" Hunter asked, his attention focused wholly on the absurdly sharp knife slicing into vegetables beneath him.

"Good. We've got a new lineup coming out soon," I said. I wasn't sure if they'd told Dana anything about my rehab stint or if they assumed I had, and a little piece at the back of my mind kept worrying about it with every word spoken. "You guys will have to come to the launch party."

Lottie beamed at me as she slid her fingers across the cutting board and stole a baby carrot. "I'd love that."

She and Dana disappeared around the corner when the doorbell rang a few moments later, likely fawning over their son. As much as I was anxious to meet him, I kept myself calm, hanging back with Hunter while he cooked something on the stove that smelled incredible. "I haven't told Lottie about rehab yet," I said quietly, hoping he'd be able to hear me. "Please don't bring it up."

He shook his head, jokingly pointing his knife at me.

"Do you honestly think I'd just casually ask you about that in front of her? It's not my place to do so."

"I just didn't want you to think I'd already told her and mention it."

"I won't, man," he said, his lips forming a straight line as he leaned back against the counter, his eyes half on the food and half on me. "You know, we're thinking of forming a new section of the company."

I snorted. "Does the Harris Agricultural Empire really need another venture?"

"I didn't choose the name, okay?" he laughed. "It's still agriculture, to be fair. We've got so much farmland and so many contracted farmers, I figured, hey—why not branch into fresh produce? We could sell to local businesses, give them better, organic options for their restaurants and such."

Fresh produce. That wasn't a bad idea at all. "We'd happily add you to the suppliers list at the brewery," I grinned. "And our new lineup is infusion-based. We could work together on something, maybe even a zero percent."

Hunter's head tipped back and forth as if he were thinking about it, his lower lip between his teeth, before he broke out into a full-on smile. "Hell yeah. We could definitely make that work."

A tiny giggle chirped out behind me. I swiveled on my seat, locking eyes with a chubby little eight-month-old boy with piercing hazel eyes and a massive grin.

God, he looked just like Lottie.

"Cole, this is Brody," Lottie beamed, holding the little guy outstretched to me as if she were the monkey in The Lion King.

I stared at him in awe. It had been a long time, years on years, since I'd interacted with a child his age. They were the cutest before they could talk. And their heads smelled like heaven.

"You can take him," she laughed, her arms just barely beginning to shake from holding the weight of him.

Hesitantly, I reached out and wrapped my arms around his little torso, lifting his weight easily. He babbled incoherently, his eyes stuck on mine like glue, his smile far too wide to be anything other than cute. "Hi," I said, setting him down on my lap and bobbing my leg up and down. He giggled, his little hand wrapping around one of my fingers.

"He likes you," Hunter said from behind me.

"You're a natural," Lottie chuckled. "He didn't even like Dana the first time they met and she's—"

Dana's elbow landed square in Lottie's gut. "Oh, sorry," Dana gushed, but from where I was sitting, it looked intentional.

Odd.

I don't know how long I held him. It felt like hours, but it didn't get old. He seemed happy enough in my arms, content to play with his stuffed animal, my fingers, or a set of teething rings. All I needed to do was ensure he didn't fall from my lap and that he was sufficiently entertained.

Lottie set the table for the four of us, her eyes trained on me and Brody as she went. Occasionally, Dana would pull her to the side, whispering something urgently. As I watched the two of them, I realized I'd never really seen them together outside of Lottie's wedding and the first time I'd met Dana. Maybe this was just their relationship, whispery and secretive, weird as it was.

"You seem comfortable with Brody," Lottie grinned as she stepped around me with a handful of plates.

I chuckled. "Yeah, I guess I am. He's easy."

"Only when other people are around," Hunter quipped,

his eyes rolling as he carried a pot of steaming something to the table.

"You'd make a good dad, Cole," Lottie added. "Have you ever thought of having kids?"

Dana's head swiveled to Lottie faster than my eyes could keep up. "Lottie."

"It's fine," I chuckled, waving my hand as Brody started to coo in my lap. "I've thought about it a bit, yeah. Maybe down the line."

A glass of wine in each of our hands and a lightly snoring baby in a bassinet made for a fairly calm, post-meal hangout. Lottie idly rocked the bassinet with her foot as she babbled on about horse breeds, but all I could do was watch Dana.

The way her face lit up whenever Lottie spoke was sweet. Their friendship was odd, but in fairness, I found most female friendships to be somewhat alike in that sense. Girls had a way of connecting deeper than most men did, I suppose. But when her lips parted, her smile like something out of a fairytale, I felt something in my chest go soft.

"So Lottie's gotten into scrapbooking," Hunter declared, a little smirk crossing his cheeks as he reached for something behind him.

"Babe, no—"

"It's cute," Hunter laughed. "Every mom goes through this phase, right? And what better time to do it than when he's still little and you can keep all the memories in one place."

A loud *thunk* echoed through the room as he dropped the photo album onto the table.

This was the part of parenthood that had always seemed incredibly boring to me. I guess it would be different if it was your own kid but being made to look at photo after photo where they basically looked the same other than different clothing and covered in different food wasn't the type of thing I liked to spend my time doing. But I appreciated Lottie and Hunter for everything they'd done for me over the last seven months, and if that meant I needed to pretend like a scrapbook was the greatest thing in the world, then so be it.

"I'd love to see it," I said, doing my absolute best to sell it.

Hunter came around to my side of the table, glass of wine in hand, and flipped the book open to the first page.

Although I didn't know a whole lot about scrapbooking, I could tell that Lottie wasn't a very good scrapbooker. Random stickers and extravagant, unrelated backgrounds littered the pages, but I had to admit, the photos were cute.

Brody's first bath, one of them read, and included a handful of pictures of a very young Brody, still wrinkly and raisin-like, clinging to a toy for dear life as water was poured over him. *Brody's first walk*, another said, and I couldn't even see him in the stroller because he was so small. *Brody's first meal*, said another, and yep, there it was, the famous photo of him covered in food and laughing about it.

Hunter turned the page, and my stomach flip-flopped.
Brody's first friend.

There, on a hospital bed, sat Lottie with Brody on her

lap. Beside her, clad in a hospital gown with a smaller bundle in her arms, was Dana.

Hunter tried to turn the page but I reached out, almost bending the paper to keep it open.

It was Dana, no doubt about it. The freckles were the same, the hair, the lips, the intense hazel eyes. The only difference was the width of her face—just a tad bit rounder.

"Dana," I said, her name barely breaking past my lips. I lifted my gaze to look at her, and she looked pissed. "You have a kid?"

Chapter 14
Dana

The silence was so deafening I wondered if Cole could hear my racing heart from across the table. It was quiet enough to hear a fucking pin drop, and I was positive the thumping in my chest was far louder than that.

I swear I could actually feel the stress running through my veins. *Say something,* I screamed at myself. The silence only made it worse, solidifying the answer before I could. There wasn't the option to say no. Any normal person without a child would have already explained it away, not stare at him like a deer caught in the headlights.

Making a mental note to berate Hunter later, I cleared my far too tight throat. "Yes," I said. "My sister's watching him today."

Cole's gaze dropped back to the photo and studied it for a moment longer before seeming to nod, almost to himself. My stomach churned, full of Hunter's gumbo and bile. *Please don't put the pieces together. Please.* He couldn't find out like this. Even with Lottie and Hunter by my side for damage control, the idea of him learning that Drew was his without me actually telling him felt like hell. I should have told him. I should have—

"He's cute," Cole said, a half-assed, forced smile tugging his lips back.

"Thanks," I breathed.

"You know, Brody has started doing this thing lately where he screams at the top of his lungs because he thinks it's funny," Lottie offered. I appreciated her attempt to shift the conversation, but even I could tell there was a stiffness to her, a lurking unease at this unspoken-until-now secret. Cole had to have at least figured out that he was the only one in the room left out of this knowledge.

"He does it in the middle of the night sometimes," Hunter added. He chuckled and it sounded so forced. "Just one short screech and then a fit of giggles. It's kind of terrifying."

Cole's eyes met mine again briefly before abandoning me. "That sounds horrible," he said, huffing a light laugh as he slowly, agonizingly, turned the page to the next set of photographs.

"Dana, can you help me clean up?" Lottie asked. In her eyes, I could see a million apologies sparkling back at me, as well as an invitation.

"Of course."

We gathered the dishes strewn across the table as quietly as we could to not wake Brody as the boys idly talked about Hunter's company. A heaviness hung as I slipped my hand in front of Cole to take his plate and bowl, a brief second of eye contact making my stomach lurch. He had to be at least a little confused, and confusion meant he was thinking about it, and thinking about it would inevitably lend itself to figuring it out.

I wanted to vomit.

"I'm sorry," Lottie said, her voice so quiet I could barely hear her over the running water of the sink. She rinsed each dish as I handed them to her before putting them on the rack in the dishwasher. "I've made so many of those stupid scrapbooks, I didn't even think for a second it would be the one with that photo in it."

I watched as Cole slowly started to relax in his seat across the room. He laughed at something Hunter said, his tone more animated now. "Maybe I should just tell him," I sighed.

"Is that what you want to do? Or is it because you feel like you have to?"

"I don't know. Both?"

Lottie's lips pressed into a thin line as she watched me. "I'll support you either way. You know that."

"I just... I don't know, Lots." I passed her another plate, staring at the water as it dripped off the edge of it. "A part of me wants to. But the other part of me—the sane part of me—remembers what happened a year ago. And the rumors I keep hearing at work—"

"What rumors?" She instantly cut me off.

"That he's an alcoholic," I said. "It makes sense after last year. I just don't know if I can have that around Drew, not after the shit I went through growing up."

Lottie was one of the few people I'd allowed myself to open up to fully about what happened in my childhood. We'd shared a room in Hawaii during the few months we'd worked there on a ranch, and not having cell service or Wi-Fi in the apartment had meant we'd had to actually talk to one another.

"Some people say he was in rehab, others are saying he was in Vegas on a binge for months on end," I told her. "Either way, I know how that ends."

Lottie avoided looking at me. She took the dishes quietly, reaching out blindly, and something in my gut told me she knew something.

"Lottie," I deadpanned.

"What?"

"What do you know?"

She took a deep breath and met my gaze. There was a sadness in her eyes, a glistening that confirmed for me that she knew things I didn't. "It's not my place—"

An ear-piercing shriek rippled from the bassinet next to Hunter's chair, followed by a fit of giggles. Hunter reached in and plucked out a wide-awake Brody, not a hint of glee on his face, and looked across the room at us. "Told you he likes to randomly scream."

"He's probably hungry," Lottie said. She wiped her hands on a dishtowel and shut off the water, abandoning the conversation, and walked across the room to snatch her little boy from her husband. "If your mom fed him at the right time, then he's not eaten for hours."

"We should probably head off, anyway," Cole added, pushing his chair back with a deafening screech of wood-on-wood. He glanced back at me as he stood. "If you're okay with that, I mean."

"Uh, yeah, sure." I shoved off from where I was leaning against the counter. That awkward unease was back between the four of us, too many unspoken words to count hanging in the air.

Lottie grabbed a jar of something small and red from the cabinet. "Honestly, that's probably in your best interest. He's not very cute when he eats and this shit gets everywhere," she laughed, pulling out the high chair from the corner with her foot and plopping Brody down into it.

Another little scream, another fit of giggles. "Plus, I think he's running out of good-behavior-energy."

Cole and I quickly gathered our things and slid on our muddied boots, a silence between us that felt far too charged for my liking. I wished I hadn't agreed to ride with him, at least then I wouldn't have to sit in the car next to him on the way back into town. That gave him far too much time and opportunity to ask me questions.

We said our brief goodbyes, and I kissed Brody on the top of his head just seconds before the jar of food was opened. Quick hugs were dispersed filled with silent apologies from both Hunter and Lottie. I wasn't mad at either of them, I was mad at myself.

I still wasn't entirely sure what had possessed Cole to drive his Mercedes-Maybach down Lottie's dirt road. Surely, he had something less fancy, something that he wouldn't mind getting covered in mud and grass, but he didn't seem to care that the rims and lower end of the shiny black car was slick with dirt. He hit a button on his key fob and the car beeped twice then unlocked. All I could do was stare at the handle of the passenger side door, worried I'd ruin the leather interior with my boots.

"It's fine," he said, and for a split second, I wondered if he could read my mind. I'd be seven levels of fucked if he could. "I'll get it detailed tomorrow."

Hesitantly, I slid into the passenger seat, careful to keep my boots outside of the car. Knocking my feet together, I tried to get as much dirt as I could off the soles, but as I finally brought them into the car, I couldn't help but notice that Cole hadn't even tried to clean his off before sitting down. The footwell on his side was covered in mud.

We didn't say a word as he turned the car around and started the long drive back down Lottie's dirt road. With the insane suspension on his car, we barely felt any bumps, but an uncomfortableness still hung between us, blaring at us from all angles.

I had to say something, anything. If I didn't, I knew in my gut he'd bring it up first.

"So the new summer range," I offered. I tugged at the seatbelt across my chest, loping it under my breast to give me a little more breathing room—it felt like there wasn't enough oxygen in the fucking car. "I heard you and Hunter talking about it."

"Dana," he sighed.

"You said something about a non-alcoholic range?" I added. *Please take the fucking bait.*

He went quiet for a minute, his eyes focused on the road in front of him. "Yeah, we've only got one that's zero percent at the moment, and to be honest, it tastes like shit."

I let out a sigh of relief. "Yeah, it does."

He chuckled lightly, a little less stiffly than he did back at Lottie's. "I want to make a good one. One that people will actively reach for instead of Bud Light zero, or the Peroni zero, or any other zero, for that matter."

"That's fair," I said. "Probably better for you to drink that other than the shit you used to drink."

He hit his brakes, stopping far more violently than a normal person at a red light. *Why the fuck did you say that?*

Silence hung over us for a moment, charged and angry, but when he finally spoke, it was as if the question hadn't even phased him. "I like what I drink. I'm not picky, but I prefer shit that tastes good instead of having to mask it with juices and syrups. I wouldn't say the non-alcoholic option would be better for me."

I stared at him. Openly. "You wouldn't get violently

drunk on non-alcoholic beer," I retorted, the words falling from my lips before I could even process them.

"I wouldn't get violently drunk anyway," he said. The words were spoken so fucking casually that I thought I'd misunderstood.

"What?" I blurted, turning in my seat and wincing from the seat belt digging into my rib cage. The light turned green and he took off, the car revving in anger as he picked up speed far more quickly than necessary. "You can't apologize for what happened last year and then try to say that you didn't get insanely drunk. You were drinking fistfuls at seven in the morning—"

"Yeah, because my friends had just gotten married and I wanted to keep celebrating into the next day," he interrupted, glancing at me briefly with a warning in his eyes. "I wasn't proud of that. But you don't have to make it sound like I did that all the time."

I stared at him in disbelief, my lips parted, my nostrils flaring. Why was he avoiding the obvious? Or worse, was he being truthful? Was that genuinely just a one-time thing that got out of control, and all the talk about him being an alcoholic was completely unfounded?

"Why did you stop drinking then?" I asked, deciding that confronting him head-on was the best solution.

Another glance, another warning. "Who said I stopped?"

"Like, half the girls at work," I snapped. "They think you've either been in rehab or went on a binge in Vegas for six months."

His nose scrunched, a scoff echoing in the small space, but I caught how white his knuckles were as they gripped the steering wheel. "And you honestly believe there's truth in their gossip?"

I didn't know what to say. A part of me wanted to push him more, tell him how I'd heard story after story about how he'd shown up drunk to work on more than one occasion. Or the time he tried to lead a tour when he could barely walk. But there was a part of me that wanted to trust him, wanted to give him the benefit of the doubt.

But I also knew how fucking good alcoholics were at hiding their addiction.

"Can you drop me off at Safeway?" I asked, killing the conversation. "I've got to pick up a few things then I can Uber home afterward."

He glanced at me again, that air of warning wiped away. "I'll just go with you."

―――

"Since when is milk this expensive?"

I glared at him as I leaned over the handle of the cart. The casual conversations going on around us while we communicated in tight, irritated sentences was definitely odd. It felt like we were some old married couple that hated each other's guts, forced to work together on a grocery trip before spending the next week avoiding one another in our own house.

Either that or just two people who almost dated and had a baby together but one of them didn't know.

Guess which one?

"Do you not do your own shopping?" I grunted, plucking the gallon with the latest expiration date off the shelf and dropping it in the cart.

"Not really."

"Shocking," I mumbled. I glanced down at the list in my hand, filled with necessities, and knew damn well that this would leave me strapped for cash until the end of the month. Exhaling an annoyed sigh, I noticed him looking at it before pulling the front of the cart toward the meat section.

"Is all of that just for you?" he asked, glancing back at me warily before staring down at the selection of ground beef I had placed in the cart.

"No, my sister's staying with me at the moment."

"To watch your son?"

I swallowed. We hadn't brought him up until now. I wondered if that was on purpose, if he had planned to discuss it here, in public, where I couldn't openly berate him if he pissed me off. "Yes. To watch Drew."

His gaze lingered on the pack of ground beef. "That's his name?"

And there it was again, that feeling of wanting to hurl my guts all over the floor of Safeway. "Well, it's Andrew, but I call him Drew for short," I explained, my throat closing, forcing my voice to come out as a squeak.

"It's cute," he said as he pulled me and the cart toward the other end of the store.

To the fucking baby section.

He'd either read further down the list than I thought or decided to head there on his own. I wasn't sure but either way I felt unsettled, and the heat in my cheeks was nearly burning as we turned down the aisle.

"What do we need?" he asked, his voice a bit gruff as he met my stare over the cart.

We. I knew he didn't mean it like that, but god fucking dammit, the brief idea of my son having two parents made my chest ache. Clumsily, I unfolded the list again. "Two boxes of diapers," I said, pointing toward the massive boxes on the shelves.

"Size?"

"One in size two and one in size three."

"He's growing?"

"Well yeah, Cole, that's what babies do," I sighed, helping him load the boxes to the bottom of the cart. "He's almost grown out of size two, so I need to be prepared."

"Right, yeah, that makes sense."

"Can you grab a couple of boxes of baby wipes? Store brand is fine." I kicked the box of size three a little further back and grabbed for the list again. I couldn't remember if I'd put diaper cream on there, and for the life of me, I had no idea if I had any left at home.

A few packs of baby wipes landed in the cart, my attention barely picking it up.

"Can I get him this?"

I glanced up from the list. Cole stood with a box in his hands roughly the size of his torso. On the front of it was a baby about Drew's size, sitting on a play mat in front of a short tower with buttons covering the front. *Music With Me,* it said across the top, and the more I looked at the nautical-themed item, it looked like something he could press buttons on to make different sounds.

Then I glanced at the price tag on the shelf.

"Cole, that's a hundred and fifty bucks."

He shrugged. "So?"

He didn't wait until I'd said yes to find space for it in the cart. He took the time to move things out of the way gently, carefully shifting them so he didn't damage any items and slipped it into the empty space.

"Okay," I breathed.

I stared at the massive toy knowing damn well I wouldn't have been able to afford that on my own. I hoped he hadn't already put the pieces together and was buying it as a gesture of goodwill or an offering of a truce. I needed to tell him, needed to just spit the words out, but by the time they'd barely formed in my mind he spoke again.

"What's next on the list?"

Chapter 15

Cole

Two weeks had passed in the blink of an eye with how much work I'd been doing on the new range of products. With a preliminary launch date in the spring and a ramp-up and push at the start of summer, we had a lot of shit to get done in the coming months.

And that meant less time for other things.

The revelation about Dana having a son had been in the back of my mind but I'd decided it wasn't worth dwelling on or overthinking the weird feeling in my gut questioning the timing of it all. Yes, the diapers said up to four months, and the math added up to the approximate time of the incident between Dana and me. But I also knew that we weren't anywhere close to exclusive and Lottie had said she wasn't exactly shy when it came to sex. Lingering on possibilities wasn't good for me, and besides, it was too far-fetched that it didn't matter.

Instead of thinking about things that wouldn't help me in the long run, I'd spent my time working and going to the gym, attended two more AA meetings, and cashed in on opportunities with Dana when they presented themselves. I would have preferred to take her out properly, but stolen glances as we passed each other at work and the occasional makeout session in my office were enough to keep me hooked on her.

In truth, I wasn't sure anything would *unhook* me from her.

Every time I touched her I wanted more. But we'd held off, and although she'd been receptive to every move I made with her since our talk, a part of me wondered if our schedules not aligning was more on her than it was on me. But again, I couldn't focus on that. I'd take what I could get for now and deal with the stress of everything else going on. That's what Emily, my sponsor, had suggested, and I wanted to take as much of her advice as I reasonably could.

Everything except not pursuing things with Dana. That was one I wouldn't budge on.

My nerves started to get to me as I stepped into the open space in the center of the brew house. I still wasn't accustomed to handling these types of talks with my staff without a drink, and every single time I had to, I'd found myself more and more tempted. It was the location—anywhere else not surrounded by massive vats of alcohol and I would have been fine.

"Thank you all for coming," I said, my voice booming over the group. Waitresses and cooks from the restaurant stood to my left, the brewing gang in the center, and to the right, the tour guides and bar staff. Behind them were the office workers, the ones making everything run behind the scenes. Somewhere smushed between the tour guides and the office staff, Dana's head of deep brown hair poked out, her hazel eyes fixed on me. "I appreciate that many of you who weren't scheduled for today still took time out of your lives to come in."

Grumbles and stares were the only reply.

"In celebration of all of the work you've done toward our new range and ahead of the upcoming chaos of the summer, including spending six months under different management and adjusting incredibly, I have a gift for you all."

The grumbles and whispers stopped. Only stares remained.

"Three weeks from today, we'll be shutting down all operations for ten days apart from the absolute necessities, for which I've hired in. All of you will continue to be paid your normal salary for those ten days we'll be shut down," I explained. I clicked a button on the tiny remote I'd been given by IT and directed the group's attention to the projector behind me. "Those of you who wish to spend those days doing what I have planned are welcome to join me in Costa Rica."

And just like that, all hell broke loose.

Questions and murmurs poured at me from every angle, stunned looks on every face. "A company retreat?" someone asked, and I nodded.

"Paid for?" another questioned. I nodded again.

"Flights and everything?"

Another nod.

"Anyone who wishes to join will be paid for and accommodated," I explained. The stares were beginning to bore into my skin, making me feel like instead of being covered in gazes, I was covered in spiders. Resisting the temptation to scratch at the nonexistent arachnids, I cleared my throat instead. "I can't help you if you don't have a passport, though. You'll need to sort that out yourselves."

"What about meals?"

"We'll be staying at an all-inclusive resort," I replied,

plastering a smile on my face that I hoped would sell my excitement. In truth, I was happy to be doing this for them—they'd worked incredibly hard and it was barely a dent to my bank account to cover it. But I was also overworked and overstressed, so it was something I greatly looked forward to as well.

I found myself searching for Dana's face in the crowd only to come up empty.

———

"You're coming, right?"

Dana's lips pressed together as she pulled the previously cake-covered spoon from her mouth, her lipstick not even budging. I'd finally gotten her out for dinner but still hadn't received confirmation from her on whether or not she was coming to Costa Rica.

She sighed. "I want to," she admitted. "But I haven't quite worked out the details."

"Baby. We leave in a week."

She winced whenever I called her that. I'd noticed it a handful of times now, maybe I should stop. "That, right there, is the problem."

"What?"

"The baby. Drew. I can't just leave him with my sister for ten days, Cole. And I don't think I'd trust the nanny to watch him for that long, either. I mean, what if something happens?" she babbled, her words nearly running into each other as she tried to emphasize them by waving the spoon around. I tried not to crack a grin, tried not to laugh at what she was saying. "I'd be an almost nine-hour flight away, and that's if I can get on the first one out without any layovers. Drew's never been away from me for that long—"

"Dana," I interrupted, wrapping my fingers around her wrist to keep her from flinging her spoon more. My lips twitched up as her brows knitted, a hint of irritation playing on that beautiful fucking face. "Drew's invited. I never said he couldn't come."

"What?"

"Do you think for one second that I didn't consider how that would work for you?" I continued. I plucked the spoon from her hand and buried it into her slice of cake before holding out the bite for her. Suspicious, she opened her mouth, letting me feed her. "I assumed Drew would be coming."

"But everyone else isn't bringing their kids," she said around the mouthful of cake.

"You're not everyone else."

Her cheeks heated. "Because we've had sex?"

"Because I care about you."

The plush rug beneath my feet did absolutely nothing to calm my racing mind. I didn't know exactly when I'd gotten out of bed; one minute, I couldn't sleep, the next, I was pacing. The moon hung low in the sky outside of my window, the metal surfaces on my balcony shining brightly in its reflection. Beyond that were the peaks, the stars, the tops of the trees, and the babbling brooks that would soon freeze over when the temperatures dropped. I swallowed.

I wanted a drink.

I was so close to eight months. So fucking close. I needed to remember that and I knew in my bones that I couldn't jeopardize it. I'd removed every bit of alcohol from this place weeks ago. The kitchen alone hadn't been enough. The wine cellar, full to the brim with aged fine wines, had been auctioned off locally with every cent of the proceeds going to recovery groups. I'd hired a team to sweep the house of any bottles I might have stashed in my drunken stupors. I'd removed temptation as much as I could.

And still, despite that, I craved.

Pressing my forehead to the glass doors of the balcony, I tried to concentrate on my breathing. More than anything, I needed someone to talk to, but it was nearing ten in the evening and I felt awful bothering anyone at this time.

Bobby should be awake, though.

It was like I blinked and then I was in front of his door, a deafening silence bleeding out from beneath it.

I tried not to panic at the loss of time. It was something I'd experienced a lot while I was drinking and more so when I'd first started to get sober. I'd go through the halls of rehab and end up in places I didn't remember getting to. But it had been months since the last time it had happened.

I knocked on Bobby's door and got nothing in reply. Hesitantly, I pushed it open and switched on the light.

The room was a fucking mess. Diet Coke cans littered the floor along with boxes of takeout and half-eaten bags of chips. Clothes were *everywhere*. And the bed, unmade and dirty, was empty.

I was happy he had a social life. But my god he needed to clean this up before he gave my house a rat problem.

I blinked again and I was in the kitchen, my phone ringing against my ear. I jumped at the realization that time had slipped again, and when I glanced down, my hands were shaking.

"Hello?"

Oh, thank fuck, I called my sponsor. "Em," I said, the single syllable of her name cracking.

"Craving?"

"Yes," I breathed. I wrapped my fingers around the handle of a drawer to steady them, my knuckles immediately turning white. "I've had water. I've tried sleeping, walking, watching TV. It won't go away."

"That's okay, Cole. It happens," Emily sighed. "Have you done the grounding techniques you've learned?"

"Yeah. And deep breathing. And changing my environment." Instinctually, I pulled open the drawer, barely paying attention to the keys I clasped in my hand. "I think a drive might help."

"Maybe try a walk outside instead?" Emily offered, her voice suddenly a bit more alert.

"There's bears out here near me."

"Do you not have a fence?"

"I do but you know damn well they can climb," I chuckled, the tension in my body slowly starting to calm. "Honestly, just talking to someone is already making me feel better."

"Good. I'm glad."

"Do you get calls like this often?" I asked, and suddenly I was moving without realizing it.

I was at my front door before I knew it, slippers on and a light jacket around my shoulders. Emily was babbling on about some TV show she'd watched recently that she thought might be enough to distract me.

I blinked, and I was in my car, my phone in my pocket, the call ended, halfway down my driveway.

I blinked, and I was in the liquor store.

I blinked, and a bottle of Lagavulin was in my left hand as I stood three people back in line for the checkout.

I blinked, and it was bagged up.

My heart thundered in my chest as I stepped out the chiming door of the store. Little droplets of rain hit my forehead, just a drizzle. I stared at the brown bag in my hand, knowing that the freedom from what ached in my throat was just inside.

What the fuck had I done? How had I taken such a drastic turn from how solid I was hours ago at dinner with Dana?

Teeth chattering and hands beginning to shake violently, I fished my phone from my pocket, pulling up my contacts as quickly as I could. I didn't know who to call; I'd already exhausted my opportunity with Em, Bobby was out doing god knows what, and Grayson had his daughter tonight. Lottie and Hunter were out at an event and outside of those options, there was only one decent one left.

My thumb hesitated over Dana's name. If I called her, if I asked her for help, the facade would break. She'd know. Not to mention she had a four-month-old at home and was likely strapped for sleep to begin with.

But I was almost eight months sober. I was so close. And I... I was fucking proud of that. But I wasn't strong enough on my own to deal with it and I was slipping, my mind was fogging, and I knew there was a chance I'd lose time again and wouldn't come to until the morning, hungover, broken, and damaged.

I tapped on her name.

It only rang once.

"Cole?"

"I need help," I said, the words breaking as my fingers spasmed, the bag slipping from my grip. The glass shattered as it slammed against the concrete, little shards of glass spraying out the top and the scent of slaved-over whiskey filling the air. "Please. I'm sorry."

I heard shuffling over the phone before she spoke again. "Where are you?" Keys jingled, and a few words were spoken to someone else, something that sounded like, *watch Drew, I need to go.* I breathed in shakily as I realized that she was coming. "Cole?"

"Flagstaff Spirits," I trembled. I wasn't far from her home. I could just go to her—

"I'm on my way."

Chapter 16

Dana

Panic. Pure, raw panic coursed through me as I clutched my phone in my hand. Down the line, the sound of shattering glass made me jump from the bed.

Please. I'm sorry.

I'd never heard him sound so broken. *"Where are you?"* I demanded, plucking Drew from his crib as he cooed playfully at me before pushing my way out the bedroom door.

Cole sniffled down the line, his breathing shaky. I stepped into the living room and placed Drew in his bassinet, nudging my sister to wake her up from where she slept on the couch.

"Vee," I whispered, angling the phone away from my mouth. Her eyes flickered open, widening the moment she saw the fear on my face. "Watch Drew. I need to go."

"O-okay," Vee said, scrambling until she was sitting up.

"Cole?" I pushed. Grabbing my keys from the hook beside the door, I yanked the front door open and raced down the front steps toward my Camry.

"*Flagstaff Spirits*," he had answered, his voice shaking violently.

My heart dropped into the pit of my stomach. He'd lied to me. It *was* a problem.

But at that moment I didn't care.

"I'm on my way," I said. I ended the call and slid into the driver's seat, backing down my driveway far too fast. Flagstaff wasn't far from me at all, a five-minute drive at most.

———

The rain pelted me as I slammed my car door. Cole sat on the curb, his feet stretched out in front of him. His arms were wrapped around his middle, his jacket and jeans soaked. Behind him, near the front door of the liquor store, was a damp, brown paper bag with glass shards protruding from it.

Oh my god.

Darting across the parking lot I ran toward him, nearly tripping over the hump of the sidewalk to kneel down next to him.

"Cole," I rasped, gently touching the back of his head with my palm.

Slowly, he looked up at me, his eyes red and raw. I realized then that the quivering beneath my fingertips wasn't from the chill of the rain, it was from him. He was rocking himself back and forth and my chest ached for him. "I don't know what happened," he broke. He relinquished his grasp on himself only to push his hands through his hair instead.

"Time kept fucking hopping and before I could stop it, I'd bought a bottle. I don't even remember doing it. It just happened, Dana, and I'm sorry I lied to you. I have a fucking problem."

"Hey, hey, it's okay," I insisted. I wrapped my fingers around his and pried them from his hair, replacing them with the softer touch of mine. "It's okay. Did you drink any?"

He shook his head. "I don't think so."

"Good. That's good," I said. "Deep breaths, Cole. You're okay."

"I lied to you," he gulped.

"I know."

"You came anyway," he whispered. A hand snuck around my waist and pulled me into him, tight and unwavering, and I couldn't have cared less that he was wet. The rain was picking up anyway and we'd both likely come out of this soaked to the bone. All I cared about was making sure he was okay. "Thank you."

I nodded into the crook of his neck and wrapped my arms around him, squeezing him back.

"You were right," he said. His fingers dug into my side, his grip almost bruising. "That night—last year—that was only the tip of the iceberg. I was fucked, baby. I couldn't stop. I spiraled further after that, got worse, drank myself into fucking oblivion every chance I had."

I swallowed and pulled back enough to look at him. The realization of his words slowly began to seep into me, creating a tidal wave inside that challenged the unwavering support I wanted to give him.

"The rumors are true. I was in rehab," he sniffled. His eyes met mine, striking and bloodshot. "I'm almost at eight months. Almost. I don't want to throw it away."

"I know you don't," I breathed. But worry reared its ugly head again, screaming at me to run away and never look back, to block him from my life in every way possible, take my son and go. He was like Mom, though Mom had never made it eight months. But I didn't want to leave him, not like this. "What can I do?"

"Stay," he croaked.

I shook my head. "I'm not going anywhere. What else?"

His eyes left mine, veering off to the broken bottle behind him. "Can you check the seal?"

I let out a shaky breath and nodded, pushing out of his grasp with relative ease. The paper bag fell apart the moment I touched it, waterlogged and fragile, and as I peeled back the layer that covered the top of the bottle, I breathed a sigh of relief when I saw that the seal hadn't been broken. "You're good, Cole. You didn't open it."

"Oh, thank fuck." He laid back on the sidewalk, clutching the sides of his head again as he half-submerged himself in a puddle. "Thank fuck, thank fuck, thank fuck."

I kneeled down next to him again, taking his hand and forcing him to sit back up. "Do you have a sponsor?"

He nodded. "Yeah, calling her was the first thing I did," he sighed. "I thought it had helped. But then I ended up here."

Slowly, I interlaced my fingers with his. I could tell he needed the grounding comfort. "Okay. Good. You did all the right things."

He shook his head. "I haven't been to a meeting in days. I didn't do all the right things."

"We can find you a meeting," I offered. "If you think that will help, we'll do that. I'll take you."

His eyes met mine again. Every feature in his face that had been tense seconds ago released. "You'll do that?"

"If that's what you want."

"Please," he breathed, squeezing my hand so tight I thought it might break. "I don't want to go home and fuck up all over again."

With his hand still locked in mine in a convention center in downtown Denver, we listened as the others spoke. It was nearing midnight. I had no idea that AA meetings ran so late, but apparently they were available for people needing them at desperate hours. We'd had to drive almost an hour but I was happy to do that for him. With him.

Even though every second of it was breaking my heart.

He'd changed into a fresh set of clothes in my car after pulling out a gym bag from the trunk of his. I wasn't nearly as soaked as he was, but he'd offered me a fresh shirt and hoodie anyway. I glanced down at it as a man across from us spoke about his struggle after losing his wife, and remembered I still needed to give back the hoodie I'd stolen from him weeks ago.

It wasn't my first time at an AA meeting. I'd been once before during Mom's longest stint of sobriety when I was eighteen, when she'd made it a whole six months. We'd all gone in support of her but the next morning, the booze on her breath had stunk up the breakfast table.

"Do you want to share?" I whispered to Cole, careful to keep my voice low enough that it wouldn't disturb anyone else.

Cole shook his head. "No, just listen."

He squeezed my hand again, his thumb tracing the back of it. When I'd first heard about his alcoholism and put the pieces together, I wished I could have gone back and changed things. I didn't mean in the way of Drew, not in a million years, but if I could have had him with someone else...

But sitting there with him and knowing how hard he was trying, how much further he'd gotten than Mom, I was fighting it. I didn't want Drew to grow up with an alcoholic father in his life, but if Cole was genuinely making improvements and could be one of the few who could make it out the other side, who was I to demonize him? And if he struggled occasionally, did that make him a horrible person? Surely not. My gut instinct was to help him but I couldn't quite tell what my mind thought of him. But I knew how my heart felt. I knew that I cared about him no matter what —he was the father of my son.

A woman across the circle spoke about how she was almost eight months sober and I could feel Cole relax in his seat. Another person almost at the same milestone as him, struggling with the same issues, speaking her mind for him. "It's overwhelming," she sighed. "Sometimes I don't feel like I have control when the cravings hit. Shit happens and all I can do is hope for the best."

Cole squeezed my hand again, a silent *me too*.

"Tell me about him."

I cracked a grin as I shoveled a mouthful of pan-fried

hash browns into my mouth. The saying was true, "You don't plan to go to Denny's. You end up at Denny's." Either way, breakfast at half past midnight was a solid choice. "Drew?"

Cole nodded and sliced into his stack of chocolate-chip pancakes. "I want to know."

"Well, he's four months old," I began around a mouthful. "Almost five. He lost the last of the hair he was born with the other day, so he's looking a bit like a bald old man."

Cole chuckled and shoved a bite of pancakes into his mouth. It was the first real, happy sound he'd made in hours.

"He only babbles right now. I thought he said mama once but Vee said it sounded more like la-la so I'm not counting it."

"Is he a handful?" Cole asked. His foot tapped against mine and a little wave of fondness washed over me.

"A bit but for the most part, he's fairly good. He doesn't shriek for attention like Brody," I laughed. "He sleeps through the night about half the time. He's... he's great, honestly."

"Do you like being a mom?" Cole asked, his words a little hesitant as he watched me.

I leaned forward onto the table, resting my head in my hand. "Yeah," I grinned. "More than I thought I would. Though that answer could change once he starts teething."

He laughed and the weight I'd felt on my shoulders when all this began suddenly felt lighter.

———

His house loomed high above though I could only make out points of it with my headlights off. The drive back had taken us well into the morning hours—it was almost two o'clock—and I didn't feel comfortable leaving him back at the liquor store where he'd left his car.

My phone dinged in my bag and instinctively Cole reached down to grab it. He passed it to me, and my screen lit up with a text from Vee.

"He's finally asleep," I sighed, flicking the screen off and leaning my head back on the headrest.

"That's good." I turned my head on the cushion, looking across the center console at Cole. He'd calmed down so much since I'd met him at the liquor store. There seemed to be an ease now between us, something that felt far more like comfort instead of the underlying tension since he'd found out I had a kid.

"The last time you were here," Cole started, his hand creeping across the center console and coming to rest on my bare mid-thigh, "When you left, was it because of him?"

"In a roundabout way, yes." I shifted, turning onto my side. "I needed to pump but I'd left it in my car back at the restaurant."

"And you didn't want me to know that?"

"It wasn't that I didn't want you to know," I lied. Thinking on my feet, I threw out the one plausible thing I could come up with that wasn't *I didn't want you to figure out he's your kid*. "I just... I don't know. People get weird about having sex with a new mom, you know? They think things aren't quite right down there, or that it's like throwing a sausage down a hallway, and I didn't want you to get weirded out, I guess."

His bloodshot eyes softened. Gently, his hand tightened its grip on my thigh just a little more, and my thoughts turned somewhere much darker. "I wouldn't have been weirded out, Dana."

I wanted to believe that I did. But when it came with the possibility of him putting those goddamn pieces together, it was hard. The lie wasn't entirely a lie—there had been men I'd met since Drew had been born, and the moment a baby was brought up, it was as if I were spoiled goods. There was no telling if he wouldn't have been the same.

"Are you okay to be by yourself now?" I asked. The twisting in my gut had only amplified, and although I was happy to be able to talk about Drew and my life casually now, that stone still sat at the bottom of my stomach, constantly waiting for the other shoe to drop. Part of me wanted to run for too many reasons, but the other wanted to stay as long as he needed me.

His hand tightened again on my thigh as he leaned a little closer. "Do you want me to be honest, or do you need to get home?"

My chest tightened, his face just inches from mine. I wrapped my fingers around the seatbelt, needing something, anything, for support. "Honest," I breathed.

The warmth of his breath ghosted my lips, sending my pulse skyrocketing. Why the hell did he have this much power over me? Why was I incapable of controlling my attraction to him? Why did my chest fucking ache for him when his hand cupped my jaw, his thumb so gentle as it swiped back and forth over my cheek?

"I still need you, Dana."

A switch flipped inside of me. As if by primal instinct, I warmed so wholly to him that it almost frightened me. His lips met mine and I sank into him, something in my gut aching for his touch. "Then use me," I mumbled against his mouth.

He kissed me gently, almost hesitantly. His hand inched higher up my thigh, the skin-on-skin contact making me tremble, and I knew damn well that the heat building between my legs would be my undoing. My shorts were already riding up from the cheap leather of my Camry, and all it would take was the lightest touch—

His kiss turned deeper, his tongue delving into my mouth, his hand shifting to the back of my neck as his other crept higher, ghosting the frayed hem of my shorts. I pressed lightly against his chest, fisting his shirt in my palm. His heart beat erratically beneath it, thumping almost in time with my own.

Until his fingers slid up and inside my underwear.

My pulse hit a peak and I sucked in a shaky breath, gaining nothing but his air. "Cole," I hissed.

"Fuck, you want me," he replied. The tip of his finger slid down my cotton-covered slit, forcing a tremble through my body. "You still want me."

I did.

I really fucking did.

"Inside," he huffed, and within a second, his hand was gone, focused wholly on unbuckling our seatbelts.

Chapter 17
Cole

I couldn't keep myself away from her. Certainly not now, not after what I'd gone through and after what she'd seen. Maybe not ever. I didn't know, and I didn't fucking care.

All that mattered was her mouth on mine and the raw ache at the base of my core. Maybe I'd misjudged before—maybe it wasn't alcohol I had been craving but *her*.

No. I still craved booze.

But it was enough to keep me satiated. It was enough to drag my thoughts away, to keep me clean, to keep me centered.

I shoved the master bedroom door open, the wood clanging off the wall, and forced her backward into the space. Half of her clothing had been discarded on the way up to the second floor, lost somewhere in the grand foyer or on the stairs, and she stood before me in just her bra and underwear. The little black set at any other time would have been my undoing. But she was ripping me apart with just her presence.

I'd felt how warm, how slick she was through that little

black set. I'd felt how much she wanted me. It had almost been surreal, after all, what kind of woman would still want me after witnessing what she'd seen tonight? What kind of woman would see me at my absolute lowest and still ache for me? She hadn't gotten that wet last time and it made all the more sense now.

Her fingers worked at the button of my jeans, fumbling and frantic, and all I could think to do was help her. She gratefully accepted and went up on her tiptoes, hooking one hand behind my neck, kissing me again. And again. And again.

I freed myself from the stiff material, my cock aching instead against the soft cotton of my boxers and kicked the jeans off behind me as I led her to the bed. It took everything in me, absolutely everything, not to take her the moment she laid back on the plush comforter, her lips tilted up in a soft, far too sultry grin.

Maybe I was shifting from one addiction to another.

Maybe she was salvation.

Grabbing the back of my shirt with one hand, I pulled it up and over my head, leaving myself bare except for my boxers. I wanted her in any way she'd give me. I wanted to taste her, devour her, sink myself inside of her and never leave. I wanted to worship the fucking ground she walked on.

She lifted up on her elbows and stretched her neck up to me, her mouth searching for mine, and I gave it to her on a silver platter.

Something bloomed in my veins as I kissed her, changing me, shredding me. I begged time not to shift like it did earlier that evening and plucked her bra from her body, mumbling an apology as the fabric grazed her sensitive nipples. Her neck tasted of vanilla, soft and warm, but I was aching to taste her between her thighs. I wanted every inch of her that she would allow, and from the way her body was responding, I knew she'd give it.

My breath caught when her slender fingers wrapped themselves around the base of my cock. I didn't think I could get any harder but *fuck*, the way she touched me, so gentle yet so fucking needy, only made me swell more. I needed her. I needed to be inside of her.

I pushed my boxers down over her hand and let her work at me while I sucked at the side of her neck, something primal screaming at me to mark her. I felt like a goddamn teenager, not caring who sees a hickey from an intense make out session on the football field. With her free hand she removed her own underwear, and within seconds, I had my fingers buried inside of her warmth.

"Do you want the lube this time?" I mumbled, eyeing my dresser where I kept it stashed. It didn't feel like she needed it, but I was playing by her rules, taking this at the speed she was comfortable with.

"Does it feel like I do?" she laughed.

"No."

"Then there's your answer."

Pushing her legs up by her breasts, I removed my fingers and pressed the tip of my cock against her entrance. I could already feel the burning at the base of my throat ease just a little, but I had to have more. "Watch me," I rasped, dropping my forehead to hers and staring down at where we connected over the bridge of her nose. "I want you to fucking see how perfectly I fit."

The moan that broke through her as I buried every inch of me inside of her made me quiver. I felt like I couldn't breathe, like I didn't need to, like she was the only thing I needed. No air, no water, no food, no sleep. Just her, and this.

I kissed her and the fucking world shattered around me.

I fucked her and she came undone.

Every kiss, every cry, every whimper she made felt like more than what it should have. She was just a woman I'd met last year, just someone I'd slept with a handful of times, just someone I'd destroyed a potential relationship with because of my drinking.

Just someone who'd appeared back in my life, just a woman who'd truly lived while I drowned.

But the connection we'd had last year hadn't gone away. If anything, in that moment, it felt like it had grown tenfold. When I kissed her, it wasn't out of want but desperation. We were connected in ways I couldn't comprehend. It was as if she had been the only one I could count on to show up when I needed someone, like she had done everything in her power to make sure I didn't drown again.

I didn't deserve any of it.

But I was going to lose myself with her.

"You're everything," I rasped, my lips against her ear, my chest against her breasts, my cock so far inside of her I didn't think I'd ever leave.

She whimpered a little moan as I touched her, my fingers thrumming against her clit with every drive of my hips. I wondered what she'd been worried about, there wasn't a single thing about her that felt wrong. It hadn't changed her fundamentally to have a child. It didn't make her any less worthy of feeling so fucking good.

Her head turned, seeking out my lips again, but she didn't kiss me. "Cole," she whispered, our heated breaths mixing. I could feel the way her body began to tremble, the way her walls started to close in on me. "I..."

Her hand sought out mine, her fingers wrapping around my wrist, and slowly, shyly, led me to her breast. She'd pushed me away the last time I'd gone for them.

Gently, I ghosted a finger across her swollen nipple, watching in fucking awe as the tiniest bead of white prickled to the surface. She moaned louder, and I did it again, taking it between my fingers and rolling it.

Every part of her stiffened before breaking, a shriek rippling from her throat. I covered my mouth with hers, drinking in the reverberations of her noises as she came around my cock, her walls trembling and clenching around me. It was the sweetest fucking thing I'd ever felt, and it dragged me closer to joining her.

"Fuck, oh my god," she cried, the overstimulation forcing her wild eyes to lock onto mine as I moved down her body.

I didn't even think about it. I just did it.

Closing my lips around her nipple, the intensely sweet drop of milk hit my tongue. My hips stuttered, my mind went fucking numb, and oh god, I was close. I was so goddamn close.

"Cole, you don't have to—"

"I want to," I rasped, and as if by magic, my tongue moving against her produced another little drop, and then another. Her fingers knotted in my hair, her trembling body taking all that it could from me. Just a little more, a little longer, I could hold out. I could make it last. I could take her, I could claim her, I could fill her up then do it again. I had to. I didn't want to stop.

I lost all control and rocketed over the edge, emptying everything I had inside of her, shaking as I fucked her, as I claimed her. I wouldn't recover from it this time. I knew I was ruined, ruined for every other fucking woman.

I didn't want anyone else.

The warmth of the sun on my bare back coaxed me gently from sleep. I hadn't slept so well since she'd last been in my bed, and even then, it wasn't like this. I felt rested, satiated.

Reaching across the sheets, I searched for her. But I came up empty, my eyes peeling open, only to find nothing more than a blank space where she'd been before.

My stomach dropped. *Not again.*

The panic in my gut forced me from the bed. There wasn't a single part of me that had fallen asleep worried that she'd leave again but here I was, my throat aching, boxers in hand, heading out my bedroom door to look out the front window from the top of the stairwell.

Her Camry was still parked outside.

The realization that I was standing in the middle of my hallway completely naked set in as the panic slipped away. I wasn't that concerned about Bobby stumbling across me, but I wasn't exactly one to show my cock to anyone that happened to pass by.

I pulled my boxers on and checked the guest room, then the gym, then the upstairs living area. In each space I came up empty. It was when I stumbled into the bathroom two doors down from my bedroom that I finally found her, hunched over the bathroom sink with two devices stuck to her breasts and one of my button-ups around her shoulders.

The words almost left my mouth.

I thought you'd left.

She gave me a soft little smile and held up the controller for the device. "Sorry," she said, her voice still thick with sleep. "Remembered it this time."

Something about seeing her like that, in my house, caring for her child even without him there, made my chest feel full. "Is there anything I can do to help?" I offered, stepping past the threshold. I glanced at the machine but I didn't want to stare at it, so instead, I watched her eyes, her lips.

"A glass of water would be amazing," she grinned.

By the time I'd retrieved it and come back, the bottles and the attachments were resting on the sink. Instead, she'd replaced them with her hands, her face scrunched in concentration as she massaged each breast. "Does it hurt?"

"Hmm? Oh. No, it's just... weird," she laughed.

I set the glass down in front of her and saddled up behind her, wrapping my arms around her waist. I watched as she worked at them in the mirror. Each little squeeze and push, each little grunt she made churned something inside of my chest.

She reached for the pump again but I held her back, grasping her wrist gently in my palm and plucking the two little suction attachments from her. Her look of surprise softened as she glanced back at me in the mirror, the smallest little smile tugging at her lips.

Dana guided me, showing me how to place them and what button to press on the device, explaining how she needed to coax more out halfway through to get a good pump.

I took in every word.

I took in every goddamn second.

Bad & Bossy

Any other morning I would have opted to go back to bed with Dana or join her in the shower. But I knew the state of my own house, knew that Bobby had no sense of control when it came to keeping things clean, and I didn't want her to inevitably end up in one of the living spaces or the kitchen and walk into a disaster.

So instead of taking my time with her, I took the time to impress her.

I picked up every scrap of trash Bobby had left behind and stuffed it into a bag before dumping it in the outside bin. I washed the dishes, wiped the counters, I even fucking vacuumed. There wasn't a single thing left behind, not a single crumb or morsel. I wanted to prove to her that after last night, I wasn't too far gone.

I shot a message to Bobby. He still hadn't come home, at least not that I could tell. A part of me was almost jealous of how much his social life in Boulder had seemed to take off, but I didn't let it sour me.

Hope you had a good night. I had Dana over.

By the time she finally emerged, taking the steps carefully from what I could only imagine was a good ache between her thighs, I was halfway through making her breakfast.

Still in my button-up shirt but with the buttons actually fastened and nothing underneath, she looked like a goddamn dream. Her wet, wavy hair hung over one shoulder, dampening the white material and giving me a peek of her breast. The leftover makeup from last night was gone, nothing but her bare, tanned skin and freckles left behind.

The temptation to throw her over the counter and take her again was nearly maddening.

"Smells good," she grinned. "What are you making?"

"Honestly?" I laughed, reaching out an arm and tucking her into my side. "It's just bacon. I'm not exactly the best chef in the world."

"Well, most mornings I barely have time for a bagel before Drew starts up so bacon is a goddamn luxury," she chuckled. Her face pressed against the side of my bare chest, warming me with her skin while chilling me with the cold of her damp hair. I only pulled her in tighter.

"Then you'll be even more excited to learn that there are frozen hash browns in the oven."

"Mmm, I love hash browns."

"Eggs?" I offered. "I've got so many damn eggs. Bobby keeps buying them."

She lifted her chin, poking me with it in the side of my pec as she looked up at me. "I could go for some eggs."

I planted a quick kiss against her cheek before slipping out of her embrace. "Scrambled? Sunny side up? Fried?" I asked, fishing out the pack from the refrigerator.

"Scrambled with cheese, if you're capable." Her wicked little grin as she hopped her ass up onto the counter had my cock twitching in my pajama bottoms. *Don't.*

I grabbed a pack of pre-grated cheddar and dropped it onto the counter next to her. "So picky."

"Just wait until Costa Rica," she giggled. "I'm not exactly good with foreign foods. I'll eat Mexican once in a blue moon, but even then, I'm happy with just a quesadilla."

Grabbing a fresh pan from the cabinet, I cranked up the gas burner and got started on her cheesy scrambled eggs. "So you're coming then?"

She leaned back against the varnished wood cabinet

behind her, bare legs dangling over the edge of the counter. I couldn't stop myself from placing an absent-minded hand on her thigh, just enough to feel her softness. "Mm-hm," she grinned.

The more I considered Dana bringing Drew, the more I found myself excited for the trip. It would be interesting to see her in her true element outside of work, and I'd be lying if there wasn't a part of me that wanted to meet the little guy, especially after meeting Brody. I only hoped he didn't scream his head off the entire flight. "Does Drew have a passport?"

She nodded. "I applied for one a few days after he was born. Lottie had been talking about a trip up to Canada with just us and our kids, so I got one just in case." Her little smile tripled in force, almost taking up the entirety of her face. "You should see the picture on it. He's just a wrinkly little thing."

Shoving my hand into the cheese packet and tossing a load into the pan, I glanced at her for approval. She shook her head and pushed the packet back into my hands. *So picky.*

"Will the tickets you bought work for him?" she asked. Still unhappy with the amount of cheese I'd given her, she tipped the packet upside down over the pan, emptying the entire contents.

"Tickets?"

"Yeah. For the flights."

"Baby," I chuckled, resuming my grasp on her thigh and squeezing it. "You're not flying commercial."

She blinked at me, the empty cheese packet hanging limply in her hand. "What do you mean?"

"You'll fly with me," I said simply. I took it from her grasp and tossed it aside, creeping my other hand up her thigh just a little more. "You don't need a ticket for that."

"Cole."

"Don't worry about it," I cooed, taking the pan off the heat so I could give her my full attention. "A few others are flying with me as well. I doubt anyone will ask questions."

Her brows came together as I slotted my hips between her knees, for once looking up at her instead of down. "Who else?"

"Just a handful of executives."

"And no one will find it weird that a tour guide is joining you?"

Her body quivered as my fingers ghosted the warmth between her thighs. "If they do, they can take it up with me."

"But they'll—"

I pressed my lips to hers, preventing her from saying anything else and did my absolute best not to fuck her next to the burning stove.

Driving her Camry was like trying to control that goddamn horse back at Lottie's. I wasn't used to the clunkiness of it. I hadn't driven something in that bad of shape since I was sixteen, occasionally driving my friend's cars instead of my own. It didn't maneuver as easily as my Tesla or my Maybach, but that could have just been a testament to its age.

Either way, I made a note to book her Camry for a full service.

I pulled into her driveway, the quaint little house sitting like a Lego amongst the rest of the identical homes. A few houses back, my driver parked on the side of the road, waiting for me to finish dropping her off so he could take me to collect my Maybach from the liquor store.

"You sure you'll be okay to get your car?" she asked, her fingers hesitant on the buckle of her seatbelt.

I nodded. "I'd have someone pick it up for me if I wasn't."

"Promise me you'll call your sponsor if you feel even the slightest inkling to go inside."

I chuckled. "I'll call her if I need to. If I did every time I felt the tiniest little want, Dana, she'd never be off the phone with me."

The joke didn't quite land. Her lips pursed into a fine line, more worry than amusement coating her features. "Cole."

"I'll call her if I need to," I repeated.

It took her a moment, but she finally nodded and pushed the door open. I followed her out, locking the car behind me, and placed the keys into her waiting hands.

I walked her to the front door, not quite ready to let her go just yet, and before she could wrap her fingers around the handle I had her face in my hands, her lips on mine. One last kiss, one last moment before we had to go back to the monotony of our day-to-day lives. I could steal as many moments as I wanted at work, but after last night, none of those would even come close to feeling as real as the last twelve hours had. I wanted *this* part to last.

She chuckled against my lips, her demeanor calming. "I'm still not going to date you," she breathed, the grin across her cheeks feeling far too mischievous for her own good.

"Keep telling yourself that baby."

The sound of the latch coming undone made us both jump, and as we turned, the door slowly opened.

There stood a woman a couple of inches taller than Dana, her shoulder-length brown hair wild and her eyes bloodshot. But that wasn't what stood out. It was the little bundle in her arms.

The smiling, eager little boy giggled the second he saw his mother. Bald head and green eyes, chubby but smaller than Brody. Something about him made the emptiness in my chest ache, made me want to reach out and take him from who I could only assume to be Vee.

I couldn't take my goddamn eyes off of him.

Chapter 18

Dana

For days, I couldn't stop worrying about that moment.

Cole had looked at my son in awe—he hadn't been able to take his eyes off of him in the few seconds it took for me to grab Drew from Vee and shuffle inside the house, saying a quick goodbye to him. I wasn't even sure he'd said it back to me, and it had taken far too long for his form to walk back down the driveway and be collected by his driver.

The longer I waited to tell him the worse it would be. I needed to keep reminding myself of that. I needed to tell him, needed to air it out and just come clean, but with the confirmation of his issues and the near-relapse of last night, I couldn't find the guts to get the words out. It was one thing for him to see the photo of a newborn Drew wrapped tightly in the hospital-issued blanket back at Lottie's, but seeing him in person, in all his little Cole-like glory, only made the possibility of Cole putting the pieces together that much more likely.

And I was running out of time.

I'd been keeping a close eye on Cole at work, going out of my way to check on him in the one place I knew he'd likely be tempted the most. I couldn't imagine running a goddamn brewery and not being able to touch an ounce of the stock we kept in the massive campus. But every time I'd seen him he'd been fine, smelling of cologne as opposed to booze. I could tell he was trying harder than usual, could see it in the little bags under his eyes, could feel the stress in his touch, but he was doing well. He'd even texted me that he went to his AA meeting.

"Do you need me to watch Drew today?" Vee asked, coming around the corner with towel-wrapped hair and pajamas covering her thin frame.

A knock at the door cut me off before I could answer her.

Drew squirmed in my arms at the sound, his hands locked solidly around his bottle, and I gave Vee a sympathetic look that said, *can you answer that please?*

It was only when my brain decided that it wished the person on the other side of the door was Cole that I wanted to take that look back. But Vee was already wrapping her hand around the knob and I didn't have time to move Drew before the door was opening. Although I felt a drop in my gut when it I saw that it *wasn't* Cole, I was still happy, all the same.

"You're not Dana," Lottie said, her brows nearly touching from confusion before she noticed me on the couch behind Vee.

Vee stepped to the side, shooting me a dirty look as Lottie stepped through the doorway. "Did you not tell *anyone* I was here?"

I shrugged. "I told Cole."

Lottie's face lit up as she rushed over to me and Drew, mom-mode activating. "Oh my god, he's grown!"

"You mean that guy you abandoned your son for a few nights ago?" Vee snapped, the door nearly slamming shut. There was a hesitation there that held her back, though, to not upset Drew with a loud noise.

Drew spit out his bottle and cooed at Lottie, stretching his arms out to her. Thankfully, I didn't need to tell her to make sure her hair was out of the way because of Drew's grabby hands, she'd already ensured her brown locks were swept up into an easy bun. "What did your mommy do?" Lottie giggled, kissing him on the nose, the cheeks, his bald little head. "How could she abandon such a perfect little boy like you?"

"Oh my god, I didn't abandon him," I groaned, sinking deeper into the couch. Lottie shot me a questioning look. "I'll explain later."

"And now you're not even going to introduce me," Vee griped.

"Vee, this is Lottie. Lottie, Vee," I deadpanned. "Happy, sis?"

"Ahh, that's right. She mentioned you were staying with her," Lottie said.

"See? People know."

"Whatever," Vee mumbled.

"So," Lottie grinned, slotting in beside me on the couch and bouncing Drew on her legs. "I figured you'd probably need some new clothes for the retreat. And maybe new luggage. And definitely some new swimsuits, and a few things for Drew."

"Retreat?" Vee asked, but I ignored her.

"Where are you going with this?" I eyed Lottie carefully, watching as Drew's face lit up as she poked his little nose.

"I thought we could go on a shopping spree before you leave. On me, obviously."

"Lots, I've got things I can bring. I don't need you buying me shit—"

"It's happening whether you like it or not." She cut me off then lifted Drew up, making little plane noises as if he was the airplane and I was the mouth, landing him back in my lap. "Can you watch him, Vee?"

Vee's mouth popped open and slammed shut, her irritation evident from the way her fists clenched. "Seriously?"

"If she can't, we can drop him off with Hunter's mom," Lottie shrugged. "She's watching Brody today and he'd love a playmate."

"Do that then," Vee huffed, storming off down the hallway and slamming the door to the bathroom behind her.

"She seems feisty," Lottie mumbled, and before I could protest, she was dragging both of us out the door.

———

"Oh my god, these swimsuits are perfect," Lottie gushed, her eyes meeting mine over racks of clothing at a store I'd never have wandered into on my own. I knew the brand but damn, they were expensive.

I sighed my reluctance and came over to meet her, taking in the array of colors and shapes. She pulled a one-piece from the rack, black with mesh panels along the sides in a zig-zag formation. The cups of the breasts were reinforced, and they were maternity, the little clasps along the bottom of the cups allowing for easy access. "Drew doesn't breastfeed very often," I said.

In truth, I actually liked the swimsuit. But I didn't like the tag hanging from one side that read four-hundred and twenty dollars. Why couldn't we have just gone to Target?

"Yeah but what if you need to pump?"

"I know this might come as a shock, Lots, but I'm pretty sure most bathing suits are removable."

She rolled her eyes and threw it in the cart anyway, along with a handful of others, and one single black bikini that was clearly designed to show off my entire ass.

It wasn't until she ordered me to the fitting room and I started trying them on that the excitement of it all started to hit me. A proper vacation, something I'd needed since the two of us had come back from Hawaii, was days away. And I'd be spending at least some of it with Cole.

I was far too excited about that part.

"Okay, we're definitely getting that one," Lottie grinned, one finger pointing up and rotating as an order for me to spin. I'd been worried that the changes my body had gone through since giving birth would stick out like a sore thumb, but the longer I looked in the mirror, the less I noticed the stretch marks and instead saw newfound curves, a larger swell of my breasts and ass. I was still me, just a little bit different, a little bit more built to take care of my son.

A smile crept across my cheeks. "Fine."

I loved everything we'd bought except for the price tag. Although I told myself I'd pay Lottie back for everything she'd purchased for me and Drew, I knew there wasn't a chance in hell I'd be in a position where I could feasibly do that.

The bags lined the booth next to me. Lottie babbled on over dinner about Brody's new advancements, how he was finally putting the right-sized blocks into the right-sized holes and picking up on the sign language she was teaching him. But I found it difficult to focus on anything besides the price tags and the vacation.

"I'm worried Cole's going to find out," I blurted, cutting her off entirely.

She blinked at me, her hands halfway through ripping off a chunk of bread. "Then tell him."

"You say that like it's easy," I sighed. "What am I supposed to tell him, oh, by the way, Drew's your son? I've dug myself a fucking hole, here, Lottie. Either he's going to find out on his own or I'm going to tell him, and neither will end well. And even if it does, even if Cole is perfectly fine with me keeping his son from him until now, there's still the issue of him being a barely recovered alcoholic."

I let out a breath and sucked up the remaining half of my sex-on-the-beach through a straw.

"And yes, I know now. Thanks for keeping that from me," I added with a snooty tone.

She took a deep breath in through her nose and slowly released it out through her mouth, sinking into her side of the booth. "It wasn't my information to share."

"He's the father of my kid. I had a right to know."

Her lips pursed into a thin line. "He's doing exceptionally well for being eight months sober, Dana."

"He came *this* close to relapsing the other day," I shot

back, holding up my thumb and forefinger just an inch apart. "If there's even a *chance*—"

"Stop," Lottie insisted, cutting me off. "It's perfectly normal to almost relapse and even to actually go through a relapse. That doesn't mean there's not a desire there to recover. He decided to get sober on his own, Dana. No one forced him into that. This isn't the same situation as your mom."

I blinked at her, the blow hitting harder than I would have thought.

"You can't expect him to be perfect. You can't expect him to get better overnight, or to not be able to deal with issues like this. I know you have your trauma around alcoholics, but it's not fair to put those expectations of failure on him when he genuinely wants to be better. If anything, knowing he has a fucking son would only make him want sobriety even more."

I couldn't remember the last time Lottie had spoken to me like that, nor could I shake the sinking feeling that she was right. Every time the feeling of wanting to run as far away as I could from him flared, I knew it was coming from that deep-seated place in my childhood. I knew that.

"So what am I supposed to do?"

"Do you want a relationship with him?"

"I don't know."

"Do you want a father for your son?"

"Obviously."

"Then trust him," she sighed. "Give him a chance. He's a good guy. Genuinely. He may be an obnoxious man-child occasionally, but he's doing so much better than he was. You didn't see him after what happened between you two. You didn't see how bad it got, how low he got, or how much he was drinking. He's come such a long way, and I fucking love you, Dana, but I'm not going to let you insinuate that he's worse than he is."

"Would you have gotten with Hunter if he was like this at the beginning?" I asked. They'd been through hell and back, from a fake relationship to a fake wedding, all in order to please her father before he passed. It had taken them forever to actually succumb to their feelings, and deep down, if Hunter was like Cole, I didn't think she would have ended up with him.

"Yes," she huffed. "Of fucking course I would have."

"Are you expecting me to watch Drew for two weeks?" Vee hissed, her irritation clear the moment Drew and I stepped through the front door.

"What? No."

"Why didn't you tell me you were fucking off to Costa Rica?"

I sighed and set my bags down before gently placing Drew in his little swing. "Because I'm taking him with me and I didn't want you to freak out. But apparently, that was going to happen anyway."

"You're taking Drew to South America?"

"Costa Rica is its own country."

"Whatever. Toe-may-toe, toe-mah-toe."

"It's perfectly safe," I added. "We'll be at an all-inclusive with everyone else from work. Why are you so concerned?"

"Because you don't have to take him. You could leave

him here with me and our parents, Dana," she snapped, grabbing a bottle out of the fridge the second Drew began to make a fuss. "You act like you couldn't possibly fathom them watching him, but they're more than capable. Instead, you pawn him off on me or the fucking nanny."

I stared at her in disbelief. She'd managed to keep her massive mouth quiet for a week about Mom and Dad, but now, on the same day that Lottie had berated me for my thought process when it came to Cole, Vee wanted to berate me for my thought process when it came to them. "I can't do this with you right now," I bit back, swallowing the horrible things I wanted to spit at her.

"I don't care," Vee said. "I mean, for Christ's sake, Dana, take him with you. But keeping him from Mom and Dad is just fucking cruel at this point."

"Cruel?" I laughed. I snatched the bottle from her hands before she could give it to Drew herself and plucked the plastic cap off. "You know what's cruel? Fucking over your daughter so badly she had to repeat her sophomore year of high school."

Vee's brows shot up. "Don't tell me you're still mad about that. It was an honest mistake!"

"Sure. Believe that all you want," I snapped, kneeling down on the carpet by Drew's swing and switching off the motor that rocked him back and forth. He gratefully accepted the bottle. "But you and I know damn well Mom knew what she was doing. She told me she'd talked to the school!"

"She probably did and forgot what they'd said," Vee countered, crossing her arms over her chest as she loomed over me. "How was she supposed to navigate that? Call them again?"

"She could have just listened to my protests when I told

her I couldn't go on a fucking cross-country road trip because I had exams! She could have trusted me when I said I'd fail if I didn't turn up for them!"

"You know how much that trip meant to her," Vee hissed.

"No, I don't, because she was drunk the entire goddamn time." I stood from Drew, taking a step toward my sister and forcing her away from us. "She was always drunk. Always relapsing. Anytime she told you she loved you, Vee, she was fucking wasted. At every soccer game of yours she attended, she had a flask in her purse. Every good moment of our lives was overshadowed by the goddamn demon hiding in the background. Do you not remember how many times she forgot to pick us up from school? Or how many times she passed out before making us dinner and Dad was on night shifts so we went to bed hungry?"

Vee's face paled as she stepped back. "You have to learn to let it go. She apologized."

"She never fucking apologized," I laughed, the sound of it far too angry to be perceived as anything else. "Not really. She doesn't give a shit, Vee, and I'm not letting her or our enabler father anywhere near my son."

The autumn wind whipped against my cheeks as I pushed through my run, uninhibited from leaving Drew with Vee. I needed to take out my anger on anything but them, and my ankles were the nearest and easiest victim.

Panting and in pain, I slowed my pace until I was walking, barely reaching the bench I liked to consider my end point before heading back home. I collapsed onto it, winded and still filled to the brim with anger, and tried to catch my breath.

Why did it always come back to this? Why was every problem in my life, every argument, every horrible thought connected to my mother? Why couldn't I have had a normal childhood instead of one where I had to worry for my imminent safety every time I got into a car with her, instead of one where I locked myself in my room every time a bottle was opened?

And why did it have to affect the swirling, confusing emotions I had for Cole?

"You okay there?"

Dragging my hands down my face and fully ready to tell the male owner of the voice to fuck off, I turned to my right, locking eyes with a man just a few inches shorter than Cole with shoulder-length black hair tied back in a ponytail. He'd been out running, too, based on his clothing. There was an unconventional handsomeness to him, an air of confidence I wished I felt. "I'm fine," I sighed.

"You sure about that?" he said, coming a little closer. He held up his palms as I shot him a glare. "Sorry, sorry. I don't really know what to do when happening upon a pretty girl that looks like she's about to cry."

"I'm not about to cry," I shot back, relaxing into the conversation just a little. "I've had a stressful evening and I thought a run would help, but that doesn't seem to be the case."

"I'm sorry about that," he offered. "I'm Robert. Just moved in down the road."

I gave him a tight smile. "Dana."

A grin spread across his lips as he offered his hand.

"Nice to meet you, Dana. I think I've seen you out running before. You've got a kid, right?"

I nodded, shaking his hand. A creeping suspicion tingled in the back of my mind, a small, minor worry that maybe I shouldn't have confirmed that to a stranger, but if he lived in my neighborhood, he was likely to know that anyway. "Honestly, I'm fine, but I appreciate you checking on me."

"Of course. I hope whatever is going on for you gets better, Dana," he said. "And at the risk of sounding too forward, I hope I get to see you around here again."

I huffed out a little laugh. The attention was nice, even if it was coming from a stranger. But still, my thoughts filtered back toward Cole, to the feelings I knew damn well were building between us. I only wished that wasn't the source of half of my stress.

"Thanks, Robert," I said, giving him a tight smile as I picked myself up off the bench. "I'm sure you will."

Chapter 19

Cole

I sat on the plush, rarely used sofa in the great foyer, my two suitcases stacked by the door. My driver was less than ten minutes away, and then it would be another forty minutes until I was at the airport with everyone else, including Dana.

Fuck, I wanted to see her.

A key turned in the lock and I sat up, watching as the door opened. A cleaned-up version of the Bobby that had moved in with me over a month ago stepped through, his button-up shirt pristine, slacks neatly pressed. His hair hung around his shoulders, combed back and freshly washed. I was proud of him, he seemed to be doing better and better every day that I saw him, making friends and taking care of himself. I wondered if he thought I was doing the same or if he knew how badly I'd spiraled just a week ago.

"Hey, man," Bobby said, dropping his keys on the tall, thin table by the door. "Didn't think I'd see you before you left."

I shrugged and stood, crossing the empty space to give

him a one-armed hug. "Driver's running behind. I feel like I haven't seen you in days," I laughed. "Where've you been, man?"

He grinned up at me. He smelled familiar, maybe he'd bought the same cologne I'd been using. "I was out in Denver for the weekend with some new friends. You should come along sometime, I think you'd like them."

"Yeah, maybe after I get back."

"Had a rough night a couple of nights back," he said candidly, shrugging against my arm. "Almost fell back into it."

That took me back a little, he'd been doing so well from what I could tell. Still, it made me feel a little better to know that I wasn't alone in that. "I did too. You should have called me."

"Yeah, I should have," he said.

"We help each other," I insisted. "Remember that. If you need me while I'm gone, you can call me."

"Same to you, man. But you've got Dana, so…"

I chuckled. "Just because I've got something going on with Dana doesn't mean I don't have time for you."

He leaned back against the little table, his grin unmatched. "But it's going well, yeah? Between you two?"

"I think so. I guess we'll see how the trip goes and who knows, maybe I'll come back with something official," I laughed. "But she's got a kid, so I'm not hedging my bets that she'll change her mind about not wanting a proper relationship with me right away."

Something glinted in his eyes as his grin faded, his entire demeanor changing. "You sure you want to get involved in that? Kids are another level, man."

I thought over his words for a moment, a little put off by the stilted nature of the conversation. Before I could dwell on it, my phone buzzed, notifying me of the arrival of my driver. "I've got to go," I sighed. "But please, Bobby, don't hesitate to reach out. And don't forget to go to meetings while I'm gone."

"Yeah, man. I won't."

By the time I'd arrived at the airport, nearly everyone had already boarded, leaving me to check in alone in the lobby and hand off my bags to the staff. I just wanted to see her, even if my nerves were firing overtime knowing that Drew would be there, too.

I climbed the steps up to the door of the jet and stepped through. Almost every seat inside my private jet was filled save for the section at the back that sat four, I'd opted to have Dana and I sit there in case Drew's carry-on necessities needed extra space. The moment I locked eyes with her and the little bundle giggling in her lap, every overworked nerve had settled.

Clearing my throat, I said my hellos to the executives and managers I'd opted to have join me on my personal flight as I made my way down the aisle toward her. I didn't give a fuck about them, didn't care for a single one of them at that moment. I just wanted to sit down with her, meet him, and pretend no one else was there.

I almost wished I'd told them all to fly commercial. At least then I wouldn't have to hold back around her.

The closer I got, the more at ease I began to feel, and as I finally reached the last four seats and the door to the plane shut, I couldn't help but laugh as she took Drew's arm in her hand and made him wave at me.

I waved back.

"Nice of you to finally show up," she chuckled, her smirk crowding my senses as I sat down next to her.

"I'm sorry I'm late." I glanced at the five rows of people ahead of us, making sure none were paying attention before pressing the smallest kiss against her cheek. "My driver hit traffic."

The engine roared to life as the pilots came over the speakers, going over the safety information I'd heard a million times before. I fished between our bodies for her seatbelt and passed it over, slipping it behind Drew's body so it sat flush against her lap.

"You'll need to hold him during takeoff, landing, and any turbulence," I said, trying not to cross any boundaries by accidentally touching him as I buckled her in. "Any other time you can have him in the car seat or... whatever else you do with babies."

She chuckled, her cheeks warming from how close I was as I tightened the belt around her. Drew watched me in fascination, his wide green eyes boring a hole into mine. "Do you not know a lot about babies?"

"Honestly? No. I'm learning as I go," I grinned. "But we've got nine hours in the air for you to fill me in."

In the spare two seats across from us, Drew slept peacefully in his foldable bassinet. He'd only kicked off once so far, and to be fair, I always wanted to do the same during takeoff when my ears ached and popped, so I didn't blame him one bit.

Dana leaned her back against my chest, no longer worried about anyone ahead of us asking questions. Whether that was her own choice or if it was a result of me leveling glares at anyone who dared look back at us was beyond me, but I was happy to be close to her, nonetheless.

"I like him," I said softly, my fingers drifting up and down her arm as she watched him breathe. The more I knew about him, the longer I watched him, the more I felt at peace with him. If there was even the slightest possibility of a long-term thing with her, I could handle a child being involved in that. At least, in theory.

Her sleepy grin as she tilted her head back at me warmed my heart. "Me too."

I chuckled quietly, careful not to make too much noise in case I woke him.

A silence settled over us as she opened her mouth but quickly closed it, deciding against whatever it was she'd wanted to say. Instead, she sank further into me, her hand fiddling with the fabric that covered my calf. "Can I ask you something?"

I buried my nose into the top of her head, drinking in the scent of her, memorizing the berries, hibiscus and vanilla. "Anything."

"How... how can you afford this?" she asked, waving her hand, gesturing at the entire plane. "The private jet, the company retreat, the house. I know Pearson Beers brings in a lot of revenue, that's clear, but *this* much?"

"A combination of the success of Pearson Beers and being born into wealth," I sighed. "My... family, if you want to call them that, comes from old money."

She went silent again, returning to fiddling with the fabric of my slacks before speaking. "Why do you say family like—"

A cry broke through from the bassinet, startling Dana into action, and I breathed a sigh of relief. I knew where her question was going, and I didn't want to go down that road with her, at least not yet. She didn't need that weighing on her along with everything else.

She plucked Drew from where he lay, his toothless mouth open and his eyes squinted shut as he let out another cry. "I know that cry," she said, rolling her eyes as she leaned over to the massive bag of baby things she'd brought with her. She fumbled for whatever it was she was looking for, grunting in frustration, before sitting back up empty-handed. "Can you hold him?"

"What?"

"I can't reach the cooler his milk is in," she said nonchalantly as if it made perfect sense and wasn't at all weird for her to be holding Drew out toward me.

I don't know why I froze. I'd had no problem taking Brody when he was given to me and had no problem in general with babies, but the longer I looked at him the more it felt like there was something that couldn't be changed after touching him. "Dana, I—"

"It's okay," she insisted. "It's just for a second."

Reluctantly, I grasped him under his little arms and took him from her gently, his wails beginning to calm. Damp eyes blinked open, that flash of green meeting mine, and I knew I was right—this couldn't be changed.

Quickly, Dana unbuckled her seatbelt and got up, fishing through the bag with a newfound determination. She glanced at us as she pulled out the mini cooler.

He wiggled in my arms, the threat of another cry on his

lips. "Hey, hey," I cooed, setting him down on my lap and letting him wrap his stubby little fingers around one of mine. "Calm down, bud. It's coming."

Drew made a little noise that sounded like a hiccup as his head tilted back to look up at me. I winced as he shoved my finger in his mouth, his gums chomping down.

"Uh, Dana?"

Clumsily, he pushed my finger to the side, up against his cheek until he seemed satisfied with the placement. He bit down again, his other hand playfully grabbing for my shirt as he seemed to calm down.

Dana stood with a bottle in her hand, her brows knitted together as she watched. "Is this normal?" I asked.

She shook her head.

"He doesn't normally bite your finger?"

She shook her head again.

Before I understood what was happening, she dropped the bottle on the seat and fished around in her bag for something else. Drew stared up at me, his little giggle far cuter than Brody's. Something about him tugged at my heartstrings—the look on his face, the light in his eyes, the way his little nose wiggled.

I only realized what it all meant when Dana sat back down beside me, a plastic, squishy giraffe in her hand, and coaxed my finger from his mouth before passing him the toy. Almost immediately it was in his mouth, its head being chomped on by the tiny baby in my lap.

"Of course, he'd choose now to start teething," she groaned, her forehead falling in defeat against my shoulder.

Chapter 20

Dana

Costa Rica was more beautiful than I could have ever imagined. The resort was massive, spanning multiple properties with independent suites, each with its own infinity pool and in-house catering. We were staying on the Peninsula Papagayo, right along the beachfront, with thick, lush forests behind us and an unwavering amount of ocean before us.

I could stay here forever.

Of course it wouldn't be a Pearson Beers retreat without Cole occasionally making us do work. We still had meetings, discussions about the upcoming launch in a few months, and the overwhelming amount of press that it would bring. Cole still had to do the rounds and answer emails, communicate with the board members who had come with us, as well as field calls and video meetings with the people he'd hired to ensure the brewery was still running efficiently. The bar, tours, and restaurant had all been shut down, but the brewery needed to continue to run.

Cole still made time to see me and Drew, almost going out of his way to do so.

Unbeknownst to me, he'd spoken to the resort staff in advance and ensured a nanny would be on site for me as needed. The moment she'd turned up and introduced herself, it was like every worry I'd had about Cole had dissipated—he'd done everything he could, from booking me a child-safe room to making sure that our meetings fell within Drew's schedule so I could either bring him along or put him down for a nap with the nanny. It only made the fear of falling for him that much less terrifying.

But what had surprised me more than anything was when I'd come back from a morning meeting on the third day and found Cole in my private residence, Drew on his lap with a bottle in his mouth, Cole holding onto him while speaking down the phone about some upcoming press release.

I stood in the doorway as the nanny gathered her things, my heart swelling in my chest. I wanted to tell him. I wanted to fall on my knees and apologize for keeping it from him, tell him how well he was doing without even knowing Drew was his. In a paradise away from Boulder, everything just felt right.

Drew clocked my presence before Cole did. His little smile tripled as he popped the bottle from his mouth, his giggles filling the room as he reached out toward me. The nanny shuffled beside me, mumbling a quick goodbye before she walked out the door, and only then did Cole follow Drew's line of sight.

"I've got to go," he said, hitting the end call button as muffled words filtered through the small speaker. He put the phone down on the table and took Drew's arm in one hand, making him wave to me just as I'd done to him on the plane. "Look who's back," he cooed to Drew, the baby voice he'd adopted making me laugh. "It's mommy."

"Don't call me that," I chuckled, crossing the room to them and planting a kiss on Drew's bald head. "What are you doing here? You weren't at the meeting."

He shrugged. "I figured I'd let Ben take the reins and hang out with this little guy instead."

"You've been here the whole time?"

"Since a few minutes after you left."

"And miraculously Drew's still alive," I mumbled.

"Well, the nanny helped a bit," Cole laughed. "He only got fussy once, though. I tried the bottle and it seemed to calm him down."

Tell him. Just tell him, here, where things are perfect and he won't get mad.

I opened my mouth to follow up my line of thought, but the words I wanted wouldn't come out. "I was planning on going to the beach," I said instead, that rock plummeting in my stomach from my fucking cowardice. "Do you want to come?"

He stood from his seat at the table, holding Drew the same way I did and tucking him into his arms. His lips pressed against my cheek gently, and for a moment, everything slotted into place. Cole holding Drew, his affection toward me, my reception to it... I wanted this. And I let myself want it.

"Of course I do," he said softly.

Our time together was beginning to feel easy and natural. We spent nearly the entire afternoon on the beach beneath a canopy, the waves hammering against the shore, the sun beating down around us. I'd covered Drew in a thick layer of sunscreen to be safe, despite keeping him in the shade, and as I relaxed and read a book Cole adorably tried to teach my—our—son how to build a sand castle. But Drew was only interested in trying to eat the sand.

The absurdity of it was the best part. Cole didn't understand babies, but in fairness, neither did I until I'd spent nine months carrying one while reading every parenting book I could get my hands on. I didn't expect Cole to know that Drew didn't know how to pack sand into a mold. Instead, I watched in amusement as he figured it out along the way, as he panicked when Drew shoved a handful of sand against his mouth, as he gently beat against his back to get him to spit it out. He learned as he went.

It was only when Drew started to drift off that we decided our beach trip was done. We decided it would be better for him to cry the way back up to my residence than to fall asleep on the beach and not be able to take a proper nap, so Cole held him in his arms as we walked, distracting him and shoving toys at him to keep him somewhat happy.

"I'll put him down," Cole said as I shut the door.

After everything, that shouldn't have surprised me. But still, I found myself freezing in the doorway, my legs covered in a layer of sand, looking at him in fucking awe. "Are you sure?"

"Yeah, I've got it," he said, flashing me a little grin. "You should rinse off."

I took his lead and let him take Drew, listening to his tiny little cries that always broke my heart as I hopped into the shower. The sand fell from my body, from places I didn't know sand could get stuck in, and I slowly let myself relax after I heard the last little cry.

Drew was fast asleep by the time I wandered back out in a plush robe, my damp hair dripping onto the wood floor. He lay silently in his crib, his little giraffe on the table beside him.

The shadow of a seated figure on my balcony, the door half open so he could hear if Drew roused, put my mind at ease.

I stepped through the crack in the door. Over the water the sun was slowly beginning to set, the sky colored in pinks and oranges and shades of blue I'd never seen before, almost as if it were painted by hand.

"Thank you," I breathed. Something familiar was urging me toward Cole but far more intense than I'd felt before.

"For what, baby?" he asked. He welcomed me with open arms, pulling me into his lap and wrapping his hands around my robe-covered waist.

I shook my head, unsure of what I wanted to say. *For being so good with him. For making sure he was out like a light. For feeding him when he needed it. For playing with him. For being what I need.* "Everything."

He pressed a kiss against my damp hair, his features darkening as he looked out at the setting sun. Silence filled the space, the only sound the chirping of the crickets and the low bass of a booming party somewhere below us on the beach.

"My parents took me to a beach in Mexico just like this when I was kid," he said, the words so quiet I almost didn't hear them.

I looked up at him, watching as he avoided my gaze but holding onto me just as tightly. "How old were you?"

"Six, maybe," he sighed. "My dad tried to teach me how to surf, but I couldn't figure it out. So instead, he took me out into the water with nothing but our bodies and spent hour after hour trying to teach me how to body surf."

His hands squeezed me a little tighter, but even through the seemingly good memory, the darkness on his face didn't fade.

"It took me a really long time to get it. But when I did, when I finally caught a wave and rode it all the way into shore, he'd hollered like I'd won a fucking gold medal. He picked me up, spun me around, the works. He said he was proud of me."

Slowly, solemnly, his eyes met mine.

"I think that might have been the only time he said that to me."

I swallowed, my chest aching for him, nearly splitting in half. I opened my mouth to speak but his lips found mine instead, silencing any hope for a reassuring word.

Taking his face in my hands, I tried to say what I wanted with my kiss instead. I held him, tasted him, conveyed everything, everything I'd been holding back with that kiss. I told him with my lips that I was proud of him, that I was falling for him, that he was enough and that I wanted this, wanted him.

I just wished I could've said it with words, instead. Wished he could understand.

His hand tightened around the belt of the robe, tugging

at the loose knot until it broke free, splitting down the center and exposing every part of me to him. His cock hardened beneath his swim trunks as he deepened the kiss with every swipe of his lips and tongue. I hadn't had him in nearly a week, and if it meant here on the balcony, I was more than willing.

I moaned into his mouth as his hand cupped my breast, his fingers brushing against my hardened, almost aching nipples. I needed to pump but it could wait.

His lips found my neck instead, kissing and sucking against the spot that made me lose my mind. My mouth was free and I could say what I wanted but still, the words wouldn't form. I found myself getting completely lost in his touch, any hope of the truth coming out falling flat. *Tell him*, I silently screamed at myself, nothing but a sigh passing my fucking lips.

His fingers trailed from my breast down my stomach, dipping below, tracing the folds around my clit instead. Little teases and gentle brushes against the bundle of nerves that was beginning to ache turned my mind further into mush.

"You have no idea what you do to me," he rasped, snaking his free hand between the robe and my skin and wrapping it around the small of my back.

"I'm still not going to date you," I teased, pushing my hips forward and guiding his fingers toward my entrance. I shuddered as they slid inside, curling forward, pressing against the spot inside that made me feel like fucking heaven.

"Keep telling yourself that," he laughed, repeating what he'd said to me just before Vee had opened the door a week ago, "while you fuck yourself on my fingers."

I moaned at his words, sinking myself further onto them and tilting my hips forward. His thumb jutted out, pressing lightly against my clit for added stimulation with every thrust I made. "More," I breathed, digging my nails into the side of his neck, pulling a little hiss from him.

"More what?"

"More," I repeated through clenched teeth. "You, this, everything. All of it. *More.*"

A sudden, wailing cry shook me back into reality.

Cole froze beneath me and my hips locked, each of us waiting for the inevitable follow-up. It could have just been in his sleep, could have been someone else's baby in another residence—

A sharper, needier one bled out from the cracked door, and god fucking dammit, I wanted to join him in wailing my brains out.

Cole slid his fingers from me and held me closer as he lifted us both from the chair. "I've got him," he said, absentmindedly sticking his digits in his mouth and cleaning them off before stepping around me.

"Cole—"

But he had already stepped through the door and was rushing over to the crib, leaving me there on the balcony exposed and wanting. I watched through the glass as he picked up Drew, holding him against his bare chest and bobbing up and down, soothing him the way they say to in every parenting book. He offered him his giraffe but he batted it away. Instead, he fetched a bottle, holding it up to his lips and swiping the little bit of milk at the tip against his mouth. Drew sucked it in, problem solved.

What was stopping me from telling him? Why couldn't I put those words together, why couldn't I just tell him and face the consequences? It didn't make sense to me. I hated secrets, always had, and yet here I was keeping the biggest one I could've ever dreamed of.

Maybe Cole had already put the pieces together. Maybe it wasn't some big realization he needed to have.

Maybe he'd already accepted that Drew was his son.

Chapter 21

Cole

Day seven, and we'd made it to our final meeting. The last three days of the trip were to be spent in whatever way each person wanted. I'd offered to pay for outings, day trips, excursions... whatever the staff wanted to do was on me.

I hadn't had a better seven days in as long as I could remember. I'd been in either my penthouse or Dana's suite, spending nearly every second that wasn't dedicated to working with her and Drew. We'd had the occasional dinner and trip down to the beach, but outside of that, I just wanted to be around her. I didn't sleep or function nearly as well when she wasn't next to me, and as much as I worried that maybe my sponsor was right and I was chasing a high I'd replaced with Dana, I didn't give myself the space to think about it.

I checked her suite once I was finally able to leave the executives behind but came up empty. Instead, I made my way up to the penthouse, hoping maybe she and Drew would be there but no trace of them.

Sighing, I collapsed on the bed, eyeing the stash of

alcohol the hotel had left as a present for me. But I didn't even crave it, didn't want it. I wanted her.

I'd barely been able to keep her off my mind, and when my thoughts weren't swirling with her, they were filled with Drew. Something about being with him, even when Dana wasn't around, had brought me a sense of peace that I wasn't used to. Sure, he screamed like a banshee sometimes and didn't always smell like sunshine and daisies, but there was something about him. Something I didn't feel when I held Brody. Something that felt familiar, like I wanted to slot him into my life right alongside Dana.

Maybe it was my growing sense of ease around kids. Or maybe it was because he was hers, therefore, he was a part of her.

I'd never given as much thought to having a family as I had in the last couple of months. I was never entirely against the idea; if I was I would have gone above and beyond to get a vasectomy the moment I was legally able to. I just didn't think having a family was a good idea unless and until I'd overcome my issues and gave up the resentment I had for my parents.

Though I wasn't sure that was something that would ever go away.

How was I supposed to be a parent when I had never learned how? How could I raise a family when my own wanted nothing to do with me? In fairness, until I was about eight years old, my parents did treat me like I was worthy of their time and attention when they were capable of giving it to me. But after I stopped believing in Santa Claus, the Tooth Fairy, and the Easter Bunny, after I outgrew watching kiddie cartoons and wanting sugary cereal for breakfast, it was as if I'd become nothing more than a crumpled-up piece of paper, my purpose served, already formed and broken.

If they hadn't driven me to my aunt's and left me for good, I probably would have turned out worse. I probably would have gotten that vasectomy, swore off a family of my own, and gone down the rabbit hole with alcohol harder, faster, and angrier. But Aunt Kathy took pity on me, saw my parents for what they were, and treated me as her own. Even through the chaos of my teenage years and the fuck-ups I made along the way, she cared. I could still hear her screaming her head off at my high school graduation, her pride far too big to keep in.

Her death a few months after I graduated college hit me hard. I'd only just invested in the property that would become Pearson Beers and I left it on the back burner, choosing instead to bury my grief in the bottom of a bottle. I'd started running with the wrong crowd again after a few years of being on the straight and narrow. I'd let it all slip. But Brody Hammersmith, Lottie's father and little Brody's namesake, had helped me figure out how to become successful on my own.

He'd also taken pity on me.

Thinking about them, Aunt Kathy and Brody, lit something inside of me. It had been far too long since I'd let myself dwell on my past for fear that it would spark up that burn at the top of my chest, the want to drink. But it didn't this time.

Instead, it made me want to appreciate what I had, made me want to live more in the moment and not take for granted what I'd been given.

It made me want to take a step further with Dana.

I'm still not going to date you. Her voice echoed in my head, tugging my lips up. She'd made that decision before

I'd met Drew, before either of us had delved deeper than we thought we would. A fresh start might have been the initial goal, with the occasional hookup and an uncertain future, but that's no longer what I wanted. And even though she teased me, even though she kept saying it, I wasn't sure she meant it. *Keep telling yourself that.*

But taking things to the next level meant commitments, commitments that I wasn't sure I could reliably keep. If I made it official with her, and things progressed further, would I be setting myself up for a life raising another man's child? Was that something I had an issue with? It didn't feel like it right now but how would it affect me as he grew, as Drew began to ask questions and resemble whomever he came from?

And would I be able to stay clean for all of it?

Would Dana still want me if I slipped?

I swallowed down the worry. With Dana by my side, I'd be solid. She'd come through like a knight in shining fucking armor for me last time. The better I got, the less she'd have to be there, picking up and piecing the shattered remains back together. I could handle it as long as she was there.

I slipped my phone from my pocket, scrolling through my contacts until the resort manager's name popped up.

The nerves flitting about in my gut didn't seem to want to let up. I raked the pomade through my hair, pushing it back and out of my face. It was nearing seven in the evening, and Dana and Drew would be up here any second.

I took the five minutes I had remaining to triple-check that my buttons were in the right holes and that the living room of my penthouse suite looked suitable. An elaborate dinner had been brought up, and although they'd offered to bring up each course individually, I'd declined. I didn't want anyone else here. Just Dana, Drew, and me.

The glass dining table had been laid out perfectly—plates, cutlery, glasses, and a bottle of sparkling juice on ice. I'd laughed when they'd brought it in under special orders from me that nothing contained alcohol. I imagined maybe they'd bring sparkling water or an array of local specialties, but no, juice it was.

A knock sounded on my door.

Drew's little grin hit me first when I opened it, but quickly and overwhelmingly, I took in every inch of Dana. The dark green dress she wore split halfway down her thigh, hanging just below her knees and hugging every goddamn curve. Her hair, swept over to one side, was perfectly coiled in loose waves despite Drew's little fist gripping onto it.

And those fucking lips.

Deep red, crisp, and begging to be used.

"Are you going to let us in or just stare at me?" she laughed, adjusting Drew's weight on her hip. A hint of a blush settled across her cheeks.

"I think I might keep staring."

She rolled her eyes dramatically and took a step toward me, almost daring me to step aside, but I didn't want to move. I wanted to memorize her just like this, dressed up entirely for me, with a baby on her hip and a smirk on her lips. I leaned forward, pressing the lightest little kiss on her cheek, and finally relented.

I took Drew from her as she stepped through, allowing

myself to fully take her in from behind as well. Drew cooed in my arms, his lips and gums gnawing down on his little plastic giraffe.

I couldn't stop looking at her fucking ass.

God, I didn't deserve her.

"Smells good," she said, the lilt in her voice telling me all that I needed to know.

"There's backup food in case you don't like it," I chuckled, stepping around her and pulling out the resort-issued high chair for Drew so he could join us at the table. Dana let out a sigh of relief.

"When you say backup food—"

"It's not dinosaur-shaped chicken nuggets, if that's what you're asking."

"There is nothing wrong with dino-nuggets." She shot a playful glare at me. "They're delicious and nutritious and frankly, if you ask me, better tasting than regular-shaped nuggets."

I laughed as I set Drew into his high chair, his feet kicking out as he giggled. "I wasn't shitting on dino-nuggets, Dana."

She plucked a single cocktail shrimp from the rim of one of the martini glasses and popped it in her mouth as she sat down. "You better not be unless you want to be blue-balled."

"Oh no, not the scary, fictitious disease teenage boys use to guilt trip girls into fucking them. I'm quaking in my boots." I pushed Drew's high chair closer to the table before realizing how easily he could reach out and knock over literally *anything* before deciding that some distance would be better. "Honestly, baby, I thought you'd have outgrown your belief in that by twenty-eight."

Her little smirk made me want to spread her out on the glass table and enjoy a different meal instead.

I slotted into my seat, watching her carefully across the array of food. "I tried to make sure everything was at least a *little* bland."

"Oh my god," she laughed. "I don't hate flavor."

"Sure you don't, baby. Either way, they brought up all of the least scary dishes they had," I grinned, expanding the cloth napkin with a flick of my wrist before laying it out over my suit slacks. There were plates of oysters, martini glasses of cocktail shrimp that she'd already got her hands on, an array of different types of rice and beans, various salads, different glazed meats, fried plantains and potatoes cooked in every way possible, anything I could think of on the menu that might work well for her.

But hidden in the fridge was a jar of spaghetti sauce and a stash of fresh noodles. *Just in case.*

"I think I can find enough here to eat," she said, her eyes still catching on the cocktail shrimp as she helped herself to one of the salads and a massive scoop of rice and beans.

Drew seemed entertained enough with a handful of toys and a bottle at the ready in case he kicked off. We ate, drank the sparkling grape juice, laughed and teased. I didn't even find myself wishing that the aforementioned juice was something else. All I wanted was to be present in the moment with her, to not be startled when time slipped away, to remember every little detail from the way she hummed around the foods she tried and liked to the way she giggled when I called her baby.

I didn't want it to end. And it didn't have to.

"Why tonight?" she asked, leaning back in her chair after devouring a small plate of chocolate cake. "We still have another three days. What's so special about today?"

"Why does it have to be special?"

She leveled a glare at me that said *cut the shit*.

"Alright," I chuckled, sitting back in my seat and trying to relax. In truth, the nerves had kicked up again, once forgotten about in the peace she brought me but now screaming at me again in full force. "You got me."

She motioned with her hand to continue, her glee from being right barely hidden.

I took a deep breath, trying to work out what I wanted to say, how I wanted to sell it to her. But it wasn't another product I was offering, wasn't a financial investment. She was Dana, and I was me, and Drew was a tiny human shaking his toy keyring about with reckless abandon.

"Tell me," she said, her voice a little softer.

"I know you said that it isn't what you want," I sighed, already hating the way I'd started. "That you didn't want to consider it after what had happened between us last year."

I could see her body stiffen, her hand half outstretched toward the martini glass of cocktail shrimp. She hesitated before retracting it.

"And I know it hasn't been that long since then, but so much has changed," I continued. "And fuck, Dana, I can't pretend this is just casual. I can't keep pretending like I don't want more with you because I do. I'll keep going like this if it's what you need, but I wanted to lay my cards on the table. I wanted to tell you because it's getting so much harder to keep it in every time I touch you."

She swallowed, her throat bobbing. She glanced at Drew as he babbled, his little noises so easy to tune out when it mattered, but I knew this wasn't something that only involved her. She had to consider him, too. "What are you saying, exactly?" she asked.

"I want a relationship with you," I rasped. "I want *everything* with you."

Chapter 22

Dana

Drew slept so deeply I wondered if he'd ever wake up.

I turned off the light to the small spare room in Cole's penthouse after setting up the nanny cam I'd brought up just in case. I couldn't help but wonder if I'd made a mistake, if I hadn't thought it through enough, if I'd made my decision on a whim. But how could I have? I hadn't been able to stop thinking about the positives and negatives for weeks. I'd thought it through.

He was on me the second I shut the door to the master.

His arm around my waist, his hand cupping my cheek, his lips just a hairsbreadth from my own. I leaned into him, drinking in the scent of his cologne and the hint of ocean spray, the smile far too strong to try to hold back.

"I don't deserve you," he said casually, as if he genuinely believed it but couldn't give a shit.

"You do, though," I breathed. Our noses touched as I looked up at him, a lone, dusty blonde curl falling forward into his face. "I wouldn't have said yes if you didn't."

His fingers tightened around my waist, so hard they

were almost bruising. "It still doesn't feel real," he chuckled, his lips pressing against mine briefly before pulling away, only to kiss me again. And again.

Somewhere between the fourth and twentieth kiss, I deepened it, holding him to me instead of letting him back away. A stifled groan of relief seeped from his throat, his body springing into action. He fisted the fabric of my dress so hard it nearly tore, and with any other garment I wouldn't have cared, but Lottie had spent too much on it and I didn't want to ruin it.

"Off," I mumbled, reaching around my back for the zipper. Cole's hand followed mine, grasping the dangling piece of metal before I could and pulling it down. He pushed the straps of my dress off my shoulders, and within seconds the soft, dark green fabric was on the floor, leaving me entirely bare before him.

"You fucking tease," he growled, the words guttural as he walked me backward toward the wall. "You spent the entirety of dinner wearing nothing underneath that?"

I giggled, gasping as his mouth met my collarbone, his teeth baring down on me. "Maybe," I said. I watched him as he devoured my skin, still fully clothed with a bulge between his thighs. Being this exposed when he wasn't made me feel even more naked.

"You're lucky I haven't had my dessert," he mumbled, and before I could even blink he was on his knees. "*Yet.*"

He kissed up and down the inside of my thigh, making my breath hitch as he looked up at me. His fingers dug into my hips, his free hand pushing my legs apart. I leaned against the wall for balance, watching as patches of my skin turned red from his nibbles and nips. His mouth moved higher, dangerously close to where I could already feel a pool of liquid heat forming.

"Tell me what you want, baby," he said, his nose flitting against the short patch of hair between my thighs. "Beg me for it."

With shaking hands, I pushed his hair back from his face, cupping his cheeks. "Please," I whispered. "Please, Cole, touch me."

With a grunt, his mouth latched onto my most sensitive spot. I tilted my hips forward, giving him easier access, sinking into him. I'd never get over this, over him, and the way he seemed to know my body better than I did. It was as if he picked up on cues I didn't even know I was giving, as if he understood the way my body ached for him, giving it exactly what it wanted.

With one hand gripping my ass for support, he squeezed, his nails digging into my skin. His other slid up between my thighs, the warmth of his tongue dragging along my clit, vicious in its movements, before dipping down to my entrance and drinking in every last ounce of me.

"You're too much," I whined, shifting my hips again in search of the fingers I knew were close by. "Too good."

"And you're everything," he said, the words muffled, the vibrations sending a little shockwave through me. He chuckled darkly, his fingers finally teasing my entrance, his others releasing my ass. "You like how that feels, don't you? When I speak to you like this."

I nodded weakly, my release already coiling tight in my gut.

His hand grabbed his belt, unlatching it swiftly and pulling it through each loop with a satisfying *thwack*. The same moment his thick, veiny cock sprung out from his slacks, his fingers sunk inside of me, filling me, but it still wasn't enough. They could never be enough, not when I wanted him.

He pulled his mouth away, giving me a full view of how hard he was and the droplets of precum leaking out.

And then he touched himself, and I thought I might die right there.

"Fuck," he groaned, his eyes fluttering as he tipped his head back, his Adam's apple straining. He moved from base to tip, base to tip, taking his time as he curled his digits inside of me, his thumb absently flicking against my clit. "Look how hard you make me. Look how much you make me want you."

My body tensed, the imminence of my orgasm almost too much to bear. "Cole, please, please, I'm so close—"

He sprung forward in an instant, replacing his twitching thumb with his mouth. His other arm moved with each tug he made on his cock, his grunts and groans setting off those little vibrations he'd given me before. He sucked, nipped, licked at my clit like a fucking madman, and within seconds I was crashing, my hand over my mouth to contain the shriek I knew would come as pleasure ripped through my veins like wildfire.

"That's it, baby," he said, and I fucking lost it.

Not even his hand between my thighs could keep me upright. My knees gave out, and down I went into his waiting arm, his other still pumping himself as I shook with every cascading wave. I kissed him sloppily, tasting myself, coating my lips in the same dampness that coated his.

Without thinking, I pushed him back with shaking hands to give myself access to his nearly fully clothed body. He leaned back onto the wood floor on his elbows, releasing his grip on his cock as I took over with my mouth instead. I couldn't escape the innate need to pleasure him, to take him as many times as he'd let me. We wouldn't be nearly done after this—no fucking way.

He plucked his buttons open, one by one, taking his time but I didn't want to take my time. I didn't want to hesitate.

Bowing my head, I wrapped my lips against the swollen, bulging head of his length. The darker-colored skin of his shaft disappeared inside my mouth, and as I looked up at him, his lips parted as he let out a steady moan, his vivid green eyes locked with mine.

His fingers fisted my hair, getting a good grip on my scalp to the point that it almost burned, and slowly, gently, he guided me back up. His breath shuddered as I released him entirely with a *pop*, a string of saliva hanging from my tongue and connecting me to the flesh of his glans.

"God," he rasped.

He pushed me back down again, the tip of his cock pressing against my lips to let him back in. The sounds he made, the twitches against my tongue, all made me the more ready for him. I took him into the back of my throat, cutting off my breathing for just a moment, and he fucking whimpered.

Oh, the power I had taking him like this.

Using my hand to keep him steady, I picked up speed, following his direction. He was hard as fucking stone, almost scalding hot to the touch. "Fuck, Dana, fuck—"

I slipped my mouth from him again, teasing him instead with my hand, and met his gaze. "Yes?"

"No, no, please, baby, please," he whined, his hand pushing against my head to try to get my mouth back on him. "Please. I'm so close, I need you—"

Laughing at how easily he came undone for me, I shoved

him back into my mouth, twisting just a little with each pump of my hand around the base. My tongue slid along the bottom, flicking against the little ridge that separated his shaft and head, and just as I felt him twitch again, his balls tightening and his cock fucking straining, I pushed myself down to the base.

He came in an instant, his groan a little too loud. Warmth slid down the back of my throat as heaving, shaky breaths wracked his chest. Slowly, gently, I pulled my mouth from him, panting from the loss of oxygen.

His pupils blown, he swiped his thumb over my lower lip, gently pushing the little drop of his cum that had escaped back into my mouth.

I sucked it clean.

"I was right," he grunted, his voice rough and heavy. "I don't fucking deserve you."

I hadn't been able to get my fill of him no matter how many times we'd collided.

Two days passed in a blur of pleasure, showers, and parenting. We'd barely left his penthouse save for the few times we'd needed something of Drew's from my suite. Every fucking moment he was out cold, I couldn't keep my hands off of Cole.

We barely slept. We barely ate.

What I'd originally thought was just a need for affection after far too long without it was so much more. Every kiss, every cuddle, every second he spent buried inside of me felt too damn perfect to be just that. I hadn't made a mistake in saying yes. I was sure of that now.

On the final night of the retreat, we'd collected ourselves enough to make an appearance downstairs with the rest of the group. The staff drank and toasted to a vacation well-deserved, and in solidarity with Cole, the two of us had cheers-ed with the rest of them with a glass of Diet Coke, Drew with a half-full bottle of breastmilk.

"Dana!"

Allison, my manager, pushed through the sea of people to approach me, her grin far too wide to not be suspicious.

"I've barely seen you since we got here," she said. The little smirk that tugged at her lips told me she knew exactly why that was, especially with Cole behind me, his hand protectively on the small of my back as he spoke to Ben.

"I..." I couldn't think of what to say. Instead, I let out a breathless chuckle, my cheeks heating. "Sorry."

"Don't apologize," she laughed, taking a sip of her drink and flashing me knowing eyes. "It's none of my business what goes on between consenting adults."

I readjusted Drew, shifting him further up my hip as he kicked. He was absolutely going to break another of my ribs if he got much stronger. "It's been a bit of a whirlwind," I admitted.

She nodded, waving a single hand at Drew as he animatedly waved back at her. Her voice dropped, just a little quieter than the din of the crowd of employees, and she leaned in closer. "Just be careful, okay?"

"I am."

The morning of departure, Cole met me in my room far before when he said he would. He came empty-handed, his bags already on their way to the airport, and helped me make sure I hadn't forgotten a single thing of mine or Drew's. He packed up my things as I packed Drew's, his worry over misplacing things incorrectly or confusingly making my chest warm.

And he carried *everything*.

The diaper bag, Drew's luggage, my luggage, even my purse. All I needed to worry about was the slightly snotty baby on my hip and his little plastic giraffe.

The drive to the airport was almost too short. I wasn't entirely ready to say goodbye to the little slice of paradise I'd found the last ten days, but I needed to believe I could have that back home in Boulder, too. We needed to see how we both fared in the real world—him with his temptation and us being in a relationship.

We could make it work and I truly wanted it to.

The same people who had flown down to Costa Rica with us joined us for the flight back. Drew slept almost the entire way, either in his foldable bassinet or on Cole's lap. The little dribbles of snot weren't entirely unusual for him, but I made a note in my calendar on my phone to make an appointment with his doctor just in case.

Cole didn't seem to have any problem wiping it away with a tissue.

For the millionth time in the last week alone, the weight of my secret pressed down on my shoulders. I owed it to him now more than ever; if we were going to try our hand at an actual relationship, he deserved to know instead of assuming he'd be helping raise someone else's child. He hadn't had a single blip while we were in Costa Rica, not a mention of needing to drink or a craving. I knew he was itching to get through meetings, but he seemed to be making major improvements from that night at the liquor store.

It was risky, involving him this much with his son. But it was a risk I felt ready to take. If we could get through this and make it out the other side, it would be good for us. For our family. I just needed to tell him.

No matter the reaction.

No matter if it meant an argument and turmoil.

He deserved to know.

The landing back in Boulder was a little rough with the winds coming over the mountains. Drew sobbed, his little plastic giraffe not quite enough to keep him distracted from the pain in his gums and ears. I'd said my apologies to the rest of the staff on the plane, but Cole had cut me off, insisting it wasn't anything to apologize for.

We waited for the rest of them to deplane before we gathered our things. Cole took Drew as I packed up his bag, making sure nothing was left behind, especially the giraffe.

"I think he might lose his mind if I lost that," I laughed, looking back at him over my shoulder as I walked down the steps of the plane onto the tarmac. Cole carried him against his chest, the smallest bit of saliva on his t-shirt.

"I mean, honestly, baby, does he even *need* teeth?" he laughed, joining me before the steps retracted. "It seems like a recipe for disaster if he's still occasionally breast-feeding—"

The smile on Cole's face fell, his eyes looking over my head and somewhere behind me. His hand tightened on Drew, holding him just a little bit closer, his body tensing.

I turned, following his line of sight, but came up only with a couple who looked to be in their early sixties with two teenagers on either side of them. A girl and a boy, lost in the screens of their phones as they stood still on the runway, a chartered private jet wheeling out toward them.

Cole didn't take his eyes off of them. Something unspoken hung in the air, something thick and angry. I almost wanted to take Drew from him.

"What's wrong?" I asked. His knuckles had gone white from the death grip he had on the handle of his luggage, but the arm around Drew remained calm and secure. Every bit of light I'd seen in his eyes for the last week came to a grinding halt. "Cole? Who are they?"

Blinking, he slowly turned to look at me, his mouth parted and his eyes more hollow than I'd seen in over a year.

"They're my parents," he breathed, his tone so cold, so dead, that I nearly didn't comprehend it.

Chapter 23

Cole

I tried not to look at myself in the mirror as I slid my cufflinks on. I checked my shirt for any wrinkles, careful not to look at my face, and dabbed a couple of fingers of cologne on either side of my neck and wrists before sliding the jacket of my tux over my arms and shoulders. My hair would have to fucking do—I didn't care enough to check.

The gala tonight would be a test. Without Dana by my side, the alcohol freely flowing at the event would be tempting beyond belief, but I'd have Grayson and Bobby to keep me in check. I just needed to get through tonight. Then I could go back to her and her son, wrap her in my arms, and try to forget about the overbearing reason that kept me from looking in the mirror.

I didn't want to see my parent's faces reflected back at me.

I hadn't been able to avoid them on the tarmac of the airport. Not when my driver had shouted my name across the goddamn empty space, alerting them to my presence.

I'd fought my way through the mindless exchange with

small talk, my hand firmly grasped within Dana's. Apparently, at some point, they had settled in Bali, had two more children, and only came back to the states when they had business to attend to or people to see.

And, of course, it was just my luck they had business in Boulder.

I didn't want to introduce Dana to them. I didn't want to fold her into that part of my life, not yet, not before I had the chance to explain it all to her. But when my mother asked her point-blank if she was my wife, we'd had no choice.

"No," I'd scoffed. I didn't elaborate, and looking back on it, I probably should have. I didn't want Dana to think that I was shutting that down as a possibility down the line.

"I'm his girlfriend," Dana had said, her mood far lighter than mine as she reached out her hand to shake both of theirs. "And this is Drew, my son."

My mother, always the one to put on a good show, had tried to say hello to him. I'd stepped away from her, tucking Drew in closer to my chest.

"We'll be in Boulder for the next few weeks," my father had said, his glasses halfway down his nose. He looked so much older. He'd aged less gracefully than Mom, though based on her looks, I suspected she'd probably had some work done. "We should meet up properly. It would be nice to chat and catch up."

I had to bite my fucking tongue.

I made my way down the stairs, pushing the memory as far out of my mind as I could, trying to replace it with the good ones from our vacation instead. In the downstairs living room, the massive floor-to-ceiling bay windows letting in the last of the sunlight, Bobby relaxed on the sofa, his button-up shirt clean and crisp. He had gotten a haircut—his hair was shorter, similar in length to mine.

"Are you ready?"

He pressed a button on the remote, powering down the television. "Yep. Just got to put on my shoes."

Tonight was as good a night as ever to take the BMW. Bobby and I settled into the car; Grayson was going to meet us there.

"You look stressed," Bobby said, for once seeming a little wary when he spoke instead of just word vomiting without thinking. "You okay?"

"I'm fine," I lied.

"Is it your parents?"

"Yeah, man, it's my fucking parents," I snapped, turning a little too sharply onto the main road that would take us into town and out of the mountains.

Bobby hesitated before he spoke again. "It's shitty of them," he said, his eyes locked on the side of my face as I tried to keep myself calm. "Showing up like this, not even bothering to reach out beforehand. I mean, what kind of fucking parents do that? They abandon their kid then show up unannounced years later, with two more kids they actually seem to care enough about to keep around."

"Why now?" I scoffed, my knuckles going white as I gripped the steering wheel.

"I don't know, man," Bobby sighed. "It's bullshit though. Fuck them. Clearly, they never cared about you and they certainly haven't started now."

"What the fuck is so much better about the two kids they've got now? What the fuck did *I* do?" I could feel the burning begin to ache at the base of my throat, the anger driving me mad. "Why wasn't I enough?"

I did my absolute best to hide the anger building in me from the moment we stepped foot into the gala.

The event tonight was for struggling kids in the surrounding areas. All of the local businessmen and women would be in attendance, pledging money toward the cause or raffling off something to the attendees. Pearson Beers was raffling off a home brewing kit and a personal tour from yours truly.

"So should I get the beers, or... ?" Bobby joked, his laughter cut short when Grayson shot him a glare. "God, sorry, didn't realize I couldn't joke about my own issues."

"It's not that," Grayson said.

"No, no, I get it," Bobby relented, holding his palms up as he stepped back. "Two glasses of water and a Pearson IPA, coming right up."

Grayson held up his empty glass in thanks as Bobby stalked off, his lips going tight the moment he was out of earshot. "I don't like it, Cole," Grayson said, whipping his head toward me so fast I worried he might get whiplash. "Look at him. Look at what he's wearing."

"Bobby?" I asked, leaning forward onto my palm as I watched Bobby disappear into the crowd over the table. "What do you mean?"

"His suit looks like yours. He got a haircut."

"All suits look the same, Gray," I chuckled. "He's cleaning himself up. He's doing better. I don't see the problem here."

"Just keep an eye on him," he huffed, sitting back in his

seat like an angry toddler. "Are you doing okay? With... you know..."

I sighed. "Do you want the truth or whatever will make you feel comfortable?"

"The truth."

"I'm shit but I'm getting through it. You don't need to worry."

He went silent, chewing on the inside of his cheek as he watched me. "I don't want to sound like a dick" he started, sitting forward again and leaving the angry toddler act behind, "but maybe you should hear them out. Meet up with them. They might have a lot more to say to you than you think."

My brows rose as I took in his words, the anger I'd been pushing down threatening to erupt. "You think I should hear them out?"

"I'm just saying that maybe—"

"You think it's worth it, giving a fucking moment of my time to them? You think *I* should hear *them* out when they are the biggest goddamn triggers for me when it comes to drowning myself in the one fucking thing I can't have?" I snapped, my hands balling into fists. My nails dug into my palms, the pain searing and raw. "They are fucking nothing to me. *Nothing.* They are shit on the floor. They are worthless, horrible humans who were perfectly happy to abandon their barely thirteen-year-old son but seem more than pleased to be raising two more. I don't want them in the same state as me. Hell, the same country."

Gray stared at me, his wide eyes and pursed lips only making it worse. "Cole—"

The booming voice of the announcer came over the loudspeaker, cutting him off. "The next prize comes from

Grayson Sparks, former NFL player and trainer of the UC Buffaloes!"

"Guess it's your time to shine, buddy," I said, the words biting and cold just as Bobby returned with our drinks.

Gray stood, hesitating for just a moment as he watched me, before heading to the stage.

"The fuck was that about?" Bobby asked, slotting in beside me and sliding my water across the fabric-draped table.

"Doesn't matter."

He watched me carefully, his finger tapping against the side of his glass. Maybe his hair did look a bit like mine but I had a fairly basic cut. It wasn't anything unusual. "You look like you need a drink," he said, the words hanging in the air, the hidden meaning known all too well to us both.

I dragged my tongue along the top row of my teeth, the burn in the back of my throat screaming.

"No," I said.

Chapter 24

Dana

I was running too much. I knew that. Shin splints had haunted me in the past, and I needed to calm it down, but with Cole being the way he was lately and the worry I couldn't help but feel, I needed the release.

He'd changed the moment we stepped off the plane in Boulder. Part of me knew that it had to do with his parents and whatever was lurking in the shadows there, but I also wondered if Costa Rica was a paradise we'd never get back. I didn't feel any different toward him now than I did before we left but did he? Was the vacation too much for him?

And worse than that, was there a chance he'd start drinking again with the added stress of being home? He was closing up already, speaking to me less, seeing me less. I didn't ever want him to feel as if he couldn't call me if something happened again, but I was beginning to worry that he might not.

Gasping for breath, I slowed my pace until I was walking, the trail along the manmade lake making my feet sore. I hated running on gravel, but I needed something different.

"Dana!"

Out of breath and hoarse, I glance up to see a cool-as-a-cucumber Robert jogging toward me. From this far away, I couldn't tell if his hair was pulled back or if he'd cut it, but he looked a bit different than he had before. Had he dyed his hair?

"Good to see you," he huffed, grinning from ear to ear. "You look a bit better than the last time we ran into each other."

I chuckled, the sound breathless and weak as I struggled to keep air in my lungs. "Yeah, thanks. I'm feeling better too."

He came to a stop in front of me, not a single drop of sweat on him. He'd definitely cut his hair, but I wasn't certain about the color. I couldn't remember the shade it had been the last time we'd met, and although it seemed lighter, almost the shade of Cole's, I wasn't positive. Something about him, from the hair to the way he stood, reminded me so much of the way Cole had been back in Costa Rica—all smiles and calm. But he didn't have that little, barely noticeable dimple Cole had when he grinned. "Haven't seen you for a while."

"I was... on vacation," I panted, wiping the slick sheen of sweat off my forehead. "Only been back a few days."

"Oh, nice! Where?"

"Costa Rica."

"Oh, no way! I go there once a year," he said, and as I slowly began to walk in the direction he'd come from to try to cool down, he walked backward with me. "I like Peninsula Papagayo the best."

"That's... an odd coincidence," I laughed. "That's where we were."

His mouth dropped open dramatically. "That's crazy."

"Yeah," I huffed.

"Maybe we could go some time," he said, and I stopped in my tracks.

"Excuse me?"

"To Papagayo," he clarified, as if that made it any fucking less weird.

"I... no, thank you." I took a step back, and he took one forward, setting alarm bells off in my head. I was winded, exhausted, but surely I could run back to my house if I needed to... right?

"Oh," Rob said, taking another step with me, and then another. My heart pounded in my chest and it wasn't from the run anymore. "I just thought, you know, you have a kid and all, but I've never seen anyone but you and your sister around your house. I thought maybe you were single."

"I'm not."

"You sure about that?"

I needed to get out of this. Get away from him. But I knew deep down there was a chance he was faster than me, probably stronger than me, and my brain was too goddamn exhausted to come up with a way out with words alone. All I could do was breathe, watch him watch me, watch him walk with me, panic rearing up inside.

"You know where I live?" I blurted out, his words catching up to me. *How the hell does he know Vee is my sister?*

"Yeah, doesn't everyone? The HOA has everyone's address on the boards," he said, shrugging as if it was fucking normal to keep one address in your head and pay attention to the goings on there.

"I-I need to get home," I stammered, nearly tripping over the loose gravel as I picked up my backward pace. "I need to feed my son."

Robert stopped, his arms crossing over his chest as he huffed out a sigh. "Alright, Dana. I'll see you around."

My calves screamed at me as I stretched them on the front porch. I'd run the entirety of the way home, checking over my shoulder every two seconds to make sure Robert wasn't following me. I needed to calm down before I went inside, needed to soothe my aching body and my shaking hands before I touched Drew.

Slowly, from the corner of my eye, I watched as a black Tesla approached, the windows tinted so dark I couldn't see inside. My heart thundered in my chest again, worrying that it was Robert but hoping that it was Cole.

My hope was shattered as the window rolled down.

"I'm sorry if I startled you," Rob shouted.

Oh, my god, I was going to call the fucking cops.

"Leave me alone, please," I snapped, shoving my hands into the pocket of my hoodie so he wouldn't see how badly I was shaking. If there was one thing I knew, that would only excite him more if he was trying to upset me.

He pressed on the brakes.

"I'm not interested," I shouted, the quiver in my voice giving me away.

He stared me down, his fingers tapping on the steering wheel. His shoulders shook, the ringing in my ears cutting off whatever he was doing but fuck, it looked like he was laughing. "You'll want me soon enough," he grinned.

The window rolled back up, and within seconds, he was speeding down the road away from my house.

I hadn't decided yet whether I wanted to tell Cole what had happened by the time he'd arrived to pick me up for our date. I didn't want to add stress and fuel to his already burning fire, but I didn't exactly know what to do about Robert, either. Was it worth calling the cops? He didn't actually do anything. He said things to me that made me uncomfortable, seemed to show up out of nowhere, admitted to watching my house, followed me home...

Yeah, I should probably tell the cops.

The doorbell rang and I kissed Drew on the top of his bald little head before handing him off to the nanny; Vee was with some friends for the night.

When I opened the door, the bags under Cole's eyes made my heart drop.

He immediately took me into his arms, his lips pressing against my temple. "Hey, baby," he mumbled, his fingers tightening around my waist.

He smelled of cologne and toothpaste, and the longer I looked up at him, the worse he looked. He was still handsome, still Cole, but god, he didn't look well. "Hi," I said softly, pushing the loose tendrils of hair out of his face. "Are you okay?"

He nodded. "Just haven't been sleeping well."

I hated that a part of me didn't believe him. I wanted to, desperately, but being what he was—an alcoholic—I couldn't help but wonder if he was struggling. If he was trying to fight his demons alone, the stress of his parents weighing him down and making it harder.

Or worse—he'd relapsed.

I knew the signs. I knew them inside and out from my mother. Seeing as there were only a couple of them present, I didn't want to consider it as a possibility. He'd called me and asked for my help the last time he'd almost slipped. I had to believe that he'd do that again. He trusted me.

He had to trust me.

Chapter 25

Cole

I put the car into park after pulling back into Dana's driveway. This was our third date this week, and yet, I still felt like it wasn't going right. There was something I wasn't doing right. We'd barely been physical, hardly more than a few kisses and stilted make-out sessions, and yet I'd been needing more without landing in the end zone.

"I'm sorry," I sighed, pushing against my eyes with the bottoms of my palms. "I know I've been a nightmare to be around."

Dana huffed a sigh as she twisted in her seat, her hand gently coming up to rest on my shoulder. My cock jumped at even that small gesture but my brain could not follow suit. "You have not. You're just going through a lot."

"I can't fucking sleep," I rasped. "I can't do shit. I've barely gotten anything done for the soft launch party next week. I'm falling behind at work." I took in a shaky breath, forcing myself to calm down. I was a constant lit fuse, always fucking seconds away from exploding. I wasn't used to being this vulnerable with her, at least not since that night outside Flagstaff Spirits, the night I came so close to relapsing.

Her hand gently coaxed my own away from my face, her fingers lacing in mine. "Stay the night," she whispered, and I couldn't quite tell if it was an offer or a request.

"I can't."

Her lips pressed together and she nodded in understanding. "Do you want to see Drew?"

"Please."

We stepped out of the car in unison. I checked the time, it was nearing Drew's usual down-and-out-for-the-night hour. I didn't have long to spend with him but I'd take what I could. I needed his peace.

Inside, the nanny held him on her lap on the couch, a bottle shoved between his gums. His eyes were already fluttering closed, but the moment he saw both of us, he perked right up.

Dana relieved the nanny and plucked him from her lap, getting a brief rundown of the evening's events while she was out. Dana thanked her and she was soon out the door, leaving just the three of us in peace.

Fuck, I wanted to stay.

I sat down next to her on the rickety couch, the burning in my throat subsiding just a hair, and pulled Drew into my lap. His wide green eyes looked up at me, the biggest smile crossing his face. He didn't care that I was a mess. He didn't care that I was barely holding myself together. He just liked looking at me, being held by me, cuddling with me. I wished that was enough for everyone else.

Between the cushion and the side of the couch, a little book stuck out. I pulled it from the trenches as Dana leaned against me, holding up Drew's bottle as if he still cared about it. He was far too transfixed with the stubble on my cheeks, though.

It was a copy of Winnie the Pooh.

I turned him in my lap, letting him lean back against my stomach as I opened up the book in front of all of us, Dana's watchful eyes focusing in on it. "You want to read to him?"

"Yeah," I breathed.

She took a moment, mulling it over, before she snuggled in closer and nodded against my shoulder.

The words blended together, a cacophony of harmonious phrases from my own rough voice and giggles from Drew. The more I read, the sleepier he got, his eyes closing then opening, only to close again, fighting it. Dana listened quietly, only perking up the handful of times that Drew coughed or wiggled slightly, the worry between her brows evident as only a mother's can be.

The longer I stared at the words, the more they started to blend into shapes I didn't quite recognize. It took me longer than it should have to read through a children's book, and although I played it off with feigned exhaustion, it worried me. It felt like I was falling apart at the seams; if I couldn't do something I'd been able to reliably do since childhood, what the fuck was wrong with me? Why couldn't I just handle shit the way everyone else did?

And why did it have to be Winnie the Pooh, of all things?

I knew these stories like the back of my hand. Knew them in my bones, could recite them from memory. That was my saving grace when the words blended together, when they became nothing more than garbled images chewed up and spat out by a heffalump.

By the time I gently shut the book with one hand, my other arm around Dana's shoulders, Drew had lulled himself into a snotty sleep against my stomach. I watched him longer than I needed to, taking in every breath, every little snore. I almost wished I could lie there with him all night or even forever if it meant feeling that peace and calm, just the rise and fall of his little chest with his hand clinging onto the rubber giraffe.

Gently, Dana pulled herself out from under my arm and out of my grasp, careful not to move either of us. "I'll get his pacifier before he swallows that poor giraffe whole."

She disappeared around the corner, leaving me alone with her sleeping child. I stuck the book back in its hiding spot and rested one hand below Drew's bent, stubby legs, keeping him in place.

"Who are you?"

I met the eyes of Vee when I heard the words. Dragging my attention from him, I realized I'd almost forgotten she was staying with Dana... when the hell had she come in?

I cleared my throat as gently as I could so I wouldn't wake Drew. "Cole," I said, my voice still a little craggy. "Cole Pearson. We met a few weeks ago."

Her mouth opened around the sound of a silent *ahh* as she leaned forward onto the island that divided the kitchen from the living room. "The infamous Cole. Didn't realize you were the same guy."

What the fuck did that mean? Did Dana have other guys coming around?

"You're the rich one, right?" she asked, one eye closing in a wink as she laughed a little too loud for my liking. I glanced down at Drew to make sure he was still asleep.

"If you want to boil me down to that, then sure."

She looked off in the direction of Dana's room as she unwrapped a tiny piece of chocolate. "How'd you two meet, then? You must be awfully fuckin' special if you're keeping her away from her kid this much."

I grimaced as Drew shifted, his little body leaning a little too far to one side, but I caught him before he could fall and wake himself. "I wouldn't say I'm keeping her away from him," I grumbled, tucking my arm a little tighter into him. "We met through some mutual friends early last year."

"Last year, huh?" she said, her voice muffled by the chocolate as her brows shot up. A chuckle seeped its way out, her head shaking. "Figures."

"What?" I asked. I was growing tired of her already. I could see why Dana complained about the company so often, but I also knew that Vee was her saving grace when it came to watching Drew. Sure, she had the nanny, but that wasn't something she could afford twenty-four-seven, and she'd refused when I'd offered her bonuses for it.

Vee's eyes drifted to the sleeping baby sprawled on my stomach before inching their way back up to my face. "You ever thought about how similar you look?"

I blinked.

Similar? I couldn't help but look down at Drew. The ringing in my ears grew louder, cacophonous almost, as I stared at the faint, thin dark blonde hairs that had started sprouting from his head.

"His pacifier was under my bed." Dana came around the corner, a pacifier in one hand and a blanket slung over her shoulder, but I could barely fucking hear her. He wasn't mine—the chance was so small I'd already written it off when I first found out about him. Besides, Dana wouldn't keep that from me. That is, if she even knew for sure that he was. There were too many differences, like the shape of his nose and his plump little lips.

I'd be a liar if I said I didn't wish it was true, though.

"When did you get home?"

"A few minutes ago," Vee shrugged. "Y'all were so snuggled up you didn't even see me. You'd be fucked if a burglar came in, Dana."

"Don't joke about that," Dana huffed. She slid in beside me and carefully plucked the giraffe from Drew's mouth, thankfully without waking him, before replacing it with the pacifier. He didn't even notice.

"I should head off," I breathed, keeping my voice low enough that Vee wouldn't hear.

Dana's eyes met mine briefly, a little flash of something flickering in them before she nodded softly. "Okay."

With precision and ease, she wrapped the little blanket around Drew, her fingers grazing my abdomen over the layers of fabric. She plucked him from me and he didn't even flinch.

He was down and out in his bassinet within seconds, snoring away. I didn't care that I had six-month-old snot on my shirt, didn't care that I'd read one of my favorite, but most triggering, stories to the kid. It fell to the wayside when I watched her with him.

All of it.

I almost didn't want to leave, but deep down, I knew it was better if I did. I needed to get a handle on myself—alone. If I could do that by myself, it would be ten times easier with her by my side.

She walked me out the door, her sister mumbling something about fantasy football as she stared at her phone. We walked in silence to my car, the unspoken words hanging in the air like a lit fucking firecracker about to explode. I wanted her to come with me. I wanted to ask her if there was any chance he was mine. I wanted to know if I was keeping her from him more than I should be.

I wanted to know if I still deserved her.

"I'm sorry about tonight," I sighed, the breath of air forming a little cloud in front of my face in the cooling night air. The doors of my BMW unlocked automatically as I leaned against the side of it. "All of it."

She shook her head. "There's nothing to apologize for." Her hands wrapped around each of her arms as she huddled in just a little for extra warmth. "I just wish you could stay."

Taking the warm skin of her face into my hands, I pressed my lips to hers softly, just enough to touch. "Me too."

―――

The entire drive home was one massive, horrible temptation.

Trying to concentrate on driving when liquor store after liquor store passed me by, when I knew that the two people I hated most were somewhere in town, when I couldn't stop the incessant thoughts that Vee had soured my head with. *He did look a little like me.* All of it was nearly impossible to shake. I could barely feel the tips of my fingers despite my heated steering wheel and just when I thought I'd have a moment of reprieve, my anxiety shot through the roof the moment the gates opened at the end of my driveway.

There was already a car there.

One I didn't recognize, one that from the looks of it was a high-end rental. A black Audi S7, decked out and capable of carrying four.

I almost turned around and drove back to Dana's.

Almost.

I should have.

My headlights illuminated the front of my garage as I turned with the driveway, a tall figure with his arms crossed coming into full focus.

I turned off the car.

I got out.

I slammed the door.

"Get the fuck off my property."

"Cole—"

"No," I snapped, the headlights cutting and giving me a moment of relief before the floodlights lit the cement. "You don't get to do this. You don't get to turn up out of the blue, venture onto *my* land, and insert yourself into *my* life."

"Son."

"I'm not your fucking son!" I took a step toward him, the ten feet between us feeling far too close, hoping he'd back away. He didn't. "You made that crystal clear the moment you sent me off to Aunt Kathy's."

"Do you have to do this?" my father asked. His graying hair swayed softly in the wind, loose and unkempt. The stubble on his cheeks was nearly the same level of gray, with little specks of black here and there, the color it used to be when I'd tugged on his beard as a kid.

"What?"

"Bring up the past like I don't remember it."

I blinked, almost lost for words. The chaste attitude, the callous way he spoke nearly sent me spiraling further than I already was. "Do you even want to be here?"

He didn't answer.

"Of course you don't," I scoffed. I hit the button in my pocket with a little too much anger, double-locking my car.

"What, did Mom bribe you with an extra bottle of scotch? 'Oh, honey, go make nice with Cole. He'd love a bit of closure, I'm sure.'"

"Don't act like I'm the one here with the problem," he said, and my blood fucking boiled.

"You think I didn't see that shit growing up?" I hissed. "You think I picked up a bottle on a whim? No, Conrad, I watched you. I learned from you. When things got hard, you pulled that Glenfiddich from the shelf. When I disappointed you for the millionth time that week, you poured yourself a glass."

His upper lip pulled back in disgust. "You could have made better choices."

"You could have been a fucking parent."

Silence hung in the air between, thick and accusatory. I tried to control my breathing, tried to calm myself down, but all I could think of was how much I needed a glass of anything and how much I wanted to wrap my fingers around my father's throat until his face turned blue.

"Leave," I hissed, my voice rough with bile and anger. "*Now.*"

It took twenty raspy breaths before he finally took a step toward his car.

Having enough faith that he'd leave and not look back, I raced up the front steps without a second thought. If I could just make it to the comfort of my bed without anything else, without another issue, I'd be fine. I could sleep it off and wake up a half-lit fuse in the morning as opposed to burnt embers and the sparking base of a bomb.

I slammed the door behind me and locked all three mechanisms before stepping through the grand foyer into the living room.

And into the arms of yet another problem.

Bobby sat back against the couch, an open bottle of vodka tucked between his legs and a glass of ice in his hand. Beside him, on the coffee table, was a second glass.

"Oh, fuck."

"Throw it out," I begged, my voice breaking. *Fuck, I sound pathetic.* "Please, Bobby, I can't deal with this right now."

He shook his head, the short hair looking so goddamn weird on him, but my eyes drew right back to the bottle. The quarter-empty bottle. "Not this time, man."

I couldn't move as he plucked the spare cup from the table and poured out two fingers' worth. His glass was already half full—this one wasn't for him.

"Come on."

The back of my throat burned. The backs of my eyes burned. This was too much for one day, for one person, for one barely recovering alcoholic. Temptation sizzled everywhere in my body. "Throw it out," I repeated, but the words felt like sand on my tongue. Pointless. Useless. A reflection of myself.

Bobby pushed the glass across the coffee table to the side closest to me. "Just this once."

Chapter 26

Dana

The stain of snot and drool on the breast of my robe was exactly why I was wearing it over my dress.

Drew coughed in my arms, his little mouth buried against my collarbone. The medicine his doctor had prescribed seemed to be doing nothing. "It's just a cold," Dr. Sinclair had said. "He probably picked it up in Costa Rica," adding that I just needed to give the medicine a bit more time.

I stared down at the two dozen red roses in my free hand. The stems crinkled in my grip, mangling themselves. Just the sight of them made me want to vomit regardless of who they were from. I'd never liked the smell of roses. But it was the little tassel hanging from the plastic that encased the tops of them that made it so much worse.

To Dana: I hope I didn't give you the wrong impression. Maybe I'll see you out running again soon. Love, Robert.

Fucking psycho.

If he genuinely thought I'd just gotten the wrong impression, he was out of his mind. The man was insane and incessant, and the more often these showed up—it was the fourth time this week—the more I wanted to tell Cole. But he had too much going on in his own life, too much for me to keep up with, and I didn't want to add to that. We just had to get through this evening, and then maybe, somehow, things could start to calm down.

Maybe then, I'd tell him.

Making a mental note to contact the police at some point, I shoved the bundle of roses into the garbage can and slammed the lid.

"Please don't tell me you're going to the launch wearing a robe."

Drew coughed again as I looked over my shoulder at my sister. She collapsed onto the sofa, her shorter, wavy locks flying up into her face from the movement. How she'd managed to stay here this long without moving on was beyond me. In any other scenario, she'd have gone on to the next location, following wherever her heart or phone led her, but it had been months now. I was thankful, at least.

"No," I chuckled, turning on the spot and pointing to the damp patch over my breast. "Just keeping my dress clean until I leave."

She looked me up and down. I must have looked ridiculous—my fluffy pink robe with a hint of my black dress poking out from underneath, shimmering black heels, my hair swooped up with little tendrils hanging around my face. I'd even managed to get a full-glam makeup look on while Drew was napping.

"Damn," Vee grinned, giving me a little whistle as I spun in a circle. I parted the bottom of the robe a bit to give her a better idea of what I was working with. "You look hot."

"Had a bit more time than usual," I chuckled. I shuffled

Drew on my hip, lifting him a bit higher and easing the weight. "He napped for ages."

"Probably just fighting off his cold." She shrugged and reached for the remote, flicking on the television. "When are you heading out?"

I pulled my phone from the pocket of my robe and checked the time—*shit*. "Cole's driver should be here any minute."

Carefully, I popped Drew into his swing and released the sash of my robe, shucking it from my shoulders. Before Vee could even take it in, a fit of coughs erupted from his tiny mouth, spittle and snot flying at high velocity right into the dangling fabric of the robe.

Almost using it as a shield, I kneeled down in front of Drew, my worry for him only growing. I hadn't heard him cough like that until that moment. It had all been dry and irritating, the only mucus in sight coming from his nose. But this cough was wet, deep, and angry. He sputtered out a little cry before another round of coughs hit him. "Hey, hey, you're okay," I cooed, wiping the little bits of snot hanging from the corners of his mouth.

"That's good," Vee remarked, and I swear I could have killed her.

"How is that good? He sounds worse."

"He's finally getting the phlegm out. It may sound bad, but honestly, it's probably an improvement. Poor guy's just coughing out the devil."

"You can't still think—" I cut myself off, breathing in deeply and trying to center myself. "Maybe I should stay home."

"Dana. He's fine," Vee sighed, pushing her body weight up so she could get a good look at both of us. "I'll keep a close eye on him. The thermometer's in the medicine drawer, right?"

I tightened my lips as I watched Drew. The fit ended and he calmed, his demeanor changing back to his usual, happy-go-lucky self as he reached out for his giraffe.

Things would be fine.

Vee was right.

"Yeah, it's in the drawer." I sighed and pushed myself back up to my feet at the same moment a honk came from outside.

Vee nodded toward the door. "Go. It's fine."

I hated this. Hated the conflicting feelings swirling in my gut, the need to be in two places at once to support the ones that needed me. "Promise you'll text me updates."

"Of course."

I took a deep breath and grabbed my purse from the countertop, quickly double-checking I wasn't taking anything Drew would need with me. "Alright."

Having Lottie and Hunter by my side was enough to keep me distracted from constantly worrying about Drew. I almost wished they'd brought Brody but a part of me wondered if I'd give him Drew's cold from the amount of doting I'd do on the poor kid.

The center of the brewery had been cleared of workers and their stations to make room for the soft launch party. Banners hung from the ceiling, decorated with the images that would be on our cans and bottles when the drinks landed on shelves in a few months. Shareholders and people much higher up than me littered the floor, all in suits or fancy dresses that likely cost much more than mine. The wait staff of the restaurant worked the floor with hors d'oeuvres, passing them out to whoever simply stretched out an arm.

Apart from me.

They seemed to have picked up on our relationship and weren't exactly happy for us.

"Who's that Cole's talking to?" Lottie asked, saddling up beside me as she sipped at a bottle of fruit-infused IPA. She hid her scowl fairly well, most wouldn't realize how much she hated the stuff.

"You don't have to drink that, you know," I laughed, following her line of sight until I spotted him.

His dirty blonde hair poked up from the crowd as he spoke animatedly with another man I didn't recognize. Even from where I was standing I could tell Cole looked a little better—no massive bags under his eyes, the color in his face had returned, and even the stubble that he'd neglected for weeks had been clean-shaven. The cut of his jaw was harsh again, and the way he spoke... it was like someone had breathed life back into him.

"I don't know who that is," I said, taking the bottle from Lottie when she tried to sip at it again. "Probably a shareholder."

Hunter's hand snaked its way around her waist as he presented her with a fresh IPA, no fruit this time, and she beamed back at him. "What'd I miss?"

"Just trying to figure out who that guy is," Lottie said, keeping her voice low as she pointed in Cole's direction.

"That would be our good friend, Cole," Hunter grinned. "Drunk already, sweetheart?"

Lottie's expression soured. "You're so annoying."

His lips pressed against the side of her head before he took a swig of the beer. A part of me was almost jealous— there wouldn't be a time when Cole and I could be like that: easy, free, drinking if we wanted, making jokes about it. It seemed like such a small thing in the grand scheme of things, but it felt almost as if the normalcy of it was calling out to me, shouting at me for the first time in weeks, that I was going down the wrong path with him.

"That's Dale Hawthorne," Hunter finally said. "He's been our liaison with local businesses for the agriculture stuff."

"I feel like I should know that" Lottie mumbled.

"You just stick to breeding, horse girl," Hunter laughed, resting his chin on top of his simmering wife's head.

"You're Dana, right?"

I spun on a dime, instinctively plastering on my customer service smile and came face to face with the man who'd been here the night Cole had turned up unannounced three months ago.

Tall, built, and just an inch shorter than Cole, I wondered why I couldn't have fallen for this one instead until a pretty little girl about the age of four with blonde braids poked out from behind him, a little stuffed rabbit clutched in her fingers.

"Uh, yeah," I said, giving the girl a small wave before she tucked herself further in behind him. "You're Cole's friend."

"Grayson," the man grinned, all dimples and hard lines as his cheeks shifted. I'd heard about Grayson, he's Cole's best friend. He'd picked him up from the airport when Cole came back from rehab. Did something in... sports? "It's nice to meet you. I've heard a lot about you."

He stuck his hand out to me as an offering. I took it gently, his palms making mine look as small as a doll's. "All good things, I hope?"

"You really think Cole would have a bad thing to say about you?" he laughed. Grayson placed a hand on his daughter and pulled her out from behind him. "This is Penny, my daughter."

She held up her little rabbit toward me.

"And Thomas, her rabbit."

"Nice to meet you, Penny and Thomas," I said, briefly shaking hands with the stuffed animal.

"You've not seen Bobby around, have you?" he asked, his brows creasing as he scanned the room.

Who the fuck is Bobby? I followed his gaze, watching the crowd for a moment. I wanted to ask, wanted to know who he was talking about, but if Cole hadn't told me himself maybe there was a reason. "I haven't really been paying much attention," I said instead.

"Let me know if you see him." He picked Penny up, her legs wrapping around his abdomen as she snuggled into the side of his suit-covered chest. "Cole doesn't like it, but I just can't stand the guy. And this is the last place he should be."

Wait, is Bobby the roommate?

"Why?" I asked, pressing just a little. I wanted to know more. If there was an issue with the person Cole was spending the majority of his time with, surely I should be privy to that.

"He's just... not right. Fucking leech, if you ask me," Gray said, and within a second his daughter erupted into a fit of giggles. "Don't repeat that, Pens."

"And he's living with Cole?"

"Yeah, he's—"

Grayson stopped speaking the same moment a hand

came to gently rest against my waist, and before I could even turn, Grayson's mouth warped into a smile.

"There you are."

That same hand pulled me roughly back, nearly knocking the wind out of me as my back collided with a rock-hard chest. I knew it was Cole, that much was obvious, but his cologne was different tonight, muskier. Had it not been for his voice, I almost would have panicked.

I turned, looking up at him and taking him in. He looked so fucking good, so healthy, so *Cole*. "Hey," I grinned, and he gave me a little smirk in return, his green eyes shining.

"I need to talk to you, if you don't mind," he said, the crease by his lip deepening and springing his dimple to life. "Alone."

Lottie snorted as she sipped at her IPA. "Just say you want to fuck her. We're all adults here."

My cheeks heated as he pulled me back again. "Okay." He leaned down, his lips puffing warm breath against my ear, and every part of me lit like a fucking fuse. "I'd like to fuck you in my office, if you don't mind."

Jesus fucking Christ, he is feeling better.

I didn't get a chance to answer before he turned us around and began walking me in the direction of the brewery's central elevator. "Shouldn't you stay down here? You know, lead the group and all that?" I asked, my throat going dry as he pressed the up arrow.

His cheeky grin turned on me, but the shimmer in his eyes had died. Instead, they were darker, half-lidded, and made me feel like a piece of meat.

I didn't necessarily hate that.

"They'll be fine," he said as the elevator dinged.

I didn't even have a moment to ask him how he was doing before his hands were on me, fisting the fabric of my lacy dress to lift it up to my hips. I gasped as he pressed me against the wall of windows in his office, his mouth at the base of my neck, his teeth and tongue lashing against my skin.

"Fuck," I breathed. My face heated as I watched the people mill about on the street below us, never quite looking up enough to see what was happening on the other side of the glass, grateful that it was tinted, nonetheless. "Cole—"

Gripping the back of my panties in his palm, he gave one swift tug, tearing them at the seams.

"I liked those," I mumbled, the breath of my words fogging the window in front of my face.

The rest of the cotton fell away as he tugged at the remaining threads, and before I could comment again, his fingers were reaching around the front of my hips, sliding down the bare skin between them until they met their mark.

Pleasure filled my veins in an instant.

"I was getting so fucking impatient waiting for you to arrive," he rasped, his voice gruff and deep as he dug the fingers of his free hand into my hips and pulled them further back toward him. His front pressed into me, the hardness of his cock against his slacks impossible to ignore. Already, my head began to swim. "You didn't even come over to say hello."

"You looked busy," I whined. The neediness was already growing with every swirl of his fingers over my clit. I hadn't seen him in almost a week, and although I'd had incessant thoughts of him fucking me in every way a girl could imagine, a part of me had wanted to actually talk to him, too.

His movements were preventing me from formulating any rational thought I may have had.

The sound of his belt buckle unclasping nearly had me moaning in anticipation. I pushed my bare ass back against him, rubbing against the hardness in his pants.

He pushed forward, shoving me into the glass of the window a little too hard, as his hands grasped for my arms and pulled them harshly behind my waist. "You want me to go back down there with your pussy juice staining my slacks?" he seethed. His belt slipped from the loops of his pants, and before I could say a word, the soft leather was wrapping around my forearms.

"Cole," I hissed, but the ache from my arms melted away the more he touched me, the more his fingers worked, sliding further down, teasing my entrance while he unbuttoned himself.

"I need to be inside of you." The way he spoke, the sound of his voice, it was as if something else was driving him, something more desperate.

He didn't give me a single second before sliding every inch of himself inside of me, filling me so entirely that I felt like I couldn't breathe. He grasped the leather of his belt, his fingers grazing my skin, and pulled me further up as he pushed us forward, my hips nearly touching the glass. He moved, burying himself in me as if his life depended on it, his free hand keeping up with my body and dragging me closer to release with every pass over my clit.

"So fucking beautiful," he said, the words melding together as I looked over my shoulder at him. He pressed a kiss to my temple and I lifted my chin, hoping for the same against my lips as a moan slipped past them, but he turned his head toward the window instead. "Show them how pretty you look with my cock inside of you."

I could feel the makeup on my face slipping off and staining the glass with each thrust. I pulled at my arms, meeting resistance from the leather, but with the brief help of his hand I was able to slide one out with ease, allowing me leverage to separate myself from the window and turn my body just a hair.

I tried to kiss him again as my release nearly peaked, forcing my legs to buckle, but his touch stopped just a second before I could tip over that edge. He moved, slipping from me with ease, his rigid cock dripping with my wetness.

"On the desk," he growled, grabbing me with a fistful of my dress and whipping me around. I blinked, trying to keep up, trying to make sense of his words but feeling lost in the haze of the abandoned orgasm.

"What?"

"On the desk," he repeated, the words like venom as he pushed me forward onto the wood.

The moan that shuttered through me as he sank himself into me once again shook me to the core. "Oh my god," I breathed. We hadn't fucked like this in over a year—the roughness, the callousness of it—spinning my thoughts in every goddamn direction. I didn't dislike it, and I didn't want it to end, I just wasn't expecting it when he'd dragged me up to his office. "Please, please, I was so close before."

"What's the matter? My baby doesn't want to be edged?" he mocked, beginning his onslaught once again as a hand snaked up the back of my dress. "Maybe I just shouldn't touch your clit again at all tonight. Maybe I should just leave you aching and desperate and dripping my fucking cum."

Oh, *god*, why did I want that?

"No, no, please, Cole," I rambled, searching behind me with my one free arm for his hand and grabbing it. "Please, fuck—"

A hand fisted the back of my updo and pulled at the same moment the other found my clit. I hissed in air through my teeth, the pleasure canceling out the pain, every nerve firing at once. "You beg so sweetly."

Rapidly, I shot toward my release, teetering on the edge in record time. His movements grew rougher, angrier, as if he was chasing something he couldn't quite catch up to. My muscles seized, the ecstasy of it reaching newfound heights, every sound pouring from my mouth nothing more than nonsense and babble.

"Come for me, baby," he demanded, his pace quickening with every thrust. "Come around my fucking cock right now or you're not coming at all."

My breasts ached as they slammed against the wood before everything in me broke. My orgasm tore through my body, blinding me, forcing a high-pitched sound from my throat before he covered my mouth. I shuddered, sensitive but riding each wave of it as he gave his last few thrusts, his fingers still moving against my clit and making me spiral. I couldn't think straight. Couldn't breathe. Couldn't care less about anything other than riding it out.

"Fucking hell," he hissed, his grin widening as he lost all control inside of me.

He groaned as his hips sputtered, as his fingers released my clit, as he found his release so intensely I could feel it dripping down the side of my leg.

With both hands on the desk on either side of me, he gasped for air, his cock twitching inside me but not retreating. "You okay?" he asked, his voice barely more than a breath.

"Yeah," I managed. I shimmied the leather off my forearm and sat there, feeling every muscle tightening around him, every beat of my heart. "That was... different."

He slid out of me in an instant.

Once I'd caught my breath, I pushed myself up from the desk, body aching from his desperation, and let my dress fall back down over me. His face had turned darker, a bit of red tinting his cheeks as he buttoned his slacks back up and began snaking his belt through each loop.

He was right. I had stained his slacks a little.

"Cole?" I said, but he didn't look at me. "I'm not—I'm not upset about that. You would have known if I didn't want it."

"I know that" he replied, but he didn't sound sure. He fumbled with the buckle of his belt, missing the hole, and as I wrapped my hands around his to help him, he batted them off. "I'm fine."

"You don't seem fine." I took his face in my hands and forced him to look at me in the dim light of the office. His eyes weren't dark from desire anymore, there was something else. And the bags beneath them were back. I gently reached up and touched his face, feeling the tell-tale sign of concealer. "What's wrong?"

"Nothing, baby," he said, the words coming too easily as he pressed a kiss to my forehead. "I just haven't seen you for a little bit. I'm fine now that you're here."

There was an emptiness to him, to his words, that I couldn't shake. He was lying. I could feel it in every bone in my body. I didn't know what to do as I held his face in my hands, his fingers still struggling to lay his belt buckle flat, his cum still dripping down my thigh. It didn't feel right. Something was off.

It felt like last year.

My heart hammered in my chest. "Cole," I breathed. "Have you—"

"No."

How did he know what I was going to say? "You didn't let me finish my sentence."

"I didn't need to," he grumbled, his eyes darting from mine as he pulled his face from my hands.

Chapter 27

Cole

I wanted to fucking cry.
    The look in her eyes, the way she'd stared at me with so much worry and fear behind them.
And I'd lied to her.

Lied to her so easily, just like I lied to everyone else, just like I lied to myself.

I should tell her. I knew that. I knew it as surely as I knew my last name, knew it like I knew I was an alcoholic—a no longer recovering one. I needed to tell her, I needed to apologize, beg her to forgive me for caving. I needed to tell her that I need help, I need to go to a meeting or go back to rehab or whatever the fuck the next step was.

But I couldn't. The words wouldn't come.

I knew she'd drop it because she cared. She'd let it go on the possibility I was telling the truth and how pressuring me could be a trigger, and that's what I counted on.

But that look in her eyes haunted me.

"Let's get you cleaned up," I sighed, opening a drawer of my desk and whipping out a handful of unused napkins. I separated them into two piles with my shaking hands, one for between her legs since I'd obliterated her underwear, and the other for the smeared makeup.

She leaned back against the edge of the desk, her eyes focused far too intently on me as I dabbed a napkin against my tongue for moisture. I hoped she couldn't smell it as I swiped under her eyes gently, picking up the little crumbles of mascara that had broken free from her lashes and smeared against her cheek. She still looked beautiful, fucking heavenly even, but I'd taken her too hard.

I probably shouldn't have without speaking to her about it first.

But time blipped and I lost it, and before I knew it, my belt was around her forearms and her face was pressed into the glass. I couldn't rewind and fix that without answers.

"I'm sorry," I breathed, and her eyes narrowed just a hair. "I shouldn't have fucked you like that without talking to you first."

She shook her head. "It's fine. Honestly. I like it when you're rough with me," she chuckled, the beauty and magic of her laughter not quite hitting the way it used to. "Just, maybe next time, let's not do it when we have an event we're supposed to be at going on downstairs."

I huffed out a laugh and nodded.

I didn't even have a moment to walk her back to Lottie, Hunter, Grayson, and Penny before I was grabbed by Damien Horsted.

"Cole! Been looking everywhere for you," he said, his

overgrown graying mustache damp from where it rested on his mouth.

I clutched Dana's hand, ready to pull her into the conversation so I didn't have to go it alone, but she gave me a small smile before releasing it and shooting off toward our friends. *Dammit.*

"Damien," I said, forcing a grin as I shook his hand. The bald patch on the top of his head had gotten wider since the last time I saw him, and I made a mental note not to mention that if I had any chance of securing him as an investor in the new product line. "Apologies, we had a work issue I needed to address so I stepped out for a moment."

One fluffy brow rose as he glanced at the back of Dana's form blending into the crowd. "A work issue?"

"Something like that."

The man, probably in his fifties, if not sixties, laughed as he turned back to me. "No problem, son. I know how it is. Events like these always bring out the seediest women, always wanting their own investment," he chuckled.

I bit my tongue so hard I tasted iron.

"I've heard whispers through the grapevine that you're thinking of adding a zero percent," he added.

I nodded. "One for each flavor of the new range, as well as one zero IPA and zero light," I replied. "If we're going to do it, I'd rather go big, then narrow down if the demand for certain ones aren't high enough."

His grin widened but I couldn't help but look past him, over his shoulder, at Dana laughing with a beer in her hand as she stood with our friends. I wanted to be over there, a beer in my own hand, that not being the worst thing in the world for me. I just wanted to relax and enjoy myself with her. Wanted fucking everything with her. *You've ruined it already, fuckwit.*

"If you can make that happen, I'll gladly invest," Damien said, his words barely reaching my ears. "Only wish you had some of them on offer tonight so I could try them."

"We're still perfecting them so that they taste like the real thing," I explained, the words clocking that he offered an investment. "But thank you. I'm glad you'd like to play a part in this."

He offered his hand to me and I took it, giving it a solid shake before something unexpected caught my eye.

No.

No, no, no. Not tonight. Not here. Not in the one goddamn place I had left that they hadn't sullied, not in the place I'd built on my own.

Dana's eyes met mine in a flash of worry, and before I knew it I was abandoning Damien and moving toward her, needing her, aching for her or booze or *something*, I didn't know what. She was moving toward me too, her eyes glancing back at the four of them as they slotted themselves into the crowd as if they belonged.

"I can get them to leave," she offered, her gaze caught between whatever look had plastered itself to my face and my parents in the distance behind her. "I can ask Ben to get security—"

"No," I said, the word feeling imprecise in my mouth. "Thank you, but no."

Her eyes went wide. "No?"

"It would only cause a scene." Even with her in front of me, that unmistakable ache flared again in the base of my throat. *I need a drink. I need a drink. I need a fucking drink.* But I couldn't, at least not with her here, not with the inability to cover it with toothpaste and a mint. "Maybe I should go."

"Cole, it's *your* event. Not theirs."

I watched them over the top of her head, watched as my mother and father worked the room as if this success was theirs while the two teenagers they kept in tow hung out on the sidelines. I watched as they took hors d'oeuvres from a waiter, watched as they took a free drink from the bar.

Dana squeezed my hand, and then my forearm, my bicep. I glanced down at her, watching her lips move but hearing nothing but ringing. It grew louder, blocking out anything else, minimizing the growing concern on Dana's face as Hunter and Lottie stepped up behind her.

I blinked, and once again, time blipped.

My feet were moving, a hand around my wrist pulling me back, a sea of people dividing as I beelined for my father.

I blinked, and he was backed against a wall, Dana's voice seeping through. "Get them out," she pleaded with someone.

But I didn't care.

They'd left me. Crying, barely thirteen, with a stashed bottle of top-shelf scotch in my backpack and a suitcase full of clothes at the foot of my aunt's driveway. The summer sun beating down on me from above, the mountains in the distance, a look of irritation on their faces.

"Don't bother thinking you can come back," Dad had said.

Mom looked bored as she'd adjusted her sunglasses and checked her lipstick in the mirror of the sun visor.

I blinked, and my hand was around my father's throat, pinning him to the wall.

"Conrad!" my mother shouted.

"Stop, stop, stop!"

A hand about the size of mine gripped onto my forearm, pulling me off of him, dragging me back. I didn't fight it. The adrenaline raced in me but I didn't have the will to do anything with it, to drag myself back to him and beat his face in until my knuckles were bloodied and he was mush, until I was being escorted away in a police car and charged with fucking murder.

I wanted to.

But I didn't.

"Cole," Hunter said, his face in front of me, his hands on my shoulders. "Do you understand what just happened?"

Behind him, security was escorting out my mother and father and the two little shits they'd brought with them. My father had said something about them, just before my hands wrapped around his throat.

"Dana," I rasped. The high was slowly coming down, reality settling back in. "Where's Dana?"

"I'm here."

A hand slid into mine, her fingers so fucking small between my own. I turned to her, taking in the hint of fear and trepidation in her face, the way her brows rose and her lower lip quivered. *Fuck.*

"I'm sorry," I breathed, squeezing her hand as I looked between her and Hunter, and behind them, Lottie and Gray, Penny in his arms and burying her face in his neck. He was the furthest away from me.

That hurt.

"I don't know what happened," I said, sucking in a shaky breath. "I don't... fuck, man, how badly did I mess up?"

Hunter shook his head as he slowly released my shoulders, his tie and shirt askew. "I stepped in before it got too bad. I don't think anyone heard much other than a few choice words."

"I'll get you some water," Dana offered, and although it shouldn't have, although it was just her way of trying to help, it stung.

"I need to go."

"What?" Dana said, squeezing my hand tighter, but I dropped it.

"I have to go. I'm sorry. I can't, I can't be here."

Chapter 28

Dana

"**Ben!**"

I rushed down the hallway, slipping past a woman carrying a stack of papers as she gave me a look that said, "You don't belong up here." Even though I looked the part of a tour guide, even though I technically only had clearance to be up here if I was going from point A to point B, I didn't give a shit.

Cole had been gone for four fucking days. No texts, no calls, nothing. He'd taken off so quickly at the launch that none of us could keep up with him, and by the time Grayson and I piled into a car, leaving Penny with Hunter and Lottie, we didn't even know which direction to head. We'd checked every liquor store in Boulder, checked his house, checked the apartment he'd left abandoned last year.

Gray had to calm me down when I saw the sheer amount of empty bottles scattered across the floor of it.

"He hasn't been here since before rehab," he'd said. "He gave me the only set of keys."

But something in the pit of my stomach just *knew*.

"Dana?" Ben asked in confusion, his brow raising as I

finally caught up to him. "You're not supposed to be up here."

"Have you seen Cole?" I asked, catching my breath as I clung to the loose sleeve of his ill-fitting suit jacket for support. "He's not in his office. I've checked every damn day this week—"

"He's not in." Both brows rose as he took a step back, taking away my support. "He sent me an email a few days ago saying he was taking some time off and left me to deal with all this launch shit."

Time off? "What?"

"He didn't tell you?"

"No, he didn't fucking tell me," I huffed, bearing my weight with both hands on my knees.

"But I thought you guys were like..."

"Together? Me too."

"I was going to say hooking up but I guess that's kinda the same thing." He tilted his head to the side as he watched me, his ponytail of wiry brown hair swooping along with the movement. "You should go back downstairs. And get a new vest. You've got a tear at the shoulder."

God, I was going to kill them both.

Defeated, angry, and hurt, I took the elevator back down before my next tour of the day. I'd barely had any time to spare in between them now—with the word getting out about the new flavors and us promoting testers on the tours—slots had filled up in record time. But my feelings were changing from worry to just being plain upset.

I nearly lost my mind trying to fish out the vibrating phone in my pocket.

The screen didn't show me the name I wanted it to, though. Instead, it said Grayson, and although it wasn't Cole, it was close enough.

"Please tell me you found him," I said quietly, squeezing past another tour guide before slipping into the vest room.

"Nothing yet," he sighed. "I did manage to get in contact with his parents, though. Hoped maybe they'd have some information but they didn't."

My eyes nearly bulged from my skull as I leaned against the wall, checking my watch to make sure I wasn't late. "You talked to them? What did they say?"

I could hear the sound of a crash in the background, followed by a few loud giggles from his daughter and a frustrated grunt from Gray. "Penny... no, never mind, sweetheart. It's fine," he said, his attention elsewhere. I had five minutes. I needed him to hurry this up. "Nothing that I didn't already know. They're disgusting people, if you ask me. Couldn't have cared less that their son was missing."

"What do you mean by 'nothing you didn't already know?'"

"Just that they said he was probably off at a bar somewhere. Which, if they'd said that nine months ago, I wouldn't have batted an eye. Not that I don't care, it just wouldn't surprise me."

The taste of iron burst into my mouth. Must have bit through my lip. "Have you checked them?"

"What?"

"The bars, Gray," I breathed. "His usual hang outs. Any others."

"I have. Just in case," he said. "Came up empty."

I pulled a fresh vest from the cupboard, inspecting it to keep my hands busy so I wouldn't go insane. "Do you think he's drinking again?"

He hesitated before he spoke and my stomach fucking

dropped. "No, Dana, I don't. I know what he's like when he's drinking, and this isn't it."

I clutched the vest in my hand, crumpling the fabric. "I just don't understand." In truth, it felt more like he was covering for his friend, not wanting to worry me.

"This shit with his parents, it runs deep. I'm shocked it took him this long to go off the grid, to be honest," he sighed. "Penny, please stop saying shit."

I let him wrangle his daughter as I glanced at my watch again. Three minutes.

"I don't know how much you know about it," he continued, "but they practically abandoned him, leaving him with his aunt when he was thirteen. Dropped him off and never looked back." My chest tightened. I knew he had issues with them, knew they were a painful thing for him to talk about, but I didn't know that. "Couldn't be bothered to actually parent him, wanted to spend their forties exploring the world. They didn't visit, call, or even write. They just pretended he didn't exist."

"God," I breathed. I didn't know what to say, or think, or feel. All I wanted to do was find him and hug him, tell him he didn't have to deal with this alone, and then go and beat his parents' faces in for him.

No wonder he'd wrapped his hand around his father's throat.

"He's got a lot going on, Dana. With work and now this, he's cracking under the stress."

"Are there any signs exclusive to him when he's drinking?" I asked as the clock ticked down to one minute. "So I know what to watch for."

He took a deep breath, silence hanging heavy before he spoke again. *Forty seconds.* "Aggression. Quick temper. Irritable. You'll be able to smell the booze on him, he's not good at hiding that. For the most part, he looks and acts sober, unless he's really wasted. Then he's just unhinged."

"And that's not what he is right now?"

"This is different, Dana."

"How?"

"He's—" his voice cut off for a second, and then he was swearing under his breath. "Shit. I've got to go. Cole's calling."

"He's calling you?" I snapped, the vest falling from my open palm. My breath caught in my throat. *Why isn't he calling me?*

"I'll let you know what he says. But I have to take this. Talk later."

———

I'd barely been able to contain my frustration through every stupid fucking tour of the day.

I slid into the driver's seat of my Camry, exhausted and angry. Between every tour, I'd tried to call Cole. No answer. Tried Grayson. No answer.

My phone was nearly dead from the amount of calls I'd made.

I turned the key in the ignition as I searched through my purse for my charger but came up empty. *Shit. Must have left it in the diaper bag.*

It was fine. I'd be home in twenty minutes and could resume angry calling there.

Mia Mara

Twenty minutes turned into forty. Then fifty. Then an hour.

Traffic was backed up as far as I could see down the main road that cut through the center of Boulder. My radio didn't work and my phone was long dead. I had nothing but my stupid, relentless thoughts to keep me entertained.

And boy, did they.

I couldn't stop wondering why Cole wasn't talking to me. Couldn't stop thinking the worst, wondering if he was knee-deep in a bender he couldn't get out of and didn't want my help. Had he talked to Grayson before today? Was Grayson keeping shit from me? Or was he being honest and that's why he wasn't picking up my calls anymore, because he was trying to get Cole back?

I leaned forward, resting my head on the steering wheel.

He had to have relapsed. I didn't care what Gray said. The signs were there. Aggression: he'd nearly strangled his father, though I guess I would have done the same if it were me so I could cancel that one out. The smell: I hadn't gotten the chance to smell his breath when he fucked me. He'd swerved every attempt I'd made to kiss him. The running away: Mom had done that numerous times when things got bad.

He had a lot of reasons to relapse right now.

My thoughts turned to Drew, to how I'd seen how happy both he and Cole were back in Costa Rica when we were able to play family. I should have told him then. Should have done a lot of things differently but that was the main thing I wished I could change. Part of me wanted to just call Cole right now and tell him, even if it had to be in a voicemail. I could use it as bait to get him to speak to me again, but my phone was dead and I had no way of knowing whether or not he was checking voicemails.

Was it even worth telling him anymore?

If he'd relapsed, could I even have him around Drew?

My brain hurt thinking about it all.

An hour turned into nearly two by the time I pulled into the neighborhood, the backs of my eyes burning and my hands shaking from too much time alone with my thoughts. I could have walked home in half the time.

Red and blue lights lit up my street from the main road. Maybe someone had run over Robert. One could hope.

But as I got closer to home they grew brighter, and louder, and angrier—

No.

No, no, no.

They were at my fucking house.

I slammed the brakes and sprung from the car, running past the ambulance and the two Boulder Police Department cars out front. Adrenaline and fear carried me, all of my exhaustion gone, and by the time I made it to my front lawn, two EMTs were wheeling out a stretcher through my front door.

Drew lay still in the center of it.

I didn't hear the scream that ripped from my throat, didn't feel the grass hit my knees, but my sister was on me in seconds.

"He's okay," she said, but it didn't quite reach me.

"Oh my god, oh my god," I breathed, the words falling from my mouth over and over as if I were a churchgoer desperate to redeem myself. But this wasn't church. This was my front yard and my fucking son was being put into an ambulance.

"I tried to call you, several times," Vee said as she wiped her tears. "He, you know, he spiked a fever and I couldn't wake him up, and it kept going up, and you weren't home, and I didn't know what else to do."

"Ma'am, are you the mother?"

I glanced up, meeting the eyes of a middle-aged woman in a police uniform with a younger first responder behind her. "Yes."

"We're checking your son's vitals and then heading straight to Foothills ED. You can join us in the ambulance."

What is happening?

"Ma'am?"

"Just fucking give me a moment to process," I snapped. My hands shook violently as Vee helped me from the ground. "My bag," I said to her, glancing back at the car.

"I'll get it." She took my keys from where they lay in the grass and high-tailed it to where I'd left the car in the center of the road.

I should have taken him back to the doctor. I should have gotten a second opinion. I should have. I should have. I should have.

Two more EMTs came out from my house, and behind them, two figures dressed in plain clothes. I barely gave them a passing glance as I made my way toward the ambulance, all cylinders fucking firing, all thoughts blurring and mingling, turning into my worst nightmare.

"Dana."

I turned and immediately wished I hadn't.

The two figures in plain clothes were my fucking parents, walking out of *my* house, with *my* son's giraffe in my mother's grip.

I was going to kill Vee.

Chapter 29

Cole

Colchester Ski Resort was dull in the late autumn.

There wasn't enough snow to keep my skis in check, the lobby was empty, and the bar was a drag. But it was quiet and remote, ideally the last place someone would come looking for me, so it was enough to keep me glued down.

I slung back the last of my glass of top-shelf cognac before passing it across the bar. Gray would be here soon, and if I had any chance of hiding it from him, I needed to finish it now.

Up in my room I scrubbed the shit out of my teeth, brushing every possible surface in my mouth to get the scent off. I dabbed on a lighter cologne, one that wouldn't necessarily point a big fucking red arrow at myself that said "I've been drinking," and splashed a bit of water on my face. I didn't have the energy to hide the bags under my eyes today, didn't care to shave. But I did what I could.

A knock sounded on my door. Let the show begin.

"Hey, Gray," I said, taking a deep breath to signal that I knew that running from my problems was absurd and pointless. I didn't want him to think I wasn't self-aware. I could play this the way I needed—I'm stressed, overworked, and overwhelmed. I needed time alone.

To drink.

God, I hated myself.

"What the fuck are you doing out here?" he pressed, pushing the door open before I had the chance to even let him in. I hadn't considered anger from him. "You've got everyone worried sick and you're out here at a ski resort that barely has any snow? Do you think this is funny?"

"Obviously, I don't think it's funny, Grayson," I hissed, closing the door behind him. He stepped across the room, a subtle sniff as he passed by. "I'm stressed to high-hell and need some time alone to think. To breathe. Especially after what happened at the launch."

"Is that all?" he asked, one eyebrow raising as he turned to me. His mop of black hair was unkempt, pressed down on one side like he'd been sleeping. "You think I don't know you, Cole? You think after everything we've gone through together, all of your highs and lows, that I don't see right through you?"

Well, shit.

The burn returned at the base of my throat. Ever since I'd quelled it after months of sobriety, it seemed to come back with a vengeance. It wanted more. It wanted it often. Every little aggravation made it spike.

"Just say it," Gray said, his voice dropping as he glanced toward the other side of the bed. *Fuck, did I remember to clean it up? Yes. I did.*

"I'm not drinking," I barked. "In fact, I'm trying *not* to—"

"Cole. Please. I really don't want to play the game you made me play nine months ago."

"I'm not drinking," I said again, each word slower and full of bullshit.

"Cole."

"I'm not. I'm, I'm not." *Fuck.* The words were already failing. I hadn't had that much earlier, had I? A few glasses at most. But I was a goddamn lightweight now, and he was coming closer, the drawer was opening, the empty bottles clanging inside.

"You're not, huh?" Gray said, looking from me to the drawer filled with three glass bottles.

"I'm not," I rasped, but the words broke.

"You are."

I'm not. They're not mine. They were here when I checked in. They belong to a friend. They aren't mine, they aren't, they aren't.

"Cole," Gray sighed, shoving the drawer closed before sinking onto the foot of the bed. "How long?"

"I'm not," I said again, but the words were barely a whisper. *You've thrown it all away. Nine months of sobriety, your fancy new chip, all gone for nothing.* It burned. "Fuck."

"How long, man?"

I tasted the tear on my lip before I even noticed my eyes were leaking. "Two weeks."

"Why didn't you call?" Gray asked, his brown eyes boring a hole in me that only made me feel smaller. "I would have done whatever I could—"

"You had Penny that night." I leaned against the door of my too-small room, feeling like a spotlight was being shined directly at me, like I was airing my failures to the world. "Please, don't tell Dana. I'll stop. I did it before, I can do it again. Just don't tell her."

His lips pursed together as his head tilted, a look of stubborn disappointment painting his face. "You have to tell her."

"I will, I promise. I just need to get a handle on myself before I see her. I can't fuck up again with her. I was too rough with her at the launch, too angry, too needy. I don't want to do that to her ever again." Words just kept falling from my mouth, whether they made sense or repeated themselves or not. All I could think about was her, and the look of dismay she'd no doubt give me the moment she knew.

"If you're going to go through this again, you need to be open with the people that care about you," Gray said, a hint of despondency in his voice. "You can't shut everyone out and disappear for six months again. You need all the support you can get."

"I know."

"You've got to do it right this time."

"I know."

"So you have to tell her."

"She'll hate me," I said, my voice cracking.

"She has enough going on right now that I don't think she'll cast you out for it," he scoffed, and as if a fucking dime had dropped, I snapped into action.

"What do you mean?"

"She didn't call you?"

"I haven't been answering, obviously," I hissed. "What's happening?"

"Her kid's in the hospital," he said, his brows knitting together as I pushed myself from the door.

"*What?* You didn't think to fucking lead with that?"

As if powered by anger alone, I grabbed my belongings in handfuls, clumsily and shakily shoving them into the duffel bag I'd brought with me. I could feel the sweat building on my back, could feel the worry already enveloping my bones.

I should have answered.

"I didn't realize that was all it would take to get you home," Gray snapped, but before I could turn on him, he was helping me pack.

He wouldn't let me drive, probably for the best. A driver would bring my car back home. But that didn't mean I was going to be useless.

I spent the entire drive chugging water to sober myself up, researching the top pediatricians in Colorado.

I would put my issues on the back burner, handle myself later. Right now, I needed to help Drew, and that meant helping Dana, and helping Dana meant keeping this from her so she could focus on her son. I'd tell her eventually but not while this was happening.

Red rocks and ponderosa pines zoomed past the window as Gray drove. I secured Drew a spot in Denver's premier children's hospital along with the best fucking pediatrician I could find. I just needed to secure transportation, and that should be easy seeing as I had the main contact for Life Light services.

There was no happy reunion.

Instead, I sat in the waiting room beside Dana in the dull and lifeless pediatric ward of Foothills. She didn't speak to me. She didn't speak to anyone. She glared harshly at the middle-aged man and woman across the room from us, daggers practically shooting from her eyes. She refused to eat or drink anything.

Still in her vest and work slacks, she sat with her head in her hands, her name tag dangling from her chest. I didn't know a single fucking thing about what was happening to Drew.

I wanted to throw up.

"Dana," I breathed, leaning just a little closer to her and sliding my hand onto her thigh. "I—"

She pulled away.

Fuck. I wanted to believe she was just worried for Drew, wanted to believe that her actions were just mixed up in fear and anger toward what was happening to her son. But a part of me thought she might have already put the pieces together, and that she wanted nothing to do with me.

Vee walked in through the doors, chatting with a nurse behind her, and within seconds, Dana was on her feet.

"I'll fucking kill you."

The words were knives as Dana spat them. It almost floored me. I'd never heard her speak like that, never heard that kind of anger from anyone except myself.

Before I realized what was happening, her hands were on Vee, driving her back. I jumped to my feet.

"If you'd have just listened to me in the first place, you wouldn't be so goddamn angry," Vee spat back.

Dana's elbow notched back, her breathing steady but heavy, and it was like the launch party all over again.

I grabbed her by the forearm, pulling her back into my chest. "Baby, calm down, calm down—"

All hell broke loose.

"It's not your goddamn place to decide who I let see my child!" Dana shrieked, her words aimed at Vee but her sudden thrashing aimed at me. I tightened my hold on her as a handful of nurses came running, their shocked faces filling the hallway as Vee took a step back.

"Dana, please," I begged, wrapping one arm around her middle, my other hand holding her arms in place. "Think this through—"

Footsteps sounded behind me, stopping me mid-speech. As a middle-aged couple came to stand beside us, Dana only thrashed harder. Her ponytail came undone, loose tendrils of wavy brown locks falling in her face. "She's a fucking alcoholic, Vee! You let her around *my* son and now look where he's ended up!"

Alcoholic.

I looked at the middle-aged woman, taking in the uncanny resemblance.

Her mother.

Bile crept up my throat and entered my mouth.

"That has nothing to do with this!" Vee shot back, the open bottle of Coke in her hand spilling onto the floor. "He's been sick for weeks, Dana. You know that. Mom is not why he's here."

Dana took in a shuddering breath, her chest shaking. I couldn't see her face, couldn't see the tears that were falling, but I knew they were there. "I told you I wanted nothing to do with them. I told you I wanted them nowhere near him. You couldn't respect my fucking boundaries and now my son, *my child*, is paying the price."

"Girls, please, don't fight over this," the man said, taking a step toward the center of them.

Dana kicked out, nearly knocking me over with the shift in weight. "Dana, breathe," I said, lowering my lips to her ear. "Breathe, baby. Breathe."

Slowly, agonizingly, she listened. She breathed. She started to calm down.

But her words hung in the air, wrapped around my mind, and squeezed. *She's a fucking alcoholic.* Maybe I shouldn't be here. Maybe I was only making things worse.

But without me to stop her, who knows what she would have done to her sister. She could have ended up leaving the hospital in a fucking cop car, landing herself in a jail cell for the night.

I knew the moment she found out about my relapse, the moment I had to tell her would haunt me. It was already.

Chapter 30

Dana

Respiratory Syncytial Virus or RSV, leading to a severe case of pneumonia.

Finally, I had answers.

On the top floor of the infant ward in Denver's Children's Hospital, I stood over my son as tubes and wires kept him alive and breathing. He would get through this. But recovery would be long, and Drew would need to stay in the hospital until he was given a full bill of health.

I still wanted to punch a hole through my sister's face.

"You'll keep him past the point when he's first recovered," Cole said, his voice low on the other side of the room as he spoke to the doctor. "Long enough to ensure there's no complications. Do you understand?"

"Stop," I sighed. "I don't even know if you guys take my insurance yet. He'll stay just as long as he needs to in order to get better and then we'll go."

"Oh, that's taken care of already, Ms. Beechings," Dr. Stanley said, her clipboard tucked in tight to her chest.

"You take my insurance then?"

"Well, of that I'm not entirely sure, but it's all been

covered by Mr. Pearson." She glanced at Cole before taking a step back. "I'll be back with some paperwork for you to sign."

She left, closing the door quietly behind her.

I didn't have the energy to fight him on that, at least not now. But fuck, it weighed heavily on me as I sat down in the plush chair beside my son's bed. He didn't even know he was the father, yet here he was offering to be financially responsible for potentially hundreds of thousands of dollars on a kid that, as far as he knew, wasn't even his.

But I was still angry with him.

He'd disappeared. He hadn't called nor had he answered any of my calls. He turned up when things got bad only because Gray had told him what happened. I knew there was a high probability he had relapsed.

Despite his generosity, every part of me screamed to tell him to leave.

"Dana," Cole began, but the little wheeze and cry from Drew was enough for me to leave whatever he wanted to say behind.

———

The silence that hung between me and Cole felt heavier by the second. The sun rose, and he stayed. It set, and he stayed. It rose again, and there he was, looking ten times worse than he did when he'd first arrived, his eyes focused intently on Drew as he tried to stick his giraffe through the oxygen mask.

A female figure at the door, sans scrubs, made my heart

rate spike before it opened. There stood Lottie in all her glory, a coffee cup in hand and a smile plastered to her face.

"I know you're having a shit time but you need a break," she said. "Come on."

I blinked at her before briefly locking eyes with Cole. "Lots, I love you, but I'm not leaving Drew."

"I know," she grinned.

Sticking her free hand into the bag at her side, she fished out a little nanny cam and stuck it to the desk opposite Drew's bed. "You can keep an eye on him while we go get bagels or something downstairs."

"But—"

"I'll watch him, Dana," Cole said, his voice thick with sleep and the weight of nearly forty-eight hours of tense silence. He sat up straight in his chair. "Go."

I stilled, glancing between the two of them. I didn't want to leave him alone with Cole if what I thought was true. But I'd also been with him nonstop for almost two days. If he was drinking, the only privacy he had was the en suite bathroom. He appeared sober, acted sober, but so did Mom when she fucked up.

Lottie gave me a single nod. "He's got it."

"Okay."

I stared at the screen of Lottie's phone, watching as Cole walked a little plastic dinosaur across Drew's legs and forced a sickly giggle from him.

"You have to eat," Lottie said, shoving a cream-cheese-filled bagel into my hand. "If you want to take care of him, you have to take care of yourself, too."

We were sitting outside, away from the stale hospital environment, trying to get some fresh air. I sighed and set the phone on the picnic table, leaving the stream running.

"I just feel fucking sick. It's all too much."

"The bagel or the world?"

"Both."

"Well, you can't fix the world," Lottie sighed, breaking off a piece of the bagel and holding it out for me. I glared at her. "But you can eat the bagel."

I plucked it from her fingers and stuffed it in my mouth, savoring the first real food I'd had in days.

"You're not a bad mother, if that's what you're worried about," Lottie said gently. "You couldn't have prevented this."

I snorted as I took another bite from my bagel. "I absolutely could have. I could have gotten a second opinion. I could have gone back to the doctor instead of waiting for the meds they gave him to work. I could have kicked my piece of shit sister out the moment she arrived. I could have stayed in Hawaii."

She shot me a glare. "If you'd stayed in Hawaii, you wouldn't have Drew."

"I wouldn't have Cole."

"You can't possibly regret Cole enough to wish your son wasn't born," she deadpanned, side-eying the monitor and taking a bite of her bagel. "I know you better than that."

"No, of course not," I sighed. "But fuck, life would be easier. And I wouldn't have all this guilt and all these problems."

"You'd have just as many problems, just different ones."

It was my turn to shoot a glare at her.

Silence fell between us for a moment as we both ate, our gazes locked on Cole as he climbed onto the side of Drew's bed, careful of the wires and tubes, and settled in next to him to read him a book. I hated the way that it tugged at my heart.

"Do you think he's relapsed?" I asked, the words hanging between us for a moment. I wished I could hear what Cole was reading him. "I can't stop thinking about it."

Lottie sighed. "I don't know. I don't think so, but it's hard to tell with him," she said, her voice small, quieter. "If you're asking if I know anything, I honestly don't. I'd tell you this time."

"I need to know for sure," I breathed. "I don't know what to do. I need to tell him the truth, but if he has fallen down that path again, I can't do it. I can't have him around Drew. Not after this, not after the shit with my mom, but I don't want to keep him from his son, either."

"I wish I knew the answer," Lottie said, her gaze breaking from the phone and turning to me. "But you know me, Dana. I lost my mom way too young. I would have taken an alive and present mom, even if she was a drunk, over a dead mom any day."

The backs of my eyes burned the longer I watched Cole and Drew together. He fit so perfectly with Drew, as if by instinct. "What if I have it wrong? What if I tell him I can't do it anymore, but he's fine, no relapse? What if I make the wrong choice?"

"Drew's still young. He won't start remembering things until he's four, five maybe."

"But Cole won't get that time back," I rasped. The back of my throat stung from the days of waterworks. "And neither will I."

Lottie took another bite as she mulled it over. "You

know, it's estimated that about fifty percent of recovering alcoholics relapse in their first year," she said, her hand reaching out to squeeze my free one. "And half of them return to sobriety afterward. They told us that when we contacted the rehab facility for him."

"But half of them don't."

"Glass half full."

"Glass half empty," I retorted. "I can't look at it like that when I know my mother."

As if conjured by the fucking devil, the doors of the hospital slid open, and there she was in all her horrible glory, looking almost as much of a mess as me. Behind her, my sister followed closely, her arms over her chest and a sour expression coating her face.

Of course, they clocked me.

I made a move to get up, but Lottie's hand kept me down.

With every step Mom took, the wind blew against her gray, thinning hair, sending it flying in the breeze. Her pudgy form seemed shorter, weaker, than the last time I'd seen her about six years ago. Her face had barely changed, just a few new wrinkles that didn't make her any less of the monster she was.

"Can we talk?" she asked, her voice as small as a fucking rodent's as she wrapped her arms around herself.

"Absolutely fucking not," I snapped. I grabbed Lottie's phone from the table, taking one last passing glance as Cole closed the book and snuggled up to my son among the wires, before shoving it into her purse.

"Honey," Mom said, causing a snort to escape out of me. "Please. I'm better now."

"She's been sober for six fucking years," Vee barked from behind her.

"Is that supposed to erase the twenty-two years before it?" I pushed myself up from the bench, shoving the last bite of my bagel into my mouth as I motioned for Lottie to join me. Without a question, she did.

"No, but I want to help, Dana," Mom bleated.

I almost had the balls to throw a punch when she took a step toward me. Almost.

The emotions took back over, running through my body like the IV drip Drew was surviving on, and before I could do anything drastic, Lottie stepped between us. "You're okay," she said to me, her wide eyes getting wider as she took me in.

I had no idea what I looked like. Didn't know if the burn behind my eyes and the well of tears was visible, didn't know if the stress and anger I was carrying on my shoulders could be seen by the naked eye. But just Mom's presence, her pushiness, her assumption that she could waltz back into my life without even an apology, was enough to spring it all back to life inside of me.

"Let's go back," Lottie said. "Let's go see Drew."

―――

I scrubbed my eyes with the base of my palms as I walked the corridors of the top floor alone. Lottie had received some kind of business call, and although she'd insisted she could let it be, I'd lied and said I'd be fine.

I felt anything but fine.

I tried to catch my breath as I approached our room, but each one was shaky at best, the tears coating my cheeks and demanding to be present. I just wanted to be able to calm down. I wanted to rewind back to relaxing on the beach in Costa Rica, wanted to watch Cole panic as Drew shoved sand in his mouth. I wanted it more than just about anything.

When I reached the doorway, I stopped. Cole was still lying beside Drew, his fingers walking up the length of his little body before stopping on the top of his head, making him giggle that sickly, snotty laugh of his since he'd gotten sick. The smile on Cole's face was the brightest I'd seen in weeks.

I had half a mind to ask him to leave, to take my son into my arms and tell him that I wouldn't accept his money and he needed to go. But the other half, the weaker half, the one that was tired and angry and missed him, wanted nothing more than to join him and Drew on the bed, to laugh and joke together. I wanted to snuggle into him. I wanted his comfort, his presence.

I couldn't choose.

I stayed there in the doorway, watching him from across the room, standing on my metaphorical fence, wishing I had a hammer to beat it to the ground.

I had a question, and a sinking stone in my stomach that knew the answer.

Chapter 31

Cole

I knew the moment I locked eyes with Dana.

I couldn't run from it anymore.

Every part of me stilled despite Drew's laughter. Every part of me locked up like a stone, falling from way too high, seconds from shattering on the pavement.

A nurse slid past Dana, barely moving her. "We need to do an X-ray on little Andrew to check on the pneumonia, see if it is improving. Do you two mind stepping out for a moment?" she asked me, and I could see the anger in Dana that they asked me instead of her.

"That's up to his mother," I said, nodding toward Dana as I carefully climbed off the bed.

I made my way to her side, already knowing where this was going, before excusing myself to the hallway. A sheen of sweat coated my skin in an instant, and the moment Dana mumbled that's fine to the nurse and shut the door behind her, I wanted to run.

But I didn't. For her, I didn't.

She swallowed as she took a step toward me, backing me further into the quiet recess at the end of the hall. Her chin held high, her shoulders back, she looked as if she was preparing herself for a war she didn't want.

"Where were you?" she asked, and the words felt less like venom and more like ice as they crawled through me. "When you left, where were you?"

This wasn't the right time. Not when Drew was still sick, not with her parents still somewhere nearby. It was all wrong.

Half-truths. "Colchester Ski Resort," I said, the words falling from me too quickly, too suddenly.

"You were skiing?"

"I was hiding," I admitted.

She swallowed again, her confidence solidified. "You've been drinking."

And there it was. My worst fucking nightmare.

"Cole."

"I'd tell you if I had." *Wrong fucking answer, idiot. You'll have to fess up eventually.* "I wasn't."

"Please don't lie to me right now," she said, and my chest fucking ached. Little tears, leftover from when she'd entered the room, dripped from the corners of her eyes.

I need a drink.

I blinked, and I was angry.

When did I become angry?

"I need the truth," she begged, and I fucking snapped.

"The truth?" I scoffed. I leaned in a little closer, and if I'd had a drink in the last forty-eight hours, she would have smelled it. "Don't I deserve the truth as well?"

Her brows knitted together as she leaned back. "What is that supposed to mean?"

"Is he or is he not my son?"

Her eyes blew wide as she took a step back, the question catching both of us off guard. I couldn't remember when I'd concluded that I more than likely was Drew's dad. I'd seen his paperwork, seen the absent information under father. But it was more of a feeling.

"Don't talk to me about the truth," I continued, pulling myself from her personal space.

"You didn't even give me a chance to answer."

"I didn't need to."

"He isn't," she said, and my world came to a halt. I studied her, watched every movement of her face, but it didn't sit right. "Why would you think that?"

"The timing. He looks like me. He's six months old tomorrow, correct? Let's rewind fifteen months," I spat, pushing my fingers through my overgrown hair to give them something to focus on. "That puts us... damn, almost exactly to the fucking day I took you out for the first time."

"We didn't have sex that night," she gulped, but the little step back she took made me think otherwise.

"We did."

She pivoted and my stomach sank further. "The timeline is murky but there were other people I was seeing then."

"Other people you were fucking?" I asked, and although she hesitated, she nodded. I raked my teeth over my bottom lip, my head swimming, her denial and resistance only confusing me more. Her body language said I'd called

her out, but I wanted to trust her, wanted to give her the benefit of the doubt that she wouldn't keep that from me. "I wasn't drinking," I added.

And so we went around again.

Back and forth, a blame game that never fucking ended. I couldn't tell her I'd relapsed—I knew that for certain and I hated myself for it. I had to wait until she was in the right headspace to hear that, and now wasn't the goddamn time to deal with this shit. It broke my heart to keep it from her, to know that she knew and not give her that truth in return, but the part of me that wanted to hide was screaming louder than the part of me that wanted her comfort.

And for once, it felt like it was right.

"Please, just say it, Cole," she snapped, one single finger jabbing into my chest.

"I have nothing to say."

She scoffed and pushed harder, her nail nearly breaking through my unwashed t-shirt as it pressed against my skin. "You're just like my mother. You know that?" she seethed, taking a step toward me and forcing me back toward the window at the end of the hall. "She was a recovering alcoholic, too. But you know what she did? She caved. Time and time again, she couldn't help herself. She ruined my fucking life."

The burn itched in the back of my throat. "Dana."

"I never, ever, in my wildest dreams thought I'd fall for a shit like her," she fumed, but the words felt too fueled with emotion to sting like she wanted them to. She choked on them, fresh tears forming, and although it fucking hurt, I just wanted to wipe them away. "I never wanted this for myself. And I certainly don't want it for my son."

I swallowed, watching the way her lips formed around the words she spoke. Why did I still want to hold her in the midst of this? Why did I just want to make it go away? I didn't have an answer for myself, so instead, I bridged the gap, reaching across the distance between us and brushing my fingers against her cheek. *So damp.* "If you knew when you met me, would you take it back? All of it?" I asked, my voice barely more than a whisper.

Her eyes slammed shut as she turned away from my touch, another tear breaking free.

"Dana," I pressed.

"Maybe," she whispered.

The longer we stood there, the wider the gap between us grew and the tenser our silence became. I just wanted this to be over, wanted us to stop fighting, but it felt like we weren't getting anywhere. I wasn't going to budge, and neither was she.

"I want you to leave," she rasped and everything came crashing down.

"I'm not leaving," I stated, removing my hand and taking a step back. I wanted to throw up, wanted to cry, wanted to run but not away. I wanted to run to Drew. "Not with Drew still needing this much medical attention. I can't."

"If you won't tell me what's going on, then I can't have you near him." Her fingers wrapped around her biceps, hugging herself tightly. "I just can't."

I can't have you near him.

"I'm not leaving him, Dana!" The words boomed around the walls of the hallway. I didn't realize how loud I'd spoken, but I couldn't take it back now. Whether he was mine or not, I felt too attached to him to leave him like this. "I can't, I won't, it's out of the fucking question."

"Please don't make me call security."

Security? Could she, would she even—

"Guys, guys, what's going on?" Lottie's voice carried down the hall as the nurses wheeled the X-ray machine from Drew's room. She caught up, glancing in before walking past.

"I don't want him here anymore," Dana said, taking a step back until she was side by side with our friend.

Lottie looked between us, her face a mixture of shock and confusion. "Why?"

Dana's eyes met mine briefly as she squeezed her arms. Behind them were storms of anger and disgust, swirling doubts, and far too much else for me to comprehend without hurting myself more. "I don't want a drunk around my son," she said, and before I could even form a rebuttal, she turned and began walking back to Drew's room.

I stood there for so long, locked and judged and embarrassed beyond belief, that I swore I could feel the dust collecting in my hair.

Fine. If she wanted me gone, if she wanted me out of her life and away from her son, I would do that. I would find it in me to drown her out, no matter how much it hurt.

———

"Cole! Cole, wait, wait, wait!"

A small hand wrapped around my wrist and pulled, spinning me two steps from my car. Lottie stood there, catching her breath, her light blue eyes wide and desperate.

"Come back. Please."

I shook her hand from me and reached into my pocket for my keys. "She doesn't want me there."

"You don't understand," Lottie urged, shifting and jumping until she stood between me and my BMW. "She'd just seen her mom downstairs. This has been a lot for her, and with her mom on top of it, she snapped, okay? She wants you there. Believe me, Cole, you need to be there with her. It's not what you think. She told me what she said to you—"

"It doesn't matter, Lots," I snapped, gently pushing her

out of the way so I could open my door. I watched her over the top of it, watched the way her face fell as she realized she wasn't stopping me. "He's not my kid, she said so herself. He's hers, and she gets to decide who sees him and who doesn't. If she doesn't want a drunk around him, then you know what? She's right. I should go."

Her lips formed a thin line as her hand came to rest on top of mine, holding the door open. She looked over her shoulder, the late autumn wind whipping through the parking garage and tugging at her clothes, before dragging her gaze back to me. "You both have secrets," she breathed, the words hanging in the air.

They felt too charged, like there was more behind them.

"And I think you're both lying."

Chapter 32

Dana

"I need to talk to you about something and I really, *really* don't want you to chew my head off for it."

Drew giggled, shoving his little giraffe into his mouth and biting down on it with his two newly formed teeth. We'd just gotten home from the hospital, and with Lottie's ever-present help, she'd insisted on driving us. He was happy as could be, and although we'd left a little earlier than Cole had originally insisted on, I didn't want to have to rely on his money for it.

I'd be sending him a check at the first possible opportunity.

"Why does that sound like you've done something shitty?" I asked, narrowing my gaze at her over Drew's head while I washed dishes. He kicked a little in the new holder that Lottie had got me that strapped him to my chest. With Vee now thoroughly kicked out of my house, the new holder would be useful to have him literally attached to me while I worked on cleaning up the house.

Lottie shifted over on the couch, her joggers tightening as she pulled her legs up. "Cause I might have."

The soapy glass in my hand slipped and fell into the sink full of water, sending bubbles and droplets flying. Drew laughed. I seethed. I could feel the fear sinking into my stomach, filling my mind with every possible thing she could say but somehow I already knew what it was.

"Just say it."

"I think Cole knows."

And there it was.

I rested my hands on the counter, digging my nails into the linoleum-wrapped cheap wood. *He was already catching on. This isn't a massive leap.* "How did this happen?" I snapped, irritation building in my gut.

I'd made my choice at the hospital. And although a part of me regretted it, I'd told him he wasn't Cole's father. I'd asked him to go. I'd told him that I couldn't have him near my son. The words behind them were clear—*we're done.* I went with my gut, and I had to stick by that, no matter how many nights I cried myself to sleep or felt like I couldn't breathe while reading Drew a story.

But we didn't need him to survive, and that's what I would have to do now—survive. Yes, he made life easier, but I couldn't care less if the next seventeen years of my life were back-breaking as a single mother if it meant keeping Drew away from the shit and the hell that I had to grow up around. My mother was the worst thing that happened to me, and my father was guilty by association. I didn't want Drew to ever know what that felt like.

"I didn't say it outright," Lottie sighed. "But I tried to get him to come back after you'd told him to leave. I'm sorry. I just—both of you are my friends, and I felt like you were both making a decision you would regret."

"So you fucking told him Drew's his son?" I accused, glaring at her over the kitchen island. She looked smaller than usual with her legs tucked up against her chest. "That wasn't your information to give."

"I just said both of you were keeping secrets," she clarified, and that didn't make it any better. "But the way he looked at me... I don't know, Dana. I think he's put the pieces together. I told him I thought he was lying about not relapsing because honestly, I think you were right about that. But I may have insinuated that he wasn't the only one lying."

"No, no, no, fuck." I pushed the bases of my palms into my eyes, trying to relieve some of the pressure building behind them. This was bad. This was fucking awful. She'd gone behind my back, she'd broken her promise, she'd told him in almost no uncertain terms.

I was screwed.

It had been two weeks. What was he waiting for, then? If he knew, if he remembered it through the likely haze of alcohol he was operating under, there was no reason for why he hadn't shown up at my door demanding to see Drew. My head spun, filling with every worst-case scenario I could think of. He was lawyering up, he was going to take me to court, he was going to demand visitation or custody, he would ask for a paternity test, he was going to take my son from me, he was dead in a ditch on the side of the road...

"I'm sorry."

"No, you're not," I croaked, wrapping one arm around the cooing baby strapped to my chest. "Do you have any idea what you've done?"

"You lost your mind when you found out I knew about Cole being in rehab," she said, her brows narrowing as she fought herself on this. "You said I should have told you. For Drew's sake. Does he not deserve the same respect?"

"Not when he's rich as shit and could crush me in court for fucking custody, Lottie!"

Drew looked up at me, his little green eyes shining, reflecting Cole right back at me. His lower lip quivered, and god, I really needed to control my anger around him. But how else was I supposed to react? How else was I supposed to feel?

Lottie shook her head. "He wouldn't. He's not that kind of person. And if for any reason he tried, you know damn well that Hunter and I would help you—"

"I wouldn't need that help if you had just kept your mouth shut in the first place!"

"He deserves to know he has a kid, Dana! And Drew deserves a father—"

A singular bang from the front door made me jump. Drew kicked off in my arms, the sounds of irritation too much for him, and as I wrapped my arm back around his bottom to calm him down, another bang shook the wood.

"That better not be Cole," I snapped, sending a glare to Lottie as I stepped around the kitchen island. Another harsh knock, followed swiftly by the sound of breaking pottery and a grunt.

"Stop, stop, you've got Drew. I'll get it," Lottie said, shooting to her feet in a second and crossing the beige carpet to the front door. She turned the handle, wrenching it open, and my stomach dropped for what had to be the millionth time in two weeks.

"You're not Dana," Robert said, a broken piece of my flower pot in his hand before he tossed it behind him. He clocked me before she could reply. "Where the hell have you been, girl? Was looking everywhere for you."

Lottie looked back at me, her brows furrowed, a silent question between us—*who the fuck is he?*

"Shut the door, Lottie," I said, taking a step toward her, but in a flash his hand was on it, holding it open. We both stopped in our tracks.

"I ask for *one* date and you disappear for weeks?" Robert pushed. Even from behind Lottie, I could smell him. It was as if he'd bathed, clothes and all, in a vat of vodka. It was almost shocking how much he reminded me of Cole—the lightly tanned skin, the lightened hair, the hint of stubble that Cole had for weeks on end. Even down to the cut of his suit, it looked like it had been taken right from Cole's closet. If I didn't know any better, at a passing glance, I'd have assumed he *was* Cole. But there were differences there too, ones that couldn't be changed. His height, his extra wide shoulders, the way his nose bent to the left. I couldn't help but wonder if he'd seen Cole a handful of times and had been trying to change his appearance under the assumption I was dating Cole. Oh my god. *Was he trying to look more like Cole in the hope that I would date him?*

"Her son was in the hospital," Lottie hissed, taking a step toward him and forcing him back. I wanted to grab her hand and pull her toward me, but the irritation from our argument stopped me before I could. "She clearly doesn't want you here, so leave."

"I called you," he barked, and Drew let out another little cry.

"And I ignored them," I shot back.

"I don't get it," Robert huffed, his fingernails digging into the cheap wood of my door and leaving a scratch. "Your precious Cole is out there drunk off his ass, spiraling—nose-diving, in fact—into his own little issues. The fucking idiot's made himself happy as a clam to never get sober again, and you're still choosing him?"

I blinked. *What was he talking about?* "I'm not choosing anybody. I'm just not agreeing to date you because you're a goddamn psychopath."

"Look at me," he laughed, something dark and almost sinister brewing in the way his voice sounded. "I'm a million times better than him."

"How do you know Cole?" Lottie asked. Her arm began to shake, the same one that was holding the door halfway shut. How much pressure is he putting on that door?

"Rehab," he said, as little bits of spittle went flying.

Rehab.

Wait.

He pushed further, and the door slammed against the wall beside it as Lottie's arm gave out. She didn't move from her spot, though, keeping herself between me, Drew, and the man before us. "You have no idea how easy it was to get him to cave," he said. A line of drool leaked from the corner of his mouth, dripping onto the neatly pressed dark grey suit. "He's *weak*. He doesn't deserve shit."

You have no idea how easy it was to get him to cave.

Oh, fuck. "You're Bobby?"

"Bobby Morgans, at your service," he chuckled, doing a little bow before nearly losing his balance.

"Leave," I hissed.

"I'm not leaving until you understand." The cut of his words almost gave me whiplash. It was terrifying how easily he slid from anger and disgust to being lighthearted and cheerful. It had terrified me the first time it happened, and now it was so much fucking worse. "You need someone who has their shit together, Dana."

"And that's you?"

"That's me."

"You look worse than Cole the last time I saw him,"

Lottie scolded, grabbing ahold of the door frame and trying to shut it before losing once again.

"I can guarantee he looks worse than I do right now," Bobby laughed. My stomach churned. "Don't you see, Dana? He caved. He caved so easily when he had so much to fucking live for. He can't handle himself. A few choice words, a few shitty situations, and he fell the moment I pulled out a bottle. Do you really want someone like that around your son?"

God, I couldn't keep up. He'd thrown Cole into his relapse?

"You think she'd want someone capable of doing that to a friend around her son?" Lottie shot back, and I couldn't think anymore. I couldn't process it all. I wanted him gone, wanted him fucking dead, and instead I had bickering at my front door the day we'd come home from the hospital.

I slipped my phone from my pocket, pushing the three little digits I needed before holding it up in plain sight. "Leave. Now."

"For fucks sake, Dana, I'm here to *help* you."

"Please don't make me call them."

A chunk of wood fell from my door as he released it, swearing under his breath. "Fine. Whatever. Fucking bitch." He stepped down off the threshold of my front door, wiping the drool from the corner of his mouth as he staggered back. "Maybe I was wrong about you. You're so goddamn blind you couldn't even see the signs."

My thumb hovered over the green call button, my hand shaking violently. He snorted a laugh as he walked down my pathway, every second feeling like hours until he stepped down the road, unlocking a car I knew for certain was Coles. His BMW.

Lottie shut the door and locked it, and it was like the

room came to life. Drew began to cry, my phone dropped to the ground, Lottie started freaking out, saying we needed to call the police anyway, she needed to check on Cole, about how this was insane and we needed to go to him.

I shut it all out. Everything but Drew. I wrapped my arms around him, soothing him, dragging my fingers across the top of his dark blonde hair. It had started sprouting weeks ago, and as I looked at him, as I really took it all in, I had a hard time not seeing Cole in him anymore. I couldn't block out the green eyes, the little dimple, the hair.

If Bobby was the one that drove him...

No. I'd made my decision. It didn't matter what the straw was that broke the camel's back. If I was okay taking him back after this, I would have been weeks ago. It didn't matter. I felt for him, truly, achingly, and as much as it would hurt me, destroy me, break me apart, I couldn't. For Drew, I had to keep myself away from him.

No matter how much it broke my heart.

Chapter 33

Cole

Everything hurt. My body, my mind, my fucking soul, if I had one. The whiskey in my pocket barely kept it under control. I'd found a happy medium that allowed me to cover up enough of the pain that I could try to be a normal person without debilitating me into a full-blown wreck.

If I didn't drink enough, I couldn't stop thinking about her and Drew.

If I drank too much, I couldn't stop thinking about her and Drew.

If I drank the perfect amount, I couldn't stop thinking about her and Drew, but it wouldn't leave me sobbing and clutching my chest in the middle of the bathroom floor.

It was the only option.

Even if it meant barely being able to function at work.

I didn't bother taking the head of the table for the shareholder meeting. Instead, I let Ben run the show, keeping to the sidelines and out of the way. The likelihood of me just messing things up was too high to risk it, and considering how many times I'd nodded off already, I'd made the right choice, even though it hurt to not be able to run my own business.

I knew it wasn't a good look, having my next in line take over while I was still around. I knew it made me look weak and incapable, knew it would likely raise questions.

But the meeting ended and they left without a word, without their questioning gazes or interrogations toward me. Either they already knew or they didn't care. Or worse—they expected it.

I waited until the room was clear to take a swig from my flask. Drive down the feeling, reach that not-so-happy medium.

The burn at the back of my throat only raged on.

I blinked, and I was almost stumbling into the hall. I'd gotten used to the blips again. They were happening more frequently, stealing patches of time from me. But time didn't mean anything anymore, not when it wasn't spent with her.

"Cole."

"Ben," I sighed, turning on my heel. "Thank you for running the meeting. I appreciate—"

"Is everything okay?" he asked, his arms crossing over the cheap suit he'd likely picked up from Goodwill. *Stop it. He's nice.* Guess the shitty thoughts were back. "Are you...?"

"I'm fine." My jaw ached from how hard I clenched it.

Ben glanced behind his shoulder, checking the hall was clear before his ponytail nearly smacked me in the face as he whipped back around. "You don't seem fine. Having me run the show while you're on site? And you're clearly day-drinking, man. I can smell it on you. We all can."

Well, that explains why the shareholders didn't talk to me. "I'm not discussing this with you," I replied, trying to keep an ounce of professionalism instead of letting my irritation cloud me. It was becoming harder than it used to be. "I said I was fine. Just leave me alone."

"Look, I know we're not close," Ben said, taking a single step toward me. Instinctually, I backed up, trying to keep my breath from him. *Pointless.* "But it's obvious you're not okay. You know the rumors around here, you know how fast they spread. Maybe it's best you take some time off again."

I scoffed. "Is this your company now?" *Well, there goes the professionalism.*

"Well, no—"

"Then don't think you can tell me what to fucking do," I snapped. "If I want to be here, I'll be here. If I don't, you'll know. I can do whatever I want here, whether that means crashing and burning it into the goddamn ground or building it up to new heights. You're *lucky* I let you play CEO for six months, but that doesn't give you a fucking title."

His wide eyes and step back told me I'd gone a little too far, but I didn't care, not about this, not about anything.

"You're also lucky I've not kicked you back down to the ground floor."

I turned on a dime, leaving him standing there, and decided maybe it was best I leave for the day. Maybe I needed more than what was in my pocket.

So what if I ended up sobbing on my bathroom floor again? I'd done it a million times by now. I was used to it, and I'd forget the gruesome details by morning.

Yellow teeth, yellower eyes, and a tall, wiry frame stood over me, a tray of shots in his hand. He sat down at the table beside me, the clear shots clinking and spilling over the lips of the glasses.

"You didn't have to pay for them," I grumbled, tipping one back and relishing in the burn of the cheap booze as it slid down my throat.

"My pleasure, bud," Adam said. He touched a glass to mine as we fired them down in rapid succession. I'd missed nights like this—though not so much the mornings after—where he and I and his group of friends would drink until the moon set and the sun rose, where I'd stumble back to my apartment on 16th Street and collapse on the bare floor.

I only wished I hadn't given Gray the keys.

"I told you it wouldn't last," Adam laughed, but it was hollow, a slight hint of sympathy to his tone. "I tried ten years ago. Don't feel bad about it."

"I don't," I lied.

In reality, I couldn't feel worse about it. This was the point I hated getting to, where the thoughts that haunted my sleep hit me in waves in my waking hours. I could get past this point, to the stage where walking was hard and driving was out of the question, and they'd quiet down again, but any further than that and I'd end up a shell of myself. I made a mental note to wait until I was home for that so I didn't end up in the bathroom here, instead.

But I couldn't stop the onslaught as I drank.

What kind of father was I? Holed up in a dark and dreary bar, music from ten years ago, at the earliest, booming over the speakers, the neon signs hurting my head. Granted, Dana hadn't confirmed it with her own mouth, but Lottie had made it more obvious than ever, and I'd felt that connection every time I was around him. I had been right. My gut had been right. Drew was mine, and I was screwing it up before he was even seven months old.

If anything, I was worse than my own father. At least he'd waited until I was thirteen to abandon me. So much for breaking that cycle.

A fist hit the table, and as I turned to look, everything in between blurred into nothing until I focused on him. Bobby practically fell into his seat, hollering hello to Adam over the music, asking him where the group was, I guess they'd met up beforehand.

I watched him as I knocked back another, watched as he took what wasn't his and plucked a shot glass from the tray. He'd been pissing me off lately in my sober bouts, in the mornings before I'd had a drink and the evenings before I drowned. My house was a fucking wreck because of him. Half of my clothes had gone missing, and even now, it was plain to see he'd been taking them as he relaxed in one of my good suits. Whether his were getting ruined in his own antics or whether he'd simply lost them in the piles of trash filling his room, I wasn't sure, but he wasn't even asking. He was just taking.

And I fucking hated his haircut.

I blinked, and he was speaking.

"Another round?" Bobby asked, his gaze cutting to me as he leaned forward onto the table.

"I don't know. I might head home," I sighed, glancing at the clock and nearly losing my mind as I realized two hours had passed. *It's fine. It happens.*

"Come on, man. It's Friday. No work tomorrow, no bitch to hold you down anymore," he laughed, placing one hand on my shoulder and giving it a squeeze.

From the sway of my body and the no longer incessant

thoughts, I'd hit the calm before the storm. Any more and I'd be a fucking shipwreck. "Don't," I breathed.

I looked to my right, hoping Adam would back me up, but the space he occupied before was empty, and the glasses he'd drunk from were gone. *When did he leave?*

"What? She's fucking insane. Keeping your kid from you? I mean, what kind of woman does that? You don't need her," he droned on and on. He knocked back the last shot left on the table before leaning into me again. "Get us another round, Cole."

"I don't want another round," I snapped, tugging my shoulder from his grip and watching as the world spun.

"Seriously? You were fine ten minutes ago."

"You didn't mention Dana ten minutes ago."

"Oh my god, man," he said, dragging one hand down his face in frustration. "Stop letting that cunt get into your fucking head—"

My hand went flying before I'd even made the decision. I grabbed him by *my* tie, wrapping it around my fist, and tugged him toward me. "Don't you *ever* call her that again," I growled, bringing his face just inches from mine, watching as the little drops of spit landed on his unshaven face. "Do you understand me?"

The laugh that bubbled from him had me pushing him back harshly into his seat, relinquishing my hold on him. "Christ, she's really got her claws in you," Bobby said.

He pushed himself to his feet, swaying a bit, before glaring down at me.

"Don't tell me what I can and can't do, Cole. You're not my fucking dad," he chuckled. "You're barely Drew's."

My hands buzzed as he walked away, the desperate temptation to beat his face in where he stood smothering me. But I wouldn't do that. We were both on edge, both suffering from a relapse. A part of me held an inch of grace for him.

Even if it meant sobbing on the bathroom floor of a rundown bar in the middle of Boulder.

My phone pinged, and I fished it from my pocket, the blind hope that it would be Dana fueling my actions. But it was a call from my sponsor. I canceled it. I couldn't be bothered lying anymore today, whether that was to myself or anyone else. Wasn't sure I even could at this stage.

How did things get this bad?

I stared at the wood of the table, memorizing the swirls in the knots and the way each piece was nailed together. I was already becoming a shell of myself tonight, but in general, I was useless. Weak. A piece of shit, a deadbeat, a failure. Dana was right to push me away. She was right to keep me from Drew. Maybe she was even right to keep the truth from me.

I waited until I heard the front door close before stumbling my way up to the bar and settling into a high top chair, passing my card over the counter, and asking the bartender to keep them coming.

Chapter 34

Dana

I stepped out of the elevator, a handful of documents tucked under my arm to deliver to Ben from my manager, Allison. I hated coming up here lately, hated the way I felt the need to look over my shoulder, to keep a constant eye out for him. I didn't know if it would happen, only that it could.

At the end of the hall, disheveled and meek, his hair a goddamn mess, Cole stood in front of the door to his office, desperately fishing in his pocket for his keys. I stood in place, my heart racing, watching as he glanced from side to side before shoving the key into the lock.

For a split second, right before he disappeared around the frame of the door, I could have sworn he spotted me. My breath caught, my heart raced, and the glint in the brief pass of green eyes nearly pulled me in.

I took a step toward his office before thinking better of it.

I had to fight to pull myself away, I knew I couldn't bend to it. A part of me loved him, I knew that much. I'd come to terms with it. But I couldn't handle all of it right now, not when I had someone who meant more to me than myself or Cole to watch after.

I just wished it didn't hurt so much.

I'd heard the rumors, how he'd randomly been in and out of work, that he'd been found passed out in his office, heard he'd been seen drinking at the bars. There were only so many things that could be exaggerations or lies, and if any of it was true, *any* of it, I wanted to cry for him. I wanted to hold him and tell him he'd be okay, wanted to take him to a meeting or help him find a new facility.

But I couldn't.

I didn't realize how much seeing Cole would throw me off for the rest of my shift.

My mind spiraled throughout my tours but I couldn't stop it. Couldn't stop thinking about whether I needed to quit, if I needed to go back to school for a degree, if I should stop trusting my gut and run upstairs to him. My future was more uncertain than ever, and most of it was my own damn fault. I'd built up an idea of it that wasn't stable for the last four months I'd been with him.

On top of that, I was operating on a level of shock and stress I'd never been under before. I had convinced myself that Cole would show up, demanding answers or visitation with his son since he'd likely figured it all out. But he hadn't. He hadn't called, he hadn't texted, he hadn't shown up at my door in a drunken fit. I wasn't sure how I should take any of it. Was he done too? Had he decided that I was right?

Or could he just not be bothered to put in an ounce of effort?

I wanted to tell him about Bobby, he deserved that much. I'd mentioned it to Gray, but Gray said Cole had basically shut him out too, and I didn't know where to go from there short of showing up at his house. I couldn't imagine he'd entertain the idea of it, considering how much I'd heard of the infamous Bobby who was helping him through his journey of recovery.

I scoffed. If he only knew what a shit Bobby truly was.

No. It was best we stayed away from each other, continued to keep the distance between us and go on with our lives. If he wanted to see Drew when he was older… ugh. I just didn't know.

I slipped into the vest room and hung mine on the wall. I didn't have a tour first thing tomorrow morning so no need to show up in it. I grabbed my bag and double-checked I had a charger with me this time before clocking out on the computer, relief already beginning to flood me knowing I'd be out of the building in minutes, away from the possibility of running into him.

But things never seem to go the way I want them to.

"Dana?"

I swallowed, my spine going rigid as I turned from the computer. Cole stood in the doorway, his hair too long, his face too scruffy. The bags under his eyes were massive, his face gaunt. His shirt buttons were off, causing the fabric to stretch and bunch in various places.

He'd somehow managed the tie.

He shut the door behind him, enclosing us in the small room alone. I could smell him across the short distance, could smell the liquor emanating from every pore.

"Please don't do this," I breathed, taking a step back and nearly knocking the monitor from the desk as I ran into it.

"I need to talk to you," he said, and *fuck*, the words felt so hollow it made my chest ache. His cheeks were reddened, his eyes bloodshot. I hated this. I hated it so much I wanted to fucking disappear into the floor.

"I can't do this with you." I held my bag to my chest, hoping somehow it would make me feel better with something between us. Maybe it would stop me from doing what I wanted, which was to make him feel better. I wanted to hold him.

His lips pursed together, the shine in his eyes intensifying before he steeled his jaw. *Please don't cry.* "I want to see my son."

Fuck.

The backs of my eyes burned. There wasn't any use in pretending anymore. Lottie had let the cat out of the bag, and I couldn't lie to him, couldn't handle it. It wasn't the right way for it to come out. The right way would have been months ago, and I should have done it then. But wishing for a time machine wouldn't get me anywhere.

"No," I croaked. Every piece of my heart fucking shattered as I watched him crumple, the shards falling in my chest and cementing their sharp sides in my stomach, churning it and making me want to vomit. "Not like this, Cole."

His lower lip quivered in the same way Drew's did, his shoulders sagging. "I'm sorry," he said quickly, covering his mouth and taking a step back toward the door. I could hear the tremble in his voice. "I didn't, I didn't mean for any of this to happen, baby. I don't understand how I got here, how any of this fucking happened." He sucked in air, his chest heaving, hyperventilation threatening to kick in. "It's all blowing up in my face."

I bit down on my lip, fighting back the tears. There was a part of me that just wanted to pull him in, lock the door, and hide with him for however long he needed. That same part of me told me to tell him about Bobby, and she was winning. "Bobby came by the other day," I breathed, taking a step toward him, flinching at the scent of whiskey on his breath. Gently, slowly, I rested a hand on his cheek. "Look, I... I know this won't be easy to hear, but he said a lot of shit and I don't want you to freak out."

Wide green eyes met mine, a hint of moisture in the inner corners.

"I know he drove you to it," I said, fingering a lock of dark blonde hair out of his face, that same face I saw reflected in Drew more and more each day. "He pushed you and pushed you, then he celebrated when you caved. This is on him."

He blinked, his jaw working, and we stood in silence for far too long before he pulled away from my touch.

No. Come on. Please.

"You're lying," he said, his voice sounding far different than before. There was nothing there, nothing behind it, no quiver to his tone, no hint of affection. "He may be insane and he may be annoying, but he wouldn't do that."

"Cole—"

"Don't." He took a deep breath in through his nose. "I shouldn't have come in here."

I watched as he turned the handle, felt the part of me that was fighting for this slowly die. Fine. If he didn't want to listen to me, if he didn't want to hear the truth, then my gut was right. "If you leave, we're done," I said, the words hurting even as I spoke them.

He hesitated. "Don't put that on me, Dana," he sighed, pushing the door open and stepping out into the hallway. "Besides, you already made it clear we were done at the hospital."

But I don't want us to be done.

He waited for a moment as I tried to find the right words to say, but the angry part of me was flaring, and I didn't want to speak because I knew she'd spew flames the moment I tried. He stood there, and I knew if he wouldn't accept what I'd said, if he *couldn't* accept it then he couldn't change, which meant he couldn't get better.

I swallowed as I stepped past him out of the room and into the sunny hallway, my emotions firing on all cylinders, confusing me and making me feel sick. "If you're not willing to listen to me then you're not willing to change," I said. His brows rose as he slammed the door behind us, making me jump.

"I'm not going to let you accuse someone I care about, someone who's going through the exact same thing I am, of being a raging, horrible monster," he snapped. He tugged at his shirt, trying to rid it of wrinkles, failing miserably as he realized none of the buttons were right.

"It's not an accusation, it's a fact."

"It's bullshit, is what it is. Just say you want to hurt me and be done with it," he hissed, coming in a little too close, a little too angry. I backed up, watching as the realization of his misstep sunk into him, watching as his eyes widened and the confused, inebriated Cole kicked back in. "I'm sorry. I—"

"No. Nope. Not doing it, Cole," I said, stepping back toward the double doors that lead to freedom. Freedom from here, from this, from him. I was tired of the tears that were already streaking down my face, tired of the fight I knew I'd never win. "I'm done."

I sat in the driver's seat, baking in the low winter sun as I idled in my driveway. Beside me was a car I recognized too well, one I'd avoided but decided I wouldn't lose my mind entirely over. I'd dealt with enough today. Couldn't I just have one fucking moment of peace?

Deciding it was better to get it over with so I could try to relax and cry alone, I opened the creaking driver's side door to the Camry and stepped up to my house. The snow was only just starting to fall as I pushed the front door open, doing my best to breathe calmly as my father sat on the floor next to my son.

I'd never been as angry at Dad as I was with Mom. He was guilty by association, yes, but he wasn't the one that ruined my childhood. He was the highlight of it, other than my sister. But I didn't understand why he was here.

"I'll go if you want," he said, his wrinkled hands raising as he took me in. I wasn't used to seeing this older version of him yet. The gray in his hair was harsher, his goatee shorter, his mustache thinner. He'd lost weight since I'd last seen him, and that was the biggest hurdle to come to terms with.

"Why are you here?"

"The nanny called me. She had a family emergency and you weren't answering," he said.

I did have a few missed calls from her but she'd followed

them up with a text message saying, "Sorted!" so I didn't think anything of it. "How did she get your number?"

"Well, she called Veronica first, and she directed her to me," he said sheepishly, pushing himself up from the carpet with a grunt. "I figured you wouldn't want Drew at our house so I came here."

I sighed and shut the door behind me, dropping my bag and keys on the little table beside it. "It's fine. You can stay."

"Are you—"

"Don't question me, Dad. I've had a hard day, and if I say you can stay, you can." I plucked Drew from his mat on the floor and tucked him into my chest as I collapsed on the couch. He giggled and wrapped his arms around my neck, trying to kick his way up my abdomen to get closer to me.

"Do you... want to talk about it?" Dad offered. He stepped behind the kitchen island that divided it from the living room, opening cabinet after cabinet until finding a kettle and pulling it out.

"You know what?" I laughed, the chaos driving me, Drew's little face cheering me up as he tried and failed to plant a kiss on my cheek. "Sure. You're probably the only one that could actually understand."

The candidness with which I spoke surprised even me. I told him everything as he sunk onto the couch beside me, two cups of peppermint tea in his hands. I told him about how Cole and I had started, how I'd met him at Lottie's as her father was dying, how we'd had an incredible time until that horrible night, when I'd left in a fit of rage, promising myself I wouldn't see him again. I told him about the turmoil I'd gone through when I'd found out I was pregnant, how I cried thinking about how the man who fathered him was a fucking dick, how I hadn't put the pieces together. I told him about my job and how Cole had returned, that I'd given him a second chance purely because of Drew. The highs of it, the lows of it, and everything in between.

Dad listened, *really* listened, for the first time in years. He let me talk about all of it, holding Drew when I needed a moment to calm myself. He offered up his own anecdotes, his struggles in trying to get mom back to rehab, how he would kick himself every time she fucked up with us because he knew damn well we'd remember it. He talked to me about how difficult it was loving someone with alcoholism, how hard it was to watch them fall when he knew she didn't want to.

"It's not something that's fixed once and for all when you go to rehab," he explained, his hand on my shoulder, his brown-eyed gaze boring a hole in my soul. For once, I didn't flinch. "It's... sweetie, it's a lifetime. It's always there. Your mother, she's been sober for six years, and although it gets easier, the fight is always going on. For both of us."

"I remember every time she stumbled," I admitted, pulling Drew back from my father's lap and watching as he desperately tried to reach for the giraffe on the coffee table. I handed it to him. "Every time she forgot something, every time she made our lives a living hell. I don't want Drew to have to go through that."

His lips pursed. "I understand that too," he sighed. "I thought about leaving your mother many times, for the sake of you and Vee. The possibility that this, what we have now, would happen. It haunted me. Sometimes I wish I'd done it. But I couldn't. I wasn't half the person you are, Dana. I wasn't strong enough for that."

"What do you mean?"

"I love your mother with every fiber of my being. I have since the moment I met her. I wasn't sure I'd be able to function without her, at least not enough to bring up two hell-raising daughters on my own," he laughed. "Maybe I was selfish for not trying. But your mother... she's my person, sweetie. I didn't think I could handle life alone, and I chose to fight it with her so I wouldn't have to."

By the time Dad left, the sun had long since set, the street lights kicking on and bouncing off the shimmering snow. I shut the door behind him, the only sound left in the house that of Drew's little snores from his bassinet on the other side of the living room. His breaths were back to normal, finally.

I was alone, for better or for worse.

I'd made my decision.

I leaned against the broken wood of my door. Everything I'd shoved down since I left work came bubbling up, every emotion, every tear, every drop of anger. I tried to stuff it down again, tried to keep myself from waking Drew, but the broken sobs took hold.

I slid down the door, burying my face in my knees, containing the sounds as best I could to keep him from waking. This was for the best. It had to be. But I felt like I was making the biggest, worst decision of my entire life.

Chapter 35

Cole

I blinked, and three months had passed.

I sat on the sofa, the sound of music coming from somewhere upstairs. Empty bottles and cans littered the floor, the couch, littered my fucking life.

I tipped the bottle back, letting every fucking drop fall down my throat. It did nothing to cure the ache, though. That wasn't from the booze anymore. No amount of alcohol killed it, no matter how much I drank. It got worse when I thought of her, when I thought of him, the ways in which he must be changing, how much bigger he must be by now.

It throbbed for the first time when I found out she'd resigned from her position. It throbbed again when I called Lottie ten minutes later, demanding she tell me where Dana had gotten a job and almost crying when she refused. It throbbed when I found myself on the bathroom floor almost every night, sick from too much booze and unable to stop thinking of her.

The binges had become worse. I couldn't remember the last time I was fully sober or the last full day of work I completed. I couldn't remember the last time I'd left my house. Everything was blurring, and she wouldn't answer my calls, she'd blocked me everywhere, and I couldn't even find a photo of my son. Lottie wouldn't tell me a single thing, wouldn't show me any recent pictures of him, instead sending me links to rehab facilities.

Everything was blurring, and I was losing my mind.

Blind hope was what led me to the door when my sensor dinged. I didn't check the camera. I knew it wasn't her, but I could pretend it was.

She'd taken every good part of me when she kicked me out of her life.

I pulled the door open, fully expecting nothing more than another package Bobby had delivered or maybe another crate from the liquor store, but instead, it was Grayson's face and black hair that filled my narrowing field of vision.

Before saying a word, he took a step back, covering his nose with the collar of his shirt. "Jesus, Cole."

I couldn't remember the last time I'd seen Gray, either. "What are... what are you doing here?"

"You're drunk," he said, and all I could do was nod. "It's one in the fucking afternoon."

"My sleep schedules fucked." I mumbled.

"You're slurring."

"If you..." I took a moment, centering myself to try to keep my words together. "If you just came here to point out my failures, you can leave."

He shook his head, the snow behind him melting as the sun sprung out from behind the clouds. "I'm not here for that. I'm sorry. I just wanted to see you if you wanted to, you know, go do something. Get out of the house."

I glanced over my shoulder at the state of the grand foyer. The sight of clothes strewn in random places, plastic bags and empty cardboard boxes from delivery after delivery, made me cringe. "Yeah. I would."

"Fishing, maybe?"

"I don't know how to fish."

"You can watch me then. Go put on clean clothes," he said, placing one hand against the center of my chest and pushing me back into the house. "If you have any."

———

It was barely spring. The trees were just beginning to grow their leaves, the birds chirping and playing in the little patches of snow that remained. The water, crystal as could be in the center of the lake, shimmered its reflection of the hanging sun and the open blue sky.

Gray had stopped at a local pizza place on the way, the level of grease nearly turning my stomach when he told me to eat half of it. I'd thrown up on the side of the road before he told me to eat some more, shoving a giant bottle of water in my face.

I was hitting the lows, that level just slightly above sobriety when I felt shaky and angry. The ache in my chest was all-consuming, but I watched as I sat across from him on the small fishing boat, taking in every stroke of his hands as he hooked a worm and cast his line. We sat in silence.

The longer we sat, the more sober I felt, and the more grounded in reality I became. *Three months.* I'd missed Drew's first Christmas, missed Dana's birthday. I'd miss Easter, too, at this rate. I couldn't help but think about how many Christmases, how many Easters and Halloweens and

Fourth of Julys and birthdays my parents had missed when they left me.

But I'd had plenty of celebrations with my aunt. Those were the holidays I cherished the most, not the ones where I was spoiled with gifts and left to play with them alone. The Christmases where it was just me and her, and she got me the things I needed and a handful of things I wanted. The ones where we watched movies and drank eggnog, laughing about something that McAllister kid did even though we'd seen it a million times.

Dana would be that for Drew. That pure kind of love where you only want the other person to thrive, to be happy, to turn out the way you hope for them. I'd had that with Aunt Kathy, and the longer I sat there on the lake, the water nearly making me sick, the stench of a bucket of worms nauseating me to my core, the more I realized that I'd had it with Dana, too.

And I'd ruined it. I'd been the one to tear it down. I'd been the one who put myself in this position. I had the chance to have a family, to have love in a way I'd been craving for most of my life, yet I'd thrown it all away. And for what?

"Cole?"

Shit. Reality rushed in again and my cheeks were damp, a lump forming in the back of my throat as I shuddered in a breath.

"Hey, man, it's okay—"

"It's not," I croaked, hastily wiping my face as if he hadn't already seen it. "Oh my god, Gray, it's not okay."

He hooked his pole into the side of the boat and crossed over to me, making my stomach churn even more with the rocking of it. He placed a hand on my shoulder, his gaze nearly ripping a hole straight through me.

"I lost her," I said, and everything became too much, too loud, too hard. That was why I drank, to avoid this. This, and the reality of my goddamn agonies being infinite when sympathy wasn't. That ran out quickly from everyone I met. Everyone but Gray. "I fucking lost her, and I lost him."

"You don't know that—"

"I didn't want this," I sniffled, wiping my eyes again as if I had any control over when they'd stop leaking. "I *don't* want this. God, Gray, I don't want this. I want my life back. I want Dana, I want my son. What the fuck has happened to me? How have I lost three months?"

Gray shifted on his feet and the boat rocked again, sending the pizza straight up my esophagus. I twisted on a dime, hurling everything up over the side of the boat. I gagged, over and over, one hand clutching the only clean shirt I had left and the other clinging to the rail of the boat. I felt like it would never end, but every second that passed with Gray holding my shoulder, it felt just a tiny, minuscule amount better.

"You need a plan," Gray said softly. "We'll do it right this time. No disappearing, no running away. You'll stay in town and you'll keep in touch, you'll be made accountable. And you'll keep up with your fucking AA meetings this time, you understand?"

I nodded as another wave of vomit spewed from me. "Okay," I coughed. A tissue entered my line of sight, and I took it from him, wiping off my mouth and chin.

"First thing we need to do is get rid of Bobby."

If I had anything left to hurl, it would have come up then.

For once, I agreed. Bobby had gone down the relapse hole with me and hadn't done a single thing to try and get better, though neither had I. But if I stood a chance at all, if

I genuinely wanted to try, I needed to be away from him and I needed him out of my fucking house.

"Yeah," I conceded, slowly turning myself back into my seat instead of staring at the water below. "Bobby has to go."

After a bit more food and zero fish caught, Grayson walked me up the driveway, a plan and an end in sight.

We both stopped in our tracks the moment we realized the front door was open.

"Did I...?" I asked, pointing to the empty space.

"No, I double-checked for you," Gray said. He took the few steps in front of me until he reached the door, peeking inside to see if anything had been broken.

"Should I call the cops?"

"No, I think Bobby might have left it open," Gray said, stepping inside and checking the table by the door. "All of your keys are still here. Anyone who wanted to break in would be an idiot if they didn't take one of your cars."

I joined him inside as I pulled up the security footage on my phone. The last motion at the door was two hours ago, and I clicked the file to open it.

Gray went on ahead as I watched the footage of Bobby stepping out onto the front porch, a bottle of whiskey clutched in his hand as he shouted something down the phone. He paced for a few minutes, practically stumbling, before slipping back inside and leaving the door wide open.

Shit, is that how I look when I'm drunk?

"Cole!"

The urgency in Gray's voice had me running. I sprinted up the stairs, taking them faster than I'd been able to in weeks. Around the corner at the top of the staircase, through the theater, into the game room—

"Call an ambulance!" Gray shouted, but oh fuck, things were blurring, and no, no, no, why was Bobby on the floor? What was the white shit coming out of his mouth?

"*Cole!*" Grayson shouted again, the fear and trepidation in his voice mixing with anger but I couldn't move, couldn't think, couldn't let myself blink and let time go—

"Nine-one-one, do you need police, fire, or ambulance?"

The sound entered my left ear and I couldn't remember dialing, but I was aware the phone was in my hand. "Ambulance," I croaked. My heart raced, my hands shook, my chest roared with far too much fear and anger.

"I'm connecting you now."

"Cole," Gray said again, his jaw fucking steel as he held two fingers to Bobby's neck and another two on the inside of his wrist. "There's no pulse."

Chapter 36

Dana

Six months.

I hadn't talked to him in six months.

No matter how much time has passed, I still found myself falling asleep questioning everything, thinking of him, and replaying the good memories over and over until sleep finally found me. I missed him with everything in my being, and with each passing day, what Dad had said to me made more and more sense.

I didn't think I could handle life alone, and I chose to fight it with her so I wouldn't have to.

Maybe Dad was the one that was stronger than me.

"Can you pass the syrup?"

I picked up the jug and passed it across the table to Mom. That was a new addition to my life—trying to work things out with her, or at least get to a point of tolerating being in the same room.

It was a slow-moving process.

"Mama!"

I grinned at Drew as he kicked in Vee's lap, one arm

outstretched to me, my mouth wrapped around a bite of pancakes. "What?" I said, the sound muffled.

He was officially one year old as of a week ago, and the party Lottie had insisted on throwing for him had ended in a screaming match between me and my mother, and a two-man food fight between Brody and Drew. Our brunch date was a sort of reconciliation.

"When do you start classes?" Mom asked, and I dragged my gaze away from my son to look at her.

It was as if I were seeing her in a new light. She looked different, better, but I supposed that was a byproduct of eating real food instead of only drinking alcohol.

"Next week."

"What's your major?"

I shrugged. "Don't have one yet. Haven't decided. I'll just study the basics this year and we'll see how it goes."

A silence hung between us for a moment as we both ate. Vee didn't make a peep, she was here to be our referee and to keep Drew happy. I hadn't quite forgiven her yet, but she seemed more than happy to pretend like nothing had happened between us. That was how she operated—what had passed was in the past. She never wallowed in it.

"I'm proud of you, you know," Mom said, and I wanted to drop my fork in frustration. "Don't give me that look, Dana. I'm being serious."

"You could have been proud of me the first time I tried to go to college ten years ago," I grumbled.

"I was then, and I am now." A sympathetic smile crept across her cheeks, reminding me far too much of the ones she'd give us when we cried about her being inebriated. "And I'm sorry, for what it's worth, that I didn't come to your high school graduation. That's one of my biggest regrets."

I took another bite, weighing whether or not to accept her apology for one of her biggest moments of disappointment for me. But I was in the spirit of forgiveness, and the more Drew giggled and tried to escape from Vee's arms, the softer I became.

Fuck it. "I forgive you," I said.

Maybe I'd learn to forgive her for more things down the line. But it was a process, and I only had so much in me in one day.

In a moment of pure calm for once in my fucking life, I stirred the soup that simmered on the stove and watched Drew on the monitor beside me as he snoozed away in his crib. I guess both of us had a bit of peace tonight.

A rerun of Friends played quietly in the background so I could still hear and Drew could still sleep. Things were getting easier the older he got. But a part of me still felt guilty every time I looked at him. I could see Cole in him so much more than before, could see it in the way he laughed and the way he smiled, in the mop of blonde hair that seemed to have sprouted overnight.

What would he think if he saw him now?

What would Drew think?

Would he call him Dada instinctually? I hadn't taught him that word like I had with Mama. Would he still cry for him like he did when we were in Costa Rica, when he wouldn't stop wailing even in my arms, wouldn't calm down until Cole held him?

I was grateful for Cole. He'd given me Drew, and that was a gift I could never repay. And he'd given me a glowing letter of recommendation when I'd resigned, a letter that had landed me a job in the head office of a soft drinks corporation with better pay and better benefits.

But I couldn't decide if I was grateful for the silence he'd given me. Three months in, he'd stopped calling me every day. He'd stopped texting. He'd stopped badgering Lottie for information about my new job. He'd relented, and although I found that life was easier when I could forget he existed, it felt more like I was losing him altogether.

I battled the urge to call him the same way I did every night.

Maybe instead of a call, I could text him. I could throw out a lifeline if he needed one. I hadn't heard anything from Lottie about his relapse, hadn't asked, but if he was still in the trenches...

I hope you're okay.

Sent.

A knock at the door nearly had me jumping out of my skin.

I moved the soup off of the hot burner and turned off the stove before anxiously making my way to the door. I was still afraid that it could be Robert, or Bobby, or whatever the hell his name was. I hadn't quite recovered from that ordeal.

I pulled open the door, making a mental note to replace the cheap wood tomorrow, and lost every bit of breath in my lungs.

Dark blonde hair, a little shaggy, but not too bad. Clean-shaven jaw, slightly tanned skin, too tall for my door, and fuck, those eyes. The same eyes I see in my son every goddamn day. "How did you...?"

Cole's brows knitted as he looked me up and down. I'd

forgotten I was only in a baggy T-shirt, shit, it was his. "How did I what?"

"I just, uh, I just sent you a text."

The laugh that came from him made my cheeks heat and my chest ache, but in a good way. Seeing that damn dimple pop out was the cherry on top. "I left my phone in the car," he said, gesturing behind him. "I had no idea."

Reality settled in as I realized this wasn't some kind of fever dream I'd conjured up from thinking about him. Cole was here, on my front porch, uninvited. He didn't smell of booze, he didn't look like he'd been through the ringer like he did the last time I saw him. He looked... healthy. I shook my head. "I'm sorry, why are you here?"

"Right. I... yeah. I brought you something, if that's okay. I just wanted to give it to you and then I'll go," he said. I couldn't think of a single time I'd seen him this nervous. If it was any other day, I would have told him to leave and then spend the rest of my night sobbing in my bed. But whatever weird coincidence was happening here was almost too laughable for me to be angry.

"Uh, yeah, okay."

He held up one finger as he jogged back to my driveway. Every step he took was precise, not a hint of swaying or stumbling. I watched as he pulled a box nearly the size of me from the trunk of his car, his slacks and button-up shirt telling me he actually went to work today. "I couldn't find big enough paper to wrap it, so you'll have to cut me a little slack," he laughed, walking back to my front door.

I stepped out of the way to let him in.

Hesitantly, he stepped across the threshold, eyeing me as he set the box down on the carpet. "I know I missed his birthday. I'm sorry about that. I was out in New York on business and I considered just having it delivered, but I, I guess I wanted to be a little selfish and try my luck seeing you."

I shut the door behind him.

"Dana?"

I didn't know what I was doing or what to think. All I could do was watch him, take him in, and note the ways that he'd changed in six months. It was overwhelming. He'd come here to see me, to drop off a gift for Drew that looked way bigger than anything he needed, to test his luck.

Why was I bending to him?

I knew why.

"How are you?" I asked, hearing the strangeness in my voice, the lump at the back of my throat.

The concern on his face morphed into something akin to understanding, but warmer than that. "I'm... getting there, Dana." Getting there. What did that mean? He took a step toward me, and I didn't move. He kept himself at a friendly distance, but we both felt the static in the air. "How's Drew? How are you?"

"Good," I answered. I took a deep breath, trying to calm the rapid beat of my heart. "He's good. I'm good. He's doing a lot better since, well, since the last time you saw him."

He nodded, his gaze flicking between me and the door. I could tell that a part of him wanted to run, but I could see the war in his eyes, could see him fighting to stick to the situation he'd ended up in. He must not have thought I'd answer the door, and maybe, if I hadn't already caved and sent him a text, I wouldn't have.

"Is, uh, is Bobby still living with you?" I asked, throwing him a curveball in an attempt to keep him locked in place.

It worked.

I watched as his eyes dropped, as his shoulders began to sag. *Oh, god, he is. He never believed me.* "No," he said quietly. The way he watched me seemed almost as if he felt like he was under a microscope, everything about him seemed so much smaller all of a sudden. He let out a breath, letting the silence hang for just a moment before he spoke. "He passed away three months ago."

"Oh my god—"

"It's okay," he swallowed, but the way he steeled his jaw, the way the ligaments in his hands flexed, told me otherwise. "I should have listened to you from the start. Shit, I should have listened to Gray from the start. You both tried to warn me."

I watched him, studying the way he avoided my eyes as he spoke. "That doesn't mean it's okay that your friend died."

"He wasn't much of a friend at the end, Dana," he sighed.

"Is that what...?"

He shook his head. "No. I, uh, made a plan with Gray right before it happened. We found him when we got back. But I won't deny that it gave me an extra push." He took another step, tentatively testing me out, breathing a sigh of relief when I didn't move. I had no reason to, he wasn't a danger to me, wasn't a danger to my son. At least not like this. "I didn't—I don't—want to go like that."

The words fell out of my mouth before I could stop them. "You've stopped drinking."

He huffed out a breathy laugh, but it didn't seem like he found it humorous. Nerves, maybe. "I don't want to lie to you. Not again. So, I'll say this—I'm trying."

Trying. Another step, and we'd move out of the friendly field and into dangerous territory. I still didn't move, didn't know what to think. What did he mean? If he wasn't sober...

"I'm back in AA. I'm doing what I can. I'm trying, but

I'm also being careful not to beat myself up when I fail," he explained, his voice quieting as he took me in. All of me.

If it was honesty hour, then I could press him harder. I jutted my chin out as I looked up at him, cementing myself to where I stood. "How often have you failed?"

He nodded, but it didn't seem like it was for me. His throat bobbed as he swallowed, his Adam's apple jumping. I knew he wasn't used to being this open about it with me, but if he was here, if he was trying to wedge himself back into Drew's life, I needed answers. I needed solutions. "Once, since I started back with AA," he admitted. "But if you want me to be harder on myself, I'll do it. I'll never fucking drink again."

Why did he have to put me between a rock and a hard place?

He took another step, closing in on me, close enough to feel the heat of him and smell his shower gel. No cologne, no masking the scent of alcohol. I couldn't even smell a hint of toothpaste or a breath mint. I felt like I was a ticking time bomb, seconds from exploding, or maybe imploding. I didn't want to push him away. A part of me was proud of him for doing this, for digging himself out of the hole he'd buried himself in, but the other part wasn't happy with knowing he'd had a fail. That part wanted none.

"I don't want you to be harder on yourself," I croaked, and dammit, could I just have one moment with him where I didn't cry? "I just, I miss—"

Before I could even breathe, his lips crashed against mine, knocking me off balance before his hands grasped my waist to keep me in place.

My heart thundered against my ribs, my body frozen as I tried to take it in. He was here, he was working on getting sober, he was kissing me. I wanted it, yet I hated that I wanted it. I wanted him.

I didn't move a single muscle when he pulled himself from me, his eyes wide, his demeanor so fucking small again. "I'm sorry," he breathed, peeling himself from me finger by finger as if he couldn't bear to let go all at once. "I... I shouldn't have come."

My body finally gave way, my layers of ice melting. I grabbed him by the collar of his white button-up and pulled him to me as if he was air and I was fucking suffocating. I wrapped a hand around the back of his neck, feeling the warmth of his skin, forcing him to close in on me again. His forehead pressed to mine, his breathing heavy and uneven, we stood in deafening silence just an inch from each other's lips.

"I missed you," he rasped, the little crack in his voice shuddering through my chest.

The pause that thickened the air between us shattered in an instant.

I kissed him as he drove me against the wall a little too roughly. A mumbled apology filled the space between our mouths but I devoured it, savoring the taste of him that I'd missed and imagined every fucking night as I fell asleep. He lifted me, slotting his hips between my legs and forcing them around his waist, desperate for contact anywhere either of us could get it.

With one arm around his neck, I pulled him in tighter, refusing to let him back away if he tried, but from the way his fingers dug into the bare flesh of my thighs and clung to my shirt, I couldn't imagine a reality where he wanted to leave. He kissed me as if he'd never get the chance to again, as if he needed this more than I did. Maybe he did.

"I'm sorry," I swallowed, his lips leaving mine only to

press against my cheeks, my chin, my jaw. "I'm so sorry. I should have told you about Drew sooner."

"Don't be."

A knot formed at the back of my throat, tainting my words as I tried to speak. "But you've missed out on so much," I said.

My shirt rode up as he held me to the wall, exposing the entirety of my lower half. He didn't even bat an eye as he pressed a kiss against the tip of my nose. "I know."

"You missed his first word," I croaked. The backs of my eyes burned. "You missed his first steps."

He huffed out a breath as his forehead rested against mine again, his eyes closed tightly, his brows furrowed.

"You missed his birthday."

"I can't tell if you're mad at me for this," he admitted, and I almost laughed. Almost.

"I'm mad at myself." I buried my face in the side of his neck, cherishing his warmth and breathing him in. I missed how he smelled. I missed everything about him. "And a little mad at you. But maybe if I'd told you sooner, if I gave you something to cling to, none of this would have—"

"Stop, baby, stop," he sighed, one hand coming to rest on the back of my head as if I were seconds from pulling away. "Neither of us knows what would have happened. I was out of my fucking mind."

The longer he held me, the more I had time and room to think, and for me, that was never a good thing.

The t-shirt rode up higher around my body, tugging and settling at my waist. The sensation of it pulled me closer to reality, to the situation at hand, to his *I'm trying*. I wanted this, I wanted him, so fucking badly I could easily lose myself in it. But I couldn't let that happen, for Drew alone. What I wanted didn't matter. What he *needed* mattered.

And Drew needed a father, yes, but more importantly, he needed a father he could rely on. He needed someone that had their shit together. Someone that wasn't just *trying* but succeeding.

I'd let my feelings for Cole cloud that.

But I didn't want to let go, didn't want to push him away again. I wanted to stay right there, in his arms, invite him back to my bedroom and shut the door to the world. I wanted to love him easily.

The tears came too quickly, too suddenly, as I realized I was making my mind up on something I wanted to live forever in vagueness with. I dug my fingers into the side of his neck, shuddered breaths wracking my chest as I took what I knew would be the last of what I'd get from him for too long.

"What's—"

"We can't," I sobbed, and his grip tightened. "I'm sorry, Cole, but we can't do this."

I could feel my weight shift heavily on the wall as he struggled to keep us upright, but I couldn't bear to pull back, to look at his face, to take in the ways that I knew I was hurting him.

"I need you to be better," I said, each word cracking the ache in my chest and increasing it tenfold. "I need you to be sober. Fully."

He held me in silence for what felt like hours but judging by the clock hanging beside my front door, it was only minutes. I cried and he shook, his fingers so deep into my skin that I was sure he'd leave little half-moon bruises from his nails.

Until slowly, finally, with every bit of restraint in both of us, he lowered my legs and set me down.

I was terrified to look at his face, to see the ways in

which I'd broken him reflecting back at me, but he was still Cole when he pulled away. Cole, but a little more tarnished. "I'm sorry," I rasped.

He steeled his jaw as he reached for the door handle, wrapping his fingers around it like he had done to me. "I get it," he said, but I wasn't sure he did.

A cry cut through the heaviness of the air, and Cole's head whipped toward my bedroom, his mouth parting. We both froze, locked in place, until he broke and his fingers released the handle, one foot turning in that direction.

I caught him by the wrist before he could try.

"No," I said, and his head dropped, his hair falling into his face.

He didn't even fight me.

He let out a shuddered breath, his chest shaking, and before I could change my mind, he was out the door and down the driveway.

I wanted to take it back for Cole's sake. Wanted to tell him that it was fine and he could tend to Drew, that he could be in our lives again, only if it ensured he wouldn't make one slip-up turn into two. But that was selfish, and Drew was crying, and the mom in me took over before I could follow him out into the black of night and stop him from irrevocably changing all of our lives for the worse.

Chapter 37

Cole

One Year Later

The sun had just barely begun its descent over the tops of the Rocky Mountains as I shut my planner and my laptop, deciding that I'd done more than enough work for one day.

The date wasn't as jarring to me as I thought it would be. One year completely sober was one thing—a thing I was thoroughly and desperately proud of—but it was also Drew's second birthday.

One year ago today, I'd woken up with one of the worst hangovers of my life after drinking myself stupid in my hotel room, the fear of missing his first birthday driving me to the bottle. But the moment it hit midnight, I'd regretted every sip. I'd vomited across the floor of the bathroom. I'd called Gray and told him I'd fucked up. I'd picked myself up and started again, telling myself it was one slip-up, and I couldn't be so hard on myself. I told myself I'd handle it if and when another came.

But it never did.

I'd been close the night I left Dana's. I'd bought a bottle, I'd sat on my bed and stared at it for upwards of an hour, but in the end, I didn't even call my sponsor. I dumped it down the drain.

The temptation to swing by her house on my way and try my luck again was overwhelming, but I had plans tonight, and I needed to not dwell on her.

She'll come to you if she changes her mind, my therapist had said.

And if she doesn't? I'd asked.

Then you can't let the hold she has on you decide your future.

I'd done my best to take it to heart. I was staying sober mostly for myself now. I'd never felt better, sans the brief periods of relief with Dana. I'd tried not to let her mailed checks for the hospital bill get under my skin, no matter how many times we played the back-and-forth game of me returning it to its sender only for it to show up again. I told myself every day that she'd likely moved on, and although it hurt every time, it helped keep the temptation at bay.

A knock sounded on my door as I stuffed my laptop into my bag. The secretary I'd hired just weeks ago stuck her head in, her braided blonde hair falling over one shoulder. "Uh, there's a kid downstairs asking to see you."

My heart leaped out of my fucking chest for a split second before remembering Drew was only two and if he was downstairs asking for me, he'd be both a prodigy and a liability.

"What do you want me to do?"

"Did he say who he is?" I asked.

"He said his name was Hayden."

Well, fuck.

"Let him up."

I collapsed into my seat, partially dumbfounded and partially impressed. *Hayden and Harley.* I'd done a bit of digging when I first sobered up, looked into the life my parents were leading and who those teenagers they'd had with them were. Twins, but fraternal. He'd be, what, fifteen now? Sixteen, maybe.

Why the hell had he come all the way from Bali to Boulder?

And why the hell did he want to see me?

My thoughts spiraled as I watched the clock tick by. I had AA in an hour. I'd need to make this fast if I had any chance of making it on time, and considering I hadn't been late in exactly one year, I didn't want to ruin my streak.

The door creaked open and in stepped a younger, spitting image of me as a teenager.

But maybe a little edgier.

His black hoodie was zipped almost all the way up, the hood of it covering his mess of dark blonde hair. His eyebrow and lip piercings told me that Mom had calmed down on her life goal for her children to look as respectable as possible. His baggy grey jeans were covered in patches from brands I didn't recognize, but the Converse on his feet were classic.

"Hi," he said as if it were the least weird thing in the world that he was there in my office.

"Uh, hey." I watched him carefully as he collapsed into the leather wingback opposite my desk.

Well, my therapist did say I needed to start bridging the gap between me and my family.

Just wasn't expecting it to happen today.

"What are you doing here?" I asked. "You're, what, sixteen now? Are you alone?"

He shrugged as he picked at something on the base of his shoe. "Almost sixteen. Mom and Dad are in Denver so I got an Uber."

I blinked, watching as he stared at me and spoke with such lighthearted indifference. As if it didn't matter if they panicked wondering where the hell he'd gone.

I snorted. "You just left?"

His sneaky little grin grew as he sunk down further into the chair. "Yeah. They've been blowing up my phone."

A weird sense of pride overwhelmed me—my kin, my brother, was doing to them exactly what my parents had done to me.

"I should probably head back soon before they put out an amber alert," he laughed.

"Do they not track your phone?"

He shrugged. "They try, but I think they're too old to realize I can just turn off my location settings. So they freak out when it goes off but they never blame me for it." His fingernail dug into a patch of dirt in his shoe before dropping it on the ground. "Dad once called our network and screamed at them for like, two hours about having unreliable tracking."

I covered my mouth with my hand, trying to keep in the absolute hilarity of it. I'd assumed my siblings would be the perfect mold of my parents. I couldn't have been more wrong. "You're lucky your sister doesn't rat you out."

"Harley wouldn't dare," he smirked. "She knows damn well I have too much dirt on her."

"Why did you come here?" I asked again, relaxing into my chair. This wasn't at all the shitstorm I imagined it to be when Laura had told me Hayden was downstairs.

He shrugged as he bounced his leg. "I don't know. Just felt like it, I guess. Wanted to see what you were all about when you didn't have Dad in a chokehold."

Heat crept into my cheeks. "I'm sorry about that. You shouldn't have had to see it."

He tongued at his lip piercing, forcing it to poke out at the front. "I know it's probably weird for you that we, like, exist and all that. But if it makes you feel any better, Mom and Dad felt bad about dropping that bomb on you. And us. We had no idea you existed, either."

It was like being burned and soothed at the same time with this kid.

Of course, I was glad to know that my parents felt like shit. And I was glad that he understood the complexities of how weird it was for me. But they hadn't even *mentioned* me to them.

Hayden's phone dinged and he glanced at it, his eyes bugging out of his skull. "Shit. Harley says Mom's calling the cops."

He scrambled up out of the chair and stuffed his phone in his pocket. "I'll have my driver take you back out to Denver," I offered, and he beamed at me over his shoulder.

"Thanks."

I didn't know what to do, whether I should hug him, just wave, or walk him out. But he beat me to it as I came around the side of my desk.

His arms wrapped around me quickly, his stature tall for his age but not quite hitting mine. "I know you hate Mom and Dad and all, but like, can we keep in touch? You're not half-bad. Harley wants to get to know you too."

Fuck. Why did that make my chest tight?

"Yeah, man. We can keep in touch."

Hurriedly, we exchanged numbers as I shot a text to my driver. I was buzzing every second of the way while I walked him to the exit, the reality of some kind of familial extension within my grasp washing over me. It was a lot, even though we'd only spent probably five minutes together. But it felt like a lifetime, and more importantly, a life*line*.

Family.

"I'm right across the street," he said down the phone. He turned toward me as he walked to the car, spinning one finger beside his head as if to indicate that our mother, on the other end of the phone, was insane. I laughed. "Mom, I'm waving at you. How do you not see me?"

He slid into the back of the car and the driver shut the door behind him, leaving me alone and unconnected once again.

But it didn't have to be like that anymore.

I'd made it a year. I'd made a connection. I was healing, I was getting better, and I was fucking capable now.

Maybe she *had* moved on. Maybe she was done with me. But she'd given me a lifeline, too, the last time I saw her.

I need you to be sober. Fully.

I was fully sober now.

I was stable.

Chapter 38

Dana

The sound of a toddler screaming was almost normal to me now. But multiple? No. That cut through like a knife to butter.

I stood on the threshold of the sliding glass door that led out to my new backyard. We'd nearly finished settling in with the help of Hunter and Lottie. Unpacking with a two-year-old was a nightmare on its own, and I'd nearly wept when they'd shown up two weeks ago with a crew of men and a distraction for Drew—their son, Brody.

Streamers and birthday hats littered the ground as the two of them ran circles around each other. The rest of his friends had gone home, but of course, Lottie and Hunter stayed to help with every aspect of the cleanup. They'd spoiled my son rotten already. They didn't need to pick up after him too.

Mom, Dad, and Vee stayed as well, but they were significantly less helpful.

But even with all of those people that I held close to my heart around me, I couldn't help but still feel alone. There was no one there to wrap an arm around my shoulder.

There was no one there to kiss me and celebrate the milestone of my son in the same way as me. No one that was feeling the same level of pride, even if they all tried.

There was a crater-shaped hole in my life, and although most of the time I was able to ignore the ache of it until the early hours of the morning, it was harder today.

"Brody!" I snapped, and the boy spun on his heel in the grass with a metal trowel in his hand. "Drop it!" He stared at me for a moment, his blue eyes sparkling in the waning sunlight.

And then he went right back to chasing Drew with it.

Lottie stepped across the lawn, her footsteps nearly reverberating through the ground before she snatched it from her son's hand. "Fucking two-year-olds," she grumbled, storming up the steps of the porch before depositing the trowel in the plastic box. "I love him, but he can be a handful."

I snorted as she wrapped her arms around me, leaning on me for support. "I'm tired," I grunted, doing my best to hold her up but close to failing. I was seconds from collapsing when she let go.

"How are you holding up?"

I narrowed my gaze at her. "I'm fine. My parents are here and we haven't argued—yet. Drew got a shit ton of gifts that will need to be opened with a box cutter, so that's fun. And he's probably going to crash in, I don't know, about an hour? So his sleep schedule is going to be in the gutter."

"You know that's not what I meant," she sighed, slotting an arm around me as she turned so we could watch them. Somehow they'd managed to find a rope, and decided tug-of-war was an original invention.

I let my mom handle that one.

"You know how I'm holding up," I muttered, steeling my jaw. "It's just a bit harder today than it usually is."

The doorbell sounded and I watched as Lottie looked inside as if fate was answering my call. But I knew better than that—it wasn't him.

I'd gotten a text about twenty minutes ago that a package was two stops away.

"I got it," I grumbled, stepping over the baby gate and making my way to the door.

A man stood there in all blue, a USPS logo across his chest, with a clipboard jutting into my personal space. Behind him, two women offloaded an oversized package, the memory of Cole dropping off a similar-looking package almost one year ago today flashing in my mind as I signed my name. That package had been a gigantic stuffed bear that Drew had lost his mind over. This, from the looks of it, was some kind of rideable monster truck.

"Sorry, ma'am, I need a signature from Drew Beechings," the man said, staring at my penmanship as if I were insane.

"He's two," I snapped. "So unless you have a crayon and some free time to teach him to write, mine, his mother's, should be good enough."

He let the conversation drop as the two women deposited the box in my living room. I waited until the three of them left before checking the note on the side of the package, my stomach dropping. I already knew who it would be from. I didn't need the reminder, not today. But I owed it to him.

I dropped to my knees and turned the small piece of cardstock paper in my hand.

. . .

Dana,

Thank you. You've done more for me, for our son, than words on a card could ever hope to describe. You're an incredible mother and I cannot even begin to try to articulate how much I appreciate the work you put into raising Drew every single day. You deserve nothing but the best, always and forever.

I hope that one day I can prove my worth to both of you.

Cole

P.S. Please stop with the check mailing game. You won't win.

The knot in the back of my throat quickly grew about ten sizes.

I choked out a sob as the tears hit me, dripping onto the little card and smudging the ink. Without thinking, I wiped it on my jeans, smearing the ink more, and fuck, that only made it worse.

"Mama!"

Drew's body slammed into the box as he took in the picture on the side of it. I covered my mouth, scooting back toward the wall, trying to keep my emotions from him. I didn't want him to see me like this, not when it felt like my fucking chest was caving in.

"Mama?" he said again, his head tilting to one side as he tugged on the zip ties wrapped around the box.

He didn't miss it this time.

A shaking, heaving sob shook my body, and within seconds, Drew was scooped up. I blinked past the tears, forcing my vision to clear, and watched as Lottie hurriedly dropped Drew off on the other side of the baby gate before calling for my mom to watch him.

He didn't miss it this time.

"Dana," Lottie said, her knees hitting the floor beside me as she placed her hands on my shoulders. "What's wrong?"

I pushed the card into her chest, hoping I hadn't ruined it too badly, and watched as she read through the smudging.

Two years. Drew was two years old, and Cole had only been in his life for three months of it.

What the fuck had I done?

"Hey, hey, it's okay," Lottie breathed. Her fingers wiped away the tears blackened from my mascara, but it was only getting worse.

Every misstep, every stupid decision I had made, laid itself out in front of me like a goddamn art gallery. I should have reconciled with my parents sooner, maybe then I wouldn't have been so hard on Cole. I shouldn't have left him to fend for himself the way I did when he relapsed. I shouldn't have pushed him away a year ago when he'd shown up at my door with a gift for Drew. The shame he must have felt when I still wouldn't let him see his son. Was that why he'd had it delivered today instead?

"I fucked up," I sobbed as Lottie wrapped her arms around me, tugging me into her chest. "I fucked it all up."

"You haven't," she whispered.

"I've kept him from Drew for a year and a half." The words came out broken, as mangled as my heart felt. If I could forgive my mother and let her back into my life, let her be around Drew, what the hell was stopping me all of these months? "I made a mistake. I made a fucking mistake, Lottie, and I can't change it. I can't take it back. I can't give him that time back."

"He needed that time," Lottie offered, but I knew she was only saying that to make me feel better. He didn't need that time. I could have helped him through any relapses he had in the last year, but I chose not to.

"No, he didn't," I shot back. I pressed the base of my palms into my eyes, smearing my makeup but needing a tiny amount of relief from the pressure building there. "I fucking abandoned him just like his parents did. I probably made him feel like a monster. I fucking loved him, Lottie. I loved him. I love him still."

Every breath I took was shaky. Every word I spoke felt like a dagger to my chest.

"I love him, Lottie, and I've ruined any semblance of an actual family with him." The part of me that wanted him gone was dead, buried deep beneath the ground in an iron cage she stood no chance of escaping from. All I was left with were the broken parts that had never wanted to leave him to begin with, and goddamn, it hurt.

"Listen to me," she said, pulling herself back to position herself in front of my face. "You haven't ruined anything."

"I have."

"You haven't. I know that for a fucking fact. And if you don't believe me, I'll take you to him," she urged. She took my face in her hands, forcing me to see the seriousness in her expression. All hard lines, with a hint of sympathy swirling in her ocean blue eyes. "I know where he is today."

Chapter 39

Cole

Grayson sat beside me in the foldable plastic chairs in the center of a middle school gymnasium, joining in as I clapped for the man who had just spoken about a lifetime of battling addiction after addiction. He was two months sober for the first time in his adult life, and every clap I made was half for him and half for the version of myself that I was both times I hit that milestone. It was hard, and he deserved every ounce of recognition.

I wanted to speak but I'd struggled to find the right moment to share my story. I wasn't often one to talk during meetings, and the regulars of this group knew that by now, skipping over me with ease as they jumped from person to person.

I opened my mouth but the leader of the meeting spoke before I had the chance to. "I think that about wraps it up for this evening," Emily said. She was still my sponsor, still my guiding light in a storm that seemed to be raging less often nowadays. Now and then I'd find myself wondering if maybe I was just in the eye of it, destined to deal with the second half and swim my way out.

"Wait," I said.

Every single eye turned to me.

"If it's okay, if you guys have time, I'd like to share."

No one moved.

"Cool. Great," I mumbled, pushing myself to my feet while wiping the sweat off my hands on my jeans.

I cleared my throat, glancing down at Grayson's wide-eyed grin for support, before beginning.

"I, uh, I started drinking when I was ten," I said, the words tasting like ash on my tongue. "I watched my father do it when he was stressed or upset or when I'd misbehaved. I saw it on the shelf, and I was worried about a vocabulary test I had the next day at school, I remember that like it was yesterday. I remember the way it tasted when I took a sip and spat it into the bathroom sink, horrified that my father was able to down it. But then I tried again, and again, and eventually, it made its way down my throat."

Gray's hand wrapped around my forearm, giving it a quick squeeze of reassurance before letting go.

"It spiraled quicker than I could have imagined," I continued. "At thirteen, rather than deal with their son's growing problem, my parents dropped me at my aunt's house two states away. Bless her, she loved me regardless, and together we managed to get it down to a normal teenage level."

I swallowed, my throat feeling far too dry. *Water. I need water.*

"I spiraled again when she died. Drowned in it for about a year before figuring out how to be stable while drinking. I could drink through the night, kill the hangover with a buzz, and start again. Always right on the edge, only occasionally letting myself go on full benders. I went years like that, running my business, making connections, making friends, and I can't remember a single fully sober moment of any of it—"

The doors of the gym opened, and although we were told to not pay any mind if people passed through during the meetings, I couldn't ignore this one.

"I..."

Hazel eyes watched me from across the room, smudges of mascara below them. It was the first time seeing them in a year and I took in a deep breath as Gray found my arm again, not letting go this time. "It's okay," he whispered.

I wiped my mouth from the nerves, massaging the muscles of my jaw. "I met someone," I faltered, the words I'd rehearsed in my mind jumbling together, reworking, rewiring. *She's here.* "And there was... there was something about her from the moment we met, something I knew I needed to pursue. But I fucked it up, royally, and I spiraled again, worse than the first time. I landed in a rehab facility out in LA for six months with help from my friends."

The doors opened again, and a slightly shorter frame stepped through, one arm reaching out to her. "Dana, we can't just, shit," Lottie whispered harshly. She grabbed for Dana's arm, but Dana took a step away from her, cementing herself in the room.

"She gave me another chance without knowing any of my problems when I returned." I closed my eyes, trying to recenter myself without seeing her gaze. "Things had changed, though. She had a child—a son. She had a life. And despite how easily I found it to slot myself in, everything else around me began to crumble, and my sobriety was teetering. It was the first time I'd ever tried to be completely sober, and I didn't know what I was doing, how to handle it, or how to get through the hard days. And the hard days just kept piling on."

I opened my eyes, meeting hers again, and it was like everything else fell away. No circle of chairs, no Gray by my side, no sponsor watching me, no gymnasium. Just her, too far away, and me.

"I slipped. I slipped and fell and ended up so far down a hole that I didn't know how to climb back out. I'd never fallen so hard before. It was a miracle I didn't drink myself to death. I had a child, now, and I had a vision for what I wanted my life to be, and I watched through a pinhole as it all crumbled, as I turned into my father. I couldn't be what I needed to be for either of them, and so I had to let go."

A knot formed in the back of my throat. I hadn't imagined it being this hard, but I also hadn't in my wildest dreams imagined she'd be standing across the room from me when I did it.

"She had so much on her plate," I croaked. "I couldn't be the father I needed to be, and she had to make the tough call on whether to allow me around our son. And ultimately, she was right. I wasn't safe." I sniffled, pushing down the crowd's stares as they slowly built up again until it was just us, "My fucking friend died, and after seeing someone sprawled out on my floor, no pulse, no breathing, because they'd choked on their own vomit after passing out from alcohol poisoning, I could have easily gone back down the hole. It was already there, neatly dug and waiting for me, but I didn't. I chose not to. I climbed out instead."

A single clap almost made me laugh.

"I'm sorry, Angie, I'm almost done," I said, huffing out a chuckle. She turned in her chair, crossed her wrinkled arms across her chest, and sat back. "I did it right this time, but I faltered. The night before my son's birthday, I drank myself stupid, cursing myself for not being strong enough to be there for it. But when morning came, when I realized that I could survive the day, I didn't want to lose it again. I picked myself up and I tried again. I gave myself grace, but I didn't need it in the end."

Dana's shaking hands covered her mouth, her hazel eyes sparkling with what I could only assume were tears. My lips twitched up at the edges as I jumbled the words around again in my mind, picking and choosing what I'd keep and what I wouldn't.

"For the woman I love endlessly, I stayed sober. For my son, I stayed sober. And most importantly, for *myself*, I stayed sober. One year ago today, I made that choice. And for the first time since I was ten, I can proudly say that I can't see myself ever touching it again."

The dullest round of applause echoed through the stupidly large space, but I didn't care.

I didn't care about the chip Emily would give me.

I didn't care about Grayson's pride.

I didn't care about Angie being the only one not clapping.

The only thing I cared about was the woman my body was already moving toward, the one I physically shoved a man-filled chair out of the way for.

She moved, too, stepping toward me, the tears streaming down her face almost making her look like some kind of horror show from the mascara, but I didn't care. I'd love horror shows for the rest of my fucking life.

Her body met mine and I wrapped my arms around her waist, digging my fingers into her, feeling her for the first time in almost a year. I held her close, a little sob breaking through as she buried herself in the crook of my neck.

I'd spent the last year of my life feeling better and better, but not a single moment of it compared to the way it felt to hold her, to have her, to touch her, even if it was only for tonight. For a moment, even. I'd take it over nothing.

"Is this part of the speech?" Angie griped.

"Shut up, Angela," Gray hissed.

I gently took her by the back of her neck, forcing her to look up at me, and pressed my lips to hers before she could change her mind. I let her go only briefly, only to take her face in my hands instead, and swiped my thumbs under her eyes. Her lips parted, and my heart nearly imploded.

"So you're not riding back with me?" Lottie laughed as she pulled open the door of her Range Rover. I spun my newly-gained gold chip between my fingers as the remnants of the meeting attendees left the gymnasium, my arm firmly around Dana as I held her to my chest.

Dana lifted her middle finger to Lottie in reply.

I chuckled into the top of her head and tightened my grip. I couldn't find it in me to let go of her, not yet. I didn't know how long it would last, and although I didn't want to tempt fate, I couldn't help but feel like maybe, *hopefully*, this was the time I'd been waiting for.

I opened the rear door of my Maybach for her and she turned to look up at me with one brow raised. She still looked like a mess—*my* mess. "In," I grinned.

"The back?"

I slipped into the seat and lifted the center console, turning it into a singular long cushion that stretched the width of the car. "In, Dana," I said again, and within seconds, she was climbing in behind me and shutting the door.

I didn't have to tell her what I wanted.

She crawled into my lap, her jeans stretching as she sat astride me. Her lips met mine, and fuck, she tasted just as I remembered, just as I'd craved for almost a year, maybe even my entire life.

Over and over, she kissed me. Over and over, she drank me in, her hands exploring more than just my neck and face. She pulled each button of my shirt, pushing until the collar gave way and hung from my shoulders, the fabric clinging to my arms and keeping its hold from where I'd tucked it in. I let her call the shots for once, eager to not take her a step too far, but she seemed just as desperate for me as I was for her.

Her forehead rested against mine as she lifted herself onto her knees, just barely gaining a height advantage while she pulled my shirt from my slacks. "You can see him," she breathed, her eyes fluttering shut as she pressed a quick kiss to my lips. "Whenever you want, Cole, you can see him. Surprise him for his birthday. It's okay if we have to wake him up."

God, it felt so much better to hear that than I thought it would.

I slid my hand beneath the back of her shirt, lifting, pulling, until it was free and lost somewhere on the floor of my car.

"Please tell me you mean that," I murmured. I kissed the side of her jaw, kissed her chin, trailed my tongue down the front of her throat as she let out a sigh that melted my fucking bones.

"I mean it."

"You won't change your mind again?" I bit at her skin

by her collarbone as I pulled the straps of her bra down, unfastening it with one quick twist around the back, watching it fall and leaving her bare from the waist up. *Not enough. Need more. Need her.*

"Not a fucking chance."

Without thinking, I shifted gears, taking her face in my hands instead and holding her just an inch from my face. Her eyes fluttered open, and I dragged my thumbs under them again, brushing away the little flecks of mascara I hadn't quite gotten before.

"Cole—"

"I love you." The words rolled off my tongue so easily, as if they'd always been there. I'd had a year to prep them, longer than that if I was being honest with myself. There wasn't a hint of anxiety that held me back. "And I've waited far too long to say that to you."

Her lower lip shook but she stilled it, clamping down on it with her upper teeth. But I caught the flash of dampness in her eyes before she closed them, breaking free of my hold to press her lips to mine again. "I love you too," she whispered. "I'm sorry I didn't make you feel safe enough to say it sooner."

Relief flooded my system as I wrapped her in my arms, shifting us, laying her down across the plush leather so I could get to work on her jeans. *A skirt would have been so much easier.* I kissed my way down her chest as I popped open the button, taking my sweet fucking time on the zipper while dragging my tongue across each breast. They seemed smaller than they were before, and I briefly wondered if it was a side effect of stopping breastfeeding before her hips were rising, helping me get her out of the dreaded pants.

"You didn't drink the night you left my house?" she

asked, and I wondered if it was really the time to get into that as I clung to the front of her underwear with my teeth.

I barked out a laugh as I released them, opting to use my hands instead. "I didn't."

"You got sober on his birthday," she said, the happy tears springing to life again.

"You're just now realizing that?" I couldn't help but grin at her as I pushed down the open front of my slacks, letting my aching cock spring free against her. She lifted her legs for me, granting me access, and oh my god, she was soaked already. I could have fucking cried at the sight.

"There's a lot going on today, okay?" she chuckled, wiping her eyes as she settled herself against me, her skin catching on the leather.

Quickly, desperately, I slid myself inside of her, unable to wait a single second longer.

"Oh my god," I groaned, crowding her as I bottomed out, every single muscle of hers clenching around me. "Christ, baby."

The shit-eating grin she flashed me was almost enough to turn me feral. "Overwhelming?" she cooed, one hand reaching up and cupping my cheek.

"Look, it may have been a year since I've had a drink, but it's been longer since I've been inside you." Already, the pleasure of her was making my head spin, and I lifted her instead, deciding I couldn't be fucking bothered trying to maneuver around the cupholders. I wanted her flush to me, and that was only going to happen one way, with her on top. "Or anyone, for that matter," I added.

The moan that dragged from her as she seated herself on every inch of me made me impossibly hard. Without hesitation, she started moving her hips, her breasts brushing against my bare chest.

I'd be lucky if I made it five fucking minutes with her after being without her for so long, after so much need and desperation had built up. But she was just as needy as me.

"Touch me," she demanded, her lips brushing against mine with every movement she made. I obliged, slipping my fingers between us, searching and finding that little bundle of nerves and circling it.

She moaned again, and I wanted to fucking fill her.

I guided her hips with my other hand, forcing her to pick up her speed, melting beneath her with every swipe of her lips against mine. Already I could feel my release tightening in my lower stomach, demanding I let it loose. But I wouldn't. Not until she was falling over the edge, too. I wanted to come undone with her, wanted to lose myself with her, wanted to feel the walls of her close in around my cock and milk me for every drop I had.

I watched as her eyes rolled, as her lips parted, as each breath came quicker and quicker. I kept my pace with one hand, digging my fingers into her flesh with the other. "So fucking perfect," I said, nudging her jaw with the tip of my nose. "So fucking beautiful."

Her cheeks reddened and her sounds hit a peak as the walls of her began to close in.

"Show me how pretty you are when you come," I said. "Show me what I've been missing."

Her nails dug into my chest as every muscle in her body locked. I bucked my hips up into her, burying myself deep, losing my goddamn mind in her, and the moment her piercing shriek broke through, pleasure ripped through my abdomen, taking me right down with her.

Chapter 40

Dana

Six Months Later

We'd only lasted seven months before Cole got tired of us picking and choosing which house to sleep in. So instead of doing the normal, sane, non-rich person thing—selling one and staying in the other—he decided we needed a new one altogether.

And of course, keep the others. *For investments,* he said.

Seeing as I had no interest in being a landlord, I'd just given it to my parents instead.

At least he'd listened to me when I insisted on something small enough that we wouldn't lose our son every day. It was still big, bigger than anything I was used to, but we had land and we had a view, so I agreed.

Drew and Brody babbled happily to each other in a language I couldn't even begin to understand as they lapped at their ice cream in unison. Over time, Drew had begun to lose the intensity of the green in his eyes, and although they still shone nearly as bright as his father's as he grinned across the lawn at me, they had a hint of me in there too.

A lot had changed since Cole had entered our lives. I could see it in the faces of the people at our home, the ones he'd insisted on inviting on our first night in the new property because apparently, christening it meant something entirely different to him. My parents, my sister who was somehow still in town, all mingled by the fire pit. Grayson and his daughter, Penny, helped Cole at the grill, and to my surprise, our son seemed to listen to her orders better than he listened to mine. Lottie and Hunter, always there, chatted away in the sun loungers behind me, catching the last rays of the sun before it dipped below the mountains.

Most surprisingly, however, was the presence of Cole's parents and his two siblings, Hayden and Harley. They had made the journey out from their quick trip to New York. That relationship was easily the rockiest of them all, but he was making an effort, and so were they. It seemed almost silly to me for them to fly out here for a housewarming party, but I wasn't about to question a rich family over how they spent their money. For all I knew, it was the same as just driving to the grocery store for them.

But Cole had been truly trying with them. Even if it meant a mental breakdown once a month where I had to talk him down from throwing away his chip.

But we were learning together, working through it together. Dad had been right—that was the best choice. Life was easier by his side even though we had to fight our demons. At least we weren't succumbing to them.

The business was looking up, too. After everything that had happened, the official launch was canceled and postponed, and instead, the new line would be making its debut by summer. This get-together he'd thrown had been more than a housewarming party—Cole and Hunter had officially partnered up and would be joining teams for the full-scale push of the lineup.

Pulling my knees to my chest as I sat in the grass, I

watched as everyone mingled. I couldn't help but feel how full circle we'd come, from where we'd started over three years ago in Lottie's backyard to now. My life had changed drastically in those three years, from tears and heartache to the happiest I'd ever been, even if it came with struggles.

"Mama!" Drew shouted across the lawn, grinning and showing his full set of baby teeth as he held up his clean popsicle stick from his ice cream with pride. "Ice cream!"

I chuckled as I set my chin on top of my knees. I'd never expected to love anyone as much as I did with that kid.

Warmth touched my skin as a hand wrapped around my front, pulling me backward into something warm and hard. I hadn't even heard him approach, let alone sit down behind me. I tilted my head back into his chest, looking up at him and his warped features from my perspective.

"You laughing at my son, Beechings?" Cole grinned, the edge of his lip pulling up on one side and accentuating his dimple. Even upside down, as he loomed over me, it made my chest ache.

"What's it to you, Pearson?" I giggled, reaching one hand up to poke him right in the crease of his dimple. He blocked out the sun for me, letting me take him in against the dimming blue background of the sky. Minutes from now, it would flood with pinks, oranges and reds, but if he stayed above me, I wouldn't see them. Just him.

And that was fine with me.

He leaned down and pressed a kiss against my lips, his nose brushing the bottom of my chin. "Not being very sociable, I see," he said, wrapping his arm around my waist instead and pulling me into the crook of his arm. I didn't have to crane my neck to see him, didn't have to stare upside down.

"Is it so bad to just sit on the sidelines and appreciate

how insane this is?" I grinned. "Everyone's here. No one's fighting. Even Brody and Drew aren't tackling each other."

Cole leaned into me, pushing his nose into the crook of my neck and pressing a kiss just below my ear. "It's only a problem when you don't include me on the sidelines."

I chuckled. "You were busy with your fancy new grill."

He rolled his eyes as he pulled away from my neck. "Gray is more than capable of grilling for me," he said. He looked out at the group, at the calmness of it. His eyes lingered on Drew as he found a stick to play with, and neither of us said a word when he started poking Brody in the side with it. "Can I run something by you?"

I glanced up at him, but he was far too lost in Drew's antics. "Sure."

"I was thinking we could go away this summer," he said, slowly dragging his gaze back to mine. He sat fully forward, motioning for me to do the same, and I watched him carefully as I angled myself in his direction. He lifted his head a little higher to block the blinding rays of the harsh angled sun before it could blind me. "After the launch, I mean."

Abso-fucking-lutely. "Costa Rica," I blurted, not wasting a single second on hesitation or consideration. "I want to go back to Costa Rica."

He flashed a grin at me that told me that was exactly what he had in mind. "Yeah. Costa Rica. We could go for a few weeks, or really however long you want. Invite whoever you want," he grinned.

"Wait, you want me to invite people?" I asked, my brows knitting as I considered that. Why the hell would I want anyone other than Drew to join us when we'd already had time there with other people?

"Well..." He laughed, the grin on his face so fucking wide it was suspicious. He glanced to the sky, one hand reaching across to grasp mine. "I probably shouldn't have said that part yet."

He leaned toward me, cupping my cheek with his free hand, and pressed the softest kiss against my lips, and then my nose, and then my cheek as he dropped his hand away.

"I was thinking we could do something else while we're there," he said, and puzzle pieces started falling into place.

I met his gaze, narrowing my brows as I studied him. "Cole," I pressed, but before I could question him further, something hard and wooden pressed into my open palm. My stomach twisted, but it wasn't like all those times before when it made nausea bubble up in my gut or made acid accumulate in the back of my throat. This was butterflies, excited but anxious nerves that almost tickled.

I knew I needed to look down, but I couldn't bring myself to do it. I knew what I'd find, knew the moment would progress, but I wanted to remember this. I wanted to remember the way he looked, the dimple that stood out like a fucking beacon, the light in his eyes that had finally returned, the nervous little grin he wore. I wanted to take a photo of it in my mind, wanted to burn it into my memory and erase every bad one with that.

But I *did* look down. And I couldn't breathe.

Just between us, out of sight of the others, he popped the little box open. Sitting on a little white cushion, a silver ring with two bright green gemstones shone in the flickering sun.

"Sapphires," he said.

Oh, my god.

A knot formed at the back of my throat, tears filling my eyes as I gently lifted the ring from its pillow. "Cole," I whispered.

"Marry me," he breathed, shutting the empty box and

placing it behind him. "I want this. I want *you*, I want Drew. I want this life we've made. We can do it in Costa Rica with whoever or no one. We can make it our place."

He pressed a kiss to my shaking lips. I frantically wiped the tears away before anyone could catch wind of what was happening. It was only minutes until they would, but I wanted to savor this. Wanted to live in this little bubble we'd made forever. I stared down at the two green sapphires, each inlaid in a circle of diamonds.

"You can say no, obviously," he added, tense green eyes meeting mine. "But I'd prefer you didn't."

"In what fucking world would I say no?" I laughed, sniffling past the tears as I slipped it onto my ring finger. Of course, it was a perfect fit.

He smiled in that stupid, annoying way that made my chest ache in the best way possible, and I pressed my lips to his, taking in the last seconds before the sun fell behind the peak of the mountains, before the world knew, before Drew inevitably came running over with sticky hands and ice cream on his face, before we had to announce it to everyone else in attendance and I had to explain the two rocks on my finger or what it meant.

"So it's a yes?" Cole asked through a laugh, his arms dragging me into his lap. It felt like *home*.

I rolled my eyes. "Of course it's a yes, Pearson."

THE END

Having a baby with my billionaire boss? That certainly wasn't in the job description when I agreed to be his pretend girlfriend.

Make a good first impression, they say, especially when you're desperate for work.

How about when you walk into the interview for executive assistant at the Colchester Mountain Resort and you come face to face with the ridiculously gorgeous, infuriating brute you just accidentally knocked over on the slopes?

I should have walked out the second he called me *Blunder Bunny*.

I shouldn't have stared at his muscles underneath his impeccable suit.

And I should definitely have run the moment he made me almost beg for the job.

But when you have a mother with Alzheimer's and unpayable medical bills, you'll do your best not to hurl insults back at the one person who can help.

The *Brute* has me managing his full calendar of ski bunnies.
Now he needs to clean up his playboy reputation for the investors.
And lucky me got chosen to deceive the world he's settled down.

So in public, we're convincing everyone we're madly in love.
In private, he's determined to melt away my ice princess facade with every touch.
And with each hot night together, it seems I'm chipping away at his damaged, frozen heart.

But then two little pink lines turn our fake relationship into a very real dilemma.
I might be falling for the very man I vowed to resist.
And I can't keep this baby bump a secret forever...

***Brute & Bossy** is Book 2 of the sizzling Boulder Billionaires series and can be read as a standalone. No cliff-hanger, no cheating, lots of steam and emotion you'll love to spice up your kindle.*

Read now on Amazon.

* * *

Chapter One
Raylene

What's a city girl like me doing in the mountains?

The bright light of my phone couldn't compete with the way the sun reflected off the piles of snow outside the Colchester Mountain Resort bar's windows. I found myself having to shield my vision from the left, the side of me facing the window, and when my hand wasn't cutting it anymore, I positioned a menu between me and the glass.

My plan was simple enough—hang around the resort for a little while, learn the ins and outs, and take a skiing lesson. It wasn't necessarily in the budget, but if I managed to sell myself well in the interview and land the job, it wouldn't matter. I'd be making more than enough to cover this and Mom's expenses.

Glasses clinked, people mingled, and the fire raging in the massive fireplace popped and crackled as I read through every little page hidden on the Colchester Ski Resort's website. The name of the owner and CEO, Wade Colchester, had flashed up numerous times throughout my research. If I'd read the job description properly—and knowing me, I absolutely did—then he would be my direct boss. I'd be his assistant. Executive Assistant, at that. That would mean a lot of time spent here and likely wherever else he roamed.

So I needed to learn all that I could about the place but, more importantly, I needed to learn about *him*, connect with him, and make a good impression.

"Afternoon, ma'am."

My head snapped to the right. A twenty-something man stood at the edge of my table, a black dress shirt tucked into black slacks, a short apron tied around his waist, and at least twenty pens hanging on for dear life.

"Can I get anything started for you?"

Shit. I wasn't a guest, per se, so this wasn't exactly a hang-out spot. *This isn't Starbucks,* I reminded myself. I'd entirely forgotten that I'd need to order something. "Uh," I started, fumbling for the menu I'd stuck against the window. I turned it rapidly in my hands, eyes searching for the beverages section. "Do you have oat milk?"

"Yes ma'am." The man shifted on his feet, his blue eyes looking between me and the menu with speculation.

"What brand?"

"Silk."

I couldn't help the grunt of irritation that slipped from me. "Do you have any Oatly?"

"I don't believe so, ma'am."

"Fine. I'll just have an oat hot chocolate, not too hot but not lukewarm. No foam, no cream, no marshmallows," I sighed. I slid the menu toward him and he nodded. "Oh, and definitely no sprinkles unless you have cinnamon."

"Yes ma'am."

His apron fluttered as he spun, taking off toward the island in the center of the room where the espresso machine sat. I cursed myself for being so picky—it wasn't necessarily something I did on purpose. It was more of an impulse, but if he and everyone else who works here eventually became my coworkers and the people I'd be around frequently, I should get myself on good terms with them.

I sighed as I turned my attention back to my phone. *Wade Colchester.* I typed his name into the search bar for the third time, fooling myself into thinking I'd maybe, somehow, find more information on him. As far as I could tell, the only thing public online was his LinkedIn, but all that gave me was a photo of the resort I was currently sitting in as well as a few photos of trophies he'd won in the past.

I couldn't help but picture him in my head, though—this mystery man I'd meet tomorrow. Older, probably; maybe in his fifties or sixties considering he didn't post photos of himself online. Maybe he didn't know how and his previous assistant had to help him set up his online accounts.

I imagine him lounging back in his office, a fireplace as large as the one in here taking up half the space. A sizable oak desk, log-cabin walls, dim lighting. Scotch in hand. A generous window to watch people ski or fall down the mountain. Gray or graying hair, a bit of a belly, and a pair of bifocal, wireframe glasses sitting on the bridge of his nose.

I might as well put him in a red velvet suit with white fur trim.

"Your oat hot chocolate, not too hot, no foam, with cinnamon," the waiter chirped as he slid the mug across the table. "Do you need anything else?"

I picked up the spoon from the saucer, pushing the back of it through the top of the hot chocolate. "Do you know anything about the owner?" I asked, batting my eyelashes to the best of my ability as I looked up at him. *Be friendly, Ray. Don't fucking flirt.*

He laughed lightly. "Mr. Colchester? I haven't actually met him yet. I only started a few days ago."

I sighed and lifted the mug to my lips. "Shame."

Skiing has never been my cup of tea.

The instructor I'd hired for the day had done his absolute best with me on the bunny hill, but I think I ate more snow than I skied on. I knew no more than the absolute basics from the one time I'd had the nerve to do this before but honestly, I'd much rather be in a pair of ice skates than the uncomfortable boots I was strapped into.

"You're leaning too far back. Your center of gravity is getting all skewed," Alex snapped.

No shit. Why did I hire you? "I'm doing what my body tells me to."

His ski kicked against mine as we rode the lift up to the top of one of the smaller slopes. Even with the bitter mountain air, my palms were sweating. I didn't want to do this, didn't want to have to potentially risk my life just to get to the bottom of this damn hill, but knowing at least some of what it took would be helpful.

"I feel like I should get every single shot updated after the amount of snow I've ingested today," I joked, trying to lighten the mood just a hair.

Alex laughed. "Yeah, probably. Tetanus, hepatitis... all of them. Oh, and don't forget rabies. Who knows how many animals piss on the slopes overnight."

I gagged just thinking about it. "Please, if I ever see you again, never say that."

"So are you here on vacation?" Alex asked, probably more out of courtesy than a real interest.

"I'm here to interview for the job as executive assistant to the CEO," I said, blowing hot air onto my gloves with the hope of defrosting my fingers.

"And so you thought you'd learn how to ski."

"Something like that," I replied.

The chair reached the top, and as my skis touched down

onto the packed-in snow beneath, I struggled to get my footing. I dug my poles into the snow, pushing myself forward as Alex hurriedly rushed toward me. His brows were furrowed, his mouth taut. "Hurry up, Raylene. You're going to cause a pileup."

"I—" I snapped my mouth shut before the abuse that sat at the edge of my tongue could drip out. I didn't want to be an asshole to him, to anyone here for that matter, but more than that, I didn't want to look like a failure. Even if he'd seen me fall on my face all day.

He helped me over to the starting line, halfway down the bigger slope, and connecting like a Y. Not only did I need to make it to the bottom without dying, I needed to make sure I wasn't going to get t-boned by someone much better than me. So basically anyone.

"You go down first. I'll watch," I offered, looking up at Alex with a smile that I absolutely did not mean.

"Not how it works," he laughed, his graying beard flying in the wind. "You go down first. That way if you fall and hurt yourself, which I'm half expecting at this point, I can ski down to you." *Ouch.* "You've got this, Ray."

I definitely didn't.

I looked up the hill, waiting for a break in the skiers coming down, and when I was well and truly in the clear, I sucked in my breath. *I can do this.*

Looked down the hill. *So steep.*

Dug my poles in. *I'm going to die.*

Aimed my skis. *Someone, please take care of Mom.*

Pushed off. *I'm so fucked.*

If my sheer lack of direction and ability to stay upright didn't warn everyone around me that I was not good at this, the scream that ripped from my throat definitely did.

Learning how to ski is so much harder than learning to

skate. Skating had come naturally to me—just an easy extension of my own feet. But *this*, this was like I was wearing clown shoes and trying to walk a tightrope. I had zero control, but I knew I needed to at least lean forward — Alex hadn't stopped hammering that in. So that's what I did.

Too fast. Way too fast, way too careless. Trees zoomed past before I could even make out their shape. I passed people much better than me, yelling out, waving their arms. Even with my goggles, the glare of the sun off the snow made it hard to tell where I was going.

Lean back, my body screamed at me. Or maybe that was someone on the slope. I couldn't tell.

A group of what looked like a blurry mess of people were in front of me, and I was rapidly approaching them. I couldn't turn, didn't know how without falling, and as the shouts and yelps got louder, I did the only thing I could think of—dig my poles into the snow.

I promptly lost them.

Before I could blink I slammed to a stop, hitting something far too hard and warm to be snow. A grunt, not from my own mouth. A loud clunk against my helmet, a snap that made me cry out because *oh my god is that my leg?*

I peeled my eyes open, adrenaline shooting through my veins like a fire. Terror filled me to the brim as I looked down at the snow, tiny droplets of blood tainting the pristine white. I didn't feel injured. Maybe I was and the adrenaline was keeping me from noticing.

"Are you okay?"

I turned to my left, my goggled eyes colliding with a far too attractive man on his knees. I couldn't see much of his tanned face because of the helmet and goggles, but I liked what I was seeing from his neck down. All hard lines and muscles. One of his poles sat beside him, broken in half. *That must have been the snap.* "I..." I breathed, blinking through the haze of confusion as I pushed my goggles up to my forehead. I looked down at my body, everything still in one piece, and thanked my lucky stars. The red in the snow below me drew my attention back. "Blood?"

"Your nose. It looks fine, I don't think it's broken," he sighed. He unlatched his boots from his skis as I stared aimlessly at him, far too in shock to do anything else. "You should really watch where you're going."

I narrowed my gaze at him, the muscles around my nose screaming in agony from my newfound source of pain. "And you shouldn't hang out at the bottom of a slope."

He grunted as he stood, brushing the excess snow off his bibs. "You do realize you're staring at me, don't you?"

"I'm not staring at you, you brute."

"Oh? Is the tree line behind me just far too interesting to take your eyes off of? Should I be worried a bear is about to maul me?"

"No, but I'm pretty sure a bear would steer clear of you anyway. Don't think their jaws open wide enough to fit your massive fucking ego inside of them."

He shook his head as he picked up his broken pole and skis from the snow. "Fucking ski bunnies," he muttered, his fingers angrily wrapping around the strap of his helmet and tugging it loose. He pulled it back over his head, taking his goggles with it, and *fuck* my first assumption was right. Far too attractive. Ash blond hair toppled down in a mess from his helmet and, even though he wasn't smiling, he had the sexiest dimples on either side of his full-lipped mouth. "Or should I call you a blunder bunny?"

"You're a dick," I snapped.

"The lengths some of you go to, I swear—"

"Ray! You good?"

I turned, my blinded eyes barely making out the form of Alex abruptly stopping in his descent, snow billowing out from his sideways skis. I wiped my nose with the back of my hand then wiped the blood on my rented bibs. "Yeah, fine."

"Eat any more snow?"

"Nah, just filled my nose with it." I turned over my shoulder, expecting to lock eyes with the obnoxiously attractive man who apparently seemed to hate me, but found him walking back into the building instead. I sighed. "Y'know, it's a good thing that skiing isn't a prerequisite for the job I'll be interviewing for."

Alex paused, his words failing, and fell into a fit of chuckles. His grin turned sly, almost mocking. "You do know who that was, don't you?"

Chapter Two
Wade

The grunt that fell from my lips wasn't exactly planned as I lifted my legs onto the desk. My ribs and left shoulder were still sore from the impact yesterday, a raging headache flaring up my neck and wrapping its fingers around my skull.

"Any plans for more kids, then?"

Jackson laughed over the phone. "God, no. Not right now at least. We've got our hands full with Cassie."

Rubbing my shoulder with the hardest part of my palm,

I groaned into the pain. "Yeah, but you can't just raise her without a sibling. I mean, you grew up with Tiana. Surely you'd want the same for your own kid."

"Mandy was an only child and turned out fine." Mandy, Jackson's wife of nearly a year, had been one of my only friends in high school. I spent half my time on the slopes training and the other half barely getting by in classes. She'd taken pity on me, thank God, and after my accident that devoured any chance of me ever competing again, she was the only one I could turn to. Did that mean picking up and moving to New York? Yes. It also meant pursuing a degree, meeting Jackson, and knowing damn well he and Mandy would be suited for one another. "Why are you groaning, anyway? Please tell me you didn't call me mid-session with one of your hookups."

I chuckled, wincing from the pain that shot through my chest. "Absolutely not. I'm not *that* depraved, Jack. I thought you knew me better than that."

Soft coos and giggles could be heard in the background. "Then what's it about? Fall on the slopes this morning?"

I sunk further in my chair. It was hard to hear things like that, innocent questions about my ability to simply stand on my skis. I wasn't anywhere close to my former glory and probably never would be again, but I took a million falls in the past as well. The trophies dotted around the room enclosed behind glass cases stared at me almost in mockery, as if I'd never fallen before today. "Some psychotic ski bunny thought the best way to get my attention would be to crash into me going thirty miles per hour."

"Aww, but I thought you loved your ski bunnies. Isn't it about time for you to settle down with one of them?"

"Ha-ha, Jackson. Love is a strong word." The glimmer of the sun reflecting off a mounted platinum ski caught my eye, and I narrowed my gaze at the writing along it. I knew what it said, of course I did. But it still made me feel like shit. *FIS World Cup - 1st Place. Wade Colchester.* "Not like I would actually have a relationship with any of them." Not like I wanted to, anyway.

Jackson grunted his distaste. "Why? They're not bad people."

"Perfect for a good time, not a long time. I'm not looking for anyone anyway."

More adorable giggles poured through the phone, a hiccup, and then Jackson's answering laugh at whatever Cassie was doing. "Not like you'd have any luck anyway. Finding a blonde, leggy woman that knows how to ski and doesn't want you for your status isn't exactly the easiest thing in the world."

If only Jack could see me roll my eyes. "They don't have to know how to ski. They just need to be amiable and have at least half a brain. The rest wouldn't hurt."

He tsk'd over the phone. "So not the psycho ski bunny from earlier, then?"

She popped up in my mind for what was easily the twentieth time today. She wasn't tall, wasn't blonde. From the little bit of hair that had escaped from beneath her helmet, she had curly chestnut hair. Curvy but fairly slim. Had she not had such a nasty mouth on her, I probably would have given her the time of day, even with the blood trickling from her nose onto the snow.

But she just had to go and call me a brute after slamming into me at full speed.

"Absolutely not Blunder Bunny."

. . .

The early afternoon sun glinted off the snowy hills and peaks outside my resort office's window. "Have all of them shown up?"

"We're only missing one. They called about an hour ago saying they got an offer elsewhere," Holly said, her nose buried in a small stack of paper as she flipped through it. "Why do people make their resumes more than one page long nowadays? It's incredibly annoying."

"Because they're desperate to sell themselves." I chuckled and leaned back in my seat, extending one hand out toward her, palm up. Her glasses slid down the bridge of her nose as her blue eyes locked with mine. "Pass me whichever one you like the most."

"There are only two decent ones," she sighed. Fighting with the papers in her grasp, she slid one out from the stack, inspecting it briefly before placing it into my waiting hand. "Douglas Conway. He has an exceptional amount of experience. He's a former ski champ like yourself and knows the area and this resort well."

"He sounds perfect—"

"He also has a lengthy criminal history with multiple charges for smuggling cocaine across the Mexican border."

Fucking great. "Let me guess. He didn't say that on his cover letter, did he?"

"Of course not," she snorted, flipping through the papers again. "We did background checks on everyone. So if you'd prefer someone who doesn't have ties to the cartel, this..." she slid another resume into my hand, "is the only other good one. Raylene Harleson."

I skimmed the first few lines of her resume as Holly spoke behind me.

"She also has an exceptional amount of experience. Fairly local. Doesn't have a history with skiing, but of course that wasn't a prerequisite."

"Any history of cocaine smuggling?" I joked, my eyes catching on one of her previous employers. *James Holman ran that business. Asshole.*

"None."

"Bring her in, then." I passed back the resumes to Holly, my gaze lingering a little too long on Raylene's CV. "She can go first."

She nodded, her long black hair falling over her shoulders, and turned to walk toward the door. "Try not to look like you take up the entire room," she added, flashing me a sarcastic grin.

The moments between Holly leaving to retrieve the candidate and coming back felt like an eternity. I'd made a point not to bring my phone into my office this morning—I knew myself better than that. Distractions were inevitable and I needed to be on my A-game. Whoever I hired needed to be someone I'd get along with, someone I'd be able to tolerate being around me the majority of the time. And that meant I needed to be observant, present, and most importantly, likable.

Not that that was difficult with women.

Two pairs of heels clacking against the ground was my only cue that Holly was returning with the candidate in question.

The door opened. One dull pair of khaki slacks and a white button-up, black pin-straight hair, and glasses. Holly. One tight, black skirt that hugged every curve, a white blouse hanging loose around her breasts and tucked in, and a head of neatly set brown curls and eyes that shone like golden honey.

Blunder Bunny.

Fucking hell.

My nostrils flared as she locked gazes with me. Her skin paled in return.

Pushing my chair back, I stood, making my way around the desk. "Raylene Harleson, I presume?" I asked, plastering an award-winning smile on my face as I held my hand outstretched for her. "I'm Wade Colchester."

She blinked up at me, her stature so slight in comparison to my height. Her lower lip, plump and stained dark red, caught itself between her teeth before she spoke. "Nice to finally meet you, Mr. Colchester."

The whites of her eyes were visible from every angle. She couldn't stop staring—exactly like she was the other day when she claimed she wasn't—and I could tell the realization was far more startling for her than it was for me. For me, this was simply a unique turn of events, a hilarious coincidence, but for her, it was more serious. She needed a job.

From the way my mouth was salivating and the way the blood was pooling in my lower half, I definitely thought she needed *more* than a job. And I probably would have given her a night of more had she not been such a mouthy little thing on the slopes yesterday.

"Have a seat," I said, stepping out of her way and motioning toward the chair opposite mine. "Let's get this show on the road."

I watched as her jaw moved, a visible gulp shifting the muscles while she stepped around me. The door behind us closed quietly, Holly's usual exit. The leather of Raylene's chair squeaked as it gave way to her hips and thighs when she sat down.

"So, Raylene," I started, making my move from behind her to my own chair. Her eyes followed me every step of the way, a nervous cat too scared to pounce. I curled my fingers around the backside of my office chair, leaning forward over it, taking up more space than I should. Holly's advice be damned.

"It's Ray, if you don't mind."

I nodded. "So, *Ray*. Tell me," I drawled, the smirk I was holding back slowly making its way to the surface. "Do you know how to ski?"

Chapter Three
Raylene

I was fucked. So entirely, utterly, horribly fucked.

I cleared my throat, sending out a silent *fuck you* to my ski instructor from yesterday for not saying a word. "No," I said. I forced myself to sound far more confident than I felt. "In all honesty, I feel much more comfortable in a pair of ice skates. But I can learn if that's a necessary prerequisite for the job."

The Brute chuckled and stared me down, his knuckles whitening around the thick leather of his chair before he abruptly released it. "It's not. But I doubt you'd pick it up very easily."

Don't say it. Don't say it. You need this job, Ray. "What's that supposed to mean?" *For fucks sake.*

"It means that after your performance yesterday, I don't think you'd be capable of standing on two feet in the snow, let alone with skis attached." I watched every muscle in his body move as he sat down in his chair, his elbows on the desk and fingers steepled.

He was every bit the asshole I saw yesterday.

His dark blonde hair was slicked back professionally, much different from his helmet hair on the slopes. The smallest dusting of stubble ghosted his cheeks and jawline, both of which were annoyingly chiseled to perfection. Hard lines made up his entire physique, and even through his suit, I could tell he had an amazing build. Hell, through his snow bibs I could tell. The man clearly worked out and likely spent more of his life out there on the slopes than he did in his office. Lucky me.

"Are you going to ask me genuine questions to find out if I'm qualified for the job or just insult my skiing abilities on my first day trying?"

Long, dark blonde lashes batted at me as he centered himself. "That was your first time?"

I nodded.

"Why were you out there?"

Shit. Might as well be honest. "I was checking out the building. Meeting some of the staff. Trying to get a leg up, really."

He nodded, his gaze wandering toward the window. "That's actually... smart. Really smart." The muscles and tendons in his hand moved as he massaged the hinge of his jaw. "Why do you want to work here? And don't give me any of that standard bullshit as in 'I love what your company stands for.' Those spiels do nothing for me."

Well, that was unexpected. "Uh," I began, racking my brain for something that didn't sound entirely rehearsed. Spiels were what I was used to in interviews, not necessarily honesty. "I need the money. I'm from Boulder. I'm a good employee and I have the experience."

"I know you do. That's why I brought you in first."

"So you didn't just desperately need to get your irritation out from yesterday?" I joked, daring him to tell me otherwise.

"Obviously I didn't know it was you until you walked in. We didn't exactly exchange pleasantries yesterday." Dark, almost black eyes clashed with mine. "Do you genuinely want this job?"

I shifted in my chair, the leather suddenly more uncomfortable than it was seconds ago. "Need and want go hand in hand."

He exhaled through his nose quickly, a little half-hearted laugh following. "That could apply to so many things, Raylene."

"It's Ray," I repeated, cursing myself internally for not being more restrained. "And please don't make this into something sexual."

Wade leaned forward onto his desk, his smirk growing bigger. "I wasn't." A ringlet of deep blonde hair fell from where it had sat neatly on his head, resting against his brow. "I was talking about your blunder on the slopes. You needed—no, wanted—to crash into me."

I narrowed my gaze. "I definitely didn't."

"Then why did you?"

"I had nowhere else to go," I insisted. "You were in my way."

"So you needed to."

I bit my tongue. I knew where he was going with this.

"You wanted to."

"How is this related at all to the job you're interviewing me for?" I snapped. My fingers tightened around the hard wooden arms of the chair, the pressure pushing against my nail beds. "Is this even an interview? You can just tell me right now if you're not going to give it to me instead of wasting my time."

His brows rose high, little wrinkles deepening on his forehead. "If this were an interview, you're not being very professional, *Ray*."

I was going to kill him. Right there in his office, blood everywhere, just like how it dripped from my nose onto the pristine snow yesterday morning. I'd do it with his own damn trophy that sat on the bookcase behind him.

I breathed in deep through my nose, then slowly out through my mouth, the same way I did when Mom wasn't doing well and I needed to keep my cool. "Neither are you, *Wade*."

His jaw hardened, his tongue rubbing against the front of his teeth. "Then maybe this isn't going to be a good fit after all."

"You haven't even given me a chance. You've barely asked me any questions, nor have you given me the opportunity to ask questions of my own. I haven't seen you look down at my resume once—"

"Because I don't need to."

"Humor me, then. Ask me an actual interview question so I don't feel like every second I've spent in here has been entirely worthless." I didn't bother to hide the venom in my voice. Anger bubbled in my blood, and I wasn't going to leave without at least giving it my best shot, even if I'd most likely ruined my chances before we'd even begun.

He grunted as he tore his gaze from me, looking instead down at my resume. "Why did you leave your last place of employment, Ms. Harleson?"

God fucking dammit.

"I didn't," I answered. I released the arms of the chair, my nails and muscles thanking me, and sat back. "I was fired."

"You're really not selling yourself," he mumbled.

"I was late twice and had to leave early a handful of times with minimal notice," I explained. "My mom has special medical needs. They weren't very understanding, to say the least."

Wade glanced at me through thick lashes, his fingers thumbing the edge of my resume. "I know James well enough to believe that."

Shit. He knew my old boss?

"He was always an asshole to his employees. We've picked up a few of his spares over the years, mostly to run the hotel side of the resort. But you were working quite closely with him, weren't you?"

I nodded. "Same role as I'm interviewing for now."

"Oh, so you *do* think it's an interview then?" He lifted his eyes back to me, his smile crooked. "Interesting. Do you have any questions for me?"

I bit my lip, my thoughts starting to mingle together. *Should I be honest? Forward? Meek?* "Salary. I want to know the salary."

"I believe it was listed on the job post."

"It was. I want it confirmed."

"The current salary for the role is seventy-one thousand," he explained. *Fuck, I need this job.* The sound of a drawer opening made me jump, and I watched the way his arm moved as he rustled through it. "Overtime is paid at two and a half times the base rate."

"And what are the hours?"

The tendons in his hands flexed as he pushed a small packet of papers across his desk toward me. "It's all in there. Ideally, I'd have you five days a week. I'm flexible on which days those are, but I'd prefer if the days off could be taken together as we have another assistant to fill those."

"You work seven days a week?" I asked, the words

falling from my lips before I could stop them. *You need this. Don't ask unnecessary questions.*

"Not always. But having someone to handle things seven days a week comes in handy."

That made sense. I knew he was a busy guy who likely had emails and phone calls all hours of the day. Unlike James, who only needed help during business hours. *You can make it work around Mom.* "How many hours per day?"

"Depends on the day. It could change if something comes up last minute." His lips twitched up at the corners, his dark eyes glinting. He knew that wasn't doable for me. He *knew*. If he hadn't put the pieces together before now, they were certainly heading that way. "You'd need to be available most of the time except for your scheduled days off."

"You're not even considering me, are you?" I blurted.

His brows rose, a little chuckle oozing from his lips. "I never said that."

Something snapped inside of me. This man, this uncaring dickhead, didn't give a shit. He wanted to toy with me, to irritate me, to waste my time because of my brief moment of understandable stupidity yesterday due to inexperience.

I wasn't going to deal with his bullshit. I wasn't going to let him walk all over me. I'd just have to figure something else out, and fast.

"You're clearly implying it." I grabbed my purse from where it sat on the hardwood floor between my feet. "You know that's not something I can do. I made that obvious when you asked why I'd been fired. You're just wasting my time, which is apparently something you care very little about doing."

"That's not—"

"Don't." Adrenaline pooled in my gut and I tightened my grip on my bag to keep from shaking as I stood. "Good luck finding someone with half of my experience who's willing to put up with you."

"Ray," he barked. One word—my name—enough to make me feel like I needed to sit down and shut up.

But I wasn't a child, and he wasn't my parent. Yes, it was an amazing salary and a cushy job that could fix half of my problems, but it was never really going to be mine to begin with.

My heels clicked against the wood floor as I headed toward his too fancy office door, my fingers wrapping around the handle.

"Ray," he tried again.

But I was already halfway down the hallway, cursing myself and cursing him.

End of first chapters

Want to see how Ray and Wade end up fake dating? Order **Brute & Bossy** *on Amazon now. Free in Kindle Unlimited.*

⭐⭐⭐⭐⭐ "One of the best meet-cutes ever, a true romantic comedy and had me laughing several times, the best explosive tension that keeps you hooked. I loved everything about this book and can't wait to read the next one!" - Goodreads reviewer

⭐⭐⭐⭐⭐ "You will enjoy their banter. You will love the teasing between the two. And the nicknames Wade gives Ray are adorable." - Goodreads reviewer

⭐⭐⭐⭐⭐ "This is a must-read for any romance lover." - Goodreads reviewer

GET BRUTE & BOSSY

Boulder Billionaires Series

Get ready to fire up your kindle with these four bossy billionaires! These swoon-throbs will impress, grovel and pleasure their way to a delicious HEA with their sassy woman. And they won't take no for an answer - not in the office and certainly not in the bedroom.

Each book follows the story of their own couple and are stand alones with a very satisfying HEA. You'll also enjoy cameo appearances of your favorite characters throughout the series.

Read the Boulder Billionaires series on Amazon:

Boulder Billionaire series page

Big & Bossy: A Fake Engagement Second Chance Romance (Jackson and Mandy)

Brute & Bossy: A Fake Relationship Opposites Attract Romance (Wade and Raylene)

Beast & Bossy: A Fake Relationship Enemies to Lovers Romance (Hunter and Lottie)

Bad & Bossy: A Secret Baby Enemies to Lovers Romance (Cole and Dana)

Happy reading!

xx

Mia

Printed in Great Britain
by Amazon